Tho

Coleridge and Opium-Eating and other Writings

SALZWASSER VERLAG

Thomas de Quincey

Coleridge and Opium-Eating and other Writings

Reprint of the original, first published in 1863.

1st Edition 2022 | ISBN: 978-3-37500-068-4

Verlag (Publisher): Salzwasser Verlag GmbH, Zeilweg 44, 60439 Frankfurt, Deutschland
Vertretungsberechtigt (Authorized to represent): E. Roepke, Zeilweg 44, 60439 Frankfurt, Deutschland
Druck (Print): Books on Demand GmbH, In de Tarpen 42, 22848 Norderstedt, Deutschland

DE QUINCEY'S WORKS.

VOLUME XI.

COLERIDGE

AND

OPIUM-EATING

AND OTHER WRITINGS

BY

THOMAS DE QUINCEY

EDINBURGH

MDCCCLXIII.

CONTENTS.

PREFATORY NOTE.

COLERIDGE.—From some misconception at the press, the account of Coleridge's personal appearance, in the paper entitled *Coleridge and Opium-Eating*, was printed off whilst yet imperfect, and, in fact, wanting its more interesting half. It had been suggested to me, as a proper off-set to a very inaccurate report characterising Coleridge's person and conversation, by an American traveller, who had, however, the excuse that his visit was a very hasty one, and that Coleridge had then become corpulent and heavy—wearing some indications that already (though, according to my present remembrance, not much more than forty-eight at that time) he had entered within the shadows of premature old age. The authorities for my counter-report are—1. A Bristol lady who with her sisters had become successors in a young ladies' boarding-school to the celebrated Hannah More; 2. Wordsworth, in his supplementary stanzas to the *Castle of Indolence;* 3. Two (if not three) artists. These shall be first called into court, as deposing to Coleridge's figure, *i.e.*, to the permanent *base* in the description—all the rest being fugitive accompaniments.

One of these artists, who is now no longer such, took down, in the year 1810, at Allan Bank, Grasmere, the exact measurements of both Samuel Taylor Coleridge and William Wordsworth (at that time the host of Coleridge and myself). His memorandum on that occasion is missing. But as he found the two poets agreeing in height to a hair's-breadth, which I myself, as an attentive bystander, can vouch for, it will be sufficient for me to refer the curious reader to the Autobiography of Haydon, in whose *studio* Wordsworth was measured with technical nicety on a day regularly dated. The report is—5 feet 10 inches, within a trifling fraction; and the same report, therefore, stands good to a nicety for Coleridge. Next, for the face and bearing of Coleridge at the time referred to by the lady (1796), an ample authority is found in Wordsworth's fine stanzas—"Ah! piteous sight it was" [I cannot recall the two or three words of filling up] "when he,"

> "This man, came back to us a wither'd flow'r."

That was perhaps in 1807, when he returned from Malta, where it was that, from solitude too intense, he first took opium in excess. But in 1796, whilst yet apparently unacquainted with opium,

> "Noisy he was, and gamesome as a boy-
> Tossing his limbs about him in delight.

Happiest and most genial he then was of all that taste the morning breezes of life. From Wordsworth we learn (what afterwards my own experience verified) that his eyes were large, and in colour were grey :—

> "Profound his forehead was, but not severe;
> And some did think" [viz., in the *Castle of Indolence*] "that *he*
> had little business there."

The lady, as *her* little contribution to this *pic-nic* portrait, insisted on his beautiful black hair, which lay in masses of natural curls half-way down his back. Among all his foibles, however, it ought to be mentioned that vanity connected with personal advantages was never one: he had been thoroughly laughed out of *that* by his long experience of life at a great public school. But that which he himself utterly ignored female eyes bore witness to; and the lady of Bristol assured me that in the entire course of her life she had not seen a young man so engaging by his exterior. He was then a very resurrection of the old knight's son in Chaucer, of him that had jousted with infidels,

> "And ridden in Bélmărie."

I should add that, whereas throughout his thirty-five years of opium he was rather corpulent, not at any period *emaciated*, as those who write romances about opium fancy to be its effect,—in 1796, when he had nearly accomplished his twenty-sixth year, he was slender in the degree most approved by ladies.

Such was Samuel Taylor Coleridge in 1796. Ask for him ten years later, and the vision had melted into air.

CEYLON.*

There is in the science and process of colonisation, as in every complex act of man, a secret philosophy—which is first respected through results, and first expounded by experience. Here, almost more than anywhere else, nature works in fellowship with man. Yet all nature is not alike suited to the purposes of the early colonist; and all men are not alike qualified for giving effect to the hidden capacities of nature. One system of natural advantages is designed to have a long precedency of others; and one race of men is selected and sealed for an eternal preference in this function of colonising to the very noblest of their brethren. As colonisation advances, that ground becomes eligible for culture—that nature becomes full of promise—which in earlier stages of the science was *not* so; because the dreadful solitude becomes continually narrower under the accelerated diffusion of men, which shortens the *space* of distance—under the strides of nautical science, which shortens the *time* of distance—and under the eternal discoveries of civilisation, which combat with elementary nature. Again, in the other element of colonisation, races of men become known for what they are; the furnace has tried them all; the truth has justi-

* *Ceylon and its Capabilities.* By J. W. Bennett.

fied itself; and if, as at some great memorial review of armies, some solemn *armilustrum*, the colonising nations, since 1500, were now by name called up—France would answer not at all; Portugal and Holland would stand apart with dejected eyes—dimly revealing the legend of *Fuit Ilium;* Spain would be seen sitting in the distance, and, like Judæa on the Roman coins, weeping under her palm-tree in the vast regions of the Orellana; whilst the British race would be heard upon every wind, coming on with mighty hurrahs, full of power and tumult, as some "hail-stone chorus,"* and crying aloud to the five hundred millions of Burmah, China, Japan, and the infinite islands, to make ready their paths before them. Already a ground-plan, or ichnography, has been laid down of the future colonial empire. In three centuries, already some outline has been sketched, rudely adumbrating the future settlement destined for the planet, some infant castrametation has been marked out for the future encampment of nations. Enough has been already done to show the course by which the tide is to flow; to prefigure for languages their proportions, and for nations to trace their distribution.

In this movement, so far as it regards man—in this machinery for sifting and winnowing the merits of races—there is a system of marvellous means, which by its very simplicity masks and hides from us the wise profundity of its purpose. Oftentimes in wandering amongst the inanimate world, the philosopher is disposed to say— this plant, this mineral, this fruit, is met with so often, not because it is better than others of the same family, perhaps it is worse, but because its resources for spreading and naturalising itself, are, by accident, greater than theirs. That

* "Hail-Stone Chorus."—*Handel's Israel in Egypt.*

same analogy he finds repeated in the great drama of colonisation. It is not, says he pensively to himself, the success which measures the merit. It is not that Nature, or that Providence has any final cause at work in disseminating these British children over every zone and climate of the earth. Oh, no! far from it! But it is the unfair advantages of these islanders, which carry them thus potently ahead. Is it so indeed? Philosopher, you are wrong. Philosopher, you are envious. You speak Spanish, philosopher, or even French. Those advantages which you suppose to disturb the equities of the case—were they not products of British energy? Those twenty-five thousands of ships, whose graceful shadows darken the blue waters in every climate—did they build themselves? That myriad of acres, laid out in the watery cities of docks—were they sown by the rain, as the fungus or the daisy? Britain *has* advantages at this stage of the race, which makes the competition no longer equal—henceforwards it has become gloriously "unfair"—but at starting we were all equal. Take this truth from us, philosopher; that in such contests the power constitutes the title; the man that has the ability to go ahead, is the man entitled to go ahead; and the nation that *can* win the place of leader, is the nation that ought to do so.

This colonising genius of the British people appears upon a grand scale in Australia, Canada, and, as we may remind the else forgetful world, in the United States of America; which States are our children, prosper by our blood, and have ascended to an overshadowing altitude from an infancy tended by ourselves. But on the fields of India it is, that our aptitudes for colonisation have displayed themselves most illustriously, because they were strengthened by violent resistance. We found many kingdoms established, and to these we have given unity; and in process of doing so, by the necessities of the general welfare, or the mere instincts of self-preservation, we have transformed them to an empire, rising like an exhalation, of our own—a mighty monument of our own superior civilisation.

Ceylon, as a virtual dependency of India, ranks in the same category. There also we have prospered by resistance; there also we have succeeded memorably where other nations memorably failed. Of Ceylon, therefore, now rising annually into importance, let us now (on occasion of this splendid book, the work of one officially connected with the island, bound to it also by affectionate ties of services rendered, not less than of unmerited persecutions suffered) offer a brief but rememberable account; of Ceylon in itself, and of Ceylon in its relations, historial or economic, to ourselves.

Mr Bennett says of it, with more or less of doubt, three things—of which any one would be sufficient to detain a reader's attention—viz., 1. That it is the Taprobanê of the Romans; 2. That it was, or has been thought to be, the Paradise of Scripture; 3. That it is "the most magnificent of the British *insular* possessions," or in yet wider language, that it is an "incomparable colony." This last count in the pretensions of Ceylon is quite indisputable; Ceylon is in fact already, Ceylon is at this moment, a gorgeous jewel in the imperial crown; and yet, compared with what it may be, with what it will be, with what it ought to be, Ceylon is but that grain of mustard-seed which hereafter is destined to become the stately tree,*

* St Mark, iv. 31, 32.

where the fowls of heaven will lodge for generations. Great are the promises of Ceylon; great already her performances. Great are the possessions of Ceylon; far greater her reversions. Rich she is by her developments, richer by her endowments. She combines the luxury of the tropics with the sterner gifts of our own climate. She is hot; she is cold. She is civilised; she is barbarous. She has the resources of the rich; and she has the energies of the poor.

But for Taprobane, but for Paradise, we have a word of dissent. Mr Bennett is well aware that many men in many ages have protested against the possibility that Ceylon could realise *all* the conditions involved in the ancient Taprobane. Milton, it is true, with other excellent scholars, has *insinuated* his belief that probably Taprobane is Ceylon; when our Saviour in the wilderness sees the great vision of Roman power, expressed, *inter alia*, by high officers of the Republic flocking to or from the gates of Rome, and "embassies from regions far remote," crowding the Appian or the Emilian roads, some

> "From the Asian kings, and Parthian amongst these;
> From India and the golden Chersonese,
> And utmost Indian isle Taprobane;
> * * * * *
> Dusk faces with white silken turbans wreathed;"

it is probable, from the mention of this island Taprobane following so closely after that of the Malabar peninsula, that Milton held it to be the island of Ceylon, and not of Sumatra. In this he does but follow the stream of geographical critics; and, upon the whole, if any one island exclusively is to be received for the Roman Taprobane, doubt there can be none that Ceylon has the superior title. But, as we know that, in regions less remote from Rome, *Mona* did not always mean the Isle of Man, nor *Ultima Thule* uniformly the Isle of Skye or of St Kilda, so it is pretty evident that features belonging to Sumatra, and probably to other oriental islands, blended (through mutual misconceptions of the parties, questioned and questioning) into one semi-fabulous object not entirely realised in any locality whatever. The case is precisely as if Cosmas Indicopleustes, visiting Scotland in the sixth century, should have placed the scene of any adventure in a town distant six miles from Glasgow and eight miles from Edinburgh. These we know to be irreconcilable conditions, such as cannot meet in any town whatever, past or present. But in such a case many circumstances might, notwithstanding, combine to throw a current of very strong suspicion upon Hamilton as the town concerned. On the same principle, it is easy to see that most of those Romans who spoke of Taprobane had Ceylon in their eye. But that all had not, and of those who really *had*, that some indicated by their facts very different islands, whilst designing to indicate Ceylon, is undeniable; since, amongst other imaginary characteristics of Taprobane, they make it extend considerably to the south of the line. Now, with respect to Ceylon, this is notoriously false. That island lies entirely in the northern tropic, and does not come within five (hardly more than six) degrees of the equator. Plain it is, therefore, that Taprobane, if construed very strictly, is an *ens rationis* made up by fanciful composition from various sources, and much like our own mediæval conceit of Prester John's country, or the fancies (which have but recently vanished) of the African river Niger, and the golden city Tombuctoo. These were lies: and yet also, in a limited sense, they were truths. They were expansions, often fabulous and impossible, engrafted upon some basis of fact by the credulity of the traveller, or subsequently by misconception of the scholar. For instance, as to Tombuctoo, Leo Africanus had authorised men to believe in some vast African city, central to that great continent, and a focus to some mighty system of civilisation. Others, improving on that chimera, asserted that this glorious city represented an inheritance derived from ancient Carthage; here, it was said, survived the arts and arms of that injured state; hither across Bilidulgerid had the children of Phœnicia fled from the wrath of Rome; and the mighty phantom of him whose uplifted truncheon had pointed its path to the carnage of Cannæ, was still the tutelary genius watching over a vast posterity worthy of himself. Here was a wilderness of lies; yet, after all, the lies were but so many voluminous *fasciæ*, enveloping the mummy of an original truth. Mungo Park came, and the city of Tombuctoo was shown to be a real existence. Seeing was believing. And yet, if, before the time of Park, you had avowed a belief in Tombuctoo, you would have made yourself an indorser of that huge forgery which had so long circulated through the forum of Europe, and, in fact, a party to the total fraud.

We have thought it right to direct the reader's eye upon this correction of the common problem as to this or that place—Ceylon for example—answering to this or that classical name, because, in fact, the problem is more subtle than it appears to be. If you are asked whether you believe in the unicorn, undoubtedly you are within the *letter* of the truth in replying that you do; for there are several varieties of large animals which carry a single horn in the forehead.* But, *virtually*, by such an answer you would countenance a falsehood or a doubtful legend, since you are well aware that, in the idea of an unicorn, your questioner included the whole traditionary character of the unicorn as an antagonist and emulator of the lion, &c.; under which fanciful description this animal is properly ranked with the griffin, the mermaid, the basilisk, the dragon, and sometimes discussed in a supplementary chapter by the current zoologies, under the idea of heraldic and apocryphal natural history. When asked, therefore, whether Ceylon is Taprobane, the true answer is, not by affirmation simply, nor by negation simply, but by both at once; it is, and it is not. Taprobane includes much of what belongs to Ceylon, but also more and also less. And this case is a type of many others standing in the same logical circumstances.

But, secondly, as to Ceylon being the local representative of Paradise, we may say, as the courteous Frenchman did to Dr Moore upon the Doctor's apologetically remarking of a word which he had used, that he feared it was not good French—"Non, Monsieur, il n'est pas; mais il mérite bien l'être." Certainly, if Ceylon was not, at least it ought to have been, Paradise; for at this day there is no place on earth which better supports the paradisiacal character (always excepting Lapland, as an Upsal professor observes, and Wapping, as an old seaman reminds us) than this Pandora of islands, which the Hindoos call Lanka, and Europe calls Ceylon. We style it the "Pan-

* *Unicorn:* and strange it is that, in ancient dilapidated monuments of the Ceylonese, religious sculptures, &c., the unicorn of Scotland frequently appears according to its true heraldic (*i.e.*, fabulous) type.

dora" of islands, because, as all the gods of the heathen clubbed their powers in creating that ideal woman—clothing her with perfections, and each separate deity subscribing to her dowery some separate gift—not less conspicuous, and not less comprehensive, has been the bounty of Providence, running through the whole diapason of possibilities, to this all-gorgeous island. Whatsoever it is that God has given by separate allotment and partition to other sections of the planet, all this he has given cumulatively and redundantly to Ceylon. Was she therefore happy, was Ceylon happier than other regions, through this hyper-tropical munificence of her Creator? No, she was not; and the reason was, because idolatrous darkness had planted curses where Heaven had planted blessings; because the insanity of man had defeated the graciousness of God. But another era is dawning for Ceylon; God will now countersign his other blessings, and ripen his possibilities into great harvests of realisation, by superadding the one blessing of a dove-like religion; light is thickening apace, the horrid altars of Moloch are growing dim; woman will no more consent to forego her birthright as the daughter of God; man will cease to be the tiger-cat that, in the *noblest* chamber of Ceylon, he has ever been; and with the new hopes that will now blossom amidst the ancient beauties of this lovely island, Ceylon will but too deeply fulfil the functions of a paradise. Too subtly she will lay fascinations upon man; and it will need all the anguish of disease, and the stings of death, to unloose the ties which, in coming ages, must bind the hearts of her children to this Eden of the terraqueous globe.

Yet if, apart from all bravuras of rhetoric, Mr Bennett seriously presses the question regarding Paradise as a question in geography, we are sorry that we must vote against Ceylon, for the reason that heretofore we have pledged ourselves in print to vote in favour of Cashmeer; which beautiful vale, by the way, is omitted in Mr Bennett's list of the candidates for that distinction already entered upon the roll. Supposing the Paradise of Scripture to have had a local settlement upon our earth, and not in some extra-terrene orb, even in that case we cannot imagine that anything could now survive, even so much as an angle or a curve, of its original outline. All rivers have altered their channels; many are altering them for ever.* Longitude and latitude might be assigned, at the most, if even those are not substantially defeated by the Miltonic "pushing askance" of the poles with regard to the equinoctial. But finally, we remark, that whereas human nature has ever been prone to the superstition of local consecrations and personal idolatries, by means of memorial relics, apparently it is the usage of God to hallow such remembrances by removing, abolishing, and confounding all traces of their punctual identities. *That* raises them to shadowy powers. By that process such remembrances pass from the state of base sensual signs, ministering only to a sensual servitude, into the state of great ideas—mysterious as spirituality is mysterious, and permanent as truth is permanent. Thus it is, and therefore it is, that Paradise has vanished; Luz is gone; Jacob's ladder is found only as an apparition in the clouds; the true cross survives no more among the Roman Catholics than the true ark is mouldering upon Ararat; no scholar can lay his hand upon Gethsemane; and for the grave of Moses the son of Amram, mightiest of law-

* See Dr Robison on *Rivers*.

givers, though it is somewhere near Mount Nebo, and in a valley of Moab, yet eye has not been suffered to behold it, and "no man knoweth of his sepulchre unto this day." *

If, however, as to Paradise in connection with Ceylon we are forced to say "*No;*" if as to Taprobane in connection with Ceylon we say both "*Yes*" and "*No,*"—not the less we come back with a reiterated "*Yes, yes, yes,*" upon Ceylon as the crest and eagle's plume of the Indies, as the priceless pearl, the ruby without a flaw, and (once again we say it) as the Pandora of oriental islands.

Yet ends so glorious imply means of corresponding power; and advantages so comprehensive cannot be sustained unless by a machinery proportionately elaborate. Part of this machinery lies in the miraculous climate of Ceylon. Climate? She has all climates. Like some rare human favourite of nature, scattered at intervals along the line of a thousand years, who has been gifted so variously as to seem

"Not one, but all mankind's epitome."

Ceylon, in order that she might become capable of products without end, has been made an abstract of the whole earth, and fitted up as a *panorganon* for modulating through the whole diatonic scale of climates. This is accomplished in part by her mountains. No island has mountains so high. It was the hideous oversight of a famous infidel in the last century, that, in supposing an Eastern prince *of necessity* to deny frost and ice as things impossible to *his* experience, he betrayed too palpably his own non-acquaintance with the grand economies of nature. To make acquaintance with cold, and the products of

* Deut. xxxiv. 6.

cold, obviously he fancied it requisite to travel northwards; to taste of polar power, he supposed it indispensable to have advanced towards the pole. Narrow was the knowledge in those days, when a master in Israel might have leave to err thus grossly. Whereas at present, few are the people amongst those not openly making profession of illiteracy, who do not know that a sultan of the tropics—ay, though his throne were screwed down by exquisite geometry to the very centre of the equator—might as surely become familiar with winter by ascending three miles in altitude, as by travelling three thousand horizontally. In that way of ascent it is that Ceylon has her regions of winter and her Arctic districts. She has her Alps, and she has her alpine tracts for supporting human life and useful vegetation. Adam's Peak, which of itself is more than seven thousand feet high (and by repute the highest range within her shores), has been found to rank only fifth in the mountain scale. The highest is a thousand feet higher. The maritime district, which runs round the island for a course of nine hundred miles, fanned by the sea-breezes, makes, with these varying elevations, a vast cycle of secondary combinations for altering the temperature and for *adapting* the weather. The central region has a separate climate of its own. And an inner belt of country, neither central nor maritime, which from the sea-belt is regarded as inland, but from the centre is regarded as maritime, composes another chamber of climates; whilst these again, each individually within its class, are modified into minor varieties by local circumstances as to wind, by local accidents of position, and by shifting stages of altitude.

With all this compass of power, however (obtained from its hills and its varyin scale of hills), Ceylon has not much of waste ground, in the sense of being irreclaimable—for of waste ground, in the sense of being unoccupied, she has an infinity. What are the dimensions of Ceylon? Of all islands in this world which we know, in respect of size it most resembles Ireland, being about one-sixth part less. But, for a particular reason, we choose to compare it with Scotland, which is very little different in dimensions from Ireland, having (by some hundred or two of square miles) a trifling advantage in extent. Now, say that Scotland contains a trifle more than thirty thousand square miles, the relation of Ceylon to Scotland will become apparent when we mention that this Indian island contains about twenty-four thousand five hundred of similar square miles. Twenty-four and a half to thirty—or forty-nine to sixty—there lies the ratio of Ceylon to Scotland. The ratio in population is not less easily remembered: Scotland has *now* (October 1843) hard upon three millions of people: Ceylon, by a late census, has just three *half* millions. But strange indeed, where everything seems strange, is the arrangement of this Ceylonese territory and people. Take a peach: what you call the flesh of the peach, the substance which you eat, is massed orbicularly around a central stone—often as large as a pretty large strawberry. Now in Ceylon, the central district, answering to this peach-stone, constitutes a fierce little Lilliputian kingdom, quite independent, through many centuries, of the lazy belt, the peach-flesh, which swathes and enfolds it, and perfectly distinct by the character and origin of its population. The peach-stone is called Kandy, and the people Kandyans. These are a desperate variety of the tiger-man, agile and fierce as he is, though smooth, insinuating, and full of subtlety as a snake, even to the moment of crouching for their last fatal spring. On the other hand, the people of the engirdling zone are called the Cinghalese, spelled according to the fancy of us authors and compositors, who legislate for the spelling of the British empire with an S or a C. As to moral virtue, in the sense of integrity or fixed principle, there is not much lost upon either race: in that point they are "much of a muchness." They are also both respectable for their attainments in cowardice; but with this difference, that the Cinghalese are soft, inert, passive cowards; but your Kandyan is a ferocious little bloody coward, full of mischief as a monkey, grinning with desperation, laughing like a hyena, or chattering if you vex him, and never to be trusted for a moment. The reader now understands why we described the Ceylonese man as a tiger-cat in his noblest division: for, after all, these dangerous gentlemen in the peach-stone are a more promising race than the silky and nerveless population surrounding them. You can strike no fire out of the Cinghalese: but the Kandyans show fight continually, and would even persist in fighting, if there were in this world no gunpowder (which exceedingly they dislike), and if their allowance of arrack were greater.

Surely this is the very strangest spectacle exhibited on earth: a kingdom within a kingdom, an *imperium in imperio*, settled and maintaining itself for centuries in defiance of all that Pagan, that Mohammedan, that Jew, or that Christian could do. The reader will remember the case of the British envoy to Geneva, who being ordered in great wrath to "quit the territories of the republic in twenty-four hours," replied, "By all means: in ten minutes." And here was a little bantam kingdom, not much bigger than the irate republic, having its separate sultan, with full-mounted establishment of peacock's feathers, white elephants, Moorish eunuchs, armies, cymbals, dulcimers, and all kinds of music, tormentors, and executioners; whilst his majesty crowed defiance across the ocean to all other kings, rajahs, soldans, kesars, "flowery" emperors, and "golden-feet" east or west, be the same more or less; and really with some reason. For though it certainly *is* amusing to hear of a kingdom no bigger than Stirlingshire with the half of Perthshire, standing erect and maintaining perpetual war with all the rest of Scotland, a little nucleus of pugnacity, sixty miles by twenty-four, rather more than a match for the lazy lubber, nine hundred miles long, that dandled it in its arms; yet as the trick was done, we cease to find it ridiculous.

For the trick *was* done: and that reminds us to give the history of Ceylon in its two sections, which will not prove much longer than the history of Tom Thumb. Precisely three centuries before Waterloo,—viz., *Anno Domini* 1515,—a Portuguese admiral hoisted his sovereign's flag, and formed a durable settlement at Columbo, which was and is considered the maritime capital of the island. Very nearly half-way on the interval of time between this event and Waterloo,—viz., in 1656 (antepenultimate year of Cromwell),—the Portuguese nation made over, by treaty, this settlement to the Dutch; which of itself seems to mark that the sun of the former people was now declining to the west. In 1796, now forty-seven years ago, it arose out of the French revolutionary war—so disastrous for Holland—that the Dutch surrendered it perforce to the British, who are not very likely to surrender it in *their* turn on any terms, or at any gentleman's request. Up to this time, when Ceylon passed under our flag, it is to be observed that no progress whatever, not the least, had been made in mastering the peach-stone, that old central nuisance of the island. The little monster still crowed, and flapped his wings on his dunghill, as had been his custom always in the afternoon for certain centuries. But nothing on earth is immortal: even mighty bantams must have their decline and fall; and omens began to show out that soon there would be a dust with the new master at Columbo. Seven years after our *debut* on that stage, the dust began. By the way, it is perhaps an impertinence to remark it, but there certainly *is* a sympathy between the motions of the Kandyan potentate and our European enemy Napoleon. Both pitched into *us* in 1803, and we pitched into both in 1815. That we call a coincidence. How the row began was thus: Some incomprehensible intrigues had been proceeding for a time between the British governor or commandant, or whatever he might be, and the Kandyan prime minister. This minister, who was a noticeable man, with large gray eyes, was called *Pilamé Tilawé*. We write his name after Mr Bennett; but it is quite useless to study the pronunciation of it, seeing that he was hanged in 1812 (the year of Moscow),—a fact for which we are thankful as often as we think of it. *Pil.* (surely *Tilawé* cannot be pronounced Garlic?) managed to get the king's head into Chancery, and then fibbed him. Why Major-General M'Dowall (then commanding our forces) should collude with Pil. Garlic is past our understanding. But so it was. *Pil.* said that a certain prince, collaterally connected with the royal house, by name Mootto Sawmé, who had fled to our protection, was, or might be thought to be, the lawful king. Upon which the British general proclaimed him. What followed is too shocking to dwell upon. Scarcely had Mootto, apparently a good creature, been inaugurated, when *Pil.* proposed his deposition, to which General M'Dowall consented, and his own (*Pil.'s*) elevation to the throne. It is like a dream to say, that this also was agreed to. King Pil. the First, and, God be thanked! the last, was raised to the—*musnud*, we suppose, or whatsoever they call it in Pil.'s jargon. So far there was little but farce; now comes the tragedy. A certain Major Davie was placed with a very inconsiderable garrison in the capital of the Kandyan empire, called by name Kandy. This officer, whom Mr Bennett somewhere calls the "gallant," capitulated upon terms, and had the inconceivable folly to imagine that a base Kandyan chief would think himself bound by these terms. One of them was, that he (Major Davie) and his troops should be allowed to retreat unmolested upon Columbo. Accordingly, fully armed and accoutred, the British troops began their march. At Wattépolowa a proposal was made to Major Davie, that Mootto Sawmé (our *protegé* and instrument) should be delivered up to the Kandyan tiger. Oh, sorrow for the British name! he *was* delivered. Soon after, a second proposal came, that the British soldiers should deliver up their arms, and should march back to Kandy. It makes an Englishman shiver with indignation to hear that even this demand was complied with. Let us pause for one moment. Wherefore is it, that in all similar cases,—in this Ceylonese case, in Major Baillie's Mysore case, in the Cabool case,—uniformly the privates are wiser than their officers? In a case of delicacy or doubtful policy, certainly the officers would have been the party best able to solve the difficulties; but in a case of elementary danger, where manners disappear and great passions come upon the stage, strange it is that poor men, labouring men, men without education, always judge more truly of the crisis than men of high refinement. But this was seen by Wordsworth: thus spoke he, thirty-six years ago, of Germany, contrasted with the Tyrol:—

> "Her haughty schools
> Shall blush; and may not we with sorrow say—
> A few strong instincts, and a few plain rules,
> Among the herdsmen of the Alps have wrought
> More for mankind at this unhappy day,
> Than all the pride of intellect and thought."

The regiment chiefly concerned was the 19th (for which regiment the word *Wattépolowa*, the scene of their martyrdom, became afterwards a memorial war-cry). Still to this hour it forces tears of wrath into our eyes when we read the recital of the case. A dozen years ago we first read it in a very interesting book, published by the late Mr Blackwood—the *Life of Alexander Alexander*. This Alexander was not personally present at the bloody catastrophe; but he was in Ceylon at the time, and knew the one sole fugitive* from that fatal day. The soldiers of the 19th, not even in that hour of horror, forgot their discipline, or their duty, or their respectful attachment to their officers. When they were ordered to ground their arms (oh, base idiot that could issue such an order!) they remonstrated most earnestly, but most respectfully. Major Davie, agitated and distracted by the scene, himself recalled the order. The men resumed their arms. Alas! again the fatal order was issued; again it was recalled; but finally, it was issued peremptorily. The men sorrowfully obeyed. We hurry to the odious conclusion. In parties of twos and of threes, our brave countrymen were called out

* *Fugitive*, observe. There were some others, and amongst them Major Davie, who, for private reasons, were suffered to survive as prisoners.

by the horrid Kandyan tiger-cats. Disarmed by the frenzy of their moonstruck commander, what resistance could they make? One after one the parties called out to suffer were decapitated by the executioner. The officers, who had refused to give up their pistols, finding what was going on, blew out their brains with their own hands, now too bitterly feeling how much wiser had been the poor privates than themselves. At length there was stillness on the field. Night had come on. All were gone—

"And darkness was the buryer of the dead."

The reader may recollect a most picturesque murder near Manchester, about thirteen or fourteen years ago, perpetrated by two brothers named M'Kean, where a servant woman, whose throat had been effectually cut, rose up, after an interval, from the ground at a most critical moment (so critical, that, by that act, and at that second of time, she drew off the murderer's hand from the throat of a second victim), staggered, in her delirium, to the door of a room where sometimes a club had been held, doubtless under some idea of obtaining aid, and at the door, after walking some fifty feet, dropped down dead. Not less astonishing was the resurrection, as it might be called, of an English corporal, cut, mangled, re-mangled, and left without sign of life. Suddenly he rose up, stiff and gory; dying and delirious, as he felt himself, with misery from exhaustion and wounds, he swam rivers, threaded enemies, and moving day and night, came suddenly upon an army of Kandyans; here he prepared himself with pleasure for the death that now seemed inevitable, when, by a fortunate accident, for want of a fitter man, he was selected as an ambassador to the English officer commanding a Kandyan garrison—and thus once more escaped miraculously.

Sometimes, when we are thinking over the great scenes of tragedy through which Europe passed from 1805 to 1815, suddenly, from the bosom of utter darkness, a blaze of light arises; a curtain is drawn up; a saloon is revealed. We see a man sitting there alone, in an attitude of alarm and expectation. What does he expect? What is it that he fears? He is listening for the chariot-wheels of a fugitive army. At intervals he raises his head—and we know him now for the Abbé de Pradt—the place, Warsaw—the time, early in December 1812. All at once the rushing of cavalry is heard; the door is thrown open; a stranger enters. We see, as in Cornelius Agrippa's mirror, his haggard features; it is a momentary king, having the sign of a felon's death, written secretly on his brow; it is Murat; he raises his hands with a gesture of horror as he advances to M. l'Abbé. We hear his words—"*L'Abbé, all is lost!*"

Even so, when the English soldier, reeling from his anguish and weariness, was admitted into the beleaguered fortress, his first words, more homely in expression than Murat's, were to the same dreadful purpose: "Your honour," he said, "all is dished;" and this being uttered by way of prologue, he then delivered himself of the message with which he had been charged, and *that* was a challenge from the Kandyan general to come out and fight without aid from his artillery. The dismal report was just in time; darkness was then coming on. The English officer spiked his guns; and, with his garrison, fled by night from a fort in which else he would have perished by starvation or by storm, had Kandyan forces been equal to such an effort. This corporal was, strictly speaking, the only man who *escaped*, one or two other survivors having been reserved as captives, for some special reasons. Of this captive party was Major Davie, the commander, whom Mr Bennett salutes by the title of "gallant," and regrets that "the strong arm of death" had intercepted his apology.

He could have made no apology. Plea or palliation he had none. To have polluted the British honour in treacherously yielding up to murder (and absolutely for nothing in return a prince whom we ourselves had seduced into rebellion—to have forced his men and officers into laying down their arms, and suing for the mercy of wretches the most perfidious on earth; these were acts as to which atonement or explanation was hopeless for *him*, forgiveness impossible for England. So this man is to be called "the gallant"—is he? We will thank Mr Bennett to tell us who was that officer subsequently seen walking about in Ceylon, no matter whether in Western Columbo, or in Eastern Trincomalé, long enough for reaping his dishonour, though, by accident, not for a court-martial? Behold, what a curse rests in this British island upon those men, who, when the clock of honour has sounded the hour for their departure, cannot turn their dying eyes nobly to the land of their nativity—stretch out their hands to the glorious island in farewell homage, and say with military pride—as even the poor gladiators (who were but slaves) said to Cæsar, when they passed his chair to their death—"*Morituri te salutamus!*" This man, and Mr Bennett knows it, because he was encrusted with the leprosy of cowardice, and because upon him lay the blood of those to whom he should have been *in loco parentis*, made a solitude wherever he appeared; men ran from him as from an incarnation of pestilence; and between him and free intercourse with his countrymen, from the hour of his dishonour in the field to the hour of his death, there flowed a river of separation—there were stretched lines of interdict heavier than ever Pope ordained—there brooded a schism like that of death, a silence like that of the grave; making known for ever the deep damnation of the infamy, which on this earth settles upon the troubled resting-place of him who, through cowardice, has shrunk away from his duty, and, on the day of trial, has broken the bond which bound him to his country.

Surely there needed no arrear of sorrow to consummate this disaster. Yet two aggravations there were, which afterwards transpired, irritating the British soldiers to madness. One was soon reported, viz., that one hundred and twenty sick or wounded men, lying in an hospital, had been massacred without a motive by the children of hell with whom we were contending. The other was not discovered until 1815. Then first it became known, that in the whole stores of the Kandyan government (*à fortiori* then in the particular section of the Kandyan forces which we faced), there had not been more gunpowder remaining at the hour of Major Davie's infamous capitulation than seven hundred and fifty pounds avoirdupois; other munitions of war having been in the same state of bankruptcy. Five minutes more of resistance, one inspiration of English pluck, would have placed the Kandyan army in our power—would have saved the honour of the country—would have redeemed our noble soldiers—and to Major Davie, would have made the total difference between lying in a traitor's grave, and lying in Westminster Abbey.

Was there no vengeance, no retribution, for these things? Vengeance there was, but by accident. Retribution there was, but partial and remote. Infamous it was for the English government at Columbo, as Mr

Bennett insinuates, that having a large fund disposable annually for secret service, between 1796 and 1803, such a rupture *could* have happened and have found us unprepared. Equally infamous it was that summary chastisement was not inflicted upon the perfidious court of Kandy. What *real* power it had, when unaided by villany amongst themselves, was shown in 1804; in the course of which year one brave officer, Lieutenant Johnstone of the 19th, with no more than one hundred and fifty men, including officers, marched right through the country, in the teeth of all opposition from the king, and resolutely took* Kandy in his route. However, for the present, without a shadow of a reason, since all reasons ran in the other direction, we ate our leek in silence; once again, but now for the last time, the bloody little bantam crowed defiance from his dunghill, and tore the British flag with his spurs. What caused his ruin at last was literally the profundity of our own British humiliation; had *that* been less, had it not been for the natural reaction of that spectacle, equally hateful and incredible, upon a barbarian chief, as ignorant as he was fiendish, he would have returned a civil answer to our subsequent remonstrances. In that case our government would have been conciliated; and the monster's son, who yet lives in Malabar, would now be reigning in his stead. But *Diis aliter visum est*—earth was weary of this Kandyan nuisance, and the infatuation which precipitated its doom took the following shape:—In 1814, certain traders, ten in number, not British, but

* "*Took* Kandy in his route." This phrase is equivocal; it bears two senses—the traveller's sense and the soldier's. But we rarely make such errors in the use of words; the error is original in the Government documents themselves.

Cinghalese, and therefore British subjects entitled to British protection, were wantonly molested in their peaceable occupations by this Kandyan king. Three of these traders one day returned to our frontier, wearing upon necklaces, inextricably attached to their throats, their own ears, noses, and other parts of their own persons, torn away by the pincers of the Kandyan executioners. The seven others had sunk under their sufferings. Observe that there had been no charge or imputation against these men, more or less; *stet pro ratione voluntas.* This was too much even for our all-suffering* English administration. They sent off a kind of expostulation, which amounted to this—"How now, my good sir? What are you up to?" Fortunately for his miserable subjects (and, as this case showed, by possibility for many who were *not* such), the vain-glorious animal returned no answer; not because he found any diplomatic difficulty to surmount, but in mere self-glorification and in pure disdain of *us.* What a commentary was *that* upon our unspeakable folly up to that hour!

We are anxious that the reader should go along with the short remainder of this story, because it bears strongly upon the true moral of our Eastern policy, of which, hereafter, we shall attempt to unfold the casuistry in a way that will be little agreeable to the calumniators of Clive and Hastings. We do not intend that these

* Why were they "all-suffering?" will be the demand of the reader; and he will doubt the fact simply because he will not apprehend any sufficient motive. That motive we believe to have been this: war, even just or necessary war, is costly; now, the governor and his council knew that their own individual chances of promotion were in the exact ratio of the economy which they could exhibit.

men shall have it all their own way in times to come. Our Eastern rulers have erred always, and erred deeply, by doing too little rather than too much. They have been *too* long-suffering, and have tolerated many nuisances, and many miscreants, when their duty was—when their power was—to have destroyed them for ever. And the capital fault of the East India Company—that greatest benefactor for the East that ever yet has arisen—has been in not publishing to the world the grounds and details of their policy. Let this one chapter in that policy, this Kandyan chapter, proclaim how great must have been the evils from which our "usurpations" (as they are called) have liberated the earth. For let no man dwell on the rarity or on the limited sphere of such atrocities, even in Eastern despotisms. If the act be rare, is not the anxiety eternal? If the personal suffering be transitory, is not the outrage upon human sensibilities, upon the majesty of human nature, upon the possibilities of light, order, commerce, civilisation, of a duration and a compass to make the total difference between man viler than the brutes, and man a little lower than the angels?

It happened that the first noble, or "Adikar," of the Kandyan king, being charged with treason at this time, had fled to our protection. That was enough. Vengeance on *him* in his proper person had become impossible, and the following was the vicarious vengeance adopted by God's vicegerent upon earth, whose pastime it had long been to study the ingenuities of malice, and the possible refinements in the arts of tormenting. Here follows the published report on this one case:—"The ferocious miscreant determined to be fully revenged, and immediately sentenced the Adikar's wife and children together with his brother and the brother's wife, to death after the following fashion—the children were ordered to be decapitated before their mother's face, and their heads to be pounded in a rice-mortar by their mother's hands; which, to save herself from a diabolical torture and exposure" (concealments are here properly practised in the report for the sake of mere human decency), "she submitted to attempt. The eldest boy shrunk (shrank) from the dread ordeal, and clung to his agonized parent for safety; but his younger brother stepped forward and encouraged him to submit to his fate, placing himself before the executioner by way of setting an example. The last of the children to be beheaded was an infant at the breast, from which it was forcibly torn away, and its mother's milk was dripping from its innocent mouth as it was put into the hands of the grim executioner." Finally, the Adikar's brother was executed, having no connection (so much as alleged) with his brother's flight; and then the two sisters-in-law, having stones attached to their feet, were thrown into a tank. These be thy gods, O Egypt! such are the processes of Kandyan law, such is its horrid religion, and such the morality which it generates! And let it not be said these were the excesses of a tyrant. Man does not brutalize, by possibility, in pure insulation. He gives and he receives. It is by sympathy, by the contagion of example, by reverberation of feelings, that every man's heart is moulded. A prince, to have been such as this monster, must have been bred amongst a cruel people: a cruel people, as by other experience we know them to be, naturally produce an inhuman prince, and such a prince reproduces his own corruptors.

Vengeance, however, was now at hand: a better and

more martial governor, Sir Robert Brownrigg, was in the field since 1812. On finding that no answer was forthcoming, he marched with all his forces. But again these were inadequate to the service; and once again, as in 1803, we were on the brink of being sacrificed to the very lunacies of retrenchment. By a mere god-send, more troops happened to arrive from the Indian continent. We marched in triumphal ease to the câpital city of Kandy. The wicked prince fled: Major Kelly pursued him—to pursue was to undertake—to overtake was to conquer. Thirty-seven ladies of his *zenana*, and his mother, were captured elsewhere: and finally the whole kingdom capitulated by a solemn act, in which we secured to it what we had no true liberty to secure, viz., the *inviolability* of their horrid idolatries. Render unto Cæsar the things which are Cæsar's—but this was *not* Cæsar's. Whether in some other concessions, whether in volunteering certain civil privileges of which the conquered had never dreamed, and which, for many a long year, they will not understand, our policy were right or wrong—may admit of much debate. Oftentimes, but not always, it is wise and long-sighted policy to presume in nations higher qualities than they have, and developments beyond what really exist. But as to religion, there can be no doubt, and no debate at all. To exterminate their filthy and bloody abominations of creed and of ritual practice, is the first step to any serious improvement of the Kandyan people: it is the *conditio sine quâ non* of all regeneration for this demoralized race. And what we ought to have promised, all that in mere civil equity we had the right to promise, was—that we would *tolerate* such follies, would make no war upon such superstitions as should not be openly immoral. One word more than this covenant was equally beyond the powers of one party to that covenant, and the highest interests of all parties.

Philosophically speaking, this great revolution may not close perhaps for centuries: historically, it closed about the opening of the Hundred Days in the *annus mirabilis* of Waterloo. On the 13th of February 1815, Kandy, the town, was occupied by the British troops, never again to be resigned. In March followed the solemn treaty by which all parties assumed their constitutional stations. In April occurred the ceremonial part of the revolution, its public notification and celebration, by means of a grand processional entry into the capital, stretching for upwards of a mile; and in January 1816, the late king, now formally deposed, "a stout, good-looking Malabar, with a peculiarly keen and roving eye, and a restlessness of manner, marking unbridled passions," was conveyed in the governor's carriage to the jetty at Trincomalee, from which port H.M.S. Mexico conveyed him to the Indian continent: he was there confined in the fortress of Velore, famous for the bloody mutiny amongst the Company's sepoy troops, so bloodily suppressed. In Velore, this cruel prince, whose name was Sree Wickremé Rajah Singha, died some years after; and one son whom he left behind him, born during his father's captivity, may still be living. But his ambitious instincts, if any such are working within him, are likely to be seriously baffled in the very outset by the precautions of our diplomacy; for one article of the treaty proscribes the descendants of this prince as enemies of Ceylon, if found within its precincts. In this exclusion, pointed against a single family, we are reminded of the Stuart dynasty in England, and the Bonaparte dynasty in France. We cannot, however, agree with Mr Bennett's view of this parallelism—either in so far as it points our pity towards Napoleon, or in so far as it points the regrets of disappointed vengeance to the similar transportation of Sree.

Pity is misplaced upon Napoleon, and anger is wasted upon Sree. He ought to have been hanged, says Mr Bennett; and so said many of Napoleon. But it was not our mission to punish either. The Malabar prince had broken no faith with *us:* he acted under the cursed usages of a cruel people and a bloody religion. These influences had trained a bad heart to corresponding atrocities. Courtesy we did right to pay him, for our own sakes as a high and noble nation. What we could not punish judicially, it did not become us to revile. And finally, we much doubt whether hanging upon a tree, either in Napoleon's case or Sree's, would not practically have been found by both a happy liberation from that bitter cup of mortification which both drank off in their latter years.

At length, then, the entire island of Ceylon, about a hundred days before Waterloo, had become ours for ever. Hereafter Ceylon must inseparably attend the fortunes of India. Whosoever in the East commands the sea, must command the southern empires of Asia; and he who commands those empires, must for ever command the Oriental islands. One thing only remains to be explained; and the explanation, we fear, will be harder to understand than the problem: it is—how the Portuguese and Dutch failed, through nearly three centuries, to master this little obstinate *nucleus* of the peach. It seems like a fairy tale to hear the answer: Sinbad has nothing wilder. "They were," says Mr Bennett, "repeatedly masters of the capital." What was it, then, that stopped them from going on? "At one period, the former (*i.e.*, the Portuguese) had conquered all but the impregnable position called *Kandi Udda.*" And what was it, then, that lived at Kandi Udda? The dragon of Wantley? or the dun cow of Warwick? or the classical Hydra? No; it was thus:—*Kandi* was "in the centre of the mountainous region, surrounded by impervious jungles, with secret approaches for only one man at a time." Such tricks might have answered in the time of Ali Baba and the forty thieves; but we suspect that even then an "*open sesame*" would have been found for this pestilent defile. Smoking a cigar through it, and dropping the sparks, might have done the business in the dry season. But, in very truth, we imagine that political arrangements were answerable for this long failure in checkmating the king, and not at all the cunning passage which carried only one inside passenger. The Portuguese permitted the Kandyan natives to enter their army; and that one fact gives us a short solution of the case. For, as Mr Bennett observes, the principal features of these Kandyans are merely "human imitations of their own indigenous leopards—treachery and ferocity," as the circumstances may allow them to profit by one or the other. Sugar-candy, how ever, appears to have given very little trouble to *us;* and, at all events, it is ours now, together with all that is within its gates. It is proper, however, to add, that since the conquest of this country in 1815, there have been three rebellions, viz.: in 1817–18, in 1834, and finally in 1842. This last comes pretty well home to our own times and concerns; so that we naturally become curious as to the causes of such troubles. The two last are said to have been inconsiderable in their extent. But the earlier of the three, which broke out so soon after the conquest as 1817, must, we conceive, have owed something to intrigues promoted on behalf of the exiled king. His direct lineal descendants are excluded, as we have said, from the island for ever; but his relatives, by whom we presume to be meant his *cognati* or kinspeople in the female line, not his *agnati*, are allowed to live in Kandy, suffering only the slight restriction of confinement to one street out of five, which compose this ancient metropolis. Meantime, it is most instructive to hear the secret account of those causes which set in motion this unprincipled rebellion. For it will thus be seen how hopeless it is, under the present idolatrous superstition of Ceylon, to think of any attachment in the people by means of good government, just laws, agriculture promoted, or commerce created. More stress will be laid by the Ceylonese on our worshipping a carious tooth two inches long, ascribed to the god Buddha (but by some to an ourang-outang), than to every mode of equity, good faith, or kindness. It seems that the Kandyans and we reciprocally misunderstood the ranks, orders, precedences, titular distinctions, and external honours attached to them in our several nations. But none are so deaf as those that have no mind to hear. And we suspect that our honest fellows of the 19th regiment, whose comrades had been murdered in their beds by the cursed Kandyan "nobles," neither did nor would understand the claim of such assassins to military salutes, to the presenting of arms, or to the turning out of the guard. Here, it is said, began the ill-blood, and also on the claim of the Buddhist priests to similar honours. To say the simple truth, these soldiers ought not to have been expected to show respect towards the murderers of their brethren. The priests, with their shaven crowns and yellow robes, were objects of mere mockery to the British soldier. "Not to have been kicked," it should have been said, "is gain; not to have been cudgelled, is for you a ground of endless gratitude. Look not for salutes; dream not of honours." For our own part—again we say it—let the government look ahead for endless insurrections. We tax not the rulers of Ceylon with having caused the insurrections. We hold them blameless on that head; for a people so fickle and so unprincipled will never want such matter for rebellion as would be suspected, least of all, by a wise and benevolent man. But we *do* tax the local government with having ministered to the possibility of rebellion. We British have not sowed the ends and objects of conspiracies; but undoubtedly, by our lax administration, we have sowed the *means* of conspiracies. We must not transfer to a Pagan island our own mild code of penal laws: the subtle savage will first become capable of these when he becomes capable of Christianity. And to this we must now bend our attention. Government must make no more offerings of musical clocks to the Pagan temples; for such propitiations are understood by the people to mean—that we admit their god to be naturally stronger than ours. Any mode or measure of excellence but that of power they understood not as applying to a deity. Neither must our government any longer wink at such monstrous practices as that of children ejecting their dying parents, in their last struggles, from the shelter of their own roofs, on the plea that death would pollute their dwellings. Such compliances with Paganism make Pagans of ourselves. Nor, again, ought the professed worship of devils to be tolerated, more than the Fetish worship or the African witchcraft was tolerated in the West Indies. Having at last obtained secure possession of the entire island, with no reversionary fear over our heads (as, up to Waterloo, we always had), that possibly at a general peace we might find it diplomatically prudent to let it return under Dutch possession, we have no excuse for any longer neglecting the jewel in our power. We gave up to Holland, through unwise generosity, already one splendid island, viz., Java. Let one such folly suffice for one century.

For the same reason—namely, the absolute and undivided possession which we now hold of the island—it is at length time that our home government should more distinctly invite colonists, and make known the unrivalled capabilities of this region. So vast are our colonial territories, that for every class in our huge framework of society we have separate and characteristic attractions. In some it is chiefly labour that is wanted, capital being in excess. In others these proportions are reversed. In some it is great capitalists that are wanted for the present; in others almost exclusively small ones. Now, in Ceylon either class will be welcome. It ought also to be published everywhere, that immediately after the conquest of Kandy, the government entered upon the Roman career of civilisation, and upon that also which may be considered peculiarly British. Military roads were so carried as to pierce and traverse all the guilty fastnesses of disease, and of rebellion by means of disease. Bridges, firmly built of satin-wood, were planted over every important stream. The Kirimé canal was completed in the most eligible situation. The English institution of mail-coaches was perfected in all parts of the island. At this moment there are three separate modes of itinerating through the island, viz., by mail-coach, by buggy, or by palanquin; to say nothing of the opportunities offered at intervals, along the maritime provinces, for coasting by ships or boats. To the botanist, the mineralogist, the naturalist, the sportsman, Ceylon offers almost a virgin Eldorado. To a man wishing to combine the lucrative pursuits of the colonist with the elegances of life and with the comforts of compatriot society, not (as in Australia or in American back settlements) to weather the hardships of Robinson Crusoe, the invitations from the infinite resources of Ceylon are past all count or estimate. "For my own part," says Mr Bennett, who is *now* a party absolutely disinterested, "having visited all but the northern regions of the globe, I have seen nothing to equal this incomparable country." Here a man may purchase land, with secure title and of a good tenure, at five shillings the acre; this, at least, is the upset price, though in some privileged situations it is known to have reached seventeen shillings. A house may be furnished in the Morotto style, and with luxurious contrivances for moderating the heat in the hotter levels of the island, at fifty pounds sterling. The native furniture is both cheap and excellent in quality; every way superior, intrinsically, to that which, at five times the cost, is imported from abroad. Labour is pretty uniformly at the rate of sixpence English for twelve hours. Provisions of every sort and variety are poured out in Ceylon from an American *cornucopia* of some Saturnian age. Wheat, potatoes, and many esculent plants or fruits, were introduced by the British in the great year—(and for this island, in the most literal sense, the era of a new earth and new heavens)—the year of Waterloo. From that year dates, for the Ceylonese, the day of equal laws for rich and poor, the day of development out of infant and yet unimproved advantages; finally,—if we are wise, and if *they* are docile,—the day of a heavenly religion displacing the *avowed* worship of devils, and giving to the people a new nature, a new heart, and hopes as yet not dawning upon their dreams. How often has it been said by the vile domestic calumniators of British policy, by our own anti-national deceivers, that if to-morrow we should leave India, no memorial would attest that ever we had been there. Infamous falsehood! damnable slander! Speak, Ceylon, to *that*. True it is, that the best of our gifts,—peace, freedom, security, and a new standard of public morality,—these blessings are like sleep, like health, like innocence, like the eternal revolutions of day and night, which sink inaudibly into human hearts, leaving behind (as sweet vernal rains) no flaunting records of ostentation and parade: we are not the nation of triumphal arches and memorial obelisks; but the sleep, the health, the innocence, the grateful vicissitudes of seasons, reproduce themselves in fruits and products, enduring for generations, and overlooked by the slanderer only because they are too general to be noticed as extraordinary, and benefiting by no light of contrast, simply because our own beneficence has swept away the ancient wretchedness that could have furnished the mass. Ceylon, of itself, can reply victoriously to such falsehoods. Not yet fifty years have we held this island; not yet thirty have we had the *entire* possession of the island; and (what is more important to a point of this nature) not yet thirty have we had that secure possession which results from the consciousness that our government is not meditating to resign it. Previously to Waterloo, our tenure of Ceylon was a provisional tenure. With the era of our Kandyan conquest coincides the era of our absolute appropriation, signed and countersigned for ever. The arrangements of that day at Paris, and by a few subsequent congresses of revision, are like the arrangements of

Westphalia in 1648,—valid until Christendom shall be again convulsed to her foundations. From that date is, therefore, justly to be inaugurated our English career of improvement. Of the roads laid open through the island we have spoken. The attempts at improvement of the agriculture and horticulture furnish matter already for a romance, if told of any other than this wonderful labyrinth of climates. The openings for commercial improvement are not less splendid. It is a fact infamous to the Ceylonese, that an island which might easily support twenty millions of people has been liable to famine, not unfrequently, with a population of fifteen hundred thousand. This has already ceased to be a possibility: is *that* a blessing of British rule? Not only many new varieties of rice have been introduced, and are now being introduced, adapted to opposite extremes of weather and soil,—some to the low grounds, warm and abundantly irrigated—some to the dry grounds, demanding far less of moisture; but also other and various substitutes have been presented to Ceylon. Manioc, maize, the potato, the turnip, have all been cultivated. Mr Bennett himself would, in ancient Greece, have had many statues raised to his honour for his exemplary bounties of innovation. The food of the people is now secure. And, as regards their clothing or their exports, there is absolutely no end to the new prospects opened before them by the English. Is *cotton* a British gift? Is sugar? Is coffee? We are not the men lazily and avariciously to anchor our hopes on a pearl fishery; we rouse the natives to cultivate their salt fish and shark fisheries. Tea will soon be cultivated more hopefully than in Assam. Sugar, coffee, cinnamon, pepper, are all cultivated already. Silk-worms and mulberry-trees were tried with success, and opium with *virtual* success (though in that instance defeated by an accident), under the auspices of Mr Bennett. Hemp (and surely it is wanted!) will be introduced abundantly: indigo is not only grown in plenty, but it appears that a beautiful variety of indigo, a violet-coloured indigo, exists as a weed in Ceylon. Finally, in the running over hastily the *summa genera* of products by which Ceylon will soon make her name known to the ends of the earth, we may add that salt provisions in every kind, of which hitherto Ceylon did not furnish an ounce, will now be supplied redundantly: the great mart for this will be in the vast bosom of the Indian Ocean; and at the same time we shall see the scandal wiped away that Ceylon, the head-quarters of the British navy in the East, could not supply a cock-boat in distress with a week's salt provisions, from her own myriads of cattle—zebus, buffaloes, or cows.

Ceylon has this one disadvantage for purposes of theatrical effect; she is like a star rising heliacally, and hidden in the blaze of the sun: any island, however magnificent, becomes lost in the blaze of India. But *that* does not affect the realities of the case. She has *that* within which passes show. Her one calamity is in the laziness of her native population; though in this respect the Kandyans are a more hopeful race than the Cinghalese. But the evil for both is, that they want the *motives* to exertion. These will be created by a new and higher civilisation. Foreign labourers will also be called for; a mixed race will succeed in the following generations; and a mixed breed in man is always an improved breed. Witness everywhere the people of colour contrasted with the blacks. Then will come the great race between man indefinitely exalted, and a glorious tropical nature indefinitely developed. Ceylon will be born again: in our hands she will first answer to the great summons of nature; and will become, in fact, what by providential destiny she is,—the queen lotus of the Indian seas, and the Pandora of islands.

THE KING OF HAYTI.

FROM THE GERMAN.

CHAPTER I.

Six weeks after his death stood the bust of the late stamp-distributor Goodchild, exposed to public view in the china-manufactory of L——. For what purpose? Simply for this—that he might call heaven and earth to witness, that, allowing for some little difference in the colours, he looked just as he did heretofore in life: a proposition which his brother and heir, Mr Goodchild the merchant, flatly denied. For this denial Mr Goodchild had his private reasons. "It is true," said he, "my late brother, the stamp-distributor, God rest him! did certainly bespeak three dozen copies of his own bust at the china-works; but surely he bespoke them for his use in this life, and not in the next. His intention, doubtless, was to send a copy to each of those loose companions of his who helped him to run through his fine estate: natural enough for him to propose as a spendthrift, but highly absurd for me to ratify as executor to so beggarly an inheritance; and therefore assuredly I shall not throw so much money out of the windows."

This was plausible talking to all persons who did not happen to know that the inheritance amounted to twenty-five thousand dollars; and that the merchant Goodchild, as was unanimously affirmed by all the Jews, both Christian and Jewish, in L——, weighed, moreover, in his own person, independently of that inheritance, one entire ton of gold.

CHAPTER II.

The Ostensible Reason.

The china-works would certainly never have been put off with this allegation; and therefore, by the advice of his attorney, he had in reserve a more special argument why he ought not to pay for the six-and-thirty busts. "My brother," said he, "may have ordered so many copies of his bust. It is possible. I neither affirm nor deny. Busts may be ordered, and my brother may have ordered them. But what then? I suppose all men will grant that he meant the busts to have some resemblance to himself, and by no means to have no resemblance. But now, be it known, they have no resemblance to him. *Ergo*, I refuse to take them. One word's as good as a thousand."

CHAPTER III.

"*In the second place*"—*Dinner is on the Table.*

But this one word, no, nor a thousand such, would satisfy Mr Whelp, the proprietor of the china-works; so he summoned Mr Goodchild before the magistracy. Unfortunately, Mr Whelp's lawyer, in order to show his ingenuity, had filled sixteen folio pages with an introductory argument, in which he laboured to prove that the art of catching a likeness was an especial gift of God, bestowed on very few portrait-painters and sculptors—and which, therefore, it was almost impious and profane to demand of a mere uninspired baker of porcelain. From this argument he went on to infer *à fortiori* in the second place, that where the china-baker *did* hit the likeness, and had done so much more than could lawfully be asked of him, it was an injustice that would cry aloud to heaven for redress, if, after all, his works were returned upon his hands; especially where, as in the present instance, so much beauty of art was united with the peculiar merit of a portrait. It was fatal, however, to the effect of this argument, that just as the magistrate arrived at—"*In the second place*,"—his servant came in and said, "If you please, sir, dinner is on the table." Naturally, therefore, conceiving that the *gite* of the lawyer's reasoning was to defend the want of resemblance as an admitted fact, which it would be useless to deny, the worthy magistrate closed the pleadings, and gave sentence against Mr Whelp, the plaintiff.

CHAPTER IV.

The Professional Verdict.

Mr Whelp was confounded at this decree; and as the readiest means of obtaining a revision of it, he sent in to the next sitting of the bench a copy of the bust, which had previously been omitted. As bad luck would have it, however, there happened on this occasion to be present an artist who had a rancorous enmity both to Mr Whelp and to the modeller of the bust. This person, being asked his opinion, declared without scruple, that the bust was as wretched a portrait as it was lamentable in its pretensions as a work of art, and that his youngest pupil would not have had the audacity to produce so infamous a performance, unless he had an express wish to be turned neck and heels out of his house.

Upon this award of the conscientious artist—out of regard to his professional judgment—the magistracy thought fit to impose silence upon their own senses, which returned a very opposite award: and thus it happened that the former decision was affirmed. Now, certainly, Mr Whelp had his remedy: he might appeal from the magistrate's sentence. But this he declined. "No, no," said he, "I know what I'm about: I shall want the magistrate once more; and I mustn't offend him. I will appeal to public opinion: *that* shall decide between me and the old rogue of a merchant."

And precisely in this way it was brought about, that the late stamp-distributor Goodchild came to stand exposed to the public view in the centre window of the china-manufactory.

CHAPTER V.

The Sinecurist.

At the corner of this china-manufactory a beggar had his daily station, which, except for his youth, which was now and then thrown in his teeth, was indeed a right pleasant sinecure. To this man Mr Whelp promised a handsome present if he would repeat to him in the evening what the passers-by had said of the bust in the day-time. Accordingly at night the beggar brought him the true and comfortable intelligence, that young and old had unanimously pronounced the bust a most admirable likeness of the late stamp-distributor Goodchild. This report was regularly brought for eight days: on the eighth Mr

Whelp was satisfied, and paid off his commissioner, the beggar.

The next morning Mr Whelp presented himself at Mr Goodchild's to report the public approbation of his brother's bust.

CHAPTER VI.

The Young Visionary.

But here there was sad commotion. Mr Goodchild was ill: and his illness arose from a little history, which must here be introduced by way of episode. Mr Goodchild had an only daughter named Ida. Now Miss Ida had begun, like other young ladies of her age, to think of marriage: nature had put it into her head to consider all at once that she was seventeen years of age. And it sometimes occurred to her that Mr Tempest, the young barrister, who occupied the first floor over the way, was just the very man she would like in the character of lover. Thoughts of the same tendency appeared to have occurred also to Mr Tempest. Ida seemed to him remarkably well fitted to play the part of a wife; and when he pretended to be reading the pandects at his window, too often (it must be acknowledged) his eyes were settled all the while upon Ida's blooming face. The glances of these eyes did certainly cause some derangement occasionally in Ida's sewing and netting. What if they did? Let her drop as many stitches as she would, the next day was long enough to take them up again.

This young man, then, was clearly pointed out by Providence as the partner of her future life. Ah! that her father would think so too! But he called him always the young visionary. And whenever she took a critical review of all their opposite neighbours, and fell as if by accident upon the domestic habits, respectable practice, and other favourable points about Mr Tempest, her father never failed to close the conversation by saying,—"Aye, but he's a mere young visionary." And why, Mr Goodchild? Simply for these two reasons: first, because once at a party where they had met, Mr Tempest had happened to say a few words very displeasing to his prejudices on the "golden age" of German poetry, to which Mr Goodchild was much attached, and on which he could bear no opposition. Secondly, and chiefly, because, at the same time, he had unfortunately talked of the King of Hayti as a true crowned head,—a monarch whom Mr Goodchild was determined never to acknowledge.

CHAPTER VII.

At last, Ida and Mr Tempest had come to form a regular correspondence together in the following way:—The young advocate had conducted a commerce of looks with the lovely girl for a long time, and hardly knowing how it began, he had satisfied himself that she looked like an angel; and he grew very anxious to know whether she also talked like one? To ascertain this point, he followed her many a time, and up and down many a street; and he bore patiently, for her sake, all the angry looks of his clients, which seemed to say that he would do more wisely to stay at home and study their causes, than to roam about in chase of a pretty girl. Mr Tempest differed from his clients on this matter: suits at law, said he, have learned to wait; they are used to it; but hearts have not learned to wait, and never will be used to it. However, all was in vain. Ida was attended constantly either by her father, or by an old governess; and in either case his scheme was knocked on the head.

At length, chance did for him more than he could ever do for himself, and placed him one night at her elbow in the theatre. True it was that her father, whose dislike to him ever since his fatal acknowledgment of the King of Hayti he had not failed to remark, sate on the other side of her; but the devil is in it, thought he, if I cannot steal a march on him the whole night through. As the overture to his scheme, therefore, he asked, in the most respectful manner, for the play-bill which Ida held in her hand. On returning it, he said,—what a pity that the vanity of the manager should disturb so many excellent parts; the part allotted to himself would have been far better played by several others in the company.

Mr Tempest was not much delighted on observing that Mr Goodchild did not receive this remark very propitiously, but looked still gloomier than before. The fact was, that the manager constantly attended all Mr Goodchild's literary parties, professed great deference for his opinions, and was in return pronounced by Mr Goodchild a man of "exceedingly good taste and accurate judgment." His first shot, Mr Tempest saw clearly, had missed fire; and he would have been very glad to have had it back again; for he was thrown into a hideous fright when he saw the deep darkness which was gathering on Mr Goodchild's face. Meantime, it was some little support to him under his panic—that in returning the play-bill to Ida, he had ventured to press her hand, and fancied (but it could only be fancy) that she slightly returned the pressure. His enemy, whose thunder now began to break, insisted on giving an importance to his remark which the unfortunate young man himself had never contemplated—having meant it only as an introduction to further conversation, and not at all valuing himself upon it. "A pity, my good sir," said Mr Goodchild· "Why so, my good sir? On the contrary, my good sir, on the contrary, I believe it is pretty generally admitted that there is no part whatsoever in which this manager fails to outshine all competitors."

"Very true, sir; as you observe, sir, he outshines all his competitors; and, in fact, that was just the very remark I wished to make."

"It was, was it? Well, then, upon my word, my good sir, you took a very odd way to express it. The fact is, young and visionary people of this day are very rash in their judgments. But it is not to be supposed that so admirable a performer as this can be at all injured by such light and capricious opinions."

Mr Tempest was confounded by this utter discomfiture of his inaugural effort, and sank dejected into silence. But his victorious foe looked abroad in all directions with a smiling and triumphant expression on his face, as if asking whether anybody had witnessed the ability with which he had taken down the conceit of the young rattlebrain.

However, Mr Tempest was not so utterly dejected, but he consoled himself with thinking that every dog has his day: his turn would come; and he might yet perhaps succeed in laying the old dragon asleep.

CHAPTER VIII.

With a view to do this as soon as possible, at the end of the first act he begged a friend who stood next to him to take his place by the side of Ida for a few minutes, and then hastened out. Under one of the lamps on the outside of the theatre, he took out from his pocket the envelope of a letter he had lately received, and with a pencil wrote upon it a formal declaration of love. His project was, to ask Ida a second time for the play-bill, and on returning it, to crush up the little note and put both together into her hand. But lord! how the wisest schemes are baffled! On returning to the pit, he found the whole condition of things changed. His faithless representative met him with an apology at the very door. The fact was, that, seeing a pretty young lady standing close by him, the devil of gallantry had led him to cede to her use in perpetuity what had been committed to his own care in trust only for a few minutes. Nor was this all; for the lady being much admired and followed, and (like comets or Highland chieftains) having her "tail" on for this night, there was no possibility of reaching the neighbourhood of Ida for the pressure of the lady's tail of followers.

CHAPTER IX.

In his whole life had Mr Tempest never witnessed a more stupid performance, worse actors, or more disgusting people about him than during the time that he was separated from Ida. With the eye of an experienced tactician, he had calculated to a hair the course he must steer, on the termination of the play, to rejoin the object of his anxious regard. But alas! when the curtain dropped, he found his road quite blocked up. No remedy was left but to press right on, and without respect of persons. But he gained nothing by the indefatigable labour of his elbows except a great number of scowling looks. His attention was just called to this, when Ida, who had now reached the door, looked back for a moment, and then disappeared in company with her father. Two minutes after he had himself reached the door; but, looking round, he exclaimed pretty loudly—"Ah, good lord! it's of no use;" and then through the moonlight and the crowd of people he shot like an arrow, leaving them all to wonder what madness had seized the young advocate, who was usually so rational and composed. However, he overtook the object of his pursuit in the street in which he lived. For, upon his turning rapidly round the corner, Mr Goodchild, alarmed at his noise and his speed, turned round upon him suddenly, and said—"Is this a man or a horse?"

CHAPTER X.

"Mr Goodchild," began the breathless barrister, "I am very much indebted to you."

"Hem!" said the other in a way which seemed to express—"What now, my good sir?"

"You have this evening directed my attention to the eminent qualifications of our manager. Most assuredly you were in the right; he played the part divinely."

Here Mr Tempest stopped to congratulate himself upon the triumphant expression which the moonlight revealed upon the face of his antagonist. On this triumph, if his plans succeeded, he meant to build a triumph of his own.

"Aye, aye: what, then, you've come to reason at last, my good sir?"

"Your judgment and penetration, Mr Goodchild, I am bound at all times to bow to as far superior to my own.'

During this compliment to the merchant's penetration, Mr Tempest gently touched the hand of Ida with his pencil note: the hand opened, and, like an oyster, closed upon it in an instant. "In which scene, Mr Tempest," said the merchant, "is it your opinion that the manager acquitted himself best?"

"In which scene!" Here was a delightful question. The advocate had attended so exclusively to Ida, that whether there were any scenes at all in the whole performance was more than he could pretend to say; and now he was to endure a critical examination on the merits of each scene in particular. He was in direful perplexity. Considering, however, that in most plays there is some love, and therefore some love-scenes, he dashed at it, and boldly said—"In that scene, I think, where he makes the declaration of love."

"Declaration of love! why, God bless my soul! in the whole part, from the beginning to end, there is nothing like a declaration of love."

"Oh, confound your accuracy, you old fiend!" thought Mr Tempest to himself; but aloud he said—"No declaration of love, do you say? Is it possible? Why, then, I suppose I must have mistaken for the manager that man who played the lover: surely *he* played divinely."

"Divinely! divine stick! what, that wretched, stammering, wooden booby? Why he would have been hissed off the stage, if it hadn't been well known that he was a stranger hired to walk through the part for that night."

Mr Tempest, seeing that the more he said the deeper he plunged into the mud, held it advisable to be silent. On the other hand, Mr Goodchild began to be ashamed of his triumph over what he had supposed the lawyer's prejudices. He took his leave, therefore, in these words "Good night, Mr Tempest; and, for the future, my good sir, do not judge so precipitately as you did on that occasion when you complimented a black fellow with the title of king, and called St Domingo by the absurd name of

Hayti. Some little consideration and discretion go to every sound opinion."

So saying, the old dragon walked off with his treasure, and left the advocate with his ears still tingling from his mortifications.

"Just to see the young people of this day," said Mr Goodchild; "what presumption and what ignorance!" The whole evening through he continued to return to this theme; and during supper nearly choked himself in an ebullition of fiery zeal upon this favourite topic.

CHAPTER XI.

The Letter-Box.

To her father's everlasting question, "Am not I in the right, then?" Ida replied in a sort of pantomime, which was intended to represent "*Yes.*" This was her outward *yes;* but in her heart she was thinking of no other *yes* than that which she might one day be called on to pronounce at the altar by the side of Mr Tempest. And therefore, at length, when the eternal question came round again, she nodded in a way which rather seemed to say, "Oh, dear sir, you are in the right for anything I have to say against it," than anything like a downright *yes.* On which Mr Goodchild quitted one favourite theme for another more immediately necessary—viz., the lukewarmness of young people towards good counsel and sound doctrine.

Meantime, Ida's looks were unceasingly directed to her neck-handkerchief: the reason of which was this. In order, on the one hand, to have the love-letter as near as possible to her heart, and, on the other, to be assured that it was in safe custody, she had converted the beautiful white drapery of her bosom into a letter-case; and she felt continually urged to see whether the systole and diastole which went on in other important contents of this letter-case, might not by chance expose it to view. The letter asked for an answer; and late as it was, when all the house were in bed, Ida set about one. On the following morning, this answer was conveyed to its destination by the man who delivered the newspapers to her father and Mr Tempest.

From this day forward there came so many letters to Miss Goodchild by the new-established post, that the beautiful letter-case was no longer able to contain them. She was now obliged to resort to the help of her writing-desk, which, so long as her father had no suspicions, was fully sufficient.

CHAPTER XII.

The paper intercourse now began to appear too little to Mr Tempest. For what can be despatched in a moment by word of mouth, would often linger unaccomplished for a thousand years when conducted in writing. True it was that a great deal of important business had already been despatched by the letters. For instance, Mr Tempest had through this channel assured himself that Ida was willing to be his for ever. Yet even this was not enough. The contract had been made, but not sealed upon the rosy lips of Ida.

This seemed monstrous to Mr Tempest. "Grant me patience," said he to himself; "grant me patience; when I think of the many disgusting old relations, great raw-boned, absurd fellows, with dusty snuff-powdered beards, that have revelled in that lip-paradise, hardly knowing—

old withered wretches!—what they were about, or what a blessing was conferred upon them; whilst I—yes, I, that am destined to call her my bride one of these days—am obliged to content myself with payments of mere paper money."

This seemed shocking; and, indeed, considering the terms on which he now stood with Ida, Mr Tempest could scarcely believe it himself. He paced up and down his study in anger, flinging glances at every turn upon the opposite house, which contained his treasure. All at once he stopped: "What's all this?" said he, on observing Mr Goodchild's servants lighting up the chandeliers in the great saloon. "What's in the wind now?" And immediately he went to his writing-table for Ida's last letter; for Ida sometimes communicated any little events in the family that could anyways affect their correspondence; on this occasion, however, she had given no hint of anything extraordinary approaching. Yet the preparations and the bustle indicated something *very* extraordinary. Mr Tempest's heart began to beat violently. What was he to think? Great fêtes, in a house where there is an only daughter, usually have some reference to *her*. "Go, Tyrrel," said he to his clerk, "go and make inquiries (but cautiously, you understand, and in a lawyer-like manner) as to the nature and tendency of these arrangements." Tyrrel came back with the following report: Mr Goodchild had issued cards for a very great party on that evening; all the seniors were invited to tea, and almost all the young people of condition throughout the town to a masqued ball at night. The suddenness of the invitations, and the consequent hurry of the arrangements, arose in this way: a rich relative who lived in the country had formed a plan for coming by surprise, with his whole family, upon Mr Goodchild. But Mr Goodchild had accidentally received a hint of his intention by some side-wind, and had determined to turn the tables on his rich relation by surprising him with a masquerade.

"Oh, heavens! what barbarity!" said Mr Tempest, as towards evening he saw from his windows young and old trooping to the fête. "What barbarity! There's hardly a scoundrel in the place but is asked; and I—I, John Tempest, that am to marry the jewel of the house, must be content to witness the preparations and to hear the sound of their festivities from the solitude of my den."

CHAPTER XIII.

Questions and Commands.

As night drew on, more and more company continued to pour in. The windows being very bright, and the curtains not drawn, no motion of the party could escape our advocate. What pleased him better than all the splendour which he saw, was the melancholy countenance of the kind-hearted girl as she stood at the centre window and looked over at him. This melancholy countenance and these looks, directed at himself, were occasioned, as he soon became aware, by a proposal which had been made to play at questions and commands. This game, in fact, soon began. "Thunder and lightning!" said Mr Tempest, discovering what it was, "is this to be endured?"

If the mere possibility of such an issue had alarmed him, how much more sensible was his affliction when he saw, as a matter of fact laid visibly before his bodily eyes, that every fool and coxcomb availed himself of the privilege of the game to give to Ida, his own destined bride, kisses* without let or hindrance; "whilst I," said he, "I, John Tempest, have never yet been blessed with one."

But if the *sight* of such liberties taken with his blooming Ida placed him on the brink of desperation, much more desperate did he become when that sight was shut out by that "consummate villain" (as he chose to style him) the footman, who at this moment took it into his head, or was ordered, to let down the curtains. Behind the curtains—ah! ye gods, what scenes might not pass!

"This must be put a stop to," said Mr Tempest, taking his hat and cane, and walking into the street. Aye; but how? This was a question he could not answer. Wandering, therefore, up and down the streets until it had become quite dark, he returned at length to the point from which he had set out, and found that one nuisance at least—viz., the kissing—had ceased, and had given place to a concert. For Ida's musical talents and fine voice were well known, and she was generally called the little Catalani. She was now singing, and a crowd of persons had collected under the window to hear her, who seemed, by their looks, to curse every passer-by for the disturbance he made.

Mr Tempest crept on tiptoe to join the crowd of listeners, and was enraptured by the sweet tones of Ida's voice. After the conclusion of the air, and when the usual hubbub of enchanting! divine! &c., had rung out its peal, the bystanders outside began to talk of the masquerade. In the crowd were some of those who had been invited; and one amongst them was flattering himself that nobody would recognise him before he should unmasque.

* The reader must remember that the scene is laid in Germany. This, and other instances of grossiérete, have been purposely retained, in illustration of German manners.

CHAPTER XIV.

The Death's-Head Masque.

Thus much information Mr Tempest drew from this casual conversation, that he found it would not be required of the masquers to announce their names to any person on their arrival. Upon this hint he grounded a plan for taking a part in the masqued ball. By good luck he was already provided with a black domino against the winter masquerades at the public rooms; this domino was so contrived that the head of the wearer was hidden under the cloak, in which an imperceptible opening was made for the eyes; the real head thus became a pair of shoulders, and upon this was placed a false head, which, when lifted up, exposed a white skull with eyeless sockets, and grinning, with a set of brilliantly white teeth, at the curious spectator.

Having settled his scheme, Mr Tempest withdrew to his own lodgings, in order to make preparations for its execution.

CHAPTER XV.

It's only I.

The company at Mr Goodchild's consisted of two divisions: No. 1, embracing the elder or more fashionable persons, and those who were nearly connected with the family, had been invited to tea, supper, and a masqued ball; No. 2, the younger and less distinguished persons, had been invited to the ball only. This arrangement, which proceeded from the penurious disposition of Mr Goodchild, had on this occasion the hearty approbation of

Mr Tempest. About eleven o'clock, therefore, when a great part of the guests in the second division had already arrived, he ordered a sedan-chair to be fetched; and then, causing himself to be carried up and down through several streets, that nobody might discover from what house the gigantic domino had issued, he repaired to the house of Mr Goodchild.

His extraordinary stature excited so much the more astonishment amongst the party-coloured mob of masquers, because he kept himself wholly aloof from all the rest, and paced up and down with haughty strides. His demeanour and air had in it something terrific to everybody except to Ida, to whom he had whispered as he passed her alone in an ante-room—"Don't be alarmed; it's only I;" at the same time giving her a billet, in which he requested a few moments' conversation with her at any time in the course of the evening.

Some persons, however, had observed him speaking to Ida; and therefore, on her return to the great saloon, she was pressed on all sides to tell what she knew of the mysterious giant. She, good heavens! how should she know anything of him? "What had he said, then?" *That*, too, she could as little answer. He spoke, she said, in such a low, hollow, and unintelligible tone, that she was quite alarmed, and heard nothing of what he uttered.

The company now betrayed more and more anxiety in reference to the unknown masque, so that Ida had no chance for answering his billet, or granting the request which it contained. Mr Tempest now began to regret much that he had not selected an ordinary masque, in which he might have conversed at his ease, without being so remarkably pointed out to the public attention.

CHAPTER XVI.

Suspicions.

The murmurs about the tall domino grew louder and louder, and gathered more and more about him. He began to hear doubts plainly expressed, whether he was actually invited. The master of the house protested that, so far from having any such giant amongst his acquaintance, he had never seen such a giant except in show booths. This mention of booths gave a very unfortunate direction to the suspicions already abroad against the poor advocate; for at that time there was a giant in the town who was exhibiting himself for money, and Mr Goodchild began to surmise that this man, either with a view to the increasing his knowledge of men and manners, or for his recreation after the tedium of standing to be gazed at through a whole day's length, had possibly smuggled himself as a contraband article into his masqued ball.

CHAPTER XVII.

Difficulties Increased.

The worthy host set to work very deliberately to count his guests, and it turned out that there was actually just one masque more than there should be. Upon this he stepped into the middle of the company and spoke as follows:—"Most respectable and respected masques, under existing circumstances, and for certain weighty causes, me thereto moving (this phrase Mr Goodchild had borrowed from his lawyer), I have to request that you will all and several, one after another, communicate your names to me, by whispering them into my ear."

Well did Mr Tempest perceive what were the existing circumstances, and what the reasons thereto moving, which had led to this measure; and very gladly he would have withdrawn himself from this vexatious examination by marching off, but it did not escape him that a couple of sentinels were already posted at the door.

CHAPTER XVIII.

Panic.

More than one-half of the guests had already communicated their names to Mr Goodchild, and stood waiting in the utmost impatience for the examination of the giant. But the giant, on his part, was so little eager to gratify them by pressing before others, that at length, when all the rest had gone through their probation honourably, he remained the last man, and thus was, *ipso facto,* condemned as the supernumerary man before his trial commenced.

The company was now divided into two great classes—those who had a marriage garment, and the unfortunate giant who had none. So much was clear; but, to make further discoveries, the host now stepped up to him hastily and said—"Your name, if you please?"

The masque stood as mute, as tall, and as immoveable as the gable end of a house. "Your name?" repeated Mr Goodchild; "I'll trouble you for your name?" No answer coming, a cold shivering seized upon Mr Goodchild. In fact, at this moment a story came across him from his childish years, that, when Dr Faustus was played, it had sometimes happened that amongst the stage devils there was suddenly observed to be one too many, and the supernumerary one was found to be no spurious devil, but a true, sound, and legitimate devil.

For the third time, while his teeth chattered, he said—"Your name, if you please?"

"I have none," said Mr Tempest, in so hollow a voice, that the heart of the worthy merchant sunk down in a moment to his knee-buckles, and an ice-wind of panic began to blow pretty freshly through the whole company.

"Your face, then, if you please, sir?" stammered out Mr Goodchild.

Very slowly and unwillingly the masque, being thus importunately besieged, proceeded to comply; but scarcely had he unmasqued and exposed the death's head, when every soul ran out of the room with an outcry of horror.

The masque sprang after them, bounding like a greyhound, and his grinning skull nodding as he moved. This he did under pretence of pursuing them, but in fact to take advantage of the general panic for making his exit.

CHAPTER XIX.

The Parting Kiss—Miss Goodchild in the arms of Death.

In an ante-room, now totally deserted, Death was met by Ida, who said to him—"Ah! for God's sake make your escape. Oh! if you did but know what anxiety I have suffered on account of your strange conceit." Here she paused, and spite of her anxiety she could not forbear smiling at the thought of the sudden *coup-de-théâtre* by which Mr Tempest had turned the tables upon every soul that had previously been enjoying his panic. In the twinkling of an eye he had inflicted a far deeper panic upon them, and she had herself been passed by the whole herd of fugitives—tall and short, corpulent and lanky, halt and lame young and old—all spinning away with equal energy before the face of the supernumerary guest.

Death, in return, told Ida how he had been an eye-witness to the game of questions and commands, and to the letting down of the curtains. This spectacle (he acknowledged) had so tortured him, that he could stand it no longer, and he had sworn within himself that he would have a kiss as well as other persons; and further, that he would go and fetch it himself from the midst of the masquerade, though not expecting to have been detected as the extra passenger or nip.* And surely, when a whole company had tasted the ambrosia of her lips, Miss Goodchild would not be so unkind as to dismiss him alone without that happiness.

No, Miss Goodchild was not so unkind; and Death was just in the act of applying his lips to the rosy mouth of Ida, when old Goodchild came peeping in at the door to see if the coast was clear of the dreadful masque, and behind him was a train of guests, all stepping gently and on tiptoe from an adjoining corridor

Every soul was petrified with astonishment on seeing the young, warm-breathing Ida on such close and apparently friendly terms with the black gigantic Death, whose skull was grinning just right above the youthful pair, and surmounting them like a crest. At this sight all became plain, and the courage of the company, which

* In England, passengers who are taken up on stage coaches by the collusion of the guard and coachman, without the knowledge of the proprietors, are called *nips*.

had so recently sunk below the freezing point, suddenly rose at once above boiling heat. Mr Goodchild levelled a blow at the Death's head which had caused him so much pain and agitation; and Mr Tempest, seeing that no better course remained, made off for the front door; and thus the uninvited masque, who had so lately chased and ejected the whole body of the invited ones, was in turn chased and ejected by them.

The festivities had been too violently interrupted to be now resumed; the guests took leave, and the weeping Ida was banished to a close confinement in her own room.

CHAPTER XX.

Here ends our episode. It was on the very morning after this *fracas* that Mr Whelp waited upon Mr Goodchild, to report to him the universal opinion of the world upon the bust of the late stamp-distributor, his brother; and upon that opinion to ground an appeal to his justice.

A worse season for his visit he could not possibly have chosen. Mr Goodchild stormed, and said,—" The case had been tried and disposed of; and he must insist on being troubled with no further explanations." And so far did his anger make him forget the common courtesies of life, that he never asked the proprietor of the china-works to sit down. Mr Whelp, on his part, no less astonished and irritated at such treatment, inquired at the footman what was the matter with his master; and the footman, who was going away, and was reckless of consequences, repeated the whole history of the preceding night with fits of laughter; and added, that the sport was not yet over, for that this morning a brisk correspondence had commenced between his master and Mr Tempest—which, by the effect produced on the manners of both, seemed by no means of the gentlest nature.

CHAPTER XXI.

The King of Hayti.

This account was particularly agreeable to Mr Whelp. Concluding that, under the present circumstances, Mr Tempest would naturally be an excellent counsellor against Mr Goodchild, he hastened over to his apartments; and said that, his last effort to bring the merchant over the way to any reasonable temper of mind having utterly failed, he had now another scheme. But first of all he wished to have the professional opinion of Mr Tempest, whether he should lay himself open to an action if he took the following course to reimburse himself the expenses of the three dozen of busts:—He had been told by some Englishman, whose name he could not at this moment call to mind, that the bust of the stamp-master was a most striking likeness of Christophe, the black King of Hayti: now this being the case, what he proposed to do was to wash over the late stamp-distributor with a black varnish, and to export one dozen and a half of the distributor on speculation to St Domingo, keeping the rest for home consumption.

When Mr Tempest heard this plan stated, in spite of his own disturbance of mind at the adventures of the last night, he could not forbear laughing heartily at the conceit; for he well knew what was the real scheme which lurked under this pretended exportation to St Domingo. Some little time back, Mr Goodchild had addressed to the German people, through the *General Advertiser*, this question:—"How or whence it came about that, in so many newspapers of late days, mention had been made of a kingdom of Hayti, when it was notorious to everybody that the island in question was properly called St Domingo?" He therefore exhorted all editors of political journals to return to more correct principles. On the same occasion he had allowed himself many very disrespectful expressions against "a certain black fellow who pretended to be King of Hayti;" so that it might readily be judged that it would not be a matter of indifference to him if his late brother the stamp-master were sold under the name of King of Hayti.

The barrister's opinion was, that as the heir of the bespeaker had solemnly deposed to the non-resemblance of the busts, and had on this ground found means to liberate himself from all obligation to take them or to pay for them, those busts had reverted in full property to the china-works. However, he advised Mr Whelp to blacken only one of them for the present, to place it in the same window where one had stood before, and then to await the issue.

CHAPTER XXII.

A week after this, the bust of the stamp-distributor, with the hair and face blackened, was placed in the window; and below it was written, in gilt letters, "*His most excellent Majesty, the King of Hayti.*"

This manœuvre operated with the very best effect. The passers-by all remembered to have seen the very same face a short time ago as the face of a white man; and they all remembered to whom the face belonged. The laughing, therefore, never ceased from morning to night before the window of the china-works.

Now Mr Goodchild received very early intelligence of what was going on, possibly through some persons specially commissioned by Mr Whelp to trouble him with the news; and straightway he trotted off to the china-works,—not, to be sure, with any view of joining the laughers, but, on the contrary, to attack Mr Whelp, and to demand the destruction of the bust. However, all his remonstrances were to no purpose; and the more anger he betrayed, so much the more did it encourage his antagonist.

Mr Goodchild hurried home in a great passion, and wrote a note to the borough-reeve, with a pressing request that he would favour him with his company to supper that evening, to taste some genuine bottled London porter.

This visit, however, did not lead to those happy results which Mr Goodchild had anticipated. True it was that he showed his discretion in not beginning to speak of the busts until the bottled porter had produced its legitimate effects upon the spirits of the borough-reeve: the worshipful man was in a considerable state of elevation; but for all *that* he would not predict any favourable issue to the action against Mr Whelp which his host was meditating. He shrugged his shoulders, and said that, on the former occasion when Mr Goodchild had urged the bench to pronounce for the *non-resemblance* of the busts, they had gone further, in order to gratify him, than they could altogether answer to their consciences; but really, to come now and call upon the same bench to pronounce for the *resemblance* of the same identical busts, was altogether inadmissible.

CHAPTER XXIII.

Mr Goodchild was on the brink of despair the whole night through; and, when he rose in the morning and put his head out of the window to inhale a little fresh air, what should be the very first thing that met him but a poisonous and mephitic blast from the window of his opposite neighbour, which in like manner stood wide open: for his sharp sight easily detected that the young barrister, his enemy, instead of the gypsum bust of Ulpian which had hitherto presided over his library, had mounted the black china bust of the King of Hayti.

Without a moment's delay Mr Goodchild jumped into his clothes and hastened down to Mr Whelp. His two principles of vitality, avarice and ambition, had struggled together throughout the night; but on the sight of his brother the stamp-master, thus posthumously varnished with lamp-black, and occupying so conspicuous a station in the library of his mortal enemy, ambition had gained a complete victory. He bought up, therefore, the whole thirty-five busts; and understanding that the only black copy was in the possession of Mr Tempest, he begged that, upon some pretext or other, Mr Whelp would get it back into his hands, promising to pay all expenses out of his own purse.

Mr Whelp shook his head; but promised to try what he could do, and went over without delay to the advocate's rooms. Meantime, the longer he stayed and made it evident that the negotiation had met with obstacles, so much the larger were the drops of perspiration which stood upon Mr Goodchild's forehead, as he paced up and down his room in torment.

At last Mr Whelp came over, but with bad news; Mr Tempest was resolute to part with the bust at no price.

CHAPTER XXIV.

Dictation.

Mr Goodchild, on hearing this intelligence, hastened to his daughter, who was still under close confinement, and, taking her hand, said,—"Thoughtless girl, come and behold!" Then, conducting her to his own room, and pointing with his finger to Mr Tempest's book-case, he said,—"See there! behold my poor deceased brother, the stamp-distributor, to what a situation is he reduced—that, after death, he must play the part of a black fellow, styling himself King of Hayti. And is it with such a man, one who aims such deadly stabs at the honour and peace of our family, that you would form a clandestine connection? I blush for you, inconsiderate child. However, sit down to my writing-desk, and this moment write what I shall dictate, *verbatim et literatim;* and in that case I shall again consider and treat you as my obedient daughter. Ida seated herself: her father laid a sheet of paper before her, put a pen into her hand, and dictated the following epistle, in which he flattered himself that he had succeeded to a marvel in counterfeiting the natural style of a young lady of seventeen:—

"Respectable and friendly Sir,—Since the unfortunate masquerade, I have not had one hour of peace. My excellent and most judicious father has shut me up in my own apartments; and, according to special information which I have had, it is within the limits of possibility that my confinement may last for a year and a day. Now, therefore, whereas credible intelligence has reached me that you have, by purchase from the china-manufactory of the city, possessed yourself of a bust claiming to be the representation of a black fellow, who (most absurdly!) styles himself King of Hayti; and whereas, from certain weighty reasons him thereunto moving, my father has a desire to sequestrate into his own hands any bust or busts purporting to represent the said black fellow; and whereas, further, my father has caused it to be notified to me, that immediately upon the receipt of the said bust, through any honourable application of mine to you, he will release me from arrest; therefore, and on the aforesaid considerations, I, Ida Goodchild, spinster, do hereby make known my request to you, that, as a testimony of those friendly dispositions which you have expressed, or caused to be expressed to me, you would, on duly weighing the premises, make over to me the bust aforesaid in consideration of certain monies (as shall be hereafter settled) to be by me paid over unto you. Which request being granted and ratified, I shall, with all proper respect, acknowledge myself your servant and well-wisher, "IDA GOODCHILD,

"*Manu propriâ.*"

The two last words the poor child knew not how to write, and therefore her father wrote them for her, and said—the meaning of these words is, that the letter was written with your own hand; upon which, in law, a great deal depends. He then folded up the letter, sealed it, and rang for a servant to carry it over to Mr Tempest. "But not from me, do you hear, William! Don't say it comes from me: and if Mr Tempest should cross-examine you, be sure you say I know nothing of it."

CHAPTER XXV.

Candour.

"For the rest," said Mr Goodchild, "never conceit that I shall lend any the more countenance, for all this, to your connection with the young visionary. As soon as the bust is once in my hands, from that moment he and I are strangers, and shall know each other no more."

Mr Goodchild had not for a long time been in such spirits as he was after this most refined *tour d'addresse* in diplomacy (as he justly conceived it). "The style," said he, "cannot betray the secret: no, I flatter myself that I have hit *that* to a hair; I defy any critic, the keenest, to distinguish it from the genuine light sentimental *billet-doux* style of young ladies of seventeen. How should he learn then? William dares not tell him for his life. And the fellow can never be such a brute as to refuse the bust to a young lady whom he pretends to admire. Lord! it makes me laugh to think what a long face he'll show when he asks for permission to visit you upon the strength of this sacrifice; and I, looking at him like a bull, shall say, "No, indeed, my good sir; as to the bust, what's that to me, my good sir? What do I care for the bust, my good sir? I believe it's all broken to pieces with a sledge-hammer, or else you might have it back again for anything I care. Eh, Ida, my girl, won't that be droll? Won't it be laughable to see what a long face he'll cut?" But, but—

CHAPTER XXVI.

Won't it be laughable to see what a long face the fellow will cut?

If Ida had any particular wish to see *how* laughable a fellow looked under such circumstances, she had very soon that gratification; for her father's under jaw dropped enormously on the return of the messenger. It did not perhaps require any great critical penetration to determine from what member of the family the letter proceeded: and independently of *that*, Mr Tempest had (as the reader knows) some little acquaintance with the epistolary style of Miss Goodchild. In his answer, therefore, he declined complying with the request; but, to convince his beloved Ida that his refusal was designed, not for her, but for her father, he expressed himself as follows:—

" Madam, my truly respectable young friend,—It gives me great concern to be under the painful necessity of stating that it is wholly out of my power to make over unto you the bust of his gracious majesty the King of Hayti, " in consideration" (as you express it) " of certain monies to be by you paid over unto me." This, I repeat, is wholly impossible: seeing that I am now on the point of ratifying a treaty with an artist, in virtue of which three thousand copies are to be forthwith taken of the said bust on account of its distinguished excellence, and to be dispersed to my friends and others throughout Europe. With the greatest esteem, I remain your most obedient and devoted servant, " JOHN TEMPEST."

CHAPTER XXVII.

Unexpected Denouement.

" Now, then," thought Mr Goodchild, " the world is come to a pretty pass." The honour and credit of his name and family seemed to stand on the edge of a razor; and, without staying for any further consideration, he shot over, like an arrow, to Mr Tempest.

Scarcely was he out of the house when in rushed the

postman with a second note to Miss Goodchild, apologizing for the former, and explaining to her the particular purpose he had in writing it.

How well he succeeded in this was very soon made evident by the circumstance of her father's coming back with him, arm-in-arm. Mr Tempest had so handsomely apologised for any offence he might have given, and with a tone of real feeling had rested his defence so entirely upon the excess of his admiration for Miss Goodchild, which had left him no longer master of his own actions or understanding, that her father felt touched and flattered—forgave everything frankly—and allowed him to hope, from his daughter's mouth, for the final ratification of his hopes.

"But this one stipulation I must make, my good sir," said Mr Goodchild, returning to his political anxieties, "that in future you must wholly renounce that black fellow, who styles himself (most absurdly!) the King of Hayti." "With all my heart," said Mr Tempest, "Miss Goodchild will be cheaply purchased by renouncing *The King of Hayti.*"

COLERIDGE AND OPIUM-EATING.

WHAT is the deadest of things dead? It is, says the world, ever forward and rash, "a door-nail." But the world is wrong. There is a thing deader than a door-nail—viz., Gillman's Coleridge, Vol. I. Dead, more dead, most dead, is Gillman's Coleridge—dead, deader, deadest, is volume the first, which is waiting vainly, and for thousands of years is doomed to wait, for its sister volume, viz., Vol. II. The man is not born whom prophetic destiny has appointed to the task of gilding those short-hand distinctions, *Vol. II.* The readers of *Vol. I.* languish in vain for the second course of their banquet; the caravan that should convey it has foundered in the Arabian wilderness,

> "And Mecca sickens at the long delay."

That Vol. I. is dead, through three degrees of comparison, appears certain to our mind, upon more arguments than one. The book has clearly not completed its elementary act of respiration; the *systole* of Vol. I. is absolutely useless and lost without the *diastole* of that Vol. II. which is never to exist. That is one argument; and perhaps this second argument is stronger. Gillman's Coleridge, Vol. I. deals rashly, unjustly, and almost maliciously, with some of our own particular friends; and yet, until late in this summer, *Anno Domini* 1844, we—that is, ourselves and our friends—never heard of its existence. Now, a sloth, even without the benefit of Mr Waterton's evidence to his character, will travel faster than that; but malice, which travels fastest of all things, must be dead and cold at starting when it can thus have lingered in the rear for six years; and therefore, though the world was so far right, that people *do* say, " Dead as a door-nail," yet henceforward the weakest of these people will see the propriety of saying, " Dead as Gillman's Coleridge."

The reader of experience, on sliding over the surface of this opening paragraph, begins to think there's mischief singing in the upper air. No, reader; not at all. We never were cooler in our days. And this we protest, that, were it not for the excellence of the subject,—*Coleridge and Opium-Eating*,—Mr Gillman would have been dismissed by us unnoticed. Indeed, we not only forgive Mr Gillman, but we have a special kindness for him; and on this account, that he was good, he was generous, he was most forbearing, through twenty years, to poor Coleridge, when thrown upon his hospitality. An excellent thing *that*, Mr Gillman, and one sufficient, in *our* estimate, to blot out a world of libels on ourselves. But still, noticing the theme suggested by this unhappy Vol. I., we are forced at times to notice its author. Nor is this to be regretted. We remember a line of Horace never yet properly translated, viz.—

" Nec scutica dignum horribili sectere flagello."

The true translation of which, as we assure the unlearned reader, is, " Nor him that is worthy of a simple rap on the knuckles, should you 'fillip' (as Jack Falstaff observes) "with a three-man beetle."* Or, to give a literal version, "Nor must you pursue with the horrid knout of Christopher that man who merits only a switching." Very true. We protest against all attempts to invoke the exterminating knout or *flagellum*, for *that* sends a man to the hospital for two months; but you see that the same judicious poet who dissuades an appeal to the knout indirectly recommends the switch, which, indeed, is rather pleasant than otherwise, amiably playful in some of its lighter caprices, and, in its very worst, suggesting only a pennyworth of diachylon.

We begin our review of this book by professing, with hearty sincerity, our fervent admiration of that extraordinary man who furnishes the theme for Mr Gillman's *coup d'essai* in biography. He was, in a literary sense, our brother; for he also was amongst the contributors to *Blackwood*, and will, we presume, take his station in that Blackwood gallery of portraits which in a century hence will possess more interest for intellectual Europe than any merely martial series of portraits, or any gallery of statesmen assembled in congress, except as regards one or two leaders; for defunct major-generals and secondary diplomatists, when their date is past, awake no more emotion than last year's advertisements or obsolete directories; whereas those who in a stormy age have swept the harps of passion, of genial wit, or of the wrestling and gladiatorial reason, become more interesting to men when they

---

* "*A three-man beetle*:"—A beetle is that heavy sort of pestle with which paviours drive home the paving-stones; and sometimes, when it is too heavy for a single man, it is fitted up by three handles at right angles to the implement, for the use of three men.

can no longer be seen as bodily agents than even in the middle chorus of that intellectual music over which, living, they presided.

Of this great camp Coleridge was a leader, and fought among the *primipili;* yet comparatively he is still unknown. Heavy, indeed, are the arrears still due to philosophic curiosity on the real merits and on the separate merits of Samuel Taylor Coleridge. Coleridge as a poet, Coleridge as a philosopher,—how extensive are those two questions, if those were all! And upon neither question have we yet any investigation, such as, by compass of views, by research, or even by earnestness of sympathy with the subject, can or ought to satisfy a philosophic demand. Blind is that man who can persuade himself that the interest in Coleridge, taken as a total object, is becoming an obsolete interest. We are of opinion that even Milton, now viewed from a distance of two centuries, is still inadequately judged or appreciated in his character of poet, of patriot, and partisan, or, finally, in his character of accomplished scholar. But if so, how much less can it be pretended that satisfaction has been rendered to the claims of Coleridge! for upon Milton libraries have been written. There has been time for the malice of men, for the jealousy of men, for the enthusiasm, the scepticism, the adoring admiration of men to expand themselves. There has been room for a "slashing Bentley with his desperate hook," for an Addison, for a Johnson, for a wicked Lauder, for an avenging Douglas, for an idolising Chateaubriand, for a wild insulting infidel Curran; and yet, after all, little enough has been done towards any comprehensive estimate of the mighty being concerned. Piles of materials have been gathered to the ground; but, for the monument which should have risen from these materials, neither the first stone has been laid nor has a qualified architect yet presented his credentials. On the other hand, upon Coleridge little comparatively has yet been written; whilst the separate characters on which the judgment is awaited are more by one than those which Milton sustained. Coleridge also is a poet. Coleridge also was mixed up with the fervent politics of his age—an age how memorably reflecting the revolutionary agitations of Milton's age! Coleridge also was an extensive and brilliant scholar. Whatever might be the separate proportions of the two men in each particular department of the three here noticed, think as the reader will upon that point, sure we are that either subject is ample enough to make a strain upon the amplest faculties. How alarming, therefore, for any *honest* critic, who should undertake this later subject of Coleridge, to recollect that, after pursuing him through a zodiac of splendours corresponding to those of Milton in kind, however different in degree,—after weighing him as a poet, as a philosophic politician, as a scholar,—he will have to wheel after him into another orbit—into the unfathomable *nimbus* of transcendental metaphysics! Weigh him the critic must in the golden balance of philosophy the most abstruse—a balance which even itself requires weighing previously—or he will have done nothing that can be received for an estimate of the composite Coleridge. This astonishing man, be it again remembered, besides being an exquisite poet, a profound political speculator, a philosophic student of literature through all its chambers and recesses, was also a circumnavigator on the most pathless waters of scholasticism and metaphysics. He had sounded, without guiding-charts, the secret deeps of Proclus and Plotinus; he had laid down buoys on the twilight or moonlight ocean of Jacob Boehmen;* he had cruised over the broad Atlantic of Kant and Schelling, of Fitch and Oken. Where is the man who shall be equal to these things?

We, at least, make no such adventurous effort; or, if ever we should presume to do so, not at present. Here we design only to make a coasting voyage of survey round the headlands and most conspicuous seamarks of our subject as they are brought forward by Mr Gillman, or collaterally suggested by our own reflections; and especially we wish to say a word or two on Coleridge as an opium-eater.

Naturally the first point to which we direct our attention is the history and personal relations of Coleridge. Living with Mr Gillman for nineteen years as a domesticated friend, Coleridge ought to have been known intimately. And it is reasonable to expect, from so much intercourse, some additions to our slender knowledge of Coleridge's adventures (if we may use so coarse a word), and of the secret springs at work in those early struggles of Coleridge at Cambridge, London, Bristol, which have been rudely told to the world, and repeatedly told as showy romances, but never rationally explained.

The anecdotes, however, which Mr Gillman has added to the personal history of Coleridge are as little advantageous to the effect of his own book as they are to the in-

---

* "*Jacob Boehmen:*"—We ourselves had the honour of presenting to Mr Coleridge Law's English version of Jacob—a set of huge quartos. Some months afterwards we saw this work lying open, and one volume, at least, overflowing, in parts, with the commentaries and the *corollaries* of Coleridge. Whither has this work, and so many others swathed about with Coleridge's manuscript notes, vanished from the world?

terest of the memorable character which he seeks to illus trate. Always they are told without grace, and generally are suspicious in their details. Mr Gillman we believe to be too upright a man for countenancing any untruth. He has been deceived. For example, will any man believe this? A certain "excellent equestrian," falling in with Coleridge on horseback, thus accosted him: "Pray, sir, did you meet a tailor along the road?" "*A tailor!*" answered Coleridge. "*I did meet a person answering such a description, who told me he had dropped his goose; that, if I rode a little farther, I should find it. And I guess he must have meant you.*" In Joe Miller, this story would read perhaps sufferably. Joe has a privilege, and we do not look too narrowly into the mouth of a Joe Millerism; "a gift horse," as the old proverb instructs us, "must not have his mouth looked into;" but Mr Gillman, writing the life of a philosopher, and no jest-book, is under a different law of decorum. That retort, however, which silences the jester, some people may fancy must be a good one; and we are desired to believe that in this case the baffled assailant rode off in a spirit of benign candour, saying aloud to himself, like the excellent philosopher that he evidently was, "Caught a Tartar!"

But another story of a sporting baronet, who was besides a member of Parliament, is much worse, and altogether degrading to Coleridge. This gentleman, by way of showing off before a party of ladies, is represented as insulting Coleridge by putting questions to him on the qualities of his horse,* so as to draw the animal's miser-

* *His Horse:*—One fact, tolerably notorious, should have whispered to Mr Gillman that all anecdotes which presuppose for their basis any equestrian skill or habits in Coleridge rest upon moonshine. Samuel Taylor Coleridge's first attempts at horsemanship were

able defects into public notice; and then closing his display by demanding what he would take for the horse, "including the rider." The supposed reply of Coleridge might seem good to those who understand nothing of true dignity; for, as an *impromptu*, it was smart, and even caustic. The baronet, it seems, was reputed to have been bought by the minister; and the reader will at once divine that the retort took advantage of that current belief, so as to throw back the sarcasm, by proclaiming that neither horse nor rider had a price placarded in the market at which any man could become their purchaser. But this

---

pretty nearly his last. What motive swayed the judgment, or what stormy impulse drove the passionate despair of Samuel Taylor Coleridge into quitting Jesus College, Cambridge, was never clearly or certainly made known to the very nearest of his friends: which lends further probability to a rumour, already in itself probable enough, that this motive which led, or this impulse which drove, the unhappy man into headlong acts of desperation, was—the reader will guess for himself, though ten miles distant—a woman. In fact, most of us play the fool at least once in our life-career; and the criminal cause of our doing so is pretty well ascertained by this time in all cases to be a woman. Coleridge was hopelessly dismissed by his proud, disdainful goddess, although really she might have gone farther and fared worse. I am able, by female aid, to communicate a pretty close description of Samuel Taylor Coleridge as he was in the year 1796. In stature, according to the severe measurement taken down in the *studio* of a very distinguished artist, he was exactly 5 feet 10 inches in height; with a blooming and healthy complexion; beautiful and luxuriant hair, falling in natural curls over his shoulders; and, as a lady (the successor of Hannah More in her most lucrative boarding-school) said to me about the year of Waterloo, "simply the most perfect realisation of a pastoral Strephon that in all her life she had looked upon." *Strephon* was the romantic name that survived from her rosy days of sweet seventeen: at present, Strephon, as well as Chloe, are at a discount; but what she meant was an Adonis. By reason of reading too much Kant and Schelling, he grew fat and corpulent towards Waterloo; but he was then slender and agile as an antelope.

was not the temper in which Coleridge either did reply or could have replied. Coleridge showed, in the *spirit* of his manner, a profound sensibility to the nature of a gentleman; and he felt too justly what it became a self-respecting person to say, ever to have aped the sort of flashy fencing which might seem fine to a theatrical blood.

Another story is self-refuted. "A hired partisan" had come to one of Coleridge's political lectures with the express purpose of bringing the lecturer into trouble; and most preposterously he laid himself open to his own snare by refusing to pay for admission. Spies must be poor artists who proceed thus. Upon which Coleridge remarked, "that, before the gentleman kicked up a dust, surely he would down with the dust." So far the story will not do. But what follows is possible enough. The *same* "hired" gentleman, by way of giving unity to the tale, is described as having hissed. Upon this a cry arose of "Turn him out!" But Coleridge interfered to protect him. He insisted on the man's right to hiss if he thought fit; it was legal to hiss; it was natural to hiss: "For what is to be expected, gentlemen, when the cool waters of reason come in contact with red-hot aristocracy, but a hiss?" *Euge!*

Amongst all the anecdotes, however, of this splendid man—often trivial, often incoherent, often unauthenticated—there is one which strikes us as both true and interesting; and we are grateful to Mr Gillman for preserving it. We find it introduced, and partially authenticated, by the following sentence from Coleridge himself:— "From eight to fourteen I was a playless day-dreamer, a *helluo librorum*, my appetite for which was indulged by a singular incident. A stranger, who was struck by my conversation, made me free of a circulating library in

King Street, Cheapside." The more circumstantial explanation of Mr Gillman is this:—"The incident, indeed, was singular. Going down the Strand in one of his day-dreams, fancying himself swimming across the Hellespont, thrusting his hands before him as in the act of swimming, his hand came in contact with a gentleman's pocket. The gentleman seized his hand: turning round and looking at him with some anger,—'What! so young, and yet so wicked?' at the same time accusing him of an attempt to pick his pocket. The frightened boy sobbed out his denial of the intention, and explained to him how he thought himself Leander swimming across the Hellespont. The gentleman was so struck and delighted with the novelty of the thing, and with the simplicity and intelligence of the boy, that he subscribed, as before stated, to the library; in consequence of which Coleridge was further enabled to indulge his love of reading."

We fear that this slovenly narrative is the very perfection of bad story-telling. But the story itself is striking, and, by the very oddness of the incidents, not likely to have been invented. The effect, from the position of the two parties,—on the one side a simple child from Devonshire, dreaming in the Strand that he was swimming over from Sestos to Abydos; and, on the other, the experienced man, dreaming only of this world, its knaves and its thieves, but still kind and generous, and still capable of distinguishing,—is beautiful and picturesque. *O, si sic omnia!*

But the most interesting to us of the *personalities* connected with Coleridge are his feuds and his personal dislikes. Incomprehensible to us is the war of extermination which Coleridge made upon the political economists. Did Sir James Steuart, in speaking of vine-dressers (not *as* vine-dressers, but generally as cultivators), tell his readers that, if such a man simply replaced his own consumption, leaving no surplus whatever or increment for the public capital, he could not be considered a useful citizen, not the beast in the Revelations is held up by Coleridge as more hateful to the spirit of truth than the Jacobite baronet. And yet we know of an author—viz., one S. T. Coleridge—who repeated that same doctrine without finding any evil in it. Look at the first part of Schiller's *Wallenstein*, where Count Isolani having said, "Poh! we are *all* his subjects," *i.e.*, soldiers (though unproductive labourers) not less than productive peasants, the emperor's envoy replies, "Yet with a difference, general;" and the difference implies Sir James's scale, his vine-dresser being the equatorial case between the two extremes of the envoy. Malthus again, in his population book, contends for a mathematic difference between animal and vegetable life in respect to the law of increase; as though the first increased by geometrical ratios, the last by arithmetical! No proposition more worthy of laughter, since both, when permitted to expand, increase by geometrical ratios, and the latter by much higher ratios; whereas Malthus persuaded himself of his crotchet simply by refusing the requisite condition in the vegetable case, and granting it in the other. If you take a few grains of wheat, and are required to plant all successive generations of their produce in the same flower-pot for ever, of course you neutralise its expansion by your own act of arbitrary limitation.* But so

* Malthus would have rejoined by saying that the flower-pot limitation was the actual limitation of Nature in our present circumstances. In America it is otherwise, he would say: but England *is* the very flower-pot you suppose; she is a flower-pot which cannot be multiplied, and cannot even be enlarged. Very well; so

you would do if you tried the case of *animal* increase by still exterminating all but one replacing couple of parents. This is not to try, but merely a pretence of trying, one order of powers against another. That was folly. But Coleridge combated this idea in a manner so obscure that nobody understood it. And leaving these speculative conundrums, in coming to the great practical interests afloat in the poor laws, Coleridge did so little real work, that he left as a *res integra* to Dr Alison the capital argument that legal and *adequate* provision for the poor, whether impotent poor or poor accidentally out of work, does not extend pauperism: no; but is the one great resource for putting it down. Dr Alison's overwhelming and *experimental* manifestations of that truth have prostrated Malthus and his generation for ever. This comes of not attending to the Latin maxim, "*Hoc* age" (mind the object before you). Dr Alison, a wise man, "*hoc* egit" (he minded the thing before him); Coleridge "*aliud* egit" (he hunted three hares at once). And we see the result. In a case which suited him, by interesting his peculiar feeling, Coleridge could command

"Attention full ten times as much as there needs."

---

be it (which we say in order to waive irrelevant disputes); but then the true inference will be, not that vegetable increase proceeds under a different law from that which governs animal increase, but that, through an accident of position, the experiment cannot be tried in England. Surely the levers of Archimedes, with submission to Sir Edward B. Lytton, were not the less levers because he wanted the *locum standi.* It is proper, by the way, that we should inform the reader of this generation where to look for Coleridge's skirmishings with Malthus. They are to be found chiefly in the late Mr William Hazlitt's work on that subject,—a work which Coleridge so far claimed as to assert that it had been substantially made up from his own conversation

But search documents, value evidence, or thresh out bushels of statistical tables, Coleridge could not, any more than he could ride with Elliot's dragoons.

Another instance of Coleridge's inaptitude for such studies as political economy is found in his fancy, by no means "rich and rare," but meagre and trite, that taxes can never injure public prosperity by mere excess of quantity. If they injure, we are to conclude that it must be by their quality and mode of operation, or by their false appropriation (as, for instance, if they are sent out of the country and spent abroad); because, says Coleridge, if the taxes are exhaled from the country as vapours, back they come in drenching showers. Twenty pounds ascend in a Scotch mist to the Chancellor of the Exchequer from Leeds; but does it evaporate? Not at all. By return of post, down comes an order for twenty pounds' worth of Leeds cloth on account of government, seeing that the poor men of the ——th regiment want new gaiters. And thus thinks S. T. Coleridge. True; but, of this return twenty pounds, not more than four will be profit—*i.e.*, surplus accruing to the public capital; whereas of the original twenty pounds every shilling was surplus. The same unsound fancy has been many times brought forward, often in England, often in France; but it is curious that its first appearance upon any stage was precisely two centuries ago, when as yet political economy slept with the pre-Adamites—viz., in the Long Parliament. In a quarto volume of the debates during 1644, printed as an independent work, will be found the same identical doctrine, supported very sonorously by the same little love of an illustration from the see-saw of mist and rain.

Political economy was not Coleridge's forte. In politics he was happier. In mere personal politics he (like every man, when reviewed from a station distant by forty years) will often appear to have erred; nay, he will be detected and nailed in error. But this is the necessity of us all. Keen are the refutations of time; and absolute results to posterity are the fatal touchstone of opinions in the past. It is undeniable, besides, that Coleridge had strong personal antipathies, for instance, to Messrs Pitt and Dundas. Yet *why*, we never could understand. We once heard him tell a story upon Windermere to the late Mr Curwen, then M.P. for Workington, which was meant apparently to account for this feeling. The story amounted to this, that, when a freshman at Cambridge, Mr Pitt had wantonly amused himself at a dinner party in smashing with filberts (discharged in showers like grape shot) a most costly dessert set of cut glass; from which Samuel Taylor Coleridge inferred a principle of destructiveness in his *cerebellum*, which, if so, was a palliation, and no aggravation. Now, if this dessert set belonged to some poor suffering Trinitarian, and not to himself, we are of opinion that he was faulty, and ought, upon his own great subsequent maxim, to have been coerced into "indemnity for the past and security for the future." But, besides that this glassy *mythus* belongs to an era fifteen years earlier than Coleridge's, so as to justify a shadow of scepticism, we really cannot find in such an *escapade* under the boiling blood of youth any sufficient justification of that withering malignity towards the name of Pitt which runs through Coleridge's famous *Fire, Famine, and Slaughter*. As this little viperous *jeu d'esprit* (published anonymously) subsequently became the subject of a celebrated after-dinner discussion in London at which Coleridge (*comme de raison*) was the chief speaker, the reader of this generation may wish to know the question at issue; and, in order to judge of *that*, he must know the outline of the devil's squib. The writer brings upon the scene three pleasant young ladies—viz., Miss Fire, Miss Famine, and Miss Slaughter. "What are you up to? What's the row?" we may suppose to be the introductory question of the poet. And the answer of the ladies makes us aware that they are fresh from larking in Ireland and France. A glorious spree they had; lots of fun, and laughter *à discretion*.* At all times *gratus puellæ risus ab angulo;* so that we listen to their little gossip with interest. They had been setting men, it seems, by the ears; and the drollest little atrocities they do certainly report. Not but we have seen better in the Nenagh paper, so far as Ireland is concerned; but the pet little joke was in La Vendée. Miss Famine, who is the girl for our money, raises the question, whether any of them can tell the name of the leader and prompter to these high jinks of hell; if so, let her whisper it.

> "Whisper it, sister, so and so,
> In a dark hint, distinct and low."

Upon which the playful Miss Slaughter replies,—

> "Letters *four* do form his name.
> * * * *
> He came by stealth and unlocked my den;
> And I have drunk the blood since then
> Of thrice three hundred thousand men."

Good; but the sting of the hornet lies in the conclusion.

---

* The laughter of girls is, and ever was, among the delightful sounds of earth. Girls do not excel in philosophy: we have ascertained that this is not their *forte*.

If this quadriliteral man had done so much for *them*, (though, really, we think 6s. 8d., which is an attorney's fee, might have settled his claim), what, says Fire, setting her arms akimbo, would they do for *him?* Slaughter replies, rather crustily, that, as far as a good kicking would go, or (says Famine) a little matter of tearing to pieces by the mob, they would be glad to take tickets at his benefit. "How, you bitches!" says Fire. "Is that all?

> 'I alone am faithful; I
> *Cling to him everlastingly.*'"

The sentiment is diabolical; and the question argued at the London dinner-table was, Could the writer have been other than a devil? The dinner was at the late excellent Mr Sotheby's, known advantageously in those days as the translator of Wieland's *Oberon*. Several of the great guns amongst the literary body were present—in particular, Sir Walter Scott; and he, we believe, with his usual good nature, took the apologetic side of the dispute; in fact, he was in the secret. Nobody else, barring the author, knew at first whose good name was at stake. The scene must have been high. The company kicked about the poor diabolic writer's head as if it had been a tennis-ball. Coleridge, the yet unknown criminal, but still as an unknown sinner, absolutely perspired and fumed in pleading for the defendant; the company demurred; the orator grew urgent; wits began to *smoke* the case, as active verbs—the advocate to *smoke*, as a neuter verb; the "fun grew fast and furious;" until at length *delinquent arose*, burning tears in his eyes, and confessed to an audience, now bursting with stifled laughter (but whom he supposed to be bursting with fiery indignation), "Lo, I am he that wrote it!"

For our own part we side with Coleridge. Malice is not always of the heart; there is a malice of the understanding and the fancy. Neither do we think the worse of a man for having invented the most horrible and old-woman troubling curse that demons ever listened to. We are too apt to swear horribly ourselves; and often have we frightened the cat—to say nothing of the kettle—by our shocking (far too shocking) oaths.

There were other celebrated men whom Coleridge detested, or seemed to detest—Paley, Sir Sidney Smith, Lord Hutchinson, and Cuvier. To Paley it might seem as if his antipathy had been purely philosophic; but we believe that partly it was personal; and it tallies with this belief that, in his earliest political tracts, Coleridge charged the archdeacon repeatedly with his own joke, as if it had been a serious saying—viz., "that he could not afford to keep a conscience;" such luxuries, like a carriage, for instance, being obviously beyond the finances of poor men.

With respect to the philosophic question between the parties as to the grounds of moral election, we hope it is no treason to suggest that both were perhaps in error. Against Paley it occurs at once that he himself would not have made consequences the *practical* test in valuing the morality of an act, since these can very seldom be traced at all up to the final stages, and in the earliest stages are exceedingly different under different circumstances; so that the same act, tried by its consequences, would bear a fluctuating appreciation. This could not have been Paley's *revised* meaning; consequently, had he been pressed by opposition, it would have come out that by *test* he meant only *speculative* test—a very harmless doctrine, certainly, but useless and impertinent to any purpose of his system. The reader may catch our meaning in the following illustration. It is a matter of general belief that happiness, upon the whole, follows in a higher degree from constant integrity than from the closest attention to self-interest. Now, happiness is one of those consequences which Paley meant by final or remotest; but we could never use this idea as an exponent of integrity or interchangeable criterion; because happiness cannot be ascertained or appreciated except upon long tracts of time, whereas the particular act of integrity depends continually upon the election of the moment. No man, therefore, could venture to lay down as a rule, Do what makes you happy; use this as your test of actions, satisfied that in that case always you will do the thing which is right; for he cannot discern independently what *will* make him happy, and he must decide on the spot. The use of the *nexus* between morality and happiness must therefore be inverted; it is not practical or prospective, but simply retrospective; and in that form it says no more than the good old rules hallowed in every cottage. But this furnishes no practical guide for moral election which a man had not before he ever thought of this *nexus*. In the sense in which it is true, we need not go to the professor's chair for this maxim; in the sense in which it would serve Paley, it is absolutely false.

On the other hand, as against Coleridge, it is certain that many acts could be mentioned which are judged to be good or bad only because their consequences are known to be so, whilst the great catholic acts of life are entirely (and, if we may so phrase it, haughtily) independent of consequences. For instance, fidelity to a trust is a law of immutable morality subject to no casuistry whatever. You have been left executor to a friend; you are to pay over his last legacy to X, though a dissolute scoundrel; and you are to give no shilling of it to the poor brother of X, though a good man and a wise man, struggling with adversity. You are absolutely excluded from all contemplation of results. It was your deceased friend's right to make the will; it is yours simply to see it executed. Now, in opposition to this primary class of actions stands another, such as the habit of intoxication, which is known to be wrong only by observing the consequences. If drunkenness did not terminate, after some years, in producing bodily weakness, irritability in the temper, and so forth, it would *not* be a vicious act; and accordingly, if a transcendent motive should arise in favour of drunkenness, as that it would enable you to face a degree of cold or contagion else menacing to life, a duty would arise, *pro hac vice*, of getting drunk. We had an amiable friend who suffered under the infirmity of cowardice; an awful coward he was when sober, but when very drunk, he had courage enough for the Seven Champions of Christendom. Therefore, in an emergency, where he knew himself suddenly loaded with the responsibility of defending a family, we approved highly of his getting drunk. But to violate a trust could never become right under any change of circumstances. Coleridge, however, altogether overlooked this distinction, which, on the other hand, stirring in Paley's mind, but never brought out to distinct consciousness, nor ever investigated nor limited, has undermined his system. Perhaps it is not very important how a man *theorises* upon morality. Happily for us all, God has left no man in such questions practically to the guidance of his understanding; but still, considering that academic bodies *are* partly instituted for the support of speculative truth as well as truth practical, we must think it a blot upon the splendour of Oxford and Cambridge that both of them, in a Christian land, make Paley the foundation of their ethics, the alternative being Aristotle. And in our mind, though far inferior as a moralist to the Stoics, Aristotle is often less of a pagan than Paley.

Coleridge's dislike to Sir Sidney Smith and the Egyptian Lord Hutchinson fell under the category of Martial's case :—

> " Non amo te, Sabidi, nec possum dicere quare ;
> Hoc solum novi—non amo te, Sabidi."

Against Lord Hutchinson we never heard him plead anything of moment except that he was finically Frenchified in his diction, of which he gave this instance: That having occasion to notice a brick wall (which was literally *that*, not more and not less), when reconnoitring the French defences, he called it a *revêtement*. And we ourselves remember his using the French word *gloriole* rather ostentatiously—that is, when no particular emphasis attached to the case. But every man has his foibles, and few, perhaps, are less conspicuously annoying than this of Lord Hutchinson. Sir Sidney's crimes were less distinctly revealed to our mind. As to Cuvier, Coleridge's hatred of *him* was more to our taste; for (though quite unreasonable, we fear) it took the shape of patriotism. He insisted on it that our British John Hunter was the genuine article, and that Cuvier was a humbug. Now, speaking privately to the public, we cannot go quite so far as *that;* but, when publicly we address that most respectable character, *en grand costume*, we always mean to back Coleridge, for we are a horrible John Bull ourselves. As Joseph Hume observes, it makes no difference to us—right or wrong, black or white—when our countrymen are concerned; and John Hunter, notwithstanding he had a bee in his bonnet,* was really a great man, though it will not follow that Cuvier must therefore have been a little one. We do not pretend to be acquainted with the tenth part of Cuvier's performances; but we suspect that Coleridge's range in that respect was not much greater than our own.

Other cases of monomaniac antipathy we might revive from our recollections of Coleridge had we a sufficient motive; but in compensation, and by way of redressing the balance, he had many strange likings,—equally monomaniac,—and, unaccountably, he chose to exhibit his whimsical partialities by dressing up, as it were, in his own clothes, such a set of scarecrows as eye has not beheld. Heavens! what an ark of unclean beasts would have been Coleridge's private *menagerie* of departed philosophers could they all have been trotted out in succession! But did the reader feel them to be the awful bores which, in fact, they were? No; because Coleridge had blown upon these withered anatomies, through the blowpipe of his own creative genius, a stream of gas that swelled the tissue of their antediluvian wrinkles, forced colour upon their cheeks and splendour upon their sodden eyes. Such a process of ventriloquism never *has* existed. He spoke by their organs; they were the tubes; and he forced through their wooden machinery his own Beethoven harmonies.

---

* *Vide*, in particular, for the most exquisite specimen of pig-headedness that the world can furnish, his perverse evidence on the once famous case at the Warwick assizes, of Captain Donelan for poisoning his brother-in-law, Sir Theodosius Boughton.

First came Dr Andrew Bell. We knew him. Was he dull? Is a wooden spoon dull! Fishy were his eyes; torpedinous was his manner; and his main idea, out of two which he really had, related to the moon—from which you infer, perhaps, that he was lunatic. By no means. It was no craze, under the influence of the moon, which possessed him; it was an idea of mere hostility to the moon. In Madras had Dr Andrew lived. The Madras people, like many others, had an idea that she influenced the weather. Subsequently the Herschels, senior and junior, systematised this idea; and then the wrath of Andrew, previously in a crescent state, actually dilated to a plenilunar orb. The Westmoreland people (for at the lakes it was we knew him) expounded his condition to us by saying that he was "maffled;" which word means "perplexed in the extreme." His wrath did not pass into lunacy; it produced simple distraction; an uneasy fumbling with the idea—like that of an old superannuated dog who longs to worry, but cannot for want of teeth. In this condition you will judge that he was rather tedious; and in this condition Coleridge took him up. Andrew's other idea, because he *had* two, related to education. Perhaps six-sevenths of that also came from Madras. No matter; Coleridge took *that* up; Southey also; but Southey with his usual temperate fervour. Coleridge, on the other hand, found celestial marvels both in the scheme and in the man. Then commenced the apotheosis of Andrew Bell; and because it happened that his opponent, Lancaster, between ourselves, really *had* stolen his ideas from Bell, what between the sad wickedness of Lancaster and the celestial transfiguration of Bell, gradually Coleridge heated himself to such an extent that people, when referring to that subject, asked each other, "Have you heard Coleridge lecture on *Bel and the Dragon?*"

The next man glorified by Coleridge was John Woolman, the Quaker. Him, though we once possessed his works, it cannot be truly affirmed that we ever read. Try to read John we often did; but read John we did not. This, however, you say, might be our fault, and not John's. Very likely; and we have a notion that now, with our wiser thoughts, we *should* read John if he were here on this table. It is certain that he was a good man, and one of the earliest in America, if not in Christendom, who lifted up his hand to protest against the slave trade; but still we suspect that, had John been all that Coleridge represented, he would not have repelled us from reading his travels in the fearful way that he did. But again we beg pardon, and entreat the earth of Virginia to lie light upon the remains of John Woolman; for he was an Israelite indeed, in whom there was no guile.

The third person raised to divine honours by Coleridge was Bowyer, the master of Christ's Hospital, London—a man whose name rises into the nostrils of all who knew him with the gracious odour of a tallow chandler's melting house upon melting day, and whose memory is embalmed in the hearty detestation of all his pupils. Coleridge describes this man as a profound critic. Our idea of him is different. We are of opinion that Bowyer was the greatest villain of the eighteenth century. We may be wrong; but we cannot be *far* wrong. Talk of knouting indeed! which we did at the beginning of this paper in the mere playfulness of our hearts,—and which the great master of the knout, Christopher, who visited men's trespasses like the Eumenides, never resorted to but in love for some great idea which had been outraged,—why, this man knouted his way through life, from bloody youth up to truculent old age. Grim idol! whose altars reeked with children's blood, and whose dreadful eyes never smiled except as the stern goddess of the Thugs smiles when the sound of human lamentations inhabits her ears So much had the monster fed upon this great idea of "flogging," and transmuted it into the very nutriment of his heart, that he seems to have conceived the gigantic project of flogging all mankind; nay, worse; for Mr Gillman, on Coleridge's authority, tells us (p. 24) the following anecdote:—

"'*Sirrah, I'll flog you,*' were words so familiar to him, that on one occasion some *female* friend of one of the boys" (who had come on an errand of intercession) "still lingering at the door, after having been abruptly told to go, Bowyer exclaimed, 'Bring that woman here, and I'll flog her.'"

To this horrid incarnation of whips and scourges, Coleridge, in his *Biographia Literaria*, ascribes ideas upon criticism and taste which every man will recognise at once as the intense peculiarities of Coleridge. Could these notions really have belonged to Bowyer, then how do we know but he wrote the *Ancient Mariner?* Yet, on consideration, no; for even Coleridge admitted that, spite of his fine theorising upon composition, Mr Bowyer did not prosper in the practice—of which he gave us this illustration; and, as it is supposed to be the one only specimen of the Bowyeriana which now survives in this sublunary world, we are glad to extend its glory. It is the most curious example extant of the melodious in sound:—

"'Twas thou that smooth'd'st the rough-rugg'd bed of pain."

"Smooth'd'st!" Would the teeth of a crocodile not

splinter under that word? It seems to us as if Mr Bowyer's verses ought to be boiled before they can be read. And when he says, *'Twas thou*, who or what is the wretch talking to? Can he be apostrophising the knout? We very much fear it. If so, then you see (reader), that, even when incapacitated by illness from operating, he still adores the image of his holy scourge, and invokes it as alone able to smooth "his rough-rugg'd bed." O thou infernal Bowyer! upon whom even Trollope (*History of Christ's Hospital*) charges "a discipline *tinctured* with more than due severity," can there be any partners found for thee in a quadrille except Draco, the bloody lawgiver, Bishop Bonner, and Mrs Brownrigg?*

The next pet was Sir Alexander Ball. Concerning Bowyer, Coleridge did not talk much, but chiefly wrote; concerning Bell, he did not write much, but chiefly talked; concerning Ball, however, he both wrote and talked. It was in vain to muse upon any plan for having Ball black-balled, or for rebelling against Bell. Think of a man who had fallen into one pit called Bell; secondly, falling into another pit called Ball. This was too much. We were obliged to quote poetry against them:

---

* Draco and the Bishop belong to history,—the first as bloody lawgiver in the days of the elder Athens, the Bishop as fiery disciplinarian to weak, relapsing *perverts* [such is the modern slang]: sneaking perverts like myself and my ever-honoured reader, who would be very willing to give the Bishop a kick in the dark, but would find ourselves too much of cowards to stand to it when the candles were brought. These men are well known; but who is Mrs Brownrigg? The reader would not have asked had he lived in the days of the Anti-Jacobin, who describes Mrs Brownrigg as the woman

> who whipp'd two female 'prentices to death,
> And hid them in the coal-hole."

"Letters four do form his name.
He came by stealth and unlock'd my den:
And the nightmare I have felt since then
Of thrice three hundred thousand men."

Not that we insinuate any disrespect to Sir Alexander Ball. He was about the foremost, we believe, in all good qualities amongst Nelson's admirable captains at the Nile. He commanded a seventy-four most effectually in that battle; he governed Malta as well as Sancho (see *Don Quixote*) governed Barataria; and he was a true practical philosopher,—as, indeed, was Sancho. But still, by all that we could ever learn, Sir Alexander had no taste for the abstract upon any subject, and would have read as mere delirious wanderings those philosophic opinions which Coleridge fastened like wings upon his respectable but astounded shoulders.

We really beg pardon for having laughed a little at these crazes of Coleridge; but laugh we did, of mere necessity, in those days, at Bell and Ball,* whenever we did not groan. And as the same precise alternative offers itself now,—viz., that in recalling the case we must reverberate either the groaning or the laughter,—we presume the reader would vote for the last. Coleridge, we are well convinced, owed all these wandering and exaggerated estimates of men—these diseased impulses, that, like the *mirage*, showed lakes and fountains where in reality there were only arid deserts—to the derangements worked by opium. But now, for the sake of change, let us pass to another topic. Suppose we say a word or two on Coleridge's accomplishments as a scholar. We are not going

* *Ball and Bell:*—*i. e.*, not to cause any misunderstanding, I mean, Bell and Ball, Ball and Bell, in order to impress the wearisome iteration

to enter on so large a field as that of his scholarship in connection with his philosophic labours—scholarship in the result; not this, but scholarship in the means and machinery, range of *verbal* scholarship, is what we propose for a moment's review.

For instance, what sort of a German scholar was Coleridge? We dare say that, because in his version of the *Wallenstein* there are some inaccuracies, those who may have noticed them will hold him cheap in this particular pretension. But to a certain degree they will be wrong. Coleridge was not *very* accurate in anything but in the use of logic. All his philological attainments were imperfect. He did not talk German; or so obscurely,—and, if he attempted to speak fast, so erroneously,—that in his second sentence, when conversing with a German lady of rank, he contrived to assure her that in his humble opinion she was a ——. Hard it is to fill up the hiatus decorously; but in fact the word very coarsely expressed that she was no better than she should be. Which reminds us of a parallel misadventure to a German, whose English education had been equally neglected. Having obtained an interview with an English lady, who, having recently lost her husband, must (as he in his unwashed German condition took for granted) be open to new offers, he opened his business thus:—"Highborn madam, since your husband have kicked de bucket ——" "Sir!" interrupted the lady, astonished and displeased. "Oh, pardon!—nine, ten tousand pardon! Now I make new beginning—quite oder beginning. Madam, since your husband have cut his stick ——" It may be supposed that this did not mend matters; and, reading so much in the lady's countenance, the German drew out an octavo dictionary, and said, perspiring with shame at having a second time missed fire, "Madam, since your husband have gone to kingdom come ——" This he said beseechingly; but the lady was past propitiation by this time, and rapidly moved towards the door. Things had now reached a crisis; and, if something were not done quickly, the game was up. Now, therefore, taking a last hurried look at his dictionary, the German flew after the lady, crying out, in a voice of despair, "Madam, since your husband—your most respected husband—your never-enoff-to-be-worshipped husband—have hopped de twig ——"* This was his sheet anchor; and, as this also *came home*, of course the poor man was totally wrecked. It turned out that the dictionary he had used—(Arnold's, we think), a work of one hundred and fifty years back, and, from mere German ignorance, giving slang translations from Tom Brown, L'Estrange, and other jocular writers—had put down the verb *sterben* (*to die*) with the following worshipful series of equivalents:—1. To kick the bucket; 2. To cut one's stick; 3. To go to kingdom come; 4. To hop the twig; to drop off the perch into Davy's locker.

But, though Coleridge did not pretend to any fluent command of conversational German, he read it with great ease. His knowledge of German literature was, indeed, too much limited by his rare opportunities for commanding anything like a well-mounted library; and particularly it surprised us that Coleridge knew little or nothing of John Paul Richter. But his acquaintance with the German philosophic masters was extensive; and his valuation of many individual German words or phrases was delicate, and sometimes profound.

---

* *Ist eben jetzt gestorben* was his German idea, which he thus rendered in classical English.

As a Grecian, Coleridge must be estimated with a reference to the state and standard of Greek literature at that time and in this country. Porson had not yet raised our ideal, *i.e.*, had not yet *told* upon that ideal. The earliest laurels of Coleridge were gathered, however, in that field. Yet no man will at this day pretend that the Greek of his prize ode is sufferable. Neither did Coleridge ever become an accurate Grecian in later times, when better models of scholarship and better aids to scholarship had begun to multiply. But still we must assert this point of superiority for Coleridge, that, whilst he never was what may be called a well-mounted nor a well-grounded scholar in any department of verbal scholarship, he yet displayed sometimes a brilliancy of conjectural sagacity and a felicity of philosophic investigation, even in this path, such as better scholars do not often attain, and of a kind which cannot be learned from books. But as respects his accuracy, again we must recall to the reader the state of Greek literature in England during Coleridge's youth; and in all equity, as a means of placing Coleridge in the balances, specifically we must recall the state of Greek metrical composition at that period.

To measure the condition of Greek literature, even in Cambridge, about the initial period of Coleridge, we need only look back to the several translations of Gray's *Elegy* by three (if not four) of the reverend gentlemen at that time attached to Eton College. Mathias, no very great scholar himself in this particular field, made himself merry, in his *Pursuits of Literature*, with these Eton translations. In that he was right. But he was *not* right in praising a contemporary translation by Cook, who (we believe) was the immediate predecessor of Porson in the Greek chair. As a specimen of this translation,* we cite one stanza; and we cannot be supposed to select unfairly, because it is the stanza which Mathias—confessedly the *proneur* of Cook's version—praises in extravagant terms. "Here," says he, "Gray, Cook, and Nature do seem to contend for the mastery." The English quatrain must be familiar to every body :—

> "The boast of heraldry, the pomp of power,
> And all that beauty, all that wealth, e'er gave,
> Await alike the inevitable hour :
> The paths of glory lead but to the grave."

And the following, we believe, though quoting from a thirty-three years' recollection † of it, is the exact Greek version of Cook :—

> 'Αχαρις εὐγενεων, χαρις ἁ βασιληιδος ἀρχας,
> Δωρα τυχης χρυσεης‡ 'Αφροδιτης καλα τα δωρα,
> Πανθ' ἁμα ταυτα τεθνηκε, και ειδεν μορσιμον ἀμαρ·
> 'Ηρωων κλε' ὀλωλε, και ἐρχεται ξυνον ἐς 'Αδην.

---

* It was printed at the end of Aristotle's *Poetics*, which Dr Cook edited.

† *A thirty-three years' recollection* in 1844 ; but now within sixty hours of the *Calender Apriles* (viz., All Fool's Festival), fourteen or fifteen years more.

‡ χρυσεης :—It is remarkable that this epithet has been everywhere assigned to τυχης. Δωρα τυχης, the gifts of Fortune, which in this place is meant to indicate *riches*, corresponding to Gray's *All that Wealth e'er gave*, might seem at first sight to justify this allocation of the epithet golden. But on this way of understanding the appropriation, we are met by a prosaic and purely mechanic fact—the gifts of golden Fortune, as the giver of golden coins—Persian darics or English guineas. Meantime this epithet has an old traditional consecration to Venus, and in such an application springs upward like a pyramid of fire into a far more illimitable and imaginative value. A truth which Shakspere caught at once by a subtle divination of his own unfathomable sensibility. Ac-

Now, really, these verses, by force of a little mosaic tessellation from genuine Greek sources, pass fluently over the tongue; but can they be considered other than a *cento?* Swarms of English schoolboys at this day would not feel very proud to adopt them. In fact, we remember (at a period say twelve years later than this) some iambic verses, which were really composed by a boy—viz., a son of Dr Prettyman (afterwards Tomline), Bishop of Winchester, and, in earlier times, private tutor to Mr Pitt. They were published by Middleton, first Bishop of Calcutta, in the preface to his work on the Greek article; and, for racy idiomatic Greek, self-originated, and not a mere mocking-bird's iteration of alien notes, are so much superior to all the attempts of these sexagenarian doctors as distinctly to mark the growth of a new era and a new generation in this difficult accomplishment within the first decennium of this century. It is singular that only one blemish is suggested by any of the contemporary critics in Dr Cook's verses—viz., in the word ξυνον· for which this critic proposes to substitute κοινον, to prevent, as he observes, the last syllable of ῳχετο from being lengthened by the ξ. Such considerations as these are necessary to the *trutinæ castigatio* (the trimming of the balance) before we can appraise Coleridge's place on the scale of his own day; which day, *quoad hoc*, be it remembered, *i. e.*, in reference to this particular accomplishment. was 1790.

As to French, Coleridge read it with too little freedom to find pleasure in French literature. Accordingly we

---

cordingly, without needing any Grecian guidance or model, how profound is the effect of that line—

What is't that takes from thee thy golden sleep?

never recollect his referring for any purpose, either of argument or illustration, to a French classic. Latin, from his regular scholastic training, naturally he read with a scholar's fluency; and indeed he read constantly in authors such as Petrarch, Erasmus, Calvin, &c., whose *prose* works he could not then have found in translations. But Coleridge had not cultivated an acquaintance with the delicacies of classic Latinity. And it is remarkable that Wordsworth, educated most negligently at Hawkshead school, subsequently, by reading the lyric poetry of Horace, simply for his own delight as a student of composition, made himself a master of Latinity in its most difficult form; whilst Coleridge, trained regularly in a great southern school, never carried his Latin to any point of classical polish.

There is another accomplishment of Coleridge's, less broadly open to the judgment of this generation, and not at all of the next—viz., his splendid art of conversation, on which it will be interesting to say a word. Ten years ago, when the music of this rare performance had not yet ceased to vibrate in men's ears, what a sensation was gathering amongst the educated classes on this particular subject! What a tumult of anxiety prevailed to "hear Mr Coleridge," or even to talk with a man who *had* heard him. Had he lived till this day, not Paganini would have been so much sought after. That sensation is now decaying, because a new generation has emerged during the ten years since his death. But many still remain whose sympathy (whether of curiosity in those who did *not* know him or of admiration in those who *did*) still reflects as in a mirror the great stir upon this subject which then was moving in the world. To these, if they should inquire for the great distinguishing principle of

Coleridge's conversation, we might say that it was the power of vast combination. He gathered into focal concentration the largest body of objects. *apparently* disconnected, that any man ever yet, by any magic, could assemble, or, *håving* assembled, could manage. His great fault was, that, by not opening sufficient spaces for reply, or suggestion, or collateral notice, he not only narrowed his own field, but he grievously injured the final impression. For when men's minds are purely passive, when they are not allowed to react, then it is that they collapse most, and that their sense of what is said must ever be feeblest. Doubtless there must have been great conversational masters elsewhere, and at many periods; but in this lay Coleridge's characteristic advantage, that he was a great natural power, and also a great artist. He was a power in the art; and he carried a new art into the power.

But now, finally,—having left ourselves little room for more,—one or two words on Coleridge as an opium-eater.

We have not often read a sentence falling from a wise man with astonishment so profound as that particular one in a letter of Coleridge's to Mr Gillman, which speaks of the effort to wean one's self from opium as a trivial task. There are, we believe, several such passages; but we refer to that one in particular, which assumes that a single "week" will suffice for the whole process of so mighty a revolution. Is, indeed, leviathan *so* tamed? In that case, the quarantine of the opium-eater might be finished within Coleridge's time and with Coleridge's romantic ease. But mark the contradictions of this extraordinary man. Not long ago we were domesticated with a venerable rustic, strongheaded, but incurably obstinate in his prejudices, who treated the whole body of medical men as ignorant pretenders, knowing absolutely nothing of the system which they professed to superintend. This, you will remark, is no very singular case. No; nor, as we believe, is the antagonist case of ascribing to such men magical powers. Nor, what is worse still, the co-existence of both cases in the same mind, as in fact happened here; for this same obstinate friend of ours, who treated all medical pretensions as the mere jest of the universe, every third day was exacting from his own medical attendants some exquisite *tour de force*, as that they should know or should do something, which, if they *had* known or done, all men would have suspected them reasonably of magic. He rated the whole medical body as infants; and yet what he exacted from them every third day, as a matter of course, virtually presumed them to be the only giants within the whole range of science. Parallel and equal is the contradiction of Coleridge. He speaks of opium excess—his own excess we mean—the excess of twenty-five years—as a thing to be laid aside easily and for ever within seven days; and yet, on the other hand, he describes it pathetically, sometimes with a frantic pathos, as the scourge, the curse, the one almighty blight which had desolated his life.

This shocking contradiction we need not press. All readers will see *that*. But some will ask, Was Mr Coleridge right in either view? Being so atrociously wrong in the first notion (viz., that the opium of twenty-five years was a thing easily to be forsworn), where a child could know that he was wrong, was he even altogether right, secondly, in believing that his own life, root and branch, had been withered by opium? For it will not follow, because, with a relation to happiness and tranquillity, a man may have found opium his curse, that therefore, as a creature of energies and great purposes, he must have been the wreck which he seems to suppose. Opium gives and takes away. It defeats the *steady* habit of exertion; but it creates spasms of irregular exertion. It ruins the natural power of life; but it developes preternatural paroxysms of intermitting power.

Let us ask of any man who holds that not Coleridge himself, but the world, as interested in Coleridge's usefulness, has suffered by his addiction to opium, whether he is aware of the way in which opium affected Coleridge; and, secondly, whether he is aware of the actual contributions to literature—how large they were—which Coleridge made *in spite* of opium. All who were intimate with Coleridge must remember the fits of genial animation which were created continually in his manner and in his buoyancy of thought by a recent or by an *extra* dose of the omnipotent drug. A lady, who knew nothing experimentally of opium, once startled us by saying that she "could tell to a certainty when Mr Coleridge had taken too much opium by his shining countenance." She was right, and we knew it; but thought the secret within narrow keeping: we knew that mark of opium excesses well, and the cause of it; or at least we believe the cause to lie in the quickening of the insensible perspiration which accumulates and glistens on the face. Be that as it may, a criterion it was that could not deceive us as to the condition of Coleridge. And uniformly in that condition he made his most effective intellectual displays. It is true that he might not be happy under this fiery animation; and we fully believe that he was not. Nobody is happy except for a very short term of years under an artificial stimulation. But in what way did that operate upon his exertions as a writer? We are of opinion that it killed

Coleridge as a poet. "The harp of Quantock"* was silenced for ever by the torment of opium; but proportionably it roused and stung by misery his metaphysical instincts into more spasmodic life. Poetry can flourish only in the atmosphere of happiness. But subtle and perplexed investigations of difficult problems are amongst the commonest resources for beguiling the sense of misery. And for this we have the direct authority of Coleridge himself, speculating on his own case. In the beautiful though unequal ode entitled *Dejection*, stanza sixth, occurs the following passage:—

> "For not to think of what I needs must feel,
> But to be still and patient all I can,
> *And haply by abstruse research to steal*
> *From my own nature all the natural man,*—
> This was my sole resource, my only plan;
> Till that which suits a part infects the whole,
> And now is almost grown the habit of my soul."

Considering the exquisite quality of some poems which Coleridge has composed, nobody can grieve (or *has* grieved) more than ourselves at seeing so beautiful a fountain choked up with weeds. But, had Coleridge been a happier man, it is our fixed belief that we should have had far less of his philosophy, and perhaps *not* much more of his general literature. In the estimate of the public, doubtless, *that* will seem a good exchange. Every man to his taste. Meantime, what we wish to show is, that the loss was not absolute, but merely relative.

---

* *The Harp of Quantock*:—Under that designation it was that Wordsworth had apostrophised Coleridge as a poet after long years of silence. The *Quantock* Hills, in southern Somersetshire, are alluded to in Wordsworth's exquisite poem of *Ruth;* and were the early scene of joint wanderings on the part of the two poets, when Wordsworth and his sister tenanted Alfoxton, during the minority of Mr St Aubyn.

It is urged, however, that, even on his philosophic speculations, opium operated unfavourably in one respect, by often causing him to leave them unfinished. This is true Whenever Coleridge (being highly charged, or saturated, with opium) had written with distempered vigour upon any question, there occurred soon after a recoil of intense disgust, not from his own paper only, but even from the entire subject. All opium-eaters are tainted with the infirmity of leaving works unfinished, and suffering reactions of disgust; but Coleridge taxed himself with that infirmity in verse before he could at all have commenced opium-eating. Besides, it is too much assumed by Coleridge and by his biographer, that to leave off opium was of course to regain juvenile health. Indeed all opium-eaters, or indulgers in alcohol, make the mistake of supposing every pain or irritation which they suffer to be the product of the stimulant used, whereas a wise man will say, Suppose you *do* leave off opium, that will not deliver you from the load of years (say sixty-three) which you carry on your back. Charles Lamb, another man of true genius, and another head belonging to the Blackwood gallery; made that mistake in his *Confessions of a Drunkard*. "I looked back," says he, "to the time when always, on waking in the morning, I had a song rising to my lips." At present, it seems, being a drunkard, he has no such song. Aye, dear Lamb, but note this, that the drunkard was fifty-six years old, while the songster was twenty-three. Take twenty-three from fifty-six, and we have heard it said that thirty-three will remain: at least Cocker, who was a very obstinate man, went to his grave in that persuasion. But that extra burthen of thirty-three years is a pretty good reason for not singing in the morning, even if brandy has been out of the question.

It is singular, as respects Coleridge, that Mr Gillman never says one word upon the event of the great Highgate experiment for leaving off laudanum, though Coleridge came to Mr Gillman's for no other purpose; and in a week, this vast creation of new earth, sea, and all that in them is, was to have been accomplished. We incline to fancy that the explosion must have hung fire. But *that* is a trifle. We have another pleasing hypothesis on the subject. Mr Wordsworth, in his exquisite lines written on a fly-leaf of his own *Castle of Indolence*, having described Coleridge as a "noticeable man with large gray eyes," goes on to say, "He" (viz., Coleridge) "did that other man entice" to view his imagery. Now, we are sadly afraid that "the noticeable man with large gray eyes" did entice "that other man," viz., Gillman, to commence opium-eating. This is droll; and it makes us laugh horribly. Gillman should have reformed *him*, viz., Samuel Taylor Coleridge; and lo, *he* corrupts Gillman! Coleridge visited Highgate by way of being converted from the heresy of opium; and the issue is, that in two months' time various grave men, amongst whom our friend Gillman marches first in great pomp, are found to have faces shining and glorious as that of Æsculapius—a fact of which we have already explained the secret meaning. And scandal says (but then, what will not scandal say?) that a hogshead of laudanum goes up every third month through Highgate tunnel. Surely one corroboration of our hypothesis may be found in the fact, that Vol. I. of Gillman's Coleridge is for ever to stand unpropped by Vol. II.; for we have already observed that opium-eaters, though good fellows upon the whole, never finish anything.

What then? A man has a right never to finish anything. Certainly he has, and by Magna Charta; but he has no right, by Magna Charta or by Parva Charta, to slander decent men like ourselves and our friend the author of the *Opium Confessions*. Here it is that our complaint arises against Mr Gillman. If he has taken to opium-eating, can we help *that?* If *his* face shines, must our faces be blackened? He has very improperly published some intemperate passages from Coleridge's letters which ought to have been considered confidential, unless Coleridge had left them for publication, charging upon the author of the *Opium Confessions* a reckless disregard of the temptations which in that work he was scattering abroad amongst men. Now, this author is connected with ourselves, and we cannot neglect his defence, unless in the case that he undertakes it himself.

We complain also that Coleridge raises (and is backed by Mr Gillman in raising) a distinction, perfectly perplexing to us, between himself and the author of the *Opium Confessions*, upon the question, why they severally began the practice of opium-eating. In himself, it seems, this motive was to relieve pain, whereas the confessor was surreptitiously seeking for pleasure. Aye, indeed! where did he learn *that?* We have no copy of the *Confessions* here, so we cannot quote chapter and verse; but we distinctly remember that toothache is recorded in that book as the particular occasion which first introduced the author to the knowledge of opium. Whether afterwards, having been thus initiated by the demon of pain, the opium confessor did not apply powers thus discovered to purposes of mere pleasure, is a question for himself; and the same question applies with the same cogency to Coleridge. Coleridge began in rheumatic pains. What then? This is no proof that he did not end in voluptuousness. For our part, we are slow to believe that ever any man did or could learn the somewhat awful truth, that in a certain ruby-coloured elixir there lurked a divine power to chase away the genius of pain, or secondly, of *ennui* (which it is, far more than pain, that saddens our human life), without sometimes, and to some extent, abusing this power. To taste but once from the tree of knowledge is fatal to the subsequent power of abstinence. True it is that generations have used laudanum as an anodyne (for instance, hospital patients), who have not afterwards courted its powers as a voluptuous stimulant; but that, be sure, has arisen from no abstinence in *them*. There are, in fact, two classes of temperaments as to this terrific drug—those which are, and those which are not preconformed to its power; those which genially expand to its temptations, and those which frostily exclude them. Not in the energies of the will, but in the qualities of the nervous organisation, lies the dread arbitration of—Fall or stand: doomed thou art to yield, or strengthened constitutionally to resist. Most of those who have but a low sense of the spells lying couchant in opium have practically none at all; for the initial fascination is for *them* effectually defeated by the sickness which nature has associated with the first stages of opium-eating. But to that other class, whose nervous sensibilities vibrate to their profoundest depths under the first touch of the angelic poison, even as a lover's ear thrills on hearing unexpectedly the voice of her whom he loves, opium is the Amreeta cup of beatitude. You know the *Paradise Lost?* and you remember from the eleventh book, in its earlier part, that laudanum must already have existed in Eden—nay, that it was used medicinally by an archangel: for, after Michael had "purged with euphrasy and rue" the eyes of Adam, lest he should be unequal to the mere *sight* of the great visions about to unfold their draperies before him, next he fortifies his fleshly spirits against the *affliction* of these visions, of which visions the first was death. And how?

> "He from the well of life three drops instilled."

What was their operation?

> "So deep the power of these ingredients pierced,
> *Even to the inmost seat of mental sight,*
> That Adam, now enforced to close his eyes,
> Sank down, and all his spirits became entranced.
> But him the gentle angel by the hand
> Soon raised———"

The second of these lines it is which betrays the presence of laudanum. It is in the faculty of mental vision—it is in the increased power of dealing with the shadowy and the dark, that the characteristic virtue of opium lies. Now, in the original higher sensibility is found some palliation for the *practice* of opium-eating; in the greater temptation lies a greater excuse. And in this faculty of self-revelation is found some palliation for *reporting* the case to the world, which palliation both Coleridge and his biographer have overlooked.

TOILETTE OF THE HEBREW LADY

EXHIBITED IN SIX SCENES.

To the Editor of a great Literary Journal.

SIR,—Some years ago you published a translation of Böttiger's *Sabina*, a learned account of the Roman toilette. I here send you a companion to that work,—not a direct translation, but a very minute abstract [weeded of that wordiness which has made the original unreadable, and therefore unread] from a similar dissertation by Hartmann on the toilette and the wardrobe of the ladies of ancient Palestine. Hartmann was a respectable Oriental scholar, and he published his researches, which occupy three thick octavos, making in all one thousand four hundred and eighty-eight pages, under the title of *Die Hebräerin am Putztische und als Braut*, Amsterdam, 1809 (*The Hebrew Woman at her Toilette, and in her Bridal Character*). I understand that the poor man is now gone to Hades, where, let us hope, that it is considered by Minos or Radamanthus no crime in a learned man to be exceedingly tedious, and to repeat the same thing ten times over, or even, upon occasion, fifteen times, provided that his own upright heart should incline him to think that course the most advisable. Certainly Mr Hartmann has the most excellent gifts at verbal expansion, and talents the most splendid for tautology, that ever came within my knowledge; and I have found no particular difficulty in compressing every tittle of what relates to his subject into a compass which, I imagine, will fill about one-twenty-eighth part at the utmost of the original work.

It was not to be expected, with the scanty materials before him, that an illustrator of the Hebrew costume should be as full and explicit as Böttiger, with the advantage of writing upon a theme more familiar to us Europeans of this day than any parallel theme even in our own national archæologies of two centuries back. United, however, with his great reading, this barrenness of the subject is so far an advantage for Hartmann, as it yields a strong presumption that he has exhausted it. The male costume of ancient Palestine is yet to be illustrated; but for the female, it is probable that little could be added to what Hartmann has collected;* and that any clever dress-maker would, with the indications here given, enable any lady at the next great masquerade in London to support the part of one of the ancient daughters of Palestine, and to call back, after eighteen centuries of sleep, the buried pomps of Jerusalem. As to the *talking*, there would be

* It is one great advantage to the illustrator of ancient costume, that when almost everything in this sort of usages was fixed and determined either by religion and state policy (as with the Jews), or by state policy alone (as with the Romans), or by superstition and by settled climate (as with both); and when there was no stimulation to vanity in the love of change from an inventive condition of art and manufacturing skill, and where the system and interests of the government relied for no part of its power on such a condition, dress was stationary for ages, both as to materials and fashion; Rebecca, the Bedouin, was dressed pretty nearly as Mariamne, the wife of Herod, in the age of the Cæsars. And thus the labours of a learned investigator for one age are valid for many which follow and precede.

no difficulty at all in that point; bishops and other "sacred" people, if they ever go a-masquing, for their own sakes will not be likely to betray themselves by putting impertinent questions in Hebrew; and for "profane" people like myself, who might like the impertinence, they would very much dislike the Hebrew; indeed, of uncircumcised Hebrews, barring always the clergy, it is not thought that any are extant. In other respects, and as a *spectacle*, the Hebrew masque would infallibly eclipse every other in the room. The upper and under chemise, if managed properly (and either you or I, Mr Editor, will be most proud to communicate our private advice on that subject, without fee or *pot-de-vin*, as the French style a bribe), would transcend, in gorgeous display, the coronation robes of queens; nose-pendants would cause the masque to be immediately and unerringly recognised; or, if those were not thought advisable, the silver ankle-bells, with their melodious chimes—the sandals, with their jewelled network—and the golden diadem, binding the forehead, and dropping from each extremity of the polished temples a rouleau of pearls, which, after traversing the cheeks, unite below the chin,—are all so unique and exclusively Hebraic, that each and all would have the same advantageous effect; proclaiming and notifying the character, without putting the fair supporter to any disagreeable expense of Hebrew or Chaldee. The silver bells alone would "bear the bell" from every competitor in the room; and she might, besides, carry a cymbal, a dulcimer, or a timbrel in her hands.

In conclusion, my dear Sir, let me congratulate you that Mr Hartmann is now in Hades (as I said before) rather than in ——; for, had he been in this latter place, he would have been the ruin of you. It was his intention, as I am well assured, just about the time that he took his flight for Elysium, to have commenced regular contributor to your journal; so great was his admiration of you, and also of the terms which you offer to the literary world. As a learned Orientalist, you could not decorously have rejected him; and yet, once admitted, he would have beggared you before any means could have been discovered by the learned for putting a stop to him. Απεραντολογια, or what may be translated literally *world-without-ending-ness*, was his forte; upon this he piqued himself, and most justly, since for covering the ground rapidly, and yet not advancing an inch, those who knew and valued him as he deserved would have backed him against the whole field of the *gens de plume* now in Europe. Had he lived, and fortunately for himself communicated his *Hebrew Toilette* to the world through you, instead of foundering (as he did) at Amsterdam, he would have flourished upon your exchequer; and you would not have heard the last of him or his Toilette for the next twenty years. He dates, you see, from Amsterdam; and, had you been weak enough to take him on board, he would have proved that "Flying Dutchman" that would infallibly have sunk your vessel.

The more is your obligation to me, I think, for sweating him down to such slender dimensions. And, speaking seriously, both of us perhaps will rejoice that, even with *his* talents for telling everything, he was obliged on this subject to leave many things untold. For, though it might be gratifying to a mere interest of curiosity, yet I believe that we should both be grieved if anything were to unsettle in our feelings the mysterious sanctities of Jerusalem, or to disturb that awful twilight which will for ever brood over Judea, by letting in upon it the "common light of day;" and this effect would infallibly take place, if any one department of daily life, as it existed in Judea, were brought, with all the degrading minutiæ of its details, within the petty finishing of a domestic portrait.

Farewell, my dear Sir, and believe me always your devoted servant and admirer,

Ω. Φ.

SCENE THE FIRST.

I. That simple body-cloth, framed of leaves, skins, flax, wool, &c., which modesty had first introduced, for many centuries perhaps sufficed as the common attire of both sexes amongst the Hebrew Bedouins. It extended downwards to the knees, and upwards to the hips, about which it was fastened. Such a dress is seen upon many of the figures in the sculptures of Persepolis; even in modern times, Niebuhr found it the ordinary costume of the lower Arabians in Hedsjas; and Shaw assures us, that, from its commodious shape, it is still a favourite dishabille of the Arabian women when they are behind the curtains of the tent.

From this early rudiment was derived, by gradual elongation, that well-known under habiliment, which in Hebrew is called *Ch'tonet,* and in Greek and Latin by words of similar sound.* In this stage of its progress, when extended to the neck and the shoulders, it represents pretty accurately the modern shirt, *camisa* or *chemise*—except that the sleeves are wanting; and during the first period of Jewish history it was probably worn as the sole

---

* *Chiton* (Χιτων), in Greek, and, by inversion of the syllables, *Tunica* in Latin; that is (1.) *Chi-ton;* then (2.) *Ton-chi.* But, if so. (3.) Why not *Ton-cha;* and (4.) Why not *Tun-cha;* as also (5.) Why not *Tun-i-ca.*—Q. E. D. Such, I believe, is the received derivation.

under-garment by women of all ranks, both amongst the Bedouin-Hebrews and those who lived in cities. A very little further extension to the elbows and the calves of the legs, and it takes a shape which survives even to this day in Asia. Now, as then, the female habiliment was distinguished from the corresponding male one by its greater length; and through all antiquity we find long clothes a subject of reproach to men, as an argument of effeminacy.

According to the rank or vanity of the wearer, this tunic was made of more or less costly materials; for wool and flax was often substituted the finest byssus, or other silky substance; and perhaps, in the latter periods, amongst families of distinction in Jerusalem, even silk itself. Splendour of colouring was not neglected; and the opening at the throat was eagerly turned to account as an occasion for displaying fringe or rich embroidery.

Böttiger remarks that, even in the age of Augustus, the morning dress of Roman ladies when at home was nothing more than this very tunic, which, if it sate close, did not even require a girdle. The same remark applies to the Hebrew women, who, during the nomadic period of their history, had been accustomed to wear no night chemises at all, but slept quite naked,* or, at the utmost, with a cestus or zone; by way of bed-clothes, however, it must be observed that they swathed their person in the folds of a robe or shawl. Up to the time of Solomon this practice obtained through all ranks, and so long the uni-

* When the little Scottish king, about 1566, was taken ill in the night at Holyrood, Pinkerton mentions that all his attendants, male and female, rushed out into the adjacent gallery, naked as they were born, and thence comes the phrase so often used in the contemporary ballads—"Even as I left my naked bed."

versal household dress of a Hebrew lady in her harem was the tunic as here described; and in this she dressed herself the very moment that she rose from bed. Indeed, so long as the Hebrew women were content with a single tunic, it flowed loose in liberal folds about the body, and was fastened by a belt or a clasp, just as we find it at this day amongst all Asiatic nations. But when a second under garment was introduced, the inner one fitted close to the shape, whilst the outer one remained full and free as before.

II. No fashion of the female toilet is of higher antiquity than that of dyeing the margin of the eye-lids and the eye-brows with a black pigment. It is mentioned or alluded to, 2 Kings ix. 30, Jeremiah iv. 30, Ezekiel xxiii. 40; to which may be added, Isaiah iii. 16. The practice had its origin in a discovery made accidentally in Egypt. For it happens that the substance used for this purpose in ancient times is a powerful remedy in cases of ophthalmia and inflammation of the eyes, complaints to which Egypt is, from local causes, peculiarly exposed. This endemic infirmity, in connection with the medical science for which Egypt was so distinguished, easily account for their discovering the uses of antimony, which is the principal ingredient in the pigments of this class. Egypt was famous for the fashion of painting the face from an early period; and in some remarkable curiosities illustrating the Egyptian toilette, which were discovered in the catacombs of Sahara in Middle Egypt, there was a single joint of a common reed containing an ounce or more of the colouring powder, and one of the needles for applying it. The entire process was as follows:—The mineral powder, finely prepared, was mixed up with a preparation of vinegar and gall-apples—sometimes with oil of almonds or other oils—sometimes, by very luxurious women, with costly gums and balsams.* And perhaps, as Sonnini describes the practice among the Mussulman women at present, the whole mass thus compounded was dried and again reduced to an impalpable powder, and consistency then given to it by the vapours of some odorous and unctuous substance. Thus prepared, the pigment was applied to the tip or pointed ferule of a little metallic pencil, called in Hebrew *Makachol*, and made of silver, gold, or ivory; the eye-lids were then closed, and the little pencil, or probe, held horizontally, was inserted between them, a process which is briefly and picturesquely described in the Bible. The effect of the black rim which the pigment traced about the eye-lid, was to throw a dark and majestic shadow over the eye; to give it a languishing and yet a lustrous expression; to increase its apparent size, and to apply the force of contrast to the white of the eye. Together with the eye-lids, the Hebrew women coloured the eye-brows, the point aimed at being twofold—to curve them into a beautiful arch of brilliant ebony, and, at the same time, to make the inner ends meet or flow into each other.

III. Ear-rings of gold, silver, inferior metals, or even horn, were worn by the Hebrew women in all ages; and in the flourishing period of the Jewish kingdom, probably by men; and so essential an ornament were they deemed,

* Cheaper materials were used by the poorer Hebrews, especially of the Bedouin tribes—burnt almonds, lamp-black, soot, the ashes of particular woods, the gall-apple boiled and pulverised, or any dark powder made into an unguent by suitable liquors. The modern Grecian women, in some districts, as Sonnini tells us, use the spine of the sea-polypus, calcined and finely pulverised, for this purpose. Boxes of horn were used for keeping the pigment by the poorer Hebrews—of onyx or alabaster by the richer.

that in the idolatrous times even the images of their false gods were not considered becomingly attired without them. Their ear-rings were larger, according to the Asiatic taste, but whether quite large enough to admit the hand is doubtful. In a later age, as we collect from the Thalmud, Part vi. 43, the Jewish ladies wore gold or silver pendants, of which the upper part was shaped like a lentil, and the lower hollowed like a little cup or pipkin. It is probable also that, even in the oldest ages, it was a practice amongst them to suspend gold and silver rings, not merely from the lower but also from the upper end of the ear, which was perforated like a sieve. The tinkling sound with which, upon the slightest motion, two or three tiers of rings would be set a-dancing about the cheeks, was very agreeable to the baby taste of the Asiatics.

From a very early age the ears of Hebrew women were prepared for this load of trinketry; for, according to the Thalmud (ii. 23), they kept open the little holes after they were pierced by threads or slips of wood, a fact which may show the importance they attached to this ornament.

IV. Nose-rings at an early period became a universal ornament in Palestine. We learn, from Biblical and from Arabic authority, that it was a practice of Patriarchal descent amongst both the African and Asiatic Bedouins, to suspend rings of iron, wood, or braided hair, from the nostrils of camels, oxen, &c.—the rope by which the animal was guided being attached to these rings. It is probable, therefore, that the early Hebrews who dwelt in tents, and who in the barrenness of desert scenery drew most of their hints for improving their personal embellishment from the objects immediately about them, were indebted for their nose-rings to this precedent of their camels. Sometimes a ring depended from both nostrils; and the size of it was equal to that of the ear-ring; so that, at times, its compass included both upper and under lip, as in the frame of a picture; and, in the age succeeding to Solomon's reign, we hear of rings which were not less than three inches in diameter. Hebrew ladies of distinction had sometimes a cluster of nose-rings, as well for the tinkling sound which they were contrived to emit, as for the shining light which they threw off upon the face.

That the nose-ring possessed no unimportant place in the Jewish toilette, is evident, from its being ranked, during the nomadic state of the Israelites, as one of the most valuable presents that a young Hebrew woman could receive from her lover. Amongst the Midianites, who were enriched by the caravan commerce, even men adopted this ornament: and this appears to have been the case in the family to which Job belonged [chap. xli. 2]. Under these circumstances, we should naturally presume that the Jewish courtezans, in the cities of Palestine, would not omit so conspicuous a trinket, with its glancing lights, and its tinkling sound: this we might presume, even without the authority of the Bible; but, in fact, both Isaiah and Ezekiel expressly mention it amongst their artifices of attraction.

Judith, when she appeared before the tent of Holofernes in the whole pomp of her charms, and apparelled with the most elaborate attention to splendour of effect, for the purpose of captivating the hostile general, did not omit this ornament. Even the Jewish proverbs show how highly it was valued; and that it continued to be valued in later times, appears from the ordinances of the Thal mud (ii. 21), in respect to the parts of the female wardrobe which were allowed to be worn on the Sabbath.

V. The Hebrew women of high rank, in the flourishing period of their state, wore NECKLACES composed of multiple rows of pearls. The thread on which the pearls were strung was of flax or woollen,—and sometimes coloured, as we learn from the Thalmud (vi. 43); and the different rows were not exactly concentric; but whilst some invested the throat, others descended to the bosom; and in many cases, even to the zone. On this part of the dress was lavished the greatest expense; and the Roman reproach was sometimes true of a Hebrew family, that its whole estate was locked up in a necklace. Tertullian complains heavily of a particular pearl necklace, which had cost about ten thousand pounds of English money, as of an enormity of extravagance. But, after making every allowance for greater proximity to the pearl fisheries, and for other advantages enjoyed by the people of Palestine, there is reason to believe that some Hebrew ladies possessed pearls which had cost at least five times that sum.* So much may be affirmed, without meaning to compare the most lavish of the ladies of Jerusalem with those of Rome, where it is recorded of some *élégantes*, that they actually slept with little bags of pearls suspended from their necks, that, even when sleeping, they might have mementoes of their pomp.

But the Hebrew necklaces were not always composed

---

* Cleopatra had a couple at that value; and Julius Cæsar had one, which he gave to Servilia, the beautiful mother of Brutus, valued by knaves who wished to buy (empturiebant) at forty-eight thousand pounds English, but by the envious female world of Rome, at sixty-three thousand.

of pearls, or of pearls only—sometimes it was the custom to interchange the pearls with little golden bulbs or berries: sometimes they were blended with the precious stones; and at other times, the pearls were strung two and two, and their beautiful whiteness relieved by the interposition of red coral.

VI. Next came the BRACELETS of gold or ivory, and fitted up at the open side with a buckle or enamelled clasp of elaborate workmanship. These bracelets were also occasionally composed of gold or silver thread; and it was not unusual for a series of them to ascend from the wrist to the elbow. From the clasp, or other fastening of the bracelet, depended a delicate chain-work or netting of gold; and in some instances, miniature festoons of pearls. Sometimes the gold chain-work was exchanged for little silver bells, which could be used, upon occasion, as signals of warning or invitation to a lover.

VII. This *bijouterie* for the arms naturally reminded the Hebrew lady of the ANKLE BELLS, and other similar ornaments for the feet and legs. These ornaments consisted partly in golden belts, or rings, which, descending from above the ankle, compressed the foot in various parts; and partly in shells and little jingling chains, which depended so as to strike against clappers fixed into the metallic belts. The pleasant tinkle of the golden belts in collision, the chains rattling, and the melodious chime of little silver ankle-bells, keeping time with the motions of the foot, made an accompaniment so agreeable to female vanity, that the stately daughters of Jerusalem, with their sweeping trains flowing after them, appear to have adopted a sort of measured tread, by way of impressing a regular cadence upon the music of their feet. The chains of gold were exchanged, as luxury advanced, for strings of pearls and jewels, which swept in snaky folds about the feet and ankles.

This, like many other peculiarities in the Hebrew dress, had its origin in a circumstance of their early nomadic life. It is usual with the Bedouins to lead the camel, when disposed to be restive, by a rope or a belt fastened to one of the fore-feet, sometimes to both; and it is also a familiar practice to soothe and to cheer the long-suffering animal with the sound of little bells, attached either to the neck or to one of the fore legs. Girls are commonly employed to lead the camels to water; and it naturally happened, that, with their lively fancies, some Hebrew or Arabian girl should be prompted to repeat, on her own person, what had so often been connected with an agreeable impression in her mute companions to the well.

It is probable, however, that afterwards, having once been introduced, this fashion was supported and extended by Oriental jealousy. For it rendered all clandestine movements very difficult in women; and by giving notice of their approach, it had the effect of preparing men for their presence, and keeping the road free from all spectacles that could be offensive to female delicacy.

From the Hebrew Bedouins, this custom passed to all the nations of Asia; Medes, Persians, Lydians, Arabs, &c., and is dwelt on with peculiar delight by the elder Arabic poets. That it had spread to the westernmost parts of Africa early in the Christian times, we learn from Tertullian, who [foolish man] cannot suppress his astonishment, that the foolish women of his time should bear to inflict such compression upon their tender feet. Even as early as the times of Herodotus, we find from his account of a Libyan nation, that the women and girls universally wore copper rings about their ankles. And at an after period, these ornaments were so much cherished by the Egyptian ladies, that, sooner than appear in public without their tinkling ankle-chimes, they preferred to bury themselves in the loneliest apartments of the harem.

Finally, the fashion spread partially into Europe; to Greece even, and to polished Rome, in so far as regarded the ankle-belts, and the other ornamental appendages, with the single exception of the silver bells: these were too entirely in the barbaresque taste, to support themselves under the frown of European culture.

VIII. The first rude sketch of the Hebrew SANDAL may be traced in that little tablet of undrest hide which the Arabs are in the habit of tying beneath the feet of their camels. This primitive form, after all the modifications and improvements it has received, still betrays itself to an attentive observer, in the very latest fashions of the sandal which Palestine has adopted.

To raw hides succeeded tanned leather, made of goat-skin, deer-skin, &c.; this, after being accurately cut out to the shape of the sole, was fastened on the bare upper surface of the foot by two thongs, of which one was usually carried within the great toe, and the other in many circumvolutions round about the ankles, so that both finally met and tied just above the instep.

The laced sole or sandal, of this form, continued in Palestine to be the universal out-of-doors protection for the foot, up to the Christian era; and it served for both sexes alike. It was not, however, worn within doors. At the threshold of the inner apartments the sandals were laid aside and visitors from a distance were presented with a vessel of water to cleanse the feet from the soiling of dust and perspiration.*

With this extreme simplicity in the form of the foot-apparel, there was no great field for improvement. The article contained two parts—the sole and the fastening. The first, as a subject for decoration, was absolutely desperate; coarse leather being exchanged for fine, all was done that could be done; and the wit of man was able to devise no further improvement. Hence it happened that the whole power of the inventive faculty was accumulated upon the fastenings, as the only subject that remained. These were infinitely varied. Belts of bright yellow, of purple, and of crimson, were adopted by ladies of distinction—especially those of Palestine, and it was a trial of art to throw these into the greatest possible varieties of convolution, and to carry them on to a nexus of the happiest form, by which means a reticulation, or trellis-work, was accomplished, of the most brilliant colouring, which brought into powerful relief the dazzling colour of the skin.

It is possible that, in the general rage for ornaments of gold which possessed the people of Palestine, during the ages of excessive luxury, the beauties of Jerusalem may have adopted gilt sandals with gilt fastenings, as the ladies of Egypt did. It is possible also, that the Hebrew ladies adopted at one time, in exchange for the sandal, slippers that covered the entire foot, such as were once worn at

* Washing the feet was a ceremony of ancient times, adopted not merely with a view, *1st*, to personal comfort, in hotter climates; or, *2d*, to decorum of appearance, where people walked about barefooted; but also, *3d*, to the reclining posture in use at meals, which necessarily brought the feet into immediate contact with the snowy swan-down cushions, squabs, &c. of couches.

Babylon, and are still to be seen on many of the principal figures on the monuments of Persepolis; and, if this were really so, ample scope would in that case have been obtained for inventive art: variations without end might then have been devised on the fashion or the materials of the subject; and by means of colour, embroidery, and infinite combinations of jewellery and pearls, an unceasing stimulation of novelty applied to the taste of the gorgeous, but still sensual and barbaresque Asiatic.

IX. The VEIL, of various texture—coarse or fine—according to circumstances, was thrown over the head by the Hebrew lady, when she was unexpectedly surprised, or when a sudden noise gave reason to expect the approach of a stranger. This beautiful piece of drapery, which flowed back in massy folds over the shoulders, is particularly noticed by Isaiah, as holding an indispensable place in the wardrobe of his haughty countrywomen; and in this it was that the enamoured Hebrew woman sought the beloved of her heart.

ADDENDA TO SCENE THE FIRST.

I. Of the Hebrew ornaments for the throat, some were true necklaces, in the modern sense, of several rows, the outermost of which descended to the breast, and had little pendulous cylinders of gold (in the poorer classes, of copper), so contrived as to make a jingling sound on the least motion of the person; others were more properly golden stocks, or throat-bands, fitted so close as to produce in the spectator an unpleasant imagination, and in the wearer as we learn from the Thalmud (vi. 43), until reconciled by use, to produce an actual feeling of constriction approaching to suffocation. Necklaces were, from the earliest times, a favourite ornament of the male sex in the East; and expressed the dignity of the wearer, as we see in the instances of Joseph, of Daniel, &c.; indeed the gold chain of office, still the badge of civic (and, until lately, of military) dignities, is no more than the outermost row of the Oriental necklace. Philo of Alexandria, and many other writers, both Persic and Arabian, give us some idea of the importance attached by the women of Asia to this beautiful ornament, and of the extraordinary money value which it sometimes bore: and from the case of the necklace of gold and amber, in the 15th Odyssey (v. 458), combined with many other instances of the same kind, there can be no doubt that it was the neighbouring land of Phœnicia from which the Hebrew women obtained their necklaces, and the practice of wearing them.

II. The fashion, however, of adorning the necklace with golden *Suns* and *Moons*, so agreeable to the Hebrew ladies of Isaiah's time (chap. iii. 18), was not derived from Phœnicia, but from Arabia. At an earlier period (Judges viii. 21), the camels of the Midianites were adorned with golden moons, which also decorated the necks of the emirs of that nomadic tribe. These appendages were not used merely by way of ornament, but originally as talismans, or amulets, against sickness, danger, and every species of calamity to which the desert was liable. The particular form of the amulet is to be explained out of the primitive religion, which prevailed in Arabia up to the rise of Mohammedanism in the seventh century of Christianity, viz., the *Sabean* religion, or worship of the heavenly host—sun, moon, and stars—the most natural of all idolatries, and especially to a nomadic people in flat and pathless deserts, without a single way-mark or guidance for their wanderings, except what they drew from the silent he ns above them. It is certain, therefore, that long before their emigration into Palestine, the Israelites had received the practice of wearing suns and moons from the Midianites; even after their settlement in Palestine, it is certain that the worship of the starry host struck root pretty deeply at different periods; and that, to the sun and moon, in particular, were offered incense and libations.

From Arabia, this fashion diffused itself over many countries;* and it was not without great displeasure that, in a remote age, Jerome and Tertullian discovered this idolatrous ornament upon the bosoms of their countrywomen.

The crescents, or *half*-moons of silver, in connection with the golden suns,* were sometimes set in a brilliant frame that represented a halo, and still keep their ground on the Persian and Turkish toilette, as a favourite ornament.

III. The GOLDEN SNAKES, worn as one of the Hebrew appendages to the necklace, had the same idolatrous derivation, and originally were applied to the same superstitious use—as an amulet, or prophylactic ornament. For minds predisposed to this sort of superstition, the serpent had a special attraction under the circumstances of the Hebrews, from the conspicuous part which this reptile sustains in the mythologies of the East. From the earliest periods to which tradition ascends, serpents of various species were consecrated to the religious feelings of Egypt, by temples, sacrifices, and formal rites of wor-

---

* Chemistry had its first origin in Arabia: and it is not impossible that the chemical nomenclature for gold and silver, viz., *sol* and *luna*, were derived from this early superstition of the Bedouin dress.

ship. This mode of idolatry had at various periods infected Palestine. According to 2 Kings xviii. 4, at the accession of King Hezekiah, the Israelites had raised peculiar altars to a great brazen serpent, and burned incense upon them. Even at this day the Abyssinians have an unlimited reverence for serpents; and the blacks in general regard them as fit subjects for divine honours. Sonnini (ii. 388) tells us, that a serpent's skin is still looked upon in Egypt as a prophylactic against complaints of the head, and also as a certain cure for them. And of the same origin, no doubt, was the general belief of antiquity (according to Pliny, 30, 12), that the serpent's skin was a remedy for spasms. That the golden serpent kept its place as an ornament of the throat and bosom after the Christian era, we learn from Clement of Alexandria. That zealous father, so intolerant of superstitious mummery under every shape, directs his efforts against this fashion as against a device of the devil.

IV. To the lowest of the several concentric circles which composed the necklace was attached a little box, exquisitely wrought in silver or gold, sometimes an onyx phial of dazzling whiteness, depending to the bosom or even to the cincture, and filled with the rarest aromas and odorous spices of the East. What were the favourite essences preserved in this beautiful appendage to the female costume of Palestine it is not possible at this distance of time to determine with certainty—Isaiah having altogether neglected the case, and Hosea, who appears to allude to it (ii. 14), having only once distinctly mentioned it (ii. 20). However, the Thalmud particularizes musk, and the delightful oil distilled from the leaf of the aromatic *malabathrum* of Hindostan. To these we may venture to add oil of spikenard, myrrh, balsams, attar of roses, and rose-water, as the perfumes usually contained in the Hebrew scent-pendants.

Rose-water, which I am the first to mention as a Hebrew perfume, had, as I presume, a foremost place on the toilette of a Hebrew *belle*. Express scriptural authority for it undoubtedly there is none; but it is notorious that Palestine availed itself of *all* the advantages of Egypt, amongst which the rose in every variety was one. *Fium*, a province of Central Egypt, which the ancients called the garden of Egypt, was distinguished for innumerable species of the rose, and especially for those of the most balsamic order, and for the most costly preparations from it. The Thalmud not only speaks generally of the mixtures made by tempering it with oil (i. 135), but expressly cites (ii. 41) a peculiar rose-water as so costly an essence, that from its high price alone it became impossible to introduce the use of it into the ordinary medical practice. Indeed this last consideration, and the fact that the highly-prized *quintessence* cannot be obtained except from an extraordinary multitude of the rarest roses, forbid us to suppose that even women of the first rank in Jerusalem could have made a very liberal use of rose-water. In our times, Savary found a single phial of it in the place of its manufacture, valued at four francs. As to the *oil of roses*, properly so called, which floats in a very inconsiderable quantity upon the surface of distilled rose-water, it is certain that the Hebrew ladies were *not* acquainted with it. This preparation can be obtained only from the balsamic roses of Fium, of Shiras, of Kerman, and of Kashmire, which surpass all the roses of the earth in power and delicacy of odour; and it is matter of absolute certainty, and incontrovertibly established by the celebrated Langlés, that this oil, which even in the four Asiatic countries just mentioned ranks with the greatest rarities, and in Shiras itself is valued at its weight in gold, was discovered by mere accident, on occasion of some festival solemnity in the year 1612.

V. To what I said in the first scene of my exhibition about the Hebrew ear-ornaments, I may add,

1. That sometimes, as Best remarked of the Hindoo dancing girls, their ears were swollen from the innumerable perforations drilled into them to support their loads of trinketry.

2. That in the large pendants of coral which the Hebrew ladies were accustomed to attach to their ears, either in preference to jewels, or in alternation with jewels, they particularly delighted in that configuration which imitated a cluster of grapes.

3. That, in ear-rings made of gold, they preferred the form of drops, or of globes and bulbs.

4. That of all varieties, however, of this appendage, pearls maintained the preference amongst the ladies of Palestine, and were either strung upon a thread, or attached by little hooks—singly, or in groups, according to their size. This taste was very early established amongst the Jews, and chiefly, perhaps, through their intercourse with the Midianites, amongst whom we find the great emirs wearing pearl ornaments of this class.

Mutatis mutandis, these four remarks apply also and equally to the case of the nose ornaments.

SCENE THE SECOND.

I. The Hair.—This section I omit altogether, though with more room at my disposal it would be well worth translating as a curiosity. It is the essay of a finished and perfect knave, who, not merely being rather bare of facts, but having literally not one solitary fact of any kind or degree, small or great, sits down to write a treatise on the mode of dressing hair amongst Hebrew ladies. Samson's hair, and the dressing it got from the Philistines, is the nearest approach that he ever makes to his subject; and being conscious that this case of Samson and the Philistines is the one sole allusion to the subject of Hebrew hair that he is possessed of—for he altogether overlooks (which surely in *him* is criminal and indictable inadvertence) the hair of Absalom—he brings it round upon the reader as often perhaps as it will bear, viz., not oftener than once every sixth page. The rest is one continued shuffle to avoid coming upon the ground; and upon the whole, though too barefaced, yet really not without ingenuity. Take, by way of specimen, his very satisfactory dissertation on the particular sort of combs which the Hebrew ladies were pleased to patronise :—

"*Combs.*—Whether the ladies of Palestine had upon their toilette a peculiar comb for parting the hair, another for turning it up, &c.; as likewise whether these combs were, as in ancient Rome, made of box-wood or of ivory, or other costly and appropriate material, all these are questions upon which I——am not able, upon my honour, to communicate the least information. But from the general silence of antiquity, prophets and all,* upon the

* The Thalmud is the only Jewish authority which mentions such a utensil of the toilette as a comb (vi. 89), but without any particular description. Hartmann adds two remarks worth quoting. 1. That the Hebrew style of the *coiffure* may probably be collected from the Syrian coins; and 2. That black hair being admired in Palestine, and the Jewish hair being naturally black, it is probable that the Jewish ladies did not colour their hair, as the Romans did.

subject of Hebrew combs, my own private opinion is, that the ladies used their fingers for this purpose, in which case there needs no more to be said on the subject of Hebrew combs." Certainly not. All questions are translated from the visionary combs to the palpable and fleshly fingers; but the comb being usually of ivory in the Roman establishments, were costly, and might breed disputes; but the fingers were a dowry of nature, and cost nothing.

II. Perfumes.—Before, however, the hair received its final arrangement from the hands of the waiting-maid, it was held open and dishevelled to receive the fumes of frankincense, aloeswood, cassia, costmary, and other odorous woods, gums, balsams, and spices of India, Arabia, or Palestine—placed upon glowing embers, in vessels of golden fretwork. It is probable also that the Hebrew ladies used amber, bisam, and the musk of Thibet; and, when fully arranged, the hair was sprinkled with oil of nard, myrrh, oil of cinnamon, &c. The importance attached to this part of the Hebrew toilette may be collected indeed from an ordinance of the Thalmud (iii. 80), which directs that the bridegroom shall set apart one-tenth of the income which the bride brings him, for the purchase of perfumes, essences, precious ointments, &c. All these articles were preserved either in golden boxes or in little oval narrow-necked phials of dazzling white alabaster, which bore the name of onyx, from its resemblance to the precious stone of that name, but was in fact a very costly sort of marble, obtained in the quarries of Upper Egypt or those of the Libanus in Syria. Indeed, long before the birth of Christ, alabaster was in such general use for purposes of this kind in Palestine, that it became the generic name for valuable boxes, no matter of what material. To prevent the evaporation of the contents, the narrow neck of the phial was re-sealed every time that it was opened. It is probable also that the *myrrhine* cups, about which there has been so much disputing, were no strangers to the Jewish toilette.

III. The Mirror was not made of glass (for glass mirrors cannot be shown to have existed before the thirteenth century), but of polished metals; and amongst these silver was in the greatest esteem, as being capable of a higher burnish than other metals, and less liable to tarnish. Metallic mirrors are alluded to by Job (xxxvii. 18). But it appears from the Second Book of Moses (xxxviii. 8), that in that age copper must have been the metal employed throughout the harems of Palestine. For a general contribution of mirrors being made upon one occasion by the Israelitish women, they were melted down and re-cast into washing vessels for the priestly service. Now the sacred utensils, as we know from other sources, were undeniably of copper. There is reason to think, however, that the copper was alloyed, according to the prevailing practice in that age, with some proportions of lead or tin. In after ages, when silver was chiefly employed, it gave place occasionally to gold. Mines of this metal were well known in Palestine; but there is no evidence that precious stones, which were used for this purpose in the ages of European luxury, were ever so used in Palestine, or in any part of Asia.

As to shape, the Hebrew mirrors were always either circular or oval, and cast indifferently flat or concave. They were framed in superb settings, often of pearls and jewels; and, when tarnished, were cleaned with a sponge full of hyssop, the universal cleansing material in Palestine.

SCENE THE THIRD.

Head-Dresses.

The head-dresses of the Hebrew ladies may be brought under three principal classes:—

The first was a NETWORK CAP, made of fine wool or cotton, and worked with purple or crimson flowers. Sometimes the meshes of the net were of gold thread. The rim or border of the cap, generally of variegated colouring, was often studded with jewellery or pearls; and at the back was ornamented with a bow, having a few ends or tassels flying loose.

Secondly, a TURBAN, managed in the following way:—First of all, one or more caps in the form of a half oval, such as are still to be seen upon the monuments of Egyptian and Persepolitan art, was fastened round the head by a ribbon or fillet tied behind. This cap was of linen, sometimes perhaps of cotton, and in the inferior ranks oftentimes of leather, or, according to the prevailing fashion, of some kind of metal; and, in any case, it had ornaments worked into its substance. Round this white or glittering ground were carried, in snaky windings, ribbons of the finest tiffany, or of lawn resembling our cambric; and to conceal the joinings, a silky substance was carried in folds, which pursued the opposite direction, and crossed the tiffany at right angles. For the purpose of calling out and relieving the dazzling whiteness of the ground, colours of the most brilliant class were chosen for the ribbons; and these ribbons were either embroidered with flowers in gold thread, or had ornaments of that description interwoven with their texture.

Thirdly, the HELMET, adorned pretty nearly as the turban; and, in imitation of the helmets worn by Chaldean generals, having long tails or tassels depending from the hinder part, and flowing loosely between the shoulders. According to the Oriental taste for perfumes, all the ribbons or fillets used in these helmets and turbans were previously steeped in perfumes.

Finally, in connection with the turban, and often with the veil, was a beautiful ornament for the forehead and the face, which the ladies of this day would do well to recall. Round the brow ran a bandeau or tiara of gold or silver, three fingers'-breadth, and usually set with jewels or pearls: from this, at each of the temples, depended a chain of pearls or of coral, which, following the margin of the cheeks, either hung loose or united below the chin.

SCENE THE FOURTH.

I. The reader has been already made acquainted with the *chemise*, or innermost under-dress. The Hebrew ladies, however, usually wore two under-dresses, the upper of which it now remains to describe. In substance it was generally of a fine transparent texture, like the muslins (if we may so call them) of Cos; in the later ages it was no doubt of silk.

The chemise sate close up to the throat; and we have already mentioned the elaborate work which adorned it about the opening. But the opening of the robe which we are now describing was of much larger compass, being cut down to the bosom; and the embroidery, &c., which enriched it was still more magnificent. The *chemise* reached down only to the calf of the leg, and the sleeve of it to the elbow: but the upper chemise or tunic, if we may so call it, descended in ample draperies to the feet, scarcely allowing the point of the foot to discover itself; and the sleeves enveloped the hands to their middle. Great pomp was lavished on the folds of the sleeves; but still greater on the hem of the robe and the fringe attached to it. The hem was formed by a broad border of purple, shaded and relieved according to patterns; and sometimes embroidered in gold thread with the most elegant objects from the animal or vegetable kingdoms. To that part which fell immediately behind the heels, there were attached thin plates of gold; or, by way of variety, it was studded with golden stars and filigree-work, sometimes with jewels and pearls interchangeably.

II. On this upper tunic, to confine the exorbitance of its draperies, and to prevent their interfering with the free motions of the limbs, a superb GIRDLE was bound about the hips. Here, if anywhere, the Hebrew ladies endeavoured to pour out the whole pomp of their splendour, both as to materials and workmanship. Belts from three to four inches broad, of the most delicate cottony substance, were chosen as the ground of this important part of female attire. The finest flowers of Palestine were here exhibited in rich relief, and in their native colours, either woven in the loom, or by the needle of the embroiderer. The belts being thirty or forty feet long, and carried round and round the person, it was in the power of the wearer to exhibit an infinite variety of forms, by allowing any fold or number of folds at pleasure to rise up more or less to view, just as fans or the coloured edges of books with us are made to exhibit landscapes, &c., capable of great varieties of expansion as they are more or less unfolded. The fastening was by a knot below the bosom, and the two ends descended below the fringe; which, if not the only fashion in use, was, however, the prevailing one, as we learn both from the sculptures at Persepolis, and from the costume of the high priest.

Great as the cost was of these girdles, it would have been far greater had the knot been exchanged for a clasp; and in fact at a later period, when this fashion did really take place, there was no limit to the profusion with which pearls of the largest size and jewellery were accumulated upon this conspicuous centre of the dress. Latterly the girdles were fitted up with beautiful chains, by means of which they could be contracted or enlarged, and with gold buckles, and large bosses and clasps, that gradually became the basis for a ruinous display of expenditure.

In conclusion, I must remark, that in Palestine, as elsewhere, the girdle was sometimes used as a purse; whether it were that the girdle itself was made hollow (as is expressly affirmed of the high priest's girdle), or that, without being hollow, its numerous foldings afforded a secure depository for articles of small size. Even in our days, it is the custom to conceal the dagger, the handkerchief for wiping the face, and other bagatelles of personal convenience, in the folds of the girdle. However, the richer and more distinguished classes in Palestine appear to have had a peculiar and separate article of that kind. And this was—

III. A PURSE, made either of metal (usually gold or silver), or of the softest leather, &c., which was attached by a lace to the girdle, or kept amongst its folds, and which, even in the eyes of Isaiah, was important enough to merit a distinct mention. It was of a conical shape, and at the broader end was usually enriched with ornaments of the most elaborate and exquisite workmanship. No long time after the Christian era, the cost of these purses had risen to such a height, that Tertullian complains, with great displeasure, of the ladies of his time, that in the mere purse, apart from its contents, they carried about with them the price of a considerable estate.

The girdle, however, still continued to be the appropriate depository for the napkin (to use the old English word) or sudatory—*i.e.*, handkerchief for clearing the forehead of perspiration. As to pocket-handkerchiefs, in our northern use of them, it has been satisfactorily shown by Böttiger, in a German Journal, that the Greek and Roman ladies knew nothing of that modern appendage to the pocket,* however indispensable it may appear to us; and the same arguments apply with equal force to the climate of Palestine.

IV. The glittering RINGS, with which (according to Isaiah iii. 21) the Hebrew ladies adorned their hands, seem to me originally to have been derived from the seal-rings, which, whether suspended from the neck, or worn upon the finger, have in all ages been the most favourite ornament of Asiatics. These splendid baubles were naturally in the highest degree attractive to women, both from the beauty of the stones which were usually selected for this purpose, and from the richness of the setting—to say nothing of the exquisite art which the ancient lapidaries displayed in cutting them. The stones chiefly

* Or rather it was required only in a catarrh, or other case of checked perspiration, which in those climates was a case of very rare occurrence. It has often struck me—that without needing the elaborate aid of Böttiger's researches, simply from one clause in Juvenal's picture of old age and its infirmities we might deduce the Roman habit of dispensing with a pocket-handkerchief. Amongst these infirmities he notices the *madidi infantia nasi*—the second childhood of a nose that needs wiping. But, if this kind of defluxion was peculiar to infancy and extreme old age, it was obviously no affection of middle age.

valued by the ladies of Palestine were rubies, emeralds, and chrysolithes; and these, set in gold, sparkled on the middle or little finger of the right hand; and in luxurious times upon *all* the fingers, even the thumb; nay, in some cases, upon the great toe.

SCENE THE FIFTH.

Upper Garment.

The upper or outer garments, which, for both sexes, under all varieties and modifications, the Hebrews expressed by the comprehensive denomination of SIMLAH, have in every age, and through all parts of the hot climates, in Asia and Africa alike, been of such voluminous compass as not only to envelope the whole person, but to be fitted for a wide range of miscellaneous purposes. Sometimes (as in the triumphal entry of Christ into Jerusalem) they were used as carpets; sometimes as coverings for the backs of camels, horses, or asses, to render the rider's seat less incommodious; sometimes as a bed coverlid or counterpane; at other times as sacks for carrying articles of value; or finally, as curtains, hangings of parlours, occasional tapestry, or even as sails for boats.

From these illustrations of the uses to which it was applicable, we may collect the form of this robe; that it was nothing more than a shawl of large dimensions, or long square of cloth, just as it came from the weaver's loom, which was immediately thrown round the person, without receiving any artificial adjustment to the human shape.

So much for the *form:* with regard to the *material*, there was less uniformity; originally it was of goats' or camels' hair; but as civilization and the luxury of cities increased, these coarse substances were rejected for the finest wool and Indian cotton. Indeed, through all antiquity, we find that pure unsullied white was the festal colour, and more especially in Palestine, where the indigenous soaps, and other cleaning materials, gave them peculiar advantages for adopting a dress of that delicate and perishable lustre.

With the advance of luxury, however, came a love of variety; and this, added to the desire for more stimulating impressions than could be derived from blank unadorned white, gradually introduced all sorts of innovations, both in form and colour; though, with respect to the first, amidst all the changes through which it travelled, the old original outline still manifestly predominated. An account of the leading varieties we find in the celebrated third chapter of Isaiah.

The most opulent women of Palestine, beyond all other colours for the upper robe, preferred purple; or, if not purple throughout the entire robe, at any rate purple flowers upon a white ground. The winter clothing of the very richest families in Palestine was manufactured in their own houses; and for winter clothing, more especially the Hebrew taste, no less than the Grecian and the Roman, preferred the warm and sunny scarlet, the puce colour, the violet, and the regal purple.*

Very probable it is that the Hebrew ladies, like those of Greece, were no strangers to the half-mantle—fastened by a clasp in front of each shoulder, and suffered to flow in free draperies down the back; this was an occasional and supernumerary garment flung over the regular upper robe—properly so called.

* By which was probably meant a colour nearer to crimson than to the blue or violet class of purples.

There was also a longer mantle, reaching to the ankles, usually of a violet colour, which, having no sleeves, was meant to expose to view the beauty, not only of the upper robe, but even of the outer tunic formerly described.

By the way, it should be mentioned that, in order to steep them in fine odour, all parts of the wardrobe were stretched on a reticulated or grated vessel—called by the Thalmud (vi. 77) *Kanklin*—from which the steams of rich perfumes were made to ascend.

In what way the upper robe was worn and fastened may be collected perhaps with sufficient probability from the modern Oriental practice, as described by travellers; but, as we have no *direct* authority on the subject, I shall not detain the reader with any conjectural speculations.

SCENE THE SIXTH.

Dress of Ceremony.

One magnificent dress remains yet to be mentioned, viz., the dress of honour or festival dress, which answers in every respect to the modern CAFTAN. This was used on all occasions of ceremony, as splendid weddings, presentations at the courts of kings, sumptuous entertainments, &c.; and all persons who stood in close connection with the throne, as favourites, crown-officers, distinguished military commanders, &c., received such a dress as a gift from the royal treasury, in order to prepare them at all times for the royal presence. According to the universal custom of Asia, the trains were proportioned in length to the rank of the wearer; whence it is that the robes of the high-priest were adorned with a train of superb dimensions; and even Jehovah is represented (Isaiah vi. 1) as filling the heavenly palace with the length of his train.* Another distinction of this festival robe was the extraordinary fulness and length of the sleeves; these descended to the knee, and often ran to the ankle or to the ground. In the sleeves and in the trains, but especially in the latter, lay the chief pride of a Hebrew *belle*, when dressed for any great solemnity or occasion of public display.

Final Notes.

I. The *Syndon*, mentioned by Isaiah, &c., was a delicate and transparent substance, like our tiffany, and in point of money value was fully on a level with the Caftan; but whether imported from Egypt or imitated in the looms of the Hebrews and Phœnicians, is doubtful. It was worn next to the skin, and consequently, in the harems of the great, occupied the place of the under tunic (or *chemise*) previously described; and, as luxury advanced, there is reason to think that it was used as a night *chemise*.

II. The *Caftan* is the *Kalaat* of the East, or *Kelaat* so often mentioned by modern travellers; thus, for example, Thevenot (tom. iii. p. 352) says—"Le Roi fait assez souvent des présens à ses Khans, &c., L'on appelle ces présens *Kalaat*." Chardin. (iii. 101), "On appelle *Calaat* les habits que le Roi donne par honneur." And lately, in Lord Amherst's progress through the northern provinces of our Indian empire, &c., we read continually of the *Khelawt*, or robe of state, as a present made by the native princes to distinguished officers.

The Caftan, or festival robe of the Hebrews, was, in my opinion, the Πεπλος of the Greeks, or *palla* of the Romans. Among the points of resemblance are these:—

1. The *palla* was flung like a cloak or mantle over the *stola* or uppermost robe, "Ad talos stola demissa et *circumdata* pallâ."

2. The *palla* not only descended in flowing draperies to the feet

* It has been doubted whether these trains were supported by train-bearers; but one argument makes it probable that they were not, viz., that they were particularly favourable to the peacock walk or strut, which was an express object of imitation in the gait of the Hebrew women.

(thus Tibullus, i. vii. C, "Fusa sed ad teneros lutea palla pedes") but absolutely swept the ground. "Verrit humum Tyrio saturatâ murice pallâ."

3. The *palla* was of the same wide compass, and equally distinguished for its splendour.

4. Like the Hebrew festival garment, the *palla* was a *vestis seposita*, and reserved for rare solemnities.

With respect to the Πεπλος, Eustathius describes it as μεγαν και περικαλλεα και ποικιλον περιβολαιον, a large and very beautiful and variegated enveloping mantle; and it would be easy in other respects to prove its identity with the *Palla*.

Salmasius, by the way, in commenting upon Tertullian *de Pallio*, is quite wrong where he says—"Palla nunquam de virili pallio dicitur." Tibullus (tom. iii. iv. 35), sufficiently contradicts that opinion.

NATIONAL TEMPERANCE MOVEMENTS.

The most remarkable instance of a combined movement in society which history, perhaps, will be summoned to notice, is that which in our own days has applied itself to the abatement of intemperance. Naturally, or by any *direct* process, the machinery set in motion would seem irrelevant to the object. If one hundred men unite to elevate the standard of temperance, they can do this with effect only by improvements in their own separate cases: each individual, for such an effort of self-conquest, can draw upon no resources but his own. One member in a combination of one hundred, when running a race, can hope for no co-operation from his ninety-nine associates; and yet, by a secondary action, such combinations are found eminently successful. Having obtained from every confederate a pledge, in some shape or other, that he will give them his support, thenceforwards they bring the passions of shame and self-esteem to bear upon each member's personal perseverance. Not only they keep alive and continually refresh in his thoughts the general purpose, which else might fade, but they also point the action of public contempt and of self-contempt at any defaulter much more potently, and with more acknowledged right to do so, when they use this influence under a license, volunteered, and signed, and sealed by the man's own hand. They first conciliate his countenance through his intellectual perceptions of what is right; and next they sustain it through his conscience (the strongest of his internal forces), and even through the weakest of his human sensibilities. That revolution, therefore, which no combination of men can further by abating the original impulse of temptations, they often accomplish happily by maturing the secondary energies of resistance.

Already in their earliest stage these temperance movements had obtained, both at home and abroad, a *national* range of grandeur. More than ten years ago,* when M. de Tocqueville was resident in the United States, the principal American society counted two hundred and seventy thousand members; and in one single state (Pennsylvania) the annual diminution in the use of spirits had very soon reached half a million of gallons. Now, a machinery must be so far good which accomplishes in that large extent its difficult purpose,—the means are meritorious for so much as they effect. Even to strengthen a feeble resolution by the aid of other infirmities, such as shame or the very servility and cowardice of deference to public opinion, becomes prudent and laudable in the service of so great an interest. Nay, sometimes to make public profession of self-distrust, by assuming the coercion of public pledges—even as we see in one large section of the Christian church men voluntarily assuming the yoke of strict sequestration, and young women sometimes, with full knowledge and absolute good faith, wooing the severest conventual restraints—

* This was written in 1845.

may become an expression of frank courage, or even of noble principle, not fearing the shame of confessing the whole vast powers of sensual temptation, when from such a confession any new or indirect aid can apparently be drawn towards a victorious resistance. Yet still, so far as it is possible, every man sighs for a still higher victory over himself, a victory not tainted by bribes, and won from no impulses but those inspired by his own higher nature and his own mysterious force of will—powers that in no creature are fully developed.

This being so, it is well that from time to time every man should throw out any hints that have occurred to his experience—suggesting such as may be new, refreshing such as may be old, towards the encouragement or the information of persons engaged in so great a struggle. My own experience had never travelled in that course which could much instruct me in the miseries from wine, or in the resources for struggling with it. I had repeatedly been obliged, indeed, to lay it aside altogether; but in this I never found room for more than seven or ten days' struggle: excesses I had never practised in the use of wine; simply the habit of using it at all, and the collateral habits formed by excessive use of opium, had produced any difficulty at resigning it even on an hour's notice. From opium I derive my right of offering hints at all upon the subjects of abstinence in other forms. But the modes of suffering from the evil, and the separate modes of suffering from the effort of self-conquest, together with errors of judgment incident to such states of transitional torment, are all nearly allied, practically analagous as regards the remedies, even if characteristically distinguished to the inner consciousness. I make no scruple, therefore, of speaking as from a station of high experience and of most watchful attention, which never remitted even under sufferings that were at times absolutely frantic.

I. The first hint which I offer, is one that has been often suggested more or less doubtfully, viz., the diminution of the particular liquor used by the introduction into each glass of some inert substance, ascertained in bulk, and equally increasing in amount from day to day. But this plan has often been intercepted by an accident: shot, or sometimes bullets, were the substances nearest at hand: an objection arose from too scrupulous a caution of chemistry as to the action upon lead of the vinous acid. Yet all objection of this kind might be removed at once by using beads in a case where small decrements were wanted, and the marbles of schoolboys, if it were thought advisable to use larger. Once for all, however, in cases deeply rooted, no advances ought ever to be made but by small stages; for the effect, which is insensible at first, by the tenth, twelfth, or fifteenth day generally accumulates unendurably under any bolder deductions. I must not stop to illustrate this point; but certain it is that by an error of this nature at the outset, most natural to human impatience under exquisite suffering, too generally the trial is abruptly brought to an end through the crisis of a passionate relapse.

II. Another object, and one to which the gladiator matched in single duel with intemperance must direct a religious vigilance, is the *digestibility* of his food: it must be digestible, not only by its original qualities, but also by its culinary preparation. In this last point we are all of us Manicheans; all of us yield a cordial assent to that Manichean proverb which refers the meats and the cooks of this world to two opposite fountains of light and of darkness. Oromasdes it is, or the good principle, that sends the food; Ahrimanes, or the evil principle, that everywhere sends the cooks. Man has been repeatedly described, or even defined, as by differential privilege of his nature, "a cooking animal." Brutes, it is said, have faces; man only has a countenance: brutes are as well able to eat as man; man only is able to cook what he eats. Such are the romances of self-flattery. I, on the contrary, maintain that many thousands of years have not availed, in this point, to raise our race generally to the level of ingenious savages. The natives of the Society and the Friendly Isles, or of New Zealand, and other favoured spots, had, and still have, an *art* of cookery, though very limited in its range; the French* have an art, and a real art, and very much more extensive; but we English are about upon a level (as regards this science) with the ape, to whom an instinct whispers that chestnuts may be roasted; or with the aboriginal Chinese of Charles Lamb's story, to whom the experience of many centuries had revealed thus much—viz., that a dish very much beyond the raw flesh of their ancestors might be had by burning down the family mansion, and thus roasting the pigsty. Rudest of barbarous devices is English cookery, and not much in advance of this primitive Chinese step—a fact which it would not be worth while to lament were it not for the sake of the poor trembling deserter from the banners of intoxication, who is thus, and by no other cause, so often thrown back beneath the yoke which he had abjured. Past counting are

* But judge not, reader, of French skill by the attempts of fourth-rate artists; and understand me to speak with respect of this skill, not as it is the tool of luxury, but as it is the handmaid of health.

the victims of alcohol that, having by vast efforts emancipated themselves for a season, are violently forced into relapsing by the nervous irritations of demoniac cookery. Unhappily for *them*, the horrors of indigestion are relieved for the moment, however ultimately strengthened by strong liquors; the relief is immediate, and cannot fail to be perceived; but the aggravation, being removed to a distance, is not always referred to its proper cause. This is the capital rock and stumbling block in the path of him who is hurrying back to the camps of temperance; and many a reader is likely to misapprehend the case through the habit he has acquired of supposing indigestion to lurk chiefly amongst *luxurious* dishes; but, on the contrary, it is amongst the plainest, simplest, and commonest dishes that such misery lurks in England. Let us glance at three articles of diet, beyond all comparison of most ordinary occurrence—viz., potatoes, bread, and butchers' meat. The art of preparing potatoes for *human* use is utterly unknown, except in certain provinces of our empire and amongst certain sections of the labouring class. In our great cities,—London, Edinburgh, &c.,—the sort of things which you see offered at table under the name and reputation of potatoes are such that, if you could suppose the company to be composed of Centaurs and Lapithæ, or any other quarrelsome people, it would become necessary for the police to interfere. The potato of cities is a very dangerous missile, and, if thrown with an accurate aim by an angry hand, will fracture any known skull. In volume and consistency it is very like a paving stone; only that, I should say, the paving stone had the advantage in point of tenderness; and upon this horrid basis, which youthful ostriches would repent of swallowing, the trembling, palpitating invalid, fresh from the scourging of alcohol, is requested to build the superstructure of his dinner. The proverb says that three flittings are as bad as a fire; and on that model I conceive that three potatoes, as they are found at the majority of British dinner tables, would be equal, in principle of ruin, to two glasses of vitriol. The same savage ignorance appears, and only not so often, in the bread of this island. Myriads of families eat it in that early state of sponge which bread assumes during the process of baking; but less than sixty hours will not fit this dangerous article of human diet to be eaten; and those who are acquainted with the works of Parmentier, of Count Rumford, or other learned investigators of bread and of the baker's art, must be aware that this quality of sponginess (though quite equal to the ruin of the digestive organs) is but one in a legion of vices to which the article is liable. A German of much research wrote a book on the conceivable faults in a pair of shoes, which he found to be about six hundred and sixty-six,—many of them, as he observed, requiring a very delicate process of study to find out; whereas the possible faults in bread, which are not less in number, being also, I conceive, about equal to the number of the beast, require no study at all for the detection—they publish themselves through all varieties of misery; but the perfection of barbarism, as regards our island cookery, is reserved for animal food; and the two poles of Oromasdes and Ahrimanes are nowhere so conspicuously exhibited. Our insular sheep, for instance, are so far superior to any which the Continent produces, that the present Prussian minister at our court is in the habit of questioning a man's right to talk of mutton as anything beyond a great idea, unless he can prove a residence in Great Britain. One sole case he cites of a dinner on the Elbe, where a particular leg of mutton really struck him as rivalling any which he had known in England. The mystery seemed inexplicable; but, upon inquiry, it turned out to be an importation from Leith. Yet this incomparable article, to produce which the skill of the feeder must co-operate with the peculiar bounty of Nature, calls forth the most dangerous refinements of barbarism in its cookery. A Frenchman requires, as the primary qualification of flesh meat, that it should be tender. We English universally, but especially the Scots, treat that quality with indifference or with bare toleration. What *we*, what *nous autres les barbares*, require is, that it should be fresh, that is, recently killed (in which state it cannot be digestible except by a crocodile, or perhaps here and there a leopard); and we present it at table in a transition state of leather, demanding the teeth of a tiger to rend it in pieces, and the stomach of a tiger to digest it.

With these habits amongst our countrymen, exemplified daily in the articles of widest use, it is evident that the sufferer from intemperance has a harder quarantine in this island to support, during the effort of restoration, than he could have anywhere else in Christendom. In Persia, and perhaps there only on this terraqueous planet, matters are even worse; for whilst we English neglect the machinery of digestion, as a matter entitled to little consideration, the people of Teheran seem unaware that there *is* any such machinery. So, at least, one might presume from cases on record, and especially from the reckless folly, under severe illness, of the three Persian princes who lately* visited this country. I take their case from

* "*Lately*:"—This was written nearly fourteen years ago. Mr Fraser, I believe, has been dead for some years.

the report of their official *mehmander*, Mr Fraser. With us, the excess of ignorance upon this subject betrays itself oftenest in that vainglorious answer made by the people who at any time are admonished of the sufferings which they are preparing for themselves by these outrages upon the most delicate of human organs. They, for *their* parts, "know not if they *have* a stomach; they know not what it is that dyspepsy means;" forgetting that, in thus vaunting their *strength* of stomach, they are at the same time proclaiming its coarseness, and showing themselves unaware that precisely those whom such coarseness of organisation reprieves from immediate and seasonable reaction of suffering, are the favourite subjects of that heavier reaction which takes the shape of *delirium tremens*, of palsy, and of lunacy. It is but a fanciful advantage which *they* enjoy, for whom the immediate impunity avails only to hide the final horrors which are gathering upon them from the gloomy rear. Better by far that more of immediate discomfort had guaranteed to them less of reversionary anguish. It may be safely asserted that few indeed are the suicides amongst us to which the miseries of indigestion have not been a large concurring cause; and, even where nothing so dreadful as *that* occurs, always these miseries are the chief hinderance of the self-reforming drunkard, and the commonest cause of his relapse. It is certain, also, that misanthropic gloom and bad temper besiege that class, by preference, to whom peculiar coarseness or obtuse sensibility of organisation has denied the salutary warnings and early prelibations of punishment which, happily for most men, besiege the more direct and obvious frailties of the digestive apparatus; and which, *by* besieging, intercept very often the ultimate more dreadful frailties in the rear.

The whole process and elaborate machinery of digestion are felt to be mean and humiliating when viewed in relation to our mere animal economy; but they rise into dignity and assert their own supreme importance when they are studied from another station,—viz., in relation to the intellect and temper: no man dares *then* to despise them. It is then seen that these functions of the human system form the essential basis upon which the strength and health of our higher nature repose; and that upon these functions, chiefly, the general happiness of life is dependent. All the rules of prudence or gifts of experience that life can accumulate, will never do as much for human comfort and welfare as would be done by a stricter attention and a wiser science directed to the digestive system. In this attention lies the key to any perfect restoration for the victim of intemperance; and, considering the peculiar hostility to the digestive health which exists in the dietetic habits of our own country, it may be feared that nowhere upon earth has the reclaimed victim of intemperance so difficult a combat to sustain; nowhere, therefore, is it so important to direct the attention upon an *artificial* culture of those resources which naturally, and by the established habits of the land, are surest to be neglected. The sheet-anchor for the storm-beaten sufferer who is labouring to recover a haven of rest from the agonies of intemperance, and who has had the fortitude to abjure the poison which ruined, but which also for brief intervals offered him his only consolation, lies, beyond all doubt, in a most anxious regard to everything connected with this supreme function of our animal economy. And, as few men that are not regularly trained to medical studies can have the complex knowledge requisite for such a duty, some printed guide should be sought of a regular professional order. Twenty years ago,* Dr Wilson Philip published a most valuable book of this class, which united a wide range of practical directions as to the choice of diet, and as to the qualities and tendencies of all esculent articles likely to be found at British tables, with some ingenious speculations (not, however, merely speculative, being aided by *experimental* investigations of the analogous digesting processes in rabbits) upon the still mysterious theory of digestion. These had originally been communicated by him to the Royal Society of London, who judged them worthy of publication in their Transactions. I notice them chiefly for the sake of remarking that the rationale of digestion, as here suggested, explains the reason of a fact which, merely *as* a fact, and altogether apart from its theory, had not been known until modern times—viz., the injuriousness to enfeebled stomachs of all fluid. Fifty years ago—and still lingering inveterately amongst nurses and other ignorant persons—there prevailed a notion that "slops" must be the proper resource of the valetudinarian; and the same erroneous notion appears in the common expression of ignorant wonder at the sort of breakfasts usual amongst women of rank in the times of Queen Elizabeth. "What robust stomachs they must have had, to support such solid meals!" As to the question of fact, whether the stomachs were more or less robust in those days than at the present, there is no need to offer an opinion; but the question of principle concerned in scientific dietetics points in the very opposite direction. But how much the organs of digestion are feebler, by so much is it the more indispensable that solid food

* "*Twenty years ago*"—but now [viz., March 31, 1859] nearer to *forty*.

and animal food should be adopted. A robust stomach may be equal to the trying task of supporting a fluid, such as tea for breakfast; but for a feeble stomach, and still more for a stomach artificially *enfeebled* by bad habits, broiled beef, or something equally solid and animal, but not too much subjected to the action of fire, is the only tolerable diet. This, indeed, is the one capital rule for a sufferer from habitual intoxication, who must inevitably labour under an impaired digestion, that as little as possible he should use of any fluid diet, and as little as possible of vegetable diet. Beef and a little bread (at least sixty hours old), or *game*—only that it is an unfeeling mockery to suggest such rare and costly articles (articles, beside, found at all only in one season of the year) to the use of those who are not rich—compose the privileged bill of fare for his breakfast. But precisely, by the way, in relatio to this earliest meal, it is that human folly has in one or two instances shown itself most ruinously inventive. The less variety there is at that meal, the more is the danger from any single luxury; and there is one, known by the name ot "muffins," which has repeatedly manifested itself to be a plain and direct bounty upon suicide. Darwin, in his Zoönomia, reports the case of an officer, holding the rank of lieutenant-colonel, who could not tolerate a breakfast in which this odious article was wanting; but, as a savage retribution invariably supervened within an hour or two upon this act of insane sensuality, he came to a resolution that life was intolerable *with* muffins, but still more intolerable *without* muffins. He would stand the nuisance no longer; but yet, being a just man, he would give Nature one final chance of reforming her dyspeptic atrocities. Muffins, therefore, being laid at one angle of the breakfast table, and loaded pistols at another, with rigid equity the colonel awaited the result. This was naturally pretty much as usual; and then the poor man, incapable of retreating from his word of honour, committed suicide—having previously left a line for posterity to the effect (though I forget the expression) "that a muffinless world was no world for *him*: better no life at all than a life dismantled of muffins." Dr Darwin was a showy philosopher, and fond of producing effect; so that some allowance must be made in construing the affair. Strictly speaking, it is probable that not the special want of muffins, but the general torment of indigestion, was the curse from which the unhappy sufferer sought relief by suicide. And the colonel was not the first by many a million that has fled from the very same form of wretchedness, or fled from its effects upon the genial spirits, to the same gloomy refuge. It should never be forgotten that, although some other more overt vexation is generally assigned as the proximate cause of suicide, and often may be so as regards the immediate occasion, too generally this vexation borrowed its whole power to annoy from the habitual atmosphere of irritation in which the system had been kept by indigestion; so that indirectly and virtually, perhaps all suicides may be traced to mismanaged digestion. Meantime, in alluding at all to so dreadful a subject as suicide, I do so only by way of giving deeper effect to the opinion expressed above upon the chief cause of relapse into habits of intemperance amongst those who have once accomplished their deliverance. Errors of digestion, either from impaired powers, or from powers not so much enfeebled as deranged, is the one immeasurable source both of disease and of secret wretchedness to the human race. Life is laid waste by the eternal fretting of the vital forces, emanating from this one cause. And it may well be conceived, that if cases so endless, even of suicide, in every generation, are virtually traceable to this main root, much more must it be able to shake and undermine the yet palpitating frame of the poor fugitive from intemperance; since indigestion in every mode and variety of its changes irresistibly upholds the temptation to that form of excitement which, though one foremost cause of indigestion, is yet unhappily its sole immediate palliation.

III. Next, after the most vigorous attention, and a scientific attention, to the digestive system in power of operation, stands *exercise*. Here, however, most people have their own separate habits with respect to the time of exercise, the duration, and the particular mode, on which a stranger cannot venture to intrude with his advice. Some will not endure the steady patience required for walking exercise; many benefit most by riding on horseback; and in days when roads were more rugged and the springs of carriages less improved, I have known people who found most advantage in the vibrations communicated to the frame by a heavy, rumbling carriage. For myself, under the ravages of opium, I have found walking the most beneficial exercise; besides that, it requires no previous notice or preparation of any kind, and this is a capital advantage in a state of drooping energies or of impatient and unresting agitation. I may mention, as possibly an accident of my individual temperament, but possibly also no accident at all, that the relief obtained by walking was always most sensibly brought home to my consciousness when some part of it (at least a mile and a half) had been performed before breakfast. In this there soon ceased to be any difficulty; for, whilst under the full oppression of opium, it was impossible for me to rise at any hour that could, by the most indulgent courtesy, be described as within the pale of morning,—no sooner had there been established any considerable relief from this oppression, than the tendency was in the opposite direction; the difficulty became continually greater of sleeping even to a reasonable hour. Having once accomplished the feat of waking at nine A.M., I backed, in a space of seven or eight months, to eight o'clock, to seven, to six, five, four, three; until at this point a metaphysical fear fell upon me that I was actually backing into "yesterday," and should soon have no sleep at all. Below three, however, I did not descend; and for a couple of years three and a-half hours' sleep was all that I could obtain in the twenty-four hours. From this no particular suffering arose, except the nervous impatience of lying in bed for one moment after awaking. Consequently the habit of walking before breakfast became at length troublesome no longer as a most odious duty, but, on the contrary, as a temptation that could hardly be resisted on the wettest mornings. As to the quantity of the exercise, I found that six miles a day formed the *minimum* which would support permanently a particular standard of animal spirits, evidenced to myself by certain apparent symptoms. I averaged about nine and a-half miles a day, but ascended on particular days to fifteen or sixteen, and more rarely to twenty-three or twenty-four—a quantity which did not produce fatigue; on the contrary, it spread a sense of improvement through almost the whole week that followed. But usually, in the night immediately succeeding to such an exertion, I lost much of my sleep—a privation that, under the circumstances explained, deterred me from trying the experiment too often; for, in addition to the sleeplessness, great distress arose for hours after one of these excesses in walking, from achings in the bones below the knee. Let me add to this slight abstract of my own experience, in a point where it is really difficult to offer any useful advice (the tastes and habits of men varying so much in this chapter of exercise), that one caution seems applicable to the case of all persons suffering from nervous irritability—viz., that a secluded space should be measured off accurately in some private grounds not liable to the interruption or notice of chance intruders; for these annoyances are unendurable to the invalid who is nervously restless. To be questioned upon trivial things is death to him, and the perpetual anticipation of such annoyances is little less distressing. Some plan must also be adopted for registering the number of rounds performed. I once walked for eighteen months in a circuit so confined that forty revolutions were needed to complete a mile. These I counted at one time by a rosary of beads—every tenth round being marked by drawing a blue bead, the other nine by drawing white beads. But this plan I found in practice more troublesome and inaccurate than that of using ten detached counters, stones, or anything else that was large enough and solid. These were applied to the separate bars of a garden chair—the first bar indicating of itself the first decade, the second bar the second decade, and so on. In fact, I used the chair in some measure as a Roman *abacus*, but on a still simpler plan; and as the chair offered sixteen bars, it followed that, on covering the last bar of the series with the ten markers, I perceived, without any trouble of calculation, the accomplishment of my fourth mile.

A necessity meantime, more painful to me by far than that of taking continued exercise, arose out of a cause which applies, perhaps, with the same intensity only to opium cases, but must also apply in some degree to all cases of debilitation from morbid stimulation of the nerves, whether by means of wine, or opium, or distilled liquors. In travelling on the outside of mails during my youthful days, for I could not endure the inside, occasionally, during the night-time, I suffered naturally from cold; no cloaks, &c., were always sufficient to relieve this; and I then made the discovery that opium, after an hour or so, diffuses a warmth deeper and far more permanent than could be had from any other known source. I mention this to explain, in some measure, the awful passion of cold which for some years haunted the inverse process of laying aside the opium. It was a perfect frenzy of misery; cold was a sensation which then first, as a mode of torment, seemed to have been revealed. In the months of July and August, and not at all the less during the very middle watch of the day, I sat in the closest proximity to a blazing fire; cloaks, blankets, counterpanes, hearth-rugs, horse-cloths, were piled upon my shoulders, but with hardly a glimmering of relief. At night, and after taking coffee, I felt a little warmer, and could sometimes afford to smile at the resemblance of my own case to that of Harry Gill.* But, secretly, I

* "*Harry Gill:*"—Many readers in this generation may not be aware of this ballad as one amongst the early poems of Wordsworth. Thirty or forty years ago it was the object of some insipid ridicule, which ought, perhaps, in another place to be noticed; and doubtless this ridicule was heightened by the false impression that the story had been some old woman's superstitious fiction, meant to illustrate a supernatural judgment on hard-heartedness. But the story was a physiologic fact; and originally it had been brought forward in a philosophic work by Darwin, who had the reputation of an irreligious man, and even of an infidel. A bold free-

was struck with awe at the revelation of powers so unsearchably new lurking within old affections so familiarly known as cold. Upon the analogy of this case it might be suspected that nothing whatever had yet been truly and seriously felt by man; nothing searched or probed by human sensibilities to a depth below the surface. If cold could give out mysteries of suffering so novel, all things in the world might be yet unvisited by the truth of human sensations. All experience worthy of the name was perhaps yet to begin. Meantime the external phenomenon by which the cold expressed itself was a sense (but with little reality) of eternal freezing perspiration. From this I was never free; and at length, from finding one general ablution insufficient for one day, I was thrown upon the irritating necessity of repeating it more frequently than would seem credible if stated. At this time I used always hot water; and a thought occurred to me very seriously that it would be best to live constantly and perhaps to sleep in a bath. What caused me to renounce this plan was an accident that compelled me for one day

---

thinker he certainly was; a Deist at the least; and, by public repute, founded on the internal evidence of his writings as well as of his daily conversation, something more. Dr Darwin, by the way, was one of the temperance fanatics long before temperance societies arose, and is supposed to have paid for his fanaticism with his life. He practised as a physician with great success and eminent reputation at Ashbourn in Derbyshire; but being a man of many crotchets, amongst them was this—that, when other men called for wine, the Doctor called (oh Bacchus!) for cream. Suddenly, on one fine golden morning, the Doctor was attacked by a spasmodic affection. A glass of old brandy was earnestly suggested. Thirty years having fled since the Doctor had tasted alcohol in *any* shape, it was imagined that old cognac would have a magical effect. But no, the Doctor called loudly for cream; and alas! Death called still more loudly for the Doctor.

to use cold water. This first of all communicated any lasting warmth; so that ever afterwards I used none *but* cold water. Now, to live in a *cold* bath in our climate, and in my own state of preternatural sensibility to cold, was not an idea to dally with. I wish to mention, however, for the information of other sufferers in the same way, one change in the mode of applying the water, which led to a considerable and sudden improvement in the condition of my feelings. I had endeavoured to procure a child's battledoor, as an easy means (when clothed with sponge) of reaching the interspace between the shoulders—which interspace, by the way, is a sort of Bokhara, so provokingly situated that it will neither suffer itself to be reached from the north,—in which direction even the czar, with his long arms, has only singed his own fingers and lost six thousand camels,—nor at all better from the south, upon which line of approach the greatest potentate in Southern Asia—viz., No. something (shall we say No. unknown?) in Leadenhall Street, has found it the best policy to pocket the little khan's murderous defiances and persevering insults.* There is no

* It is literally true that even the Khan of *Khiva*, a territory between Bokhara and the Caspian, and a much more insignificant state, relying simply on its own position and inaccessibility—too far north for England, too far south for Russia, has offered insults and outrages to that lubberly empire for one hundred and forty years, commencing its agressions in the reign of Peter the Great, as some people call him; who, being a true bully, pocketed his affronts in moody silence. The most ludicrous part of our own relations with Khiva is this:—The war with Affghanistan in 1838 and three following years, which cost us eighteen millions sterling, and pretty nearly exterminated the whole race of camels through all Central Asia [some say thirty thousand], was undertaken purely on the conceit that Russia might assault us on the Indus. Meantime, Russia was unable to reach even the little Khan of Khiva—a

battledoor long enough to reach him in either way. In my own difficulty I felt almost as perplexed as the Honourable East India Company when I found that no battledoor was to be had; for no town was near at hand. In default of a battledoor, therefore, my necessity threw my experiment upon a long hair brush; and this eventually proved of much greater service than any sponge or any battledoor; for the friction of the brush caused an irritation on the surface of the skin which, more than anything else, has gradually diminished the once continual misery of unrelenting frost; although even yet it renews itself most distressingly at uncertain intervals.

IV. I counsel the patient not to make the mistake of supposing that his amendment will necessarily proceed continuously or by equal increments; because this, which is a common notion, will certainly lead to dangerous disappointments. How frequently I have heard people encouraging a self-reformer by such language as this: "When you have got over the fourth day of abstinence, which suppose to be Sunday, then Monday will find you a trifle better; Tuesday better still,—though still it should be only by a trifle,—and so on. You may at least rely on never going back; you may assure yourself of having seen the worst; and the positive improvements, if trifles separately, must soon gather into a sensible magnitude." This may be true in a case of short standing; but as a general rule it is perilously delusive. On the

thousand miles north-west of the Indus. And it is a most laughable feature of the Affghan war, that only through the intercession of a single English cavalry officer (Sir Richmond Shakspear) was Russia able to obtain from the Khan a surrender of those unhappy Russians whom, by various accidents on the Caspian, he had treacherously made captives.

contrary, the line of progress, if exhibited in a geometrical construction, would describe an ascending path upon the whole, but with frequent retrocessions into descending curves, which, compared with the point of ascent that had been previously gained and so vexatiously interrupted, would sometimes seem deeper than the original point of starting. This mortifying tendency I can report from experience many times repeated with regard to opium; and so unaccountably, as regarded all the previous grounds of expectation, that I am compelled to suppose it a tendency inherent in the very nature of all self-restorations for animal systems. They move perhaps necessarily *per saltum*, by intermitting spasms and pulsations of unequal energy.

V. I counsel the patient frequently to call back before his thoughts—when suffering sorrowful collapses that seem unmerited by anything done or neglected—that such, and far worse perhaps, must have been his experience, and with no reversion of hope behind, had he persisted in his intemperate indulgences; *these* also suffer their own collapses, and (so far as things not co-present can be compared) by many degrees more shocking to the genial instincts.

VI. I exhort him to believe that no movement on his own part, not the smallest conceivable, towards the restoration of his healthy state, can by possibility perish. Nothing in this direction is finally lost, but often it disappears and hides itself, suddenly, however, to reappear, and in unexpected strength, and much more hopefully; because such minute elements of improvement, by reappearing at a remoter stage, show themselves to have combined with other elements of the same kind; so that, equally by their gathering tendency and their duration through intervals of apparent darkness and below the current of what seemed absolute interruption, they argue themselves to be settled in the system. There is no good gift that does not come from God; almost His greatest is health, with the peace which it inherits, and man must reap *this* on the same terms as he was told to reap God's earliest gift, the fruits of the earth, viz., "in the sweat of his brow," through labour, often through sorrow, through disappointment, but still through imperishable perseverance, and hoping under clouds when all hope seems darkened.

VII. It is difficult, in selecting from many memoranda of warning and encouragement, to know which to prefer when the space disposable is limited. But it seems to me important not to omit this particular caution: The patient will be naturally anxious, as he goes on, frequently to test the amount of his advance, and its rate, if that were possible. But this he will see no mode of doing, except through tentative balancings of his feelings, and generally of the moral atmosphere around him, as to pleasure and hope against the corresponding states, so far as he can recall them from his periods of intemperance. But these comparisons, I warn him, are fallacious when made in this way; the two states are incommensurable on any plan of *direct* comparison. Some common measure must be found, and *out of himself;* some positive fact, that will not bend to his own delusive feeling at the moment, as, for instance, in what degree he finds tolerable what heretofore was *not* so—the effort of writing letters, or transacting business, or undertaking a journey, or overtaking the arrears of labour that had been once thrown off to a distance. If in these things he finds himself improved, by tests that cannot be disputed, he may safely disregard any sceptical whispers from a wayward sensibility which cannot yet perhaps have recovered its normal health, however much improved. His inner feelings may not yet point steadily to the truth, though they may vibrate in that direction. Besides, it is certain that sometimes very manifest advances, such as any medical man would perceive at a glance, carry a man through stages of agitation and discomfort. A far worse condition might happen to be less agitated, and so far more bearable. Now, when a man is positively suffering discomfort, when he is below the line of pleasurable feeling, he is no proper judge of his own condition, which he neither will nor can appreciate. Toothache extorts more groans than dropsy.

VIII. Another important caution is, not to confound with the effects of intemperance any other natural effects of debility from advancing years. Many a man, having begun to be intemperate at thirty, enters at sixty or upwards upon a career of self-restoration; and by self-restoration he understands a renewal of that state in which he was when first swerving from temperance. But that state, for his memory, is coincident with his state of youth. The two states are coadunated. In his recollections they are intertwisted too closely. But life, without any intemperance at all, would soon have untwisted them. Charles Lamb, for instance, at forty-five, and Coleridge at sixty, measured their several conditions by such tests as the loss of all disposition to involuntary murmuring of musical airs or fragments when rising from bed. Once they had sung when rising in the morning light; now they sang no more. The *vocal* utterance of joy for *them* was silenced for ever. But these are amongst the changes that life, stern power! inflicts at any rate; these would have happened, and, above all, to men worn by the unequal irritations of too much thinking, and by those modes of care

> "That kill the bloom before its time,
> And blanch without the owner's crime
> The most resplendent hair,"

not at all the less had the one drunk no brandy nor the other any laudanum. A man must submit to the conditions of humanity, and not quarrel with a cure as being incomplete because in his climacteric year of sixty-three (*i. e.*, 7 times 9), both held dangerous numbers in the ladder of life by our dear enlightened great-grandfathers —he cannot recover entirely the vivacities of thirty-five. If, by dipping seven times in Jordan, he had cleansed his whole leprosy of intemperance—if, by going down into Bethesda, he were able to mount again upon the pinions of his youth—even then he might querulously say, "But after all these marvels in my favour, I suppose that one of these fine mornings I, like other people, shall have to bespeak a coffin." Why, yes, undoubtedly he will, or somebody *for* him. But privileges so especial were not promised, even by the mysterious waters of Palestine. Die he must; and counsels tendered to the intemperate do not hope to accomplish what might have been beyond the baths of Jordan or Bethesda. They do enough if, being executed by efforts in the spirit of earnest sincerity, they make a life of *growing* misery moderately happy for the patient, and, through that great change, perhaps more than moderately useful for others.

IX. One final remark I will make—pointed to the case, not of the yet struggling patient, but of him who is fully re established; and the more so, because I (who am no hypocrite, but rather frank to an infirmity) acknowledge in myself the trembling tendency at intervals, which would, if permitted, sweep round into currents that might be hard to overrule. After the absolute restoration to health, a man is very apt to say, "Now, then, how shall I use my health? To what delightful purpose shall I apply it? Surely it is idle to carry a fine jewel in one's watch-pocket, and never to astonish the weak minds of this world by wearing it and flashing it in their eyes." "But how?" retorts his philosophic friend. "My good fellow, are you not using it at this moment? Breathing, for instance, talking to me (though rather absurdly), and airing your legs at a glowing fire?" "Why, yes," the other confesses, "that is all true; but I am dull, and, if you will pardon my rudeness, even in spite of your too philosophic presence. It is painful to say so; but, sincerely, if I had the power at this moment to turn you by magic into a bottle of old Port wine, so corrupt is my nature, that really I fear lest the exchange might for the moment strike me as agreeable." Such a mood, I apprehend, is apt to revolve upon many of us at intervals, however firmly married to temperance; and the propensity to it has a root in certain analogies running through our nature. If the reader will permit me for a moment the use of what, without such an apology, might seem pedantic, I would call it the instinct of *focalising* which prompts such random desires. Feeling is diffused over the whole surface of the body; but light is focalised in the eye, sound in the ear. The organisation of a sense or a pleasure seems diluted and imperfect unless it is gathered by some machinery into one focus, or local centre. And thus it is that a general state of pleasurable feeling sometimes seems too superficially diffused, and one has a craving to intensify or brighten it by concentration through some sufficient stimulant. I, for my part, have tried every thing in this world except "*bang*,"* which I believe is obtained from hemp. There are other preparations of hemp which have been found to give great relief from *ennui;* not ropes, but something lately introduced, which acts upon the system as the laughing gas (nitrous oxide) acts at times. One farmer in Mid-Lothian was mentioned to me eight months ago as having taken it, and ever since annoyed his neighbours by immoderate fits of laughter; so that in January it was agreed to present him to the sheriff as a nuisance. But, for some reason, the plan was laid aside; and now, eight months later, I hear that the farmer is laughing more rapturously than ever, continues in the happiest frame of mind, the kindest of creatures, and the general torment of his neighbourhood. Now, I confess to having had a lurking interest in this extract of hemp when first I heard of it; and at intervals a desire will continue to make itself felt for some deeper compression or centralisation of the genial feelings than ordinary life affords. But old things will not avail; and new things I am now able to resist. Still, as the occasional craving does really arise in most men, it is well to notice it, and chiefly for the purpose of saying that this dangerous feeling wears off by degrees, and oftentimes for long periods it intermits so entirely as to be even displaced by a profound disgust to all modes of artificial stimulation. At those times I have remarked that the pleasurable conditions of health do *not* seem weakened by its want of centralisation. It seems to form a thousand centres. This it is well to know, because there are many who

* But, since writing this, I have received from a young friend a present of *bang*, upon which I will report hereafter.

would resist effectually if they were aware of any natural change going on silently in favour of their own efforts such as would finally ratify the success. Towards such a result they would gladly contribute by waiting and forbearing; whilst, under despondency as to this result, they might more easily yield to some chance temptation.

Finally, there is something to interest us in the *time* at which this temperance movement has begun to stir. Let me close with a slight notice of what chiefly impresses myself in the relation between this time and the other circumstances of the case. In reviewing history, we may see something more than mere convenience in distributing it into three chambers; ancient history, ending in the space between the Western Empire falling and Mohammed arising; modern history, from that time to this; and a new modern history arising at present, or from the French revolution. Two great races of men, our own in a two-headed form — British and American — and, secondly, the Russian, are those which, like rising deluges, already reveal their mission to overflow the earth. Both these races, partly through climate or through derivation of blood, and partly through the contagion of habits inevitable to brothers of the same nation, are tainted carnally with the appetite for brandy, for slings, for juleps; and no fire racing through the forests of Nova Scotia for three hundred miles in the direction of some doomed city ever moved so fiercely as the infection of habits amongst the dense and fiery populations of republican North America.

But it is remarkable that the whole *ancient* system of civilisation, all the miracles of Greece and Rome, Persia and Egypt, moved by the machinery of races that were *not* tainted with any such popular *marasmus*. The taste was slightly sowed, as an *artificial* taste, amongst luxurious individuals, but never ran through the labouring classes, through armies, through cities. The blood and the climate forbade it. In this earliest era of history, all the great races, consequently all the great empires, threw themselves, by accumulation, upon the genial climates of the south,—having, in fact, the magnificent lake of the Mediterranean for their general centre of evolutions. Round this lake, in a zone of varying depth, towered the whole grandeurs of the pagan earth. But in such climates man is *naturally*—is almost *necessarily* temperate. He is so by physical coercion and for the necessities of rest and coolness. The Spaniard, or the Moor, or the Arab, has no merit in his temperance. The effort, for *him*, would be to form the taste for alcohol. He has a vast foreground of disgust to traverse before he can reach a taste so remote and alien. No need for resistance in his will where Nature resists on his behalf. Sherbet, shaddocks, grapes,—these were innocent applications to thirst; and the great republic of antiquity said to her legionary sons, "Soldier, if you thirst, there is the river"—Nile, suppose, or Ebro. "Better drink there cannot be. Of this you may take 'at discretion.' Or, if you wait till the *impedimenta* come up, you may draw your ration of *posca*." What was *posca?* It was, in fact, acidulated water—three parts of superfine water to one part of the very best vinegar. Nothing stronger did Rome, that awful mother, allow to her dearest children, *i.e.*, her legions: truest of blessings, that, veiling itself in seeming sternness, drove away the wicked phantoms that haunt the couches of greater nations. "The blessings of the evil genii," says an Eastern proverb, "which are curses, rest upon thy head for retribution!" And the stern refusals of wisely-loving mothers,—these are the mightiest of gifts.

Now, on the other hand, our northern climates have universally the taste, latent, if not developed, for powerful liquors; and through their blood, as also through the natural tendency of the imitative principle amongst compatriots, from these high latitudes the greatest of our modern nations propagate the contagion to their brothers, though colonising warm climates. And it is remarkable that our modern preparations of liquors, even when harmless in their earliest stages, are fitted, like stepping-stones, for making the transition to higher stages that are *not* harmless. The weakest preparations from malt lead, by graduated steps, to the strongest, until we arrive at the intoxicating porter of London, which, under its local name (so insidiously delusive) of "*beer*," diffuses the most extensive ravages.

Under these marked circumstances of difference between the ruling races of antiquity and of our modern times, it now happens that the greatest era by far of human expansion is opening upon us. Two vast movements are hurrying into action by velocities continually accelerated,—the great revolutionary movement from political causes concurring with the great physical movement in locomotion and social intercourse, from the gigantic (though still infant) powers of steam. No such Titan resources for modifying each other were ever before dreamed of by nations; and the next hundred years will have changed the face of the world. At the opening of such a crisis, had no third movement arisen of resistance to intemperate habits, there would have been ground for despondency as to the amelioration of the human race; but, as the case stands, the new principle of resistance nationally to bad habits has arisen almost concurrently with the new powers of national intercourse; and henceforward, by a change equally sudden and unlooked for, that new machinery, which would else most surely have multiplied the ruins of intoxication, has become the strongest agency for hastening its extirpation.

MILTON *versus* SOUTHEY AND LANDOR.

This conversation is doubly interesting: interesting by its subject, interesting by its interlocutors; for the subject is Milton, whilst the interlocutors are *Southey* and *Landor*. If a British gentleman, when taking his pleasure in his well-armed yacht, descries in some foreign waters a noble vessel, from the Thames or the Clyde, riding peaceably at anchor,—and soon after, two smart-looking clippers, with rakish masts, bearing down upon her in company,—he slackens sail: his suspicions are slightly raised; they have not shown their teeth as yet, and perhaps all is right; but there can be no harm in looking a little closer; and assuredly, if he finds any mischief in the wind against his countryman, he will show *his* teeth also; and, please the wind, will take up such a position as to rake both of these pirates by turns. The two dialogists are introduced walking out after breakfast, "each his Milton in his pocket;" and says Southey, "Let us collect all the graver faults we can lay our hands upon, without a too minute and troublesome research;"—just so; there would be danger in *that;* help might put off from shore;—"not," says he, "in the spirit of Johnson, but in our own." Johnson, we may suppose, is some old ruffian well known upon that coast; and "*faults*" may be a flash term for what the Americans call "notions." A part of the cargo it clearly is; and one is not surprised to hear Landor, whilst assenting to the general plan of attack, suggesting in a whisper, "that they should abase their eyes in reverence to so great a man, without absolutely closing them;" which I take to mean—that, without trusting entirely to their boarders, or absolutely closing their ports, they should depress their guns and fire down into the hold, in respect of the vessel attacked standing so high out of the water. After such plain speaking, nobody can wonder much at the junior pirate (Landor) muttering, "It will be difficult for us always to refrain." Of course it will: *refraining* was no part of the business, I should fancy, taught by that same buccaneer, Johnson. There is mischief you see, reader, singing in the air,—"miching malhecho," and it is our business to watch it.

But, before coming to the main attack, I must suffer myself to be detained for a few moments by what Mr L. premises upon the "moral" of any great fable, and the relation which it bears, or *should* bear, to the solution of such a fable. Philosophic criticism is so far improved, that at this day few people, who have reflected at all upon such subjects, but are agreed as to one point—viz., that in metaphysical language the moral of an epos or a drama should be *immanent*, not *transient;* or otherwise, that it should be vitally distributed through the whole organisation of the tree, not gathered or secreted into a sort of red berry or *racemus*, pendent at the end of its boughs. This view Mr Landor himself takes, as a general view; but strange to say, by some Landorian perverseness, where there occurs a memorable exception to this rule (as in *Paradise Lost*), in that case he insists upon the rule in its rigour—the rule, and nothing *but* the rule. Where, on the contrary, the rule does really and obviously take effect (as in the *Iliad* and *Odyssey*), there he insists upon an exceptional case. There *is* a moral, in *his* opinion, hanging like a tassel of gold bullion from the *Iliad*;—and what is it? Something so fantastic that I decline to repeat it. As well might he have said that the moral of *Othello* was—"*Try Warren's Blacking!*" There is no moral, little or big, foul or fair, to the *Iliad*. Up to the 17th Book, the moral might seem dimly to be this—"Gentlemen, keep the peace: you see what comes of quarrelling." But *there* this moral ceases;—there is now a break of gauge: the narrow gauge takes place after this; whilst up to this point, the broad gauge—viz., the wrath of Achilles, growing out of his turn-up with Agamemnon—had carried us smoothly along without need to shift our luggage. There is no more quarrelling after Book XVII.; how then can there be any more moral from quarrelling? If you insist on *my* telling *you* what is the moral of the *Iliad*, I insist upon *your* telling *me* what is the moral of a rattlesnake, or the moral of a Niagara. I suppose the moral is—that you must get out of their way, if you mean to moralise much longer. The going-up (or anabasis) of the Greeks against Troy, was a *fact*, and a pretty dense fact; and, by accident, the very first in which all Greece had a common interest. It was a joint-stock concern—a representative expedition—whereas previously there had been none; for even the Argonautic expedition, which is rather of the darkest, implied no confederation except amongst individuals. How could it? For the Argo is supposed to have measured only twenty-seven tons: how she would have been classed at Lloyd's is hard to say, but certainly not as A 1. There was no state-cabin; everybody, demi-gods and all, pigged in the steerage, amongst beans and bacon. Greece was naturally proud of having crossed the herring-pond, small as it was, in search of an entrenched enemy; proud also of having licked him "into almighty smash;" this was sufficient; or if an impertinent moralist sought for something more, doubtless the moral must have lain in the booty. A peach is the moral of a peach, and moral enough; but if a man *will* have something better—a moral within a moral—why, there is the peach-stone, and its kernel, out of which he may make ratafia, which seems to be the ultimate morality that *can* be extracted from a peach. Mr Archdeacon Williams, indeed, of the Edinburgh Academy, has published an *octavo* opinion upon the case, which asserts that the moral of the Trojan war was (to borrow a phrase from children) *tit for tat*. It was a case of retaliation for crimes against Hellas, committed by Troy in an earlier generation. It may be so; Nemesis knows best. But this moral, if it concerns the total expedition to the Troad, cannot concern the *Iliad*, which does not take up matters from so early a period, nor go on to the final catastrophe of Ilium.

Now, as to the *Paradise Lost*, it happens that there is—whether there ought to be or not—a pure golden moral, distinctly announced, separately contemplated, and the very weightiest ever uttered by man or realised by fable. It is a moral rather for the drama of a world than for a human poem. And this moral is made the more prominent and memorable by the grandeur of its annunciation. The jewel is not more splendid in itself than in its setting. Excepting the well-known passage on Athenian oratory in the *Paradise Regained*, there is none even in Milton where the metrical pomp is made so effectually to aid the pomp of the sentiment. Hearken to the way in which a roll of dactyles is made to settle, like the swell of the advancing tide, into the long thunder of billows breaking for leagues against the shore:

> "That to the height of this great argument
> I may assert eternal Providence."—

Hear what a motion, what a tumult, is given by the dactylic close to each of these introductory lines! And how massily is the whole locked up into the peace of heaven, as the aërial arch of a viaduct is locked up into tranquil stability by its key-stone, through this deep spondaic close,

> "And justify the ways of God to man."

That is the moral of the Miltonic epos; and as much grander than any other moral *formally* illustrated by poets, as heaven is higher than earth.

But the most singular moral which Mr Landor anywhere discovers, is in his own poem of *Gebir*. Whether he still adheres to it, does not appear from the present edition. But I remember distinctly, in the original edition, a Preface (now withdrawn) in which he made his acknowledgments to some book read at a Welsh inn for the outline of the story; and as to the moral, he declared it to be an exposition of that most mysterious offence, *Over-colonization*. Much I mused, in my youthful simplicity, upon this criminal novelty. What might it be? Could I, by mistake, have committed it myself? Was it a felony, or a misdemeanour?—liable to transportation, or only to fine and imprisonment? Neither in the Decemviral Tables, nor in the Code of Justinian, nor the maritime Code of Oleron, nor in the Canon Law, nor the Code Napoleon, nor our own Statutes at large, nor in

Jeremy Bentham, nor in Jeremy Diddler, had I read of such a crime as a possibility. Undoubtedly the vermin, locally called *Squatters*,* both in the wilds of America and Australia, who pre-occupy other men's estates, have latterly illustrated the logical possibility of such an offence; but they were quite unknown at the era of Gebir. Even Dalica, who knew as much wickedness as most people, would have stared at this unheard-of villany, and have asked, as eagerly as *I* did—"What is it now? Let's have a shy at it in Egypt." I, indeed, knew a case, but Dalica did *not*, of shocking over-colonisation. It was the case, which even yet occurs on out-of-the-way roads, where a man, unjustly big, mounts into the inside of a stage-coach already sufficiently crowded. In streets and squares, where men could give him a wide berth, they had tolerated the iniquity of his person; but now, in a chamber so confined, the length and breadth of his wickedness shines revealed to every eye. And if the coach should upset, which it would not be the less likely to do for having *him* on board, somebody or other (perhaps myself) must lie beneath this monster, like Enceladus under Mount Etna, calling upon Jove to come quickly with a

---

* *Squatters*:—They are a sort of self-elected warming-pans. What we in England mean by the political term '*warming-pans*,' are men who occupy, by consent, some official place, or Parliamentary seat, until the proper claimant is old enough in law to assume his rights. When the true man comes to bed, the warming-pan respectfully turns out. But these ultra-marine warming-pans *wouldn't* turn out. They showed fight, and wouldn't hear of the true man, even as a bed-fellow. It is a remarkable illustration of the rapidity with which words submit to new and contradictory modifications, that a *squatter*, who is a violent intruder upon other men's rights, consequently a scoundrel, in America, ranks in Australia as a virtuous citizen, and a pioneer of colonisation.

thunderbolt and destroy both man and mountain, both *succubus* and *incubus*, if no other relief offered. Meantime, the only case of over-colonisation notorious to all Europe, is that which some German traveller (Riedesel, I think) has reported so eagerly, in ridicule of our supposed English credulity; viz., the case of the foreign swindler, who advertised that he would get into a quart bottle, filled Drury Lane theatre by his fraudulent promise, pocketed the admission-money, and decamped, protesting (in his adieus to the spectators) that "it lacerated his heart to disappoint so many noble islanders; but that on his next visit he would make full reparation by getting into a vinegar cruet." Now, here certainly was a case of over-colonisation, not perpetrated, but meditated. Yet, when one examines this case, the crime consisted by no means in doing it, but in *not* doing it. The foreign contractor would have been probably a very unhappy man had he fulfilled his contract by over-colonising the bottle; but he would have been decidedly a more virtuous man. He would have redeemed his pledge; and, if he had even died in the bottle, we should have honoured him as a "*vir bonus, cum malâ fortunâ compositus*;" as a man of honour matched in single duel with calamity, and also as the best of conjurers. Over-colonisation, therefore, except in the one case of the stage-coach, is apparently no crime; and the offence of King Gebir therefore, in my eyes, remains a mystery to this day.

What next solicits notice is in the nature of a digression; it is a kind of parenthesis on Wordsworth.

"*Landor.*—When it was a matter of wonder how Keats, who was ignorant of Greek, could have written his 'Hyperion,' Shelley, whom envy never touched, gave as a reason—'because he *was* a Greek.' Wordsworth, being asked his opinion of the same poem, called it scoffingly, 'a pretty piece of paganism;' yet he himself, in the best verses he ever wrote—and beautiful ones they are—reverts to the powerful influence of the 'pagan creed.'"

Here are nine lines exactly in the original type. Now, nine tailors are ranked, by great masters of algebra, as = one man; such is the received equation; or, as it is expressed with more liveliness in an old English drama by a man who meets and quarrels with eighteen tailors—"Come, hang it! I'll fight you *both*." But, whatever be the algebraic ratio of tailors to men, it is clear that nine Landorian lines are not always equal to the delivery of one accurate truth, or to a successful conflict with three or four signal errors. First, Shelley's reason, if it ever was assigned, is irrelevant as regards any question that must have been intended. It could not have been meant to ask—Why was the "Hyperion" so Grecian in its spirit? for it is anything but Grecian. We should praise it falsely to call it so; for the feeble, though elegant, mythology of Greece was incapable of breeding anything so deep as the mysterious portents that, in the "Hyperion," run before and accompany the passing away of divine immemorial dynasties. Nothing can be more impressive than the picture of Saturn in his palsy of affliction, and of the mighty goddess his grand-daughter, who touches the shoulder of the collapsing god—nothing more awful than the secret signs of coming woe in the palace of Hyperion. These things grew from darker creeds than Greece had ever known since the elder traditions of Prometheus—creeds that sent down their sounding plummets into far deeper wells within the human spirit. What had been meant by the question proposed to Shelley was no doubt—How so young a man as Keats, not having had the advantage of a regular classical education, could have been so much at home in the details of the *elder* mythology? Tooke's *Pantheon* might have been obtained by favour of any English schoolboy, and Dumoustier's *Lettres à Emilie sur la Mythologie* by favour of very many young ladies; but these, according to my recollection of them, would hardly have sufficed. Spence's *Polymetis*, however, might have been had by favour of any good library; and the *Bibliotheca* of Apollodorus, who is the cock of the walk on this subject, might have been read by favour of a Latin translation, supposing Keats really unequal to the easy Greek text. There is no wonder in the case; nor if there had been, would Shelley's kind remark have solved it. The *treatment* of the facts must in any case have been due to Keats's genius, so as to be the same whether he had studied Greek or not: the *facts*, apart from the treatment, must in any case have been had from a book. Secondly—Let Mr Landor rely upon it, that Wordsworth never said the thing ascribed to him here as any formal judgment, or what Scottish law would call *deliverance*, upon the *Hyperion*. As to what he might have said incidentally and collaterally, the meaning of words is so entirely affected by their position in a conversation—what followed, what went before—that five words dislocated from their context never would be received as evidence in the Queen's Bench. The court, which of all others least strictly weighs its rules of evidence, is the female tea-table; yet even that tribunal would require the deponent to strengthen his evidence, if he had only five detached words to produce. Wordsworth is a very proud man, as he has good reason to be; and perhaps it was I myself who once said in print of him—that it is not the correct way of speaking to say that Wordsworth is as proud as Lucifer, but, inversely, to say of Lucifer that some people have conceived him to be as proud as Wordsworth. But if proud, Wordsworth is not ostentatious, is not anxious for display, and least of all is he capable of descending to envy. Who or what is it that *he* should be envious of? Does anybody suppose that Wordsworth would be jealous of Archimedes if he now walked upon earth, or Michael Angelo, or Milton? Nature does not repeat herself. Be assured she will never make a second Wordsworth. Any of us would be jealous of his own duplicate; and if I had a *doppel-ganger* who went about personating me, copying me, and pirating me, philosopher as I am, I might (if the Court of Chancery would not grant an injunction against him) be so far carried away by jealousy as to attempt the crime of murder upon his carcass; and no great matter as regards HIM. But it would be a sad thing for *me* to find myself hanged; and for what, I beseech you? for murdering a sham, that was either nobody at all, or oneself repeated once too often. But if you show to Wordsworth a man as great as himself, still that great man will not be much *like* Wordsworth—the great man will not be Wordsworth's *doppel-ganger*. If not *impar* (as you say) he will be *dispar;* and why, then, should Wordsworth be jealous of him, unless he is jealous of the sun, and of Abd el Kāder, and of Mr Waghorn—all of whom carry off a great deal of any spare admiration which Europe has to dispose of. But suddenly it strikes me that we are all proud, every man of us; and I daresay with some reason for it, "be the same more or less." For I never came to know any man in my whole life intimately who could not do something or other better than anybody else. The only man amongst us that is thoroughly free from pride, that you may at all seasons rely on as a pattern of humility, is the pickpocket. That man is so admirable in his temper, and so used to pocketing anything whatever which Providence sends in his way, that he will even pocket a kicking, or anything in that line of favours which you are pleased to bestow. The smallest donations are by him thankfully received, provided only that you, whilst half-blind with anger in kicking him round a figure of eight, like a dexterous skater, will but allow *him* (which is no more than fair) to have a second "shy" at your pretty Indian pocket-handkerchief, so as to convince you, on cooler reflection, that he does not *always* miss. Thirdly—Mr Landor leaves it doubtful what verses those are of Wordsworth's which celebrate the power "of the Pagan creed;" whether that sonnet in which Wordsworth wishes to exchange for glimpses of human life, *then and in those circumstances*, "forlorn," the sight

> "—— Of Proteus coming from the sea,
> And hear old Triton wind his wreathed horn;"

whether this, or the passage on the Greek mythology in "The Excursion." Whichever he means, I am the last man to deny that it is beautiful, and especially if he means the latter. But it is no presumption to deny firmly Mr Landor's assertion, that these are "the best verses Wordsworth ever wrote." Bless the man!

> "There are a thousand such elsewhere,
> As worthy of your wonder:"—

Elsewhere, I mean, in Wordsworth's poems. In reality it is *impossible* that these should be the best; for even if, in the executive part, they were so, which is not the case, the very nature of the thought, of the feeling, and of the relation, which binds it to the general theme, and the nature of that theme itself, forbid the possibility of merits so high. The whole movement of the feeling is fanciful: it neither appeals to what is deepest in human sensibilities, nor is meant to do so. The result, indeed, serves only to show Mr Landor's slender acquaintance with Wordsworth. And what is worse than being slenderly acquainted, he is erroneously acquainted even with these two short breathings from the Wordsworthian shell. He mistakes the logic. Wordsworth does not celebrate any power at all in Paganism. Old Triton indeed! he's little better, in respect of the terrific, than a mail-coach guard, nor half as good, if you allow the guard his official seat, a coal-black night, lamps blazing back upon his royal scarlet, and his blunderbuss correctly slung. Triton would not stay, I engage, for a second look at the old Portsmouth or Bristol mail, as once I knew it. But, alas! better things than ever stood on Triton's pins are now as little able to stand up for themselves, or to startle the silent fields in darkness with the sudden flash of their glory—gone before it had fully come—as Triton is to play the Freyschütz chorus on his humbug of a horn. But the logic of Wordsworth is this—not that the Greek mythology is potent; on the contrary, that it is weaker than cowslip tea, and would not agitate the nerves of a hen sparrow; but that, weak as it is—nay, by means of that very weakness—it does but the better serve to measure the weakness of something which *he* thinks yet weaker—viz., the death-like torpor of London society in 1808, benumbed by conventional apathy and worldliness—

"Heavy as frost, and deep almost as life."

This seems a digression from Milton, who is properly the subject of this colloquy. But, luckily, it is not one of my sins. Mr Landor is lord within the house of his own book; he pays all accounts whatever; and readers that have either a bill, or bill of exceptions, to tender against the concern, must draw upon *him*. To Milton he returns upon a very dangerous topic indeed—viz., the structure of his blank verse. I know of none that is so trying to a wary man's nerves. You might as well tax Mozart with harshness in the divinest passages of *Don Giovanni*, as Milton with any such offence against metrical science. Be assured it is yourself that do not read with understanding, not Milton that by possibility can be found deaf to the demands of perfect harmony. You are tempted, after walking round a line threescore times, to exclaim at last—"Well, if the Fiend himself should rise up before me at this very moment, in this very study of mine, and say that no screw was loose in that line, then would I reply—Sir, with submission, you are ——." "What!" suppose the Fiend suddenly to demand in thunder, "What am I?" "Horribly wrong," you wish exceedingly to say; but, recollecting that some people are choleric in argument, you confine yourself to the polite answer—"That, with deference to his better education, you conceive him to lie;"—that's a bad word to drop your voice upon in talking with a fiend, and you hasten to add—"under a slight, *very* slight mistake." Aye, you might venture on that opinion even with a fiend. But how if an angel should undertake the case? And angelic was the ear of Milton. Many are the *primâ facie* anomalous lines in Milton; many are the suspicious lines, which in many a book I have seen many a critic peering into, with eyes made up for mischief, yet with a misgiving that all was not quite safe, very much like an old raven looking down a marrow-bone. In fact, such is the metrical skill of the man, and such the perfection of his metrical sensibility, that, on any attempt to take liberties with a passage of his, you feel as when coming, in a forest, upon what seems a dead lion; perhaps he may *not* be dead, but only sleeping; nay, perhaps he may *not* be sleeping, but only shamming. And you have a jealousy as to Milton, even in the most flagrant case of almost palpable error, that, after all, there may be a plot in it. You may be put down with shame by some man reading the line otherwise, reading it with a different emphasis, a different cæsura, or perhaps a different suspension of the voice, so as to bring out a new and self-justifying effect. It must be added, that, in reviewing Milton's metre, it is quite necessary to have such books as *Nares's English Orthoepy* (*in a late edition*), and others of that class lying on the table; because the accentuation of Milton's age was, in many words, entirely different from ours. And Mr Landor is not free from some suspicion of inattention as to this point. Over and above this accentual difference, the practice of our elder dramatists in the resolution of the final *tion* (which now is uniformly pronounced *shon*), will be found exceedingly important to the appreciation of a writer's verse. *Contribution*, which now is necessarily pronounced as a word of four syllables, would then, in verse, have five, being read into *con-tri-bu-ce-on*.* Many readers will recollect another word which for years brought John Kemble into hot water with the pit of Drury Lane. It was the plural of the word ache. This is generally made a dissyllable by the Elizabethan

* This is a most important *caveat:* many thousands of exquisite lines in the days of Elizabeth, James, Charles, down even to 1658 (last of Cromwell), are ruined by readers untrained to the elder dissyllabic (not monosyllabic) treatment of the *tion*.

dramatists; it occurs in the *Tempest*. Prospero says—

"I'll fill thy bones with aches."

What follows, which I do not remember *literatim*, is such metrically as to *require* two syllables for aches. But how then was this to be pronounced? Kemble thought *akies* would sound ludicrous, *aitches* therefore he called it; and always the pit howled like a famished *menagerie*, as they did also when he chose (and he constantly chose) to pronounce *beard* like *bird*. Many of these niceties must be known before a critic can ever allow *himself* to believe that he is right in *obelising*, or in marking with so much as a ? any verse whatever of Milton's. And there are some of these niceties, I am satisfied, not even yet fully investigated.

It is, however, to be borne in mind, after all allowances and provisional reservations have been madé, that Bentley's hypothesis (injudiciously as it was managed by that great scholar) has really a truth of fact to stand upon. Not only must Milton have composed his three greatest poems, the two *Paradises* and the *Samson*, in a state of blindness, but subsequently, in the correction of the proofs, he must have suffered still more from this conflict with darkness, and consequently, from this dependence upon careless readers. This is Bentley's *case:* as lawyers say, "My lord, that is my case." It is possible enough to *write* correctly in the dark, as I myself often do when losing or missing my lucifers, which, like some elder lucifers, are always rebelliously straying into places where they *can* have no business; but it is quite impossible to *correct a proof* in the dark. At least, if there *is* such an art, it must be a section of the black art. Bentley gained from Pope that admirable epithet of *slashing* ["*the rib-*

balds—from slashing Bentley down to piddling Theobalds," *i. e., Tibbalds*, as it was pronounced], altogether from his edition of the *Paradise Lost*. This the doctor founded on his own hypothesis as to the advantage taken of Milton's blindness; and corresponding was the havoc which he made of the text. In fact, on the really just allegation that Milton must have used the services of an amanuensis; and the plausible one that this amanuensis, being often weary of his task, would be likely to neglect punctilious accuracy; and the most improbable allegation that this weary person would also be very conceited, and a scoundrel, and would add much rubbish of his own; Bentley resigned himself luxuriously, without the whisper of a scruple, to his own sense of what was or was not poetic, which sense happened to be that of the adder for music. The deaf adder heareth not though the musician charm ever so wisely. No scholarship, which so far beyond other men Bentley had, could gain him the imaginative sensibility which, in a degree so far beyond average men, he wanted. Consequently, the world never before beheld such a scene of massacre as his *Paradise Lost* exhibited. He laid himself down to his work of extermination like the brawniest of reapers going in steadily with his sickle, coat stripped off and shirt sleeves tucked up, to deal with an acre of barley. One duty, and no other, rested upon *his* conscience; one voice he heard—Slash away, and hew down the rotten growths of this abominable amanuensis. The carnage was like that after a pitched battle. The very finest passages in every book of the poem were marked by italics as dedicated to fire and slaughter. "Slashing Dick" went through the whole forest like a woodman marking with white paint the giant trees that must all come down in a month or so. And one naturally reverts to a passage in the poem itself, where God the Father is supposed to say to his Filial Assessor on the heavenly throne, when marking the desolating progress of sin and death—

> "See with what havoc these fell dogs advance
> To ravage this fair world."

But still this inhuman extravagance of Bentley, in following out his hypothesis, does not exonerate *us* from bearing in mind so much truth as that hypothesis really must have had, from the pitiable difficulties of the great poet's situation.

My own opinion, therefore, upon the line, for instance, from *Paradise Regained*, which Mr Landor appears to have indicated for the reader's amazement, viz.:—

> "As well might recommend
> *Such solitude before choicest society*," *

is—that it escaped revision from some accident calling off the ear of Milton whilst in the act of having the proof read to him. Mr Landor silently prints it in italics, without assigning his objection; but, of course, that objection must be—that the line has one foot too much. It is an Alexandrine, such as Dryden scattered so profusely without asking himself why, but which Milton never tolerates except in the choruses of the *Samson*.

> "*Not difficult, if thou hearken to me*"—

is one of the lines which Mr Landor thinks that "no

---

* Mr Craik, who is a great authority on such subjects, favoured me some ten or twelve years ago with a letter on this line. He viewed it as a variety more or less irregular, but regular as regarded its model, of the dramatic or scenical verse—privileged to the extent of an extra syllable, but sometimes stretching its privilege a little further.

authority will reconcile" to our ears. I think otherwise. The cæsura is meant to fall not with the comma after *difficult*, but after *thou*, and there is a most effective and grand suspension intended. It is Satan who speaks—Satan in the wilderness; and he marks, as he wishes to mark, the tremendous opposition of attitude between the two parties to the temptation.

"Not difficult if *thou*——"

there let the reader pause, as if pulling up suddenly four horses in harness, and throwing them on their haunches—not difficult if thou (in some mysterious sense the son of God); and then, as with a burst of thunder, again giving the reins to your *quadriga*,

"—— hearken to me:"

that is, to me, that am the Prince of the Air, and able to perform all my promises for those that hearken to my temptations.

Two lines are cited under the same ban of irreconcila bility to our ears, but on a very different plea. The first of these lines is—

"*Launcelot, or Pellias, or Pellinore;*"

The other—

"*Quintius, Fabricius, Curius, Regulus.*"

The reader will readily suppose that both are objected to as "roll-calls of proper names." Now, it is very true that nothing is more offensive to the mind than the practice of mechanically packing into metrical successions, as if packing a portmanteau, names without meaning or significance to the feelings. No man ever carried that atrocity so far as Boileau, a fact of which Mr Landor is well aware; and slight is the sanction or excuse that can be drawn from *him*. But it must not be forgotten that Virgil, so scrupulous in finish of composition, committed this fault. I remember a passage ending—

"—— Noëmonaque Prytaninque;"

but, having no Virgil within reach, I cannot at this moment quote it accurately. Homer, with more excuse, however, from the rudeness of his age, is a deadly offender in this way. But the cases from Milton are very different. Milton was incapable of the Homeric or Virgilian blemish. The objection to such rolling musketry of names is, that unless interspersed with epithets, or broken into irregular groups by brief circumstances of parentage, country, or romantic incident, they stand audaciously perking up their heads like lots in a catalogue, arrow-headed palisades, or young larches in a nursery-ground, all occupying the same space, all drawn up in line, all mere iterations of each other. But in

"*Quintius, Fabricius, Curius, Regulus*,"

though certainly not a good line *when insulated* (better, however, in its connection with the entire succession of which it forms part), the apology is, that the massy weight of the separate characters enables them to stand like granite pillars or pyramids, proud of their self-supporting independency. The great names are designedly left standing in solitary grandeur, like obelisks in a wilderness that have survived all coëval buildings.

Mr Landor makes one correction by a simple improvement in the punctuation, which has a very fine effect. Rarely has so large a result been distributed through a sentence by so slight a change. It is in the *Samson*.

Samson says, speaking of himself (as elsewhere), with that profound pathos which to all hearts recalls Milton's own situation in the days of his old age, when he was composing that drama—

> "Ask for this great deliverer now, and find him
> *Eyeless in Gaza at the mill with slaves.*"

Thus it is usually printed; that is, without a comma in the latter line; but, says Landor, "there ought to be commas after *eyeless*, after *Gaza*, after *mill*." And why? because thus "the grief of Samson is aggravated at every member of the sentence." He (like Milton) was—1. blind; 2. in a city of triumphant enemies; 3. working for daily bread; 4. herding with slaves; Samson literally, and Milton with those whom politically he regarded as such.

Mr Landor is perfectly wrong, I must take the liberty of saying, when he demurs to the line in *Paradise Regained:*

> "*From that placid aspéct and meek regard,*"

on the ground that "*meek regard* conveys no new idea to *placid aspéct.*' But the difference is—as between Christ regarding, and Christ *being* regarded: *aspéct* is the countenance of Christ when passive to the gaze of others; *regard* is the same countenance in active contemplation of those others whom he loves or pities. The *placid aspéct* expresses, therefore, the divine rest; the *meek regard* expresses the radiation of the divine benignity: the one is the self-absorption of the total Godhead, the other the eternal emanation of the Filial Godhead.

By what ingenuity, says Landor, can we erect into a verse—

> "*In the bosom of bliss, and light of light?*"

Now, really, it is by my watch exactly three minutes too late for *him* to make that objection. The court cannot receive it now; for the line just this moment cited, the ink being hardly yet dry, is of the same identical structure. The usual iambic flow is disturbed in both lines by the very same ripple, viz., a trochee in the second foot, *placid* in the one line, *bosom* in the other. They are a sort of *snags*, such as lie in the current of the Mississippi. *There* they do nothing but mischief. Here, when the lines are read in their entire *nexus*, the disturbance stretches forwards and backwards with good effect on the music. Besides, if it did *not*, one is willing to take a *snag* from Milton, but one does not altogether like being *snagged* by the Mississippi. One sees no particular reason for bearing it, if one only knew how to be revenged on a river.

But, of these metrical skirmishes, though full of importance to the impassioned text of a great poet (for mysterious is the life that connects all modes of passion with rhythmus), let us suppose the casual reader to have had enough. And now at closing, for the sake of change, let us treat him to a harlequin trick upon another theme. Did the reader ever happen to see a sheriff's officer arresting an honest gentleman, who was doing no manner of harm to gentle or simple, and immediately afterwards a second sheriff's officer arresting the first—by which means that second officer merits for himself a place in history; for at one and the same moment he liberates a deserving creature (since the arrested officer cannot possibly bag his prisoner), and he also avenges the insult put upon that worthy man? Perhaps the reader did *not* ever see such a sight; and, growing personal, he asks *me*, in return, if *I* ever saw it. To say the truth, I never *did;* except once in a too-flattering dream; and though I applauded so loudly as even to waken myself, and shouted "*encore*," yet all went for nothing; and I am still waiting for that splendid exemplification of retributive justice. But why? Why should it be a spectacle so uncommon? For surely those official arresters of men must want arresting at times as well as better people. At least, however, *en attendant*, one may luxuriate in the vision of such a thing; and the reader shall now see such a vision rehearsed. He shall see Mr Landor arresting Milton—Milton, of all men!—for a flaw in his Roman erudition; and then he shall see me instantly stepping up, tapping Mr Landor on the shoulder, and saying, "Officer, you're wanted;" whilst to Milton I say, touching my hat, "Now, sir, be off; run for your life, whilst I hold this man in custody lest he should fasten on you again."

What Milton had said, speaking of the "*watchful* cherubim," was—

> "Four faces each
> Had, *like a double Janus*;"

upon which Southey—but of course Landor, ventriloquising through Southey—says, "Better left this to the imagination: double Januses are queer figures." Not at all. On the contrary, they became so common, that finally there were no other. Rome, in her days of childhood, contented herself with a two-faced Janus; but, about the time of the first or second Cæsar, a very ancient statue of Janus was exhumed, which had four faces. Ever afterwards, this sacred resurgent statue became the model for any possible Janus that could show himself in good company. The *quadrifrons Janus* was now the orthodox Janus; and it would have been as much a sacrilege to rob him of any single face, as to rob a king's statue* of its horse. One thing may recall this to Mr Landor's memory. I think it was Nero, but certainly it was one of the first six Cæsars, that built or that finished a magnificent temple to Janus; and each face was so managed as to point down an avenue leading to a separate market-place. Now, that there were *four* market-places, I will make oath before any justice of the peace. One was called the *Forum Julium*, one the *Forum Augustum*, a third the *Forum Transitorium*: what the fourth was called is best known to itself, for really I forget. But if anybody says that perhaps it was called the *Forum Landorium*, I am not the man to object; for few names have deserved such an honour more, whether from those that then looked forward into futurity with one face, or from our posterity that will look back into the vanishing past with another.

---

* *A king's statue*:—Till very lately the etiquette of Europe was, that none but royal persons could have equestrian statues. Lord Hopetoun, the reader will object, is allowed to have a horse, in St Andrew Square, Edinburgh. True, but observe that he is not allowed to mount him. The first person, so far as I remember, that, not being royal, has in our island seated himself comfortably in the saddle, is the Duke of Wellington.

THE FATAL MARKSMAN.

1.

"Listen, dame," said Bertram, the old forester of Linden, to his wife; "once for all, listen. It's not many things, thou well know'st, that I would deny to thy asking: but as for this notion, Anne, drive it clean out of thy head; root and branch lay the axe to it; the sooner the better; and never encourage the lass to think more about it. When she knows the worst, she'll settle herself down to her crying; and when that's over, all's over; she submits, and all goes right. I see no good that comes of standing shilly-shally, and letting the girl nurse herself with hopes of what must not be."

"But Bertram, dear Bertram," replied old Anne, "why not? could not our Kate live as happily with the bailiff's clerk as with the hunter Robert? Ah, you don't know what a fine lad William is; so good, so kind-hearted—"

"May be, like enough," interrupted Bertram; "kind-hearted, I dare say, but no hunter for all that. Now, look here, Anne: for better than two hundred years has this farm in the Forest of Linden come down from father to child in my family. Had'st thou brought me a son, well and good: the farm would have gone to him; and the lass might have married whom she would. But, as the case stands,—no, I say. What the devil! have I had all this trouble and vexation of mind to get the duke's allowance for my son-in-law to stand his examination as soon as he is master of the huntsman's business; and just when all's settled, must I go and throw the girl away? A likely thing, indeed! No, no, mistress Anne, it's no use talking. It's not altogether Robert that I care about. I don't stand upon trifles; and, if the man is not to your taste or the girl's, why, look out any other active huntsman that may take my office betimes, and give us a comfortable fireside in our old age. Robert or not Robert, so that it be a lad of the forest, I'll never stand upon trifles: but for the clerk—dost hear, Anne?—this hero of a crow-quill, never hang about my neck or think to wheedle me again."

For the clerk's sake old Anne would have ventured to wheedle her husband a little longer: but the forester, who knew by experience the pernicious efficacy of female eloquence, was resolved not to expose his own firmness of purpose to any further assaults or trials; and, taking down his gun from the wall, he walked out into the forest.

Scarcely had he turned the corner of the house, when a rosy light-haired face looked in at the door. It was Katharine: smiling and blushing, she stopped for a moment in agitation, and said:—"Is all right, mother? was it *yes*, dear mother?" Then, bounding into the room, she fell on her mother's neck for an answer.

"Ah Kate, be not too confident when thou should'st be prepared for the worst: thy father is a good man, as good as ever stepped, but he has his fancies; and he is resolved to give thee to none but a hunter: he has set his heart upon it; and he'll not go from his word; I know him too well."

Katharine wept, and avowed her determination to die sooner than to part from her William. Her mother comforted and scolded her by turns, and at length ended by joining her tears to her daughter's. She was promising to make one more assault of a most vigorous kind upon the old forester's heart, when a knock was heard at the door—and in stepped William. "Ah William!"—exclaimed Katharine, going up to him with streaming eyes,—"we must part: seek some other sweetheart: me you must never marry; father is resolved to give me to Robert, because he is a huntsman; and my mother can do nothing for us. But, if I am to part from you, never think that I will belong to anybody else: to my dying hour, dear William, I will remain faithful to you."

These bursts of wounded feeling were softened in the report of the mother: she explained to the bewildered clerk, who knew not what to make of Katharine's ejaculations, that Bertram had no objections to him personally; but that, simply with a view to the reversionary interest in his place as forester, he insisted on having a son-in-law who understood hunting.

"Is that all?" said William, recovering his composure, and at the same time he caught the sobbing girl to his bosom,—"Is that all? Then be of good cheer, dearest Kate. I am not unskilled in hunting: for, at one time, I was apprenticed to my uncle Finstersbusch, the forester-general; and it was only to gratify my god-father the bailiff that I exchanged the gun for the writing-desk. What care I for the reversion of the bailiff's place, unless I may take my Kate into the bailiff's house as mistress? If you can be content to look no higher than your mother did, and Will the forester is not less dear to you than Will the bailiff, then let me die if I won't quit my clerkship this instant; for, in point of pleasure, there's no comparison between the jolly huntsman's life and the formal life of the town."

"Oh! thou dear, kind lad," said Katharine, whilst all the clouds dispersed from her forehead, and her eyes swam in a shower of glittering tears, "If thou wilt do this for my sake then do so, and speak to my father without delay—before he can possibly make any promise to Robert."

"Stay, Kate: I'll go after him this moment into the forest. He's gone in search of the venison, I dare say that is to be delivered to-morrow into the office. Give me a gun and a pouch: I'll find him out—meet him with a jolly hunter's salutation—and offer my services to him as his hunting-boy."

Both mother and daughter fell upon his neck; helped to equip the new huntsman to the best of their skill; and looked after him, as he disappeared in the forest, with hope, but yet with some anxiety.

II.

"Upon my soul, but this William's a fine fellow!" exclaimed the forester as he returned home with his comrade from the chase: "Who the deuce would ever have looked for such a good shot in the flourisher of a crow-quill? Well; to-morrow I shall speak with the bailiff myself; for it would be a sad pity if he were not to pursue the noble profession of hunting. Why, he'll make a second Kuno. You know who Kuno was, I suppose?" said he, turning to William.

William acknowledged that he did not.

"Not know who Kuno was? bless my soul! to think

that I should never have told you that. Why, Kuno, you're to understand, was my great grand-father's father; and was the very first man that ever occupied and cultivated this farm. He began the world no better, I'll assure you, than a poor riding-boy; and lived servant with the young knight of Wippach. Ah! the knight liked him well, and took him to all places, battles, tournaments, hunts, and what not. Well, once upon a time it happened that this young gentleman of Wippach was present with many other knights and nobles at a great hunt held by the duke. And in this hunt the dogs turned up a stag, upon which a man was seated wringing his hands and crying piteously; for, in those days, there was a tyrannical custom among the great lords, that, when a poor man had committed any slight matter of trespass against the forest laws, they would take and bind him on the back of a stag, so that he was bruised and gored to death by the herd—or if he escaped dying that way, he perished of hunger and thirst. Well, when the duke saw this—oh lord! but he was angry; and gave command to stop the hunting; and there and then he promised a high reward to any man that would undertake to hit the stag—but threatened him with his severest displeasure in case he wounded the man; for he was resolved, if possible, to take him alive—that he might learn who it was that had been bold enough to break his law, which forbade all such murderous deeds. Now, amongst all the nobility, not a man could be found that would undertake the job on these terms. They liked the reward, mind you, but not the risk. So, at last, who should step forward but Kuno, my own great-grandfather's father—the very man that you see painted in that picture. He spoke up boldly before the duke, and said:—"My noble liege, if it is your pleasure, with God's blessing, I will run the hazard; if I miss, my life is at your grace's disposal, and must pay the forfeit; for riches and worldly goods I have none to ransom it; but I pity the poor man; and, without fee or reward, I would have exposed my life to the same hazard if I had seen him in the hands of enemies or robbers." This speech pleased the duke: it pleased him right well: and he bade Kuno try his luck; and again he promised him the reward in case he hit; but he did not repeat his threat in case he missed; that was, mind you, lest he should frighten him and make his hand unsteady. Well, Kuno took his gun, cocked it in God's name, and, commending the ball with a pious prayer to the guidance of good angels, he spent no time in taking aim—but fired with a cheerful faith right into the midst of a thicket: in the same moment out rushed the hart, staggered, and fell; but the man was unwounded, except that his hands and face were somewhat scratched by the bushes.

"The noble duke kept his word, and gave Kuno, for his reward, the farm of the forest to himself and his heirs for ever. But, lord bless us! good fortune never wanted envy; and the favour of Providence, as Kuno soon learned, is followed by the jealousy of man. Many a man there was, in those days, who would gladly have had Kuno's reward; one man for himself, perhaps; another for some poor cousin or so, or maybe something nearer of kin, but come of the wrong side the blanket: and what did they do but they persuaded the duke that Kuno's shot had hit the mark through witchcraft and black arts: "For why?" said they, "Kuno never took any aim at all, but fired at random "a devil's shot;" and a devil's shot, you're to understand, never fails of hitting the mark;

for needs must that the devil drives." So hereupon a regulation was made, and from this the custom came, that every descendant of Kuno must undergo a trial, and fire what they call his probationary shot before he is admitted tenant. However, the master of the hounds, before whom the trial takes place, can make it easy or difficult at his own pleasure. When I was admitted, guess what the master required of me: why, from the bill of a wooden bird to shoot out a ring that fastened the bird to a pole. Well, well: up to this time not one of all Kuno's descendants has failed in his trial: and he that would be my son-in-law and a worthy successor to me—let me tell you, William, that man had need to make himself a thorough huntsman."

William, who had listened to this story with lively interest (as the old forester had not failed to remark with much satisfaction), rose from his seat when it was ended, pressed the old man's hand, and promised, under his tuition, to make himself a huntsman such as even old father Kuno should have had no cause to blush for.

III.

William had scarcely lived one whole fortnight at the forest house in his capacity of huntsman, when old Bertram, who liked him better every day, gave a formal consent to his marriage with Katharine. This promise, however, was to be kept secret until the day of the probationary shot, when the presence of the ducal master of the hounds would confer a splendour on the ceremony of the betrothing which was flattering to the old man's pride. Meantime the bridegroom-elect passed his time in rapturous elevation of spirits, and forgot himself and all the world in the paradise of youthful love; so that father Bertram often said to him tauntingly, that from the day when he had hit his prime aim in obtaining Katharine's heart he had hit nothing else. The fact, however, was, that from that very day William had met with an unaccountable run of ill-luck in hunting. Sometimes his gun would miss fire; at other times, instead of a deer, he would hit the trunk of a tree. Was his hunting-bag emptied on his return home? Instead of partridges out came daws and crows, and, instead of a hare, perhaps a dead cat. At last the forester began to reproach him in good earnest for his heedlessness; and Kate herself became anxious for the event of his examination before the duke's commissioner.

William redoubled his attention and diligence; but the nearer the day of trial advanced, so much the more was he persecuted by bad luck. Nearly every shot missed; and at length he grew almost afraid of pulling a trigger for fear of doing some mischief; for he had already shot a cow at pasture, and narrowly escaped wounding the herdsman.

"Nay, I stick to my own opinion," said huntsman Rudolph one night, "somebody has cast a spell over William; for, in the regular course of nature such things could never happen; and this spell he must undo before ever he'll have any luck."

"Pooh! pooh! man, what stuff you talk!" replied Bertram. "This is nothing but superstitious foolery, such as no Christian hunter should ever so much as name. Can'st tell me now, my fine fellow, what three articles be those which make an able sportsman's stock in trade?

"Aye, my old cock of the woods, I can tell you *that*," said Rudolph clearing his throat, "or else it were a pity:

'A dog, a gun, and a skilful hand,
In the forest are better than house or land.'"

"Good," said Bertram, "and these three together are an overmatch for all the spells in Germany."

"With your leave, father Bertram," replied William, somewhat chagrined, "here is my gun; and I should be glad to see the man that has any fault to find with *that*: as to my skill, I will not boast of it; yet I think it can't be denied that I do as well as others: nevertheless, so it is, that my balls seem to fly askance, as if the wind turned them out of their course. Do but tell me what it is that I should do, and there is nothing I will not try."

"Strange, indeed!" murmured the forester, who knew not what to say.

"Take my word for it, William," repeated Rudolph, "it is just what I tell you. Go some Friday at midnight to a cross-road, and make a circle round about you with a ram-rod or a bloody sword; bless it three times in the same words as the priest uses, but in the name of Samiel"—

"Hush! hush!" interrupted the forester angrily: "dost know what that name is? why, he's one of Satan's host. God keep thee and all Christians out of his power!"

William crossed himself and would hear no more, however obstinately Rudolph persisted in his opinion. All night long he continued to clean his gun, to examine the screws, the spring, and every part of the lock and barrel; and at break of day he sallied forth to try his luck once more.

IV.

But all in vain; his pains were all thrown away; the deer flocked round him almost as it seemed in mockery of his skill. At ten paces distance he levelled at a roe-buck; twice his gun flashed in the pan; the third time it went off, but the deer darted off unhurt through the bushes. Cursing his fate, the unhappy hunter threw himself despondingly beneath a tree; at that moment a rustling was heard in the bushes, and out limped an old soldier with a wooden leg.

"Good morning to you, comrade," said the soldier; "Why so gloomy, why so gloomy? Is it body or purse that's ailing, health or wealth is it that your sighing for? Or has somebody put a charm upon your gun? Come, give us a bit of tobacco, and let's have a little chat together."

With a surly air William gave him what he asked for, and the soldier threw himself by his side on the grass. After some desultory discussion, the conversation fell upon hunting, and William related his own bad luck. "Let me see your gun," said the soldier. "Ah! I thought so. This gun has been charmed, and you'll never get a true aim with it again; and more than that, let me tell you, if the charm was laid according to the rules of art, you'll have no better luck with any other gun you take in hand."

William shuddered, and would have urged some objection against the credibility of witchcraft; but the stranger offered to bring the question to a simple test. "To old soldiers, the like of me," said he, "there's nothing at all surprising in it. Bless your soul, I could tell you stories stranger by half from this time to midnight. How do you think the sharp-shooters would come on, that must venture here, there, and everywhere, and must pick off their man from the very heart of the thickest smoke where it's clean impossible to see him—

how must they come on, I would be glad to know, if they understood no other trick than just aim and fire? Now here, for instance, is a ball that cannot fail to go true, because it's a gifted ball, and is proof against all the arts of darkness. Just try it now; give it a single trial: I'll answer for it, you'll not find it deceive you, I'll go bail for it."

William loaded his piece, and looked about for an aim. At a great height above the forest, like a moving speck, was hovering a large bird of prey. "There!" said wooden-leg, "that old devil up there, shoot *him*." William laughed, for the bird was floating in a region so elevated as to be scarcely discernible to the naked eye. "Nay, never doubt; shoot away," repeated the old soldier; "I'll wager my wooden leg you'll bring him down." William fired, the black speck was seen rapidly enlarging, and a great vulture fell bleeding to the ground.

"Oh! bless your heart, that's nothing at all," said the soldier, observing the speechless astonishment of his companion; "not worth speaking of. Indeed it's no such great matter to learn how to cast balls as good as these; little more is wanted than some slight matter of skill, and, to be sure, a stout heart; for why? the work must be done in the night. I'll teach you, and welcome, if we should chance to meet again; at present, however, I must be moving, for I've a d——d long march before me to-day, and I hear it just striking seven. Meantime, here's a few braces of my balls for you," and so saying he limped off.

Filled with astonishment, William tried a second of the balls, and again he hit an object at an inaccessible distance; he then charged with his ordinary balls, and missed the broadest and most obvious mark. On this second trial, he determined to go after the old soldier; but the soldier had disappeared in the depths of the forest, and William was obliged to console himself with the prospect of meeting him again.

V.

In the forest house all was joy and triumph when William returned, as formerly, with a load of venison, and gave practical evidence to old Bertram that he was still the same marksman he had first shown himself in his noviciate. He should now have told the reason of his late ill-luck, and what course he had taken to remove it; but, without exactly knowing why, he shrank from telling of the inevitable balls, and laid the blame upon a flaw in his gun, which had escaped his notice until the preceding night.

"Now, dame, dost a' see?" said the forester laughing; "who's wrong now, dame, I wonder? The witchcraft lay in the gun that wanted trimming; and the little devil, that by your account should have thrown down old father Kuno's picture so early this morning, I'm partly of opinion lies in a cankered nail."

"What's that you're saying about a devil?" asked William.

"Nay, nothing at all but nonsense," replied the old man; "this morning, just as the clock was striking seven, the picture fell down of itself, and so my wife will have it that all's not right about the house."

"Just as it was striking seven, eh? Ha!" And across William's thoughts flashed like a fiery arrow the old soldier, who had taken his leave at that identical time.

"Aye, sure enough, as it was striking seven: not a

very likely time for devils to be stirring; eh, my old dame? eh, Anne?" at the same time chucking her under the chin with a good-natured laugh. But old Anne shook her head thoughtfully, saying—"God grant all may turn out natural!" and William changed colour a little. He resolved to put by his balls, and, at the most, only to use one upon his day of trial, lest he might be unconsciously trifling away his future happiness at the wily suggestions of a fiend. But the forester summoned him to attendance upon the chace; and, unless he were prepared to provoke the old man, and to rouse afresh all the late suspicions in regard to his skill, he found himself obliged to throw away some of his charmed balls upon such occasions.

VI.

In a few days William had so familiarised himself to the use of his enchanted balls, that he no longer regarded it with any misgiving. Every day he roamed about in the forest, hoping to meet the wooden-leg again; for his stock of balls had sunk to a single pair, and the most rigorous parsimony became needful, if he would not put to hazard his final success on the day of trial. One day, therefore, he positively declined attending the old forester a hunting, for, on the next, the duke's commissioner was expected, and it might so happen that, before the regular probation, he would call for some exhibition of his skill. At night, however, instead of the commissioner, came a messenger from him to bespeak a very large delivery of game for court, and to countermand the preparations for his own reception until that day se'nnight.

On the receipt of this news William was ready to sink

to the ground; and his alarm would certainly have raised suspicions had it not been ascribed to the delay of his marriage. He was now under the necessity of going out to hunt, and of sacrificing at least one of his balls; with the other he vowed to himself that he would not part for any purpose on earth, except for the final shot before the commissioner which was to decide his fate for life.

Bertram scolded when William came back from the forest with only a single buck; for the quantity of venison ordered was very considerable. Next day he was still more provoked on seeing Rudolph return loaded with game and William with an empty bag. At night he threatened to dismiss him from his house, and to revoke the consent he had given to his marriage with Katharine, unless he brought home at least two roe-deer on the following morning. Katharine herself was in the greatest distress, and conjured him for love of her to apply his utmost zeal, and not to think so much about her whilst engaged in hunting.

In a despairing mood William set off to the forest. Kate, in any case, he looked upon as lost; and all that remained for him was a sad alternative between the two modes of losing her, whether by the result of this day's hunting, or of the trial before the commissioner. This was an alternative on which he felt himself incapable of deciding; and he was standing lost in gloomy contemplation of his wretched fate, when all at once a troop of deer advanced close upon him. Mechanically he felt for his last ball; it seemed to weigh a hundredweight in his hands. Already he had resolved to reserve this treasure at any price, when suddenly he saw the old wooden-leg at a distance, and apparently directing his steps towards himself. Joyfully he dropped his ball into the barrel, fired, and two roebucks fell to the ground. William left them lying, and hurried after the wooden-leg; but he must have struck into some other path, for he had wholly disappeared.

VII.

Father Bertram was well satisfied with William; but not so was William with himself. The whole day long he went about in gloomy despondency; and even the tenderness and caresses of Kate had no power to restore him to serenity. At nightfall he was still buried in abstraction; and, seated in a chair, he hardly noticed the lively conversation between the forester and Rudolph, till at length the former woke him out of his reverie.

"What, William, I say," cried Bertram, "sure you'll never sit by and hearken quietly whilst such scandalous things are said as Rudolph has just been saying of our forefather Kuno? I'm sure, I won't. If good angels stood by, and gave help to him and to the poor innocent man on the stag's back, why nothing but right: we read of such cases in the Old Testament; and let us thank God for that and all his mercies and marvels: but as to black arts and devil's shots, I'll not sit and hear such things said of our Kuno. What, man? Kuno died in his bed quietly, and with a Christian's peace, amongst his children and children's children; but the man that tampers with the powers of darkness never makes a good end. I know *that* by what I saw myself at Prague in Bohemia, when I was an apprentice lad."

"Aye! what was that?" cried Rudolph and the rest: "tell us, dear father."

"What was it? why, bad enough," said Bertram; "it makes me shudder when I think of it. There was at that time a young man in Prague, one George Smith by name, a wild, daring sort of a fellow,—not but he was a fine, active lad in his way,—that was terribly fond of hunting, and would often come and join us; indeed, I may say, whenever he could. And a very fair hunter he might have proved; but he was too hasty by far, and flung his shots away in a manner. One day, when we had been joking him on this, his pride mounted so high, that nothing would serve him but he must defy all the hunters in a body: he would beat any of them at shooting; and no game should escape him, whether in the air or in the forest. This was his boast; but ill he kept his word. Two days after comes a strange huntsman bolt upon us out of a thicket, and tells us that a little way off, on the main road, a man was lying half dead, and with nobody to look after him. We lads made up to the spot, and there, sure enough, lay poor George, torn and clawed all to pieces, just as if he had fallen amongst wild-cats: not a word could he speak; for he was quite senseless, and hardly showed any signs of life. We carried him to a house: one of us set off with the news to Prague; and thither he was soon fetched. Well, this George Smith, before he died, made confession that he had set about casting devil's balls with an old upland hunter. Devil's balls, you understand, never miss; and because he failed in something that he should have done, the devil had handled him so roughly, that what must pay for it but his precious life?"

"What was it, then, that he failed in?" asked William falteringly. "Is it always the devil that is at work in such dealings?"

"Why, who should it be?" rejoined the forester. "the devil, to be sure, who else? Some people I've heard talk of hidden powers of nature, and of the virtue of the stars. I know not: every man's free to think what he likes; but it's my opinion, and I stick to it, that it's all the devil's handicraft."

William drew his breath more freely. "But did George not relate what it was that brought such rough treatment upon him?"

"Aye, sure enough, before the magistrates he confessed all. As it drew towards midnight, it seems, he had gone with the old hunter to a cross-road: there they made a circle with a bloody sword; and in this circle they laid a skull and bones crossways. Then the old man told George what he was to do. On the stroke of eleven, he was to begin casting the balls, in number sixty-and-three, neither more nor less: one over or one under, as soon as twelve o'clock struck, he was a lost man. And during all this work he was not to speak a word, nor to step out of the circle, let what would happen. Sixty of the balls were to carry true, and only three were to miss. Well, sure enough, Smith began casting the balls; but such shocking and hideous apparitions flocked about him, that at last he shrieked out, and jumped right out of the circle. Instantly he fell down senseless to the ground; and never recovered his recollection till he found himself at Prague, as if waking out of a dream, in the hands of the surgeon, and with a clergyman by his side."

"God preserve all Christian people from such snares of Satan!" said the forester's wife, crossing herself.

"Had George, then," asked Rudolph, "made a regular contract with the devil?"

"Why, that's more than I'll undertake to say," replied

Bertram; for it is written, 'Judge not.' But, let that be as it will, it can be no slight matter of a sin for a man to meddle with things that bring the Evil One about him; and may, for aught he knows, give him power over body and soul. Satan is ready enough to come of himself, without any man's needing to summon him, or to make bargains with him. Besides, what need of any such help for a good Christian hunter? *You* know *that*, William, by your own experience: with a good gun and a skilful hand, the hunter wants no devil's balls, but hits just where he *should* hit. For my part, if I had such balls, I wouldn't fire them for any money; for the fiend is a wily devil, and might upon occasion give the ball a sly twist in its course, to serve *his* purposes instead of mine."

VIII.

The forester went to bed, and left William in the most wretched state of agitation. In vain he threw himself on his bed; sound sleep fled from his eyes. The delirium of a heated fancy presented to his eyes, by turns, in confused groups, the old wooden-legged soldier, George, Katharine, and the ducal commissioner. Now the unfortunate boy of Prague held up his hand before him, as a bloody memento of warning: then in a moment his threatening aspect would change into the face of Kate, fainting and pale as death; and near her stood the wooden-leg, his countenance overspread with a fiendish laugh of mockery. At another time he was standing before the commissioner in the act of firing his probationary shot; he levelled, took aim, fired, and—missed. Katharine fainted away, her father rejected him for ever; then came the wooden-leg, and presented him with fresh balls; but too late—no second trial was allowed him.

So passed the night with William. At the earliest dawn he went into the forest, and bent his steps, not altogether without design, to the spot where he had met the old soldier. The fresh breezy air of the morning had chased away from his mind the gloomy phantoms of the night. "Fool!" said he to himself, "because a mystery is above thy comprehension, must it therefore be from hell? And what is there so much out of the course of nature in that which I am seeking, that supernatural powers need come to help me? Man controls the mighty powers of the brute into obedience to his will; why should he not, by the same natural arts, impress motion and direction upon the course of a bit of lifeless inert metal? Nature teems with operations which we do not comprehend: and am I to trifle away my happiness for a superannuated prejudice? I will call up no spiritual beings, but I will summon and make use of the occult powers of nature, never troubling myself whether I can decipher her mysteries or not. I will go in quest of the old soldier; and, if I should not find him, I will take care to keep up my courage better than that same George of Prague; he was urged on by pride; but I by the voice of love and honour."

In this manner did William discuss his own intentions: but the old soldier was nowhere to be found. Nobody, of whom he inquired, had seen any such man as he described. The next day was spent in the same search, and with no better success.

"So be it, then!" said William internally: "the days that remain for my purpose are numbered. This very night I will go to the cross-road in the forest. It is a lonely spot; nobody will be there to witness my nocturnal labours: and I'll take care not to quit the circle till my work is done."

IX.

Twilight had set in; and William had provided himself with lead, bullet-mould, coals, and all other requisites, that he might be ready to slip out of the house unobserved immediately after supper. He was just on the point of departing, and had already wished the forester a good night, when the latter stopped him, and took his hand.

"William," said he, "I know not what is to come to me, but so it is, that this evening I have an awe upon my mind, as if from some danger, God knows what, hanging over me. Oblige me by staying this night with me. Don't look so cast down, my lad; its only to guard against possibilities."

Katherine immediately offered her services to sit up with her father, and was unwilling to intrust the care of him to anybody else, even to her own William; but father Bertram declined her offer.—"Another time," said he, "another time; to-night I feel as if I should be easier if I had William with me."

William was disposed at first to excuse himself: but Kate commended her father so earnestly to his care, that her requests were not to be resisted; and he staid with a good grace, and put off the execution of his plan until the succeeding night.

After midnight the old forester became tranquil, and slept soundly, so that, on the following morning, he laughed at his own fears. He would have gone with William into the forest; but William still clung to the hope of meeting his mysterious acquaintance with the wooden leg, and therefore opposed his wishes with a plausible pretext about his health. The wooden-leg, however, never appeared; and William, a second time resolved on the nocturnal expedition to the cross road.

At night, when he came back from the forest, Katharine ran out joyfully to meet him.—"Guess, William, only guess," she cried, "who it is that is come. There is a visitor for you, a right dear visitor; but I will not say who, for you must guess."

William had no mind for guessing, and still less for seeing visitors. On this day, the dearest in the world would have seemed in his eyes a troublesome intruder. He shrank gloomily from Katharine's welcome, and thought of turning back upon some pretence; but at that moment the house door opened, and the light of the moon discovered a venerable old man in a hunter's dress, who stepped forwards and stretched out his arms to William.

"William!" exclaimed a well-known voice, and William found himself in the arms of his uncle. A world of affecting remembrances, from the days of childhood—remembrances of love, of joy, and of gratitude, pressed with the weight of magic upon William's heart: amidst these his midnight purpose slipped away from his thoughts; and it was in the middle of the gayest conversation, upon the clock striking twelve, that William was first reminded with horror of the business he had neglected.

"Just one night more," thought he, "one single night remains: to-morrow, or never!" His violent agitation did not escape his uncle's notice; but the old man ascribed it to some little weariness in his nephew, and good-naturedly apologised for having engaged him so long in conversation, by pleading his early departure, which he could not possibly put off beyond the first dawn of the next morning.

"Think not much of an odd hour or two thrown away," said he to William on separating; "may be you'll sleep all the better for it."

These last words had a deeper import to William's thoughts than could possibly have been meant by his uncle. He saw in them an obscure allusion to his nocturnal plans, which, once executed, might (as he forboded) chase away from him for ever the comfort of tranquil slumbers.

X.

The third night came. Whatever was to be done, must be done on this day, for the next was the day of trial. From morning to night had old Anne, with her daughter Kate, bustled about the house, to make arrangements for the suitable reception of her dignified guest, the commissioner. At nightfall everything was ready, and in the most becoming order. Anne embraced William on his return from the forest, and for the first time saluted him with the endearing name of son. The eyes of Kate sparkled with the tender emotions of a youthful bride*—that loves, and is beloved. The table was decked with festal flowers, and such as rural usage has appropriated, by way of emblems, to the occasion: viands more luxurious than usual were brought out by the mother; and bottles of choice old wine by the father.

---

* *Bride*:—*We* call no woman a bride until she is irrevocably married. But in Germany she then *ceases* to be a bride. The *Braut* is she that is affianced; which sometimes she is for years. But this betrothal, which makes her a bride, is swallowed up by her nuptials.

"This night," said Bertram, "we will keep the bridal feast: to-morrow we shall not be alone, and cannot, therefore, sit so confidentially and affectionately together; let us be happy then—as happy as if all the pleasure of our lives were to be crowded into this one night."

The forester embraced his family, and was deeply moved. "But, Bertram," said his wife, "let us be as happy as we will to-night, I've a notion the young people will be happier to-morrow. Do you know what I mean?"

"Yes, love, I know what you mean; and let the children know it also, that they may enjoy their happiness beforehand. Do you hear, children? The vicar is invited to-morrow; and as soon as William has passed his examination"——

At this moment a rattling noise and a loud cry from Katharine interrupted the forester's speech. Kuno's portrait had again fallen from the wall, and a corner of the frame had wounded Katharine on the temples. The nail appeared to have been fixed too loosely in the wall, for it fell after the picture, and brought away part of the plaster. "What, in God's name, can be the reason," said Bertram with vexation, "that this picture can't be made to hang as it should do? This now is the second time that it has alarmed us. Katy, my love, art any worse?"

"No, not at all," said she, cheerfully, and wiping the blood from her tresses, "but I was sadly frightened."

William was thrown into dreadful agitation when he beheld the death-pale countenance of Kate, and the blood upon her temples. Just so had she appeared to him on the night of his hideous visions; and all the sad images of that memorable night now revived upon his mind, and tormented him afresh. The violent shock tended greatly to stagger him in his plans for the night; but the wine, which he drank in large draughts, and more hastily than usual, for the purpose of hiding his anguish, filled him with a frantic spirit of hardihood: he resolved afresh to make the attempt boldly; and no longer saw anything in his purpose but the honourable spectacle of love and courage struggling with danger.

The clock struck nine. William's heart beat violently. He sought for some pretext for withdrawing, but in vain. What pretext could a man find for quitting his young bride on their bridal festival? Time flew faster than an arrow: in the arms of love, that should have crowned him with happiness, he suffered the pangs of martyrdom. Ten o'clock was now past, and the decisive moment was at hand. Without taking leave, William stole away from the side of his bride; already he was outside the house with his implements of labour, when old Anne came after him. "Whither away, William, at this time of night?" asked she anxiously. "I shot a deer, and forgot it in my hurry," was the answer. In vain she begged him to stay: all her entreaties were flung away, and even the tender caresses of Kate, whose mind misgave her that some mystery lay buried in his hurry and agitation. William tore himself from them both, and hastened to the forest.

XI.

The moon was in the wane, and at this time was rising, and resting with a dim red orb upon the horizon. Gloomy clouds were flying overhead, and at intervals darkened the whole country, which, by fits, the moon again lit up. The silvery birches and the aspen trees rose like apparitions in the forest; and the poplars seemed, to William's fevered visions, pale shadowy forms that beckoned him to retire. He shuddered; and it suddenly struck him, that the almost miraculous disturbance of his scheme on the two preceding nights, together with the repeated and ominous falling of the picture, were the last warnings of dissuasion from a wicked enterprise, addressed to him by his better angel that was now ready to forsake him.

Once again he faltered in his purpose. Already he was on the point of returning, when suddenly a voice appeared to whisper to him: "Fool! hast thou not already accepted magical help; is it only for the trouble of reaping it that thou would'st forego the main harvest of its gifts?" He stood still. The moon issued in splendour from behind a dark cloud, and illuminated the peaceful roof of the forester's cottage. He could see Katharine's chamber window glancing under the silvery rays; in the blindness of love, he stretched out his arms towards it, and mechanically stepped homewards. Then came a second whisper from the voice; for a sudden gust of wind brought the sound of the clock striking the half hour: "Away to business!" it seemed to say. "Right, right!" he said aloud, "Away to business! It is weak and childish to turn back from a business half accomplished it is folly to renounce the main advantage, having already, perhaps, risked one's salvation for a trifle. No: let me go through with it."

He stepped forwards with long strides; the wind drove the agitated clouds again over the face of the moon; and William plunged into the thickest gloom of the forest.

At length he stood upon the cross way. At length the magic circle was drawn; the skulls were fixed; and the bones were laid round about. The moon buried herself deeper and deeper in the clouds; and no light was shed upon the midnight deed, except from the red lurid gleam of the fire, that waxed and waned by fits, under the gusty squalls of the wind. A remote church clock proclaimed that it was now within a quarter of eleven. William put the ladle upon the fire, and threw in the lead together with three bullets which had already hit the mark once: a practice, amongst those who cast the "fatal bullets," which he remembered to have heard mentioned in his apprenticeship. In the forest was now heard a pattering of rain. At intervals came flitting motions of owls, bats, and other light-shunning creatures, scared by the sudden gleams of the fire: some, dropping from the surrounding boughs, placed themselves on the magic circle, where, by their low, dull croaking, they seemed holding dialogues, in some unknown tongue, with the dead men's skulls. Their numbers increased; and amongst them were indistinct outlines of misty forms, that went and came, some with brutal, some with human faces. Their vapoury lineaments fluctuated and obeyed the motions of the wind; one only stood unchanged, and, like a shadow, near to the circle, and settled the sad light of its eyes steadfastly upon William. Sometimes it would raise its pale hands, and seem to sigh: and when it raised its hands, the fire would burn more sullenly; but a gray owl would then fan with his wings, and rekindle the decaying embers. William averted his eyes: for the countenance of his buried mother seemed to look out from the cloudy figure, with piteous expressions of unutterable anguish. Suddenly it struck eleven; and then the shadow vanished, with the action of one who prays and breathes up sighs to heaven. The owls and the night-ravens flitted croaking about;

and the skulls and bones rattled beneath their wings. William kneeled down on his coaly hearth; and with the last stroke of eleven, out fell the first bullet.

XII.

The owls and the bones were now silent; but along the road came an old crooked beldame pell-mell against the magic circle. She was hung round with wooden spoons, ladles, and other kitchen utensils, and made a hideous rattling as she moved. The owls saluted her with hooting, and fanned her with their wings. On reaching the circle, she bowed to the bones and skulls; but the coals shot forth lambent tongues of flame against her, and she drew back her withered hands. Then she paced round the circle, and with a grin presented her wares to William. "Give me the bones," said she, in a harsh guttural tone, "and I'll give thee some spoons. Give the skulls to me, love; what's the trumpery to thee, love?" and then she chaunted, with a scornful air—

"There's nothing can help: 'tis an hour too late;
Nothing can step betwixt thee and thy fate.
Shoot in the light, or shoot in the dark,
Thy bullets, be sure, shall go true to the mark.
'Shoot the dove,' says the word of command;
And the forester bold, with the matchless hand,
Levels and fires: Oh! marksman good!
The dove lies bathed in her innocent blood!
Here's to the man that shoots the dove!
Come for the prize to me, my love!"

William was aghast with horror; but he remained quiet within the circle, and pursued his labours. The old woman was one whom he well knew. A crazy old female beggar had formerly roamed about the neighbourhood in this attire, till at last she was lodged in a mad-house. He was at a loss to discover whether the object now before him were the reality or an illusion. After some little pause, the old crone scattered her lumber to the right and left with an angry air, and then tottered slowly away into the gloomy depths of the forest, singing those words:

"This to the left, and that to the right;
This and that for the bridal night.
Marksman fine, be sure and steady;
The bride she is dressed—the priest he is ready.
To-morrow, to-morrow, when day-light departs,
And twilight is spread over broken hearts;
When the fight is fought, when the race is run,
When the strife and the anguish are over and done;
When the bride-bed is decked with a winding-sheet,
And the innocent dove has died at thy feet,—
Then comes a bridegroom for me, I trow,
That shall live with me in my house of woe.
Here's to him that shoots the dove!
Come for the prize to me, my love!"

Now came all at once a rattling as of wheels and the cracking of postilions' whips. A carriage and six drove up with outriders. "What the devil's this that stops the way?" cried the man who rode the leaders. "Make way there, I say—clear the road." William looked up and saw sparks of fire darting from the horses' hoofs, and a circle of flame about the carriage wheels. By this he knew it to be a work of the fiend, and never stirred. "Push on, my lads—drive over him helter-skelter," cried the same postilion, looking back to the others; and in a moment the whole equipage moved rapidly upon the circle. William cowered down to the ground, beneath the dash of the leaders' fore-legs; but the airy train and the carriage soared into the air with a whistling sound, round and round the circle, and vanished in a hurricane which moved not a leaf of the trees. Some time elapsed before William recovered from his consternation. However, he compelled his trembling hands to keep firm, and cast a few bullets. At that moment a well-known church clock at a distance began to strike. At first the sound was a sound of comfort, connecting, as with the tones of some friendly voice, the human world with the dismal circle in which he stood, that else seemed cut off from it as by an impassable gulph; but the clock struck twice, thrice—here he shuddered at the rapid flight of time, for his work was not a third part advanced—then it struck a fourth time. He was appalled; every limb seemed palsied; and the mould slipped out of his nerveless hand. With the calmness of despair he listened to the clock until it completed the full hour of twelve; the knell then vibrated on the air, lingered, and died away. To sport with the solemn hour of midnight appeared too bold an undertaking even for the powers of darkness. However, he drew out his watch, looked, and behold! it was no more than half-past eleven.

Recovering his courage, and now fully steeled against all fresh illusions, he resumed his labours with energy. Profound quiet was all around him, disturbed only at intervals by the owls that made a low muttering, and now and then rattled the skulls and bones together. All at once a crashing was heard in the bushes. The sound was familiar to the experienced hunter's ears; he looked round, and, as he expected, a wild boar sprang out and rushed up to the circle. "This," thought William, "is no deception;" and he leaped up, seized his gun, and snapped it hastily at the wild beast; but no spark issued from the flint: he drew his hanger, but the bristly monster, like the carriage and horses, soared far above him into the air, and vanished.

XIII.

William, thus repeatedly baffled, now hastened to fetch up the lost time. Sixty bullets were already cast: he looked up; suddenly the clouds opened, and the moon again threw a brilliant light over the whole country. Just then a voice was heard from the depths of the forest crying out, in great agitation,—" William! William!" It was the voice of Kate. William saw her issue from the bushes, and fearfully look round her. Behind her panted the old woman, stretching her withered spidery arms after the flying girl, and endeavouring to catch hold of her floating garments. Katharine now collected the last remains of her exhausted strength for flight: at that moment the old wooden-leg stepped across her path; for an instant it checked her speed, and then the old hag caught her with her bony hands. William could contain himself no longer: he threw the mould with the last bullet out of his hands, and would have leaped out of the circle: but just then the clock struck twelve; the fiendish vision had vanished; the owls threw the skulls and bones confusedly together, and flew away; the fire went out, and William sank exhausted to the ground.

Now came up slowly a horseman upon a black horse. He stopped at the effaced outline of the magic circle, and spoke thus: " Thou hast stood the trial well; what would'st thou have of me?"

" Nothing of thee, nothing at all," said William: " what I want—I have prepared for myself."

" Aye; but with my help: therefore part belongs to me."

" By no means, by no means: I bargained for no help I summoned thee not."

The horseman laughed scornfully. " Thou art bolder," said he, " than such as thou are wont to be. Take the balls which thou hast cast; sixty for thee, three for me; the sixty go true, the three go askew: all will be plain, when we meet again."

William averted his face: " I will never meet thee again," said he—" leave me."

" Why turnest thou away?" said the stranger with a dreadful laugh: " do'st know me?"

" No, no"—said William, shuddering: " I know thee not! I wish not to know thee. Be thou who thou mayest, leave me!"

The black horseman turned away his horse, and said, with a gloomy solemnity—" Thou *do'st* know me: the very hair of thy head, which stands on end, confesses for thee that thou do'st. I am he—whom at this moment thou namest in thy heart with horror." So saying, he vanished, followed by the dreary sound of withered leaves, and by the echo of blasted boughs falling from the trees beneath which he had stood.

XIV.

" Merciful God! what has happened to you, William?" exclaimed Kate and her mother, as William returned, pale and agitated, after midnight: " you look as if fresh risen from the grave."

" Nothing, nothing," said William, " nothing but night air; the truth is, I am a little feverish."

" William, William!" said old Bertram, stepping up to him, " you can't deceive me: something has met you in the forest. Why would you not stop at home? Something has crossed you on the road, I'll swear."

William was struck with the old man's seriousness, and replied—"Well, yes; I acknowledge something *has* crossed me. But wait for nine days: before then, you know yourself that—"

"Gladly, gladly, my son," said Bertram: "and God be praised, that it is any thing of that kind which *can* wait for nine days. Trouble him not, wife; Kate, leave him at peace!—Beshrew me, but I had nearly done thee wrong, William, in my thoughts. Now, my good lad, go to bed, and rest thyself. 'Night,' says the proverb, 'is no man's friend.' But be of good cheer: the man that is in his vocation, and walks only in lawful paths, may bid defiance to the fiends of darkness and all their works."

William needed his utmost powers of dissimulation to disguise from the old man's penetration how little his suspicions had done him injustice. This indulgent affection of father Bertram, and such unshaken confidence in his uprightness, wrung his heart. He hurried to his bedroom, with full determination to destroy the accursed bullets. "One only will I keep, only one I will use," said he, holding out his supplicating hands pressed palm to palm, with bitter tears, towards heaven. "Oh let the purpose, let the purpose, plead for the offence; plead for me the anguish of my heart, and the trial which I could not bear! I will humble, I will abase myself in the sight of God: with a thousand, with ten thousand penitential acts I will wash out the guilt of my transgression. But can I, can I now go back, without making shipwreck of all things—of my happiness, my honour, my darling Kate?"

Somewhat tranquillised by this view of his own conduct,

he beheld the morning dawn with more calmness than he had anticipated.

XV.

The ducal commissioner arrived, and expressed a wish, previously to the decisive trial, of making a little hunting excursion in company with the young forester. "For," said he, "it is all right to keep up old usages; but, between ourselves, the hunter's skill is best shown in the forest. So, jump up, Mr Forester elect; and let's away to the forest!"

William turned pale, and would have made excuses; but, as these availed nothing with the commissioner, he begged, at least, that he might be allowed to stand his trial first. Old Bertram shook his head thoughtfully:—"William, William!" said he, with a deep tremulous tone. William withdrew instantly; and in a few moments he was equipped for the chase, and, with Bertram, followed the commissioner into the forest.

The old forester sought to suppress his misgivings, but struggled in vain to assume a cheerful aspect. Katharine, too, was dejected and agitated, and went about her household labours as if dreaming. "Was it not possible," she had asked her father, "to put off the trial?" "I also thought of that," replied he, and he kissed her in silence. Recovering himself immediately, he congratulated his daughter on the day—and reminded her of her bridal garland.

The garland had been locked up by old Anne in a drawer; and hastily attempting to open it, she injured the lock. A child was therefore despatched to a shop to fetch another garland for the bride. "Bring the handsomest they have," cried dame Anne after the child: but the child, in its simplicity, pitched upon that which glittered most: and this happened to be a bride's funeral garland of myrtle and the rosemary entwined with silver, which the mistress of the shop, not knowing the circumstances, allowed the child to carry off. The bride and the mother well understood the ominous import of this accident: each shuddered; and flinging her arms about the other's neck, sought to stifle her horror in a laugh at the child's blunder. The lock was now tried once more; it opened readily; the coronals were exchanged; and the beautiful tresses of Katharine were enwreathed with the blooming garland of a bride.

XVI.

The hunting party returned. The commissioner was inexhaustible in William's praise. "After such proofs of skill," said he, "it seems next to ridiculous that I should call for any other test: but to satisfy old ordinances, we are sometimes obliged to do more than is absolutely needful: and so we will despatch the matter as briefly as possible. Yonder is a dove sitting on that pillar: level, and bring her down."

"Oh! not *that*—not *that*, for God's sake, William," cried Katharine, hastening to the spot, "shoot not, for God's sake, at the dove. Ah! William, last night I dreamed that I was a white dove; and my mother put a ring about my neck; then came you, and in a moment my mother was covered with blood."

William drew back his piece which he had already levelled; but the commissioner laughed. "Eh, what?" said he, "so timorous? That will never do in a forester's wife: courage, young bride, courage! Or stay, may be the dove is a pet dove of your own?"

"No, it's not that," said Katharine, "but the dream has sadly sunk my spirits." "Well, then," said the commissioner, "if that's all, pluck 'em up again! and so fire away, Mr Forester."

He fired: and at the same instant, with a piercing shriek, fell Katharine to the ground.

"Strange girl!" said the commissioner, fancying that she had fallen only from panic, and raised her up; but a stream of blood flowed down her face; her forehead was shattered; and a bullet lay sunk in the wound.

"What's the matter?" exclaimed William, as the cry resounded behind him. He turned and saw Kate with a deathly paleness lying stretched in her blood. By her side stood the old wooden-leg, laughing in fiendish mockery, and snarling out—"Sixty go true, three go askew." In the madness of wrath, William drew his hanger, and made a thrust at the hideous creature. "Accursed devil!" cried he, in tones of despair; "is it thus thou hast deluded me?" More he had no power to utter; for he sank insensible to the ground close by his bleeding bride.

The commissioner and the priest sought vainly to speak comfort to the desolate parents. Scarce had the aged mother laid the ominous funeral garland upon the bosom of her daughter's corpse, when she wept away the last tears of her unfathomable grief. The solitary father soon followed her. William, the Fatal Marksman, wore away his days in a mad-house.

ON CHRISTIANITY AS AN ORGAN OF POLITICAL MOVEMENT

Forces, which are illimitable in their compass of effect, are often, for the same reason, obscure and untraceable in the steps of their movement. Growth, for instance, animal or vegetable—what eye can arrest its eternal increments? The hour-hand of a watch—who can detect the separate fluxions of its advance? Judging by the past, and the change which is registered between that and the present, we know that it must be awake; judging by the immediate appearances, we should say that it was always asleep. Gravitation, again, that works without holiday for ever, and searches every corner of the universe, what intellect can follow it to its fountains? And yet, shyer than gravitation, less to be counted than the fluxions of sun-dials, stealthier than the growth of a forest, are the footsteps of Christianity amongst the political workings of man. Nothing that the heart of man values is so secret; nothing is so potent.

It is *because* Christianity works so secretly, that it works so potently; it is *because* Christianity burrows and hides itself, that it towers above the clouds; and hence partly it is that its working comes to be misapprehended, or even lost out of sight. It is dark to eyes touched with the films of human frailty: but it is "dark with excessive bright."* Hence it has happened sometimes that minds of the highest order have entered into enmity with the Christian faith, have arraigned it as a curse to man, and have fought against it even upon Christian impulses (impulses of benignity that could not have had a birth except in Christianity). All comes from the labyrinthine intricacy in which the *social* action of Christianity involves itself to the eye of a contemporary. Simplicity the most absolute is reconcileable with intricacy the most elaborate. The weather—how simple would appear the laws of its oscillations, if we stood at their centre! and yet, because we do *not*, to this hour the weather is a mystery. Human health—how transparent is its economy under ordinary circumstances! abstinence and cleanliness, labour and rest, these simple laws, observed in just proportions, laws that may be engrossed upon a finger nail, are sufficient, on the whole, to maintain the equilibrium of pleasurable existence. Yet, if once that equilibrium is disturbed, where is the science oftentimes deep enough to rectify the unfathomable watch-work? Even the simplicities of planetary motions do not escape distortion: nor is it easy to be convinced that the distortion is in the eye which beholds, not in the object beheld. Let a planet be wheeling with heavenly science, upon arches of divine geometry: suddenly, to us, it shall appear unaccountably retrograde; flying when none pursues; and unweaving its own work. Let this planet in its utmost elongations travel out of sight, and for *us* its course will

* "Dark with excessive bright."—*Paradise Lost*, Book III.

become incoherent: because *our* sight is feeble, the beautiful curve of the planet shall be dislocated into segments, by a parenthesis of darkness; because our earth is in no true centre, the disorder of parallax shall trouble the laws of light; and, because we ourselves are wandering, the heavens shall seem fickle.

Exactly in the predicament of such a planet is Christianity: its motions are intermingled with other motions; crossed and thwarted, eclipsed and disguised, by countermotions in man himself, and by disturbances that man cannot overrule. Upon lines that are direct, upon curves that are circuitous, Christianity is advancing for ever; but from our imperfect vision, or from our imperfect opportunities for applying even such a vision, we cannot trace it continuously. We lose it, we regain it; we see it doubtfully, we see it interruptedly; we see it in collision, we see it in combination; in collision with darkness that confounds, in combination with cross lights that perplex. And this in part is irremediable; so that no finite intellect will ever retrace the total curve upon which Christianity has moved, any more than eyes that are incarnate will ever see God.

But part of this difficulty in unweaving the maze has its source in a misconception of the original machinery by which Christianity moved, and of the initial principle which constituted its differential power. In books, at least, I have observed one capital blunder upon the relations which Christianity bears to Paganism: and out of that one mistake grows a liability to others, upon the possible relations of Christianity to the total drama of this world. I will endeavour to explain my views. And the reader, who takes any interest in the subject, will not need to fear that the explanation should prove tedious;

for the mere want of space will put me under a coercion to move rapidly over the ground: I *cannot* be diffuse; and, as regards quality, he will find in this paper little of what is scattered over the surface of books.

I begin with this question: What do people mean in a Christian land by the word "*religion?*" My purpose is not to propound any metaphysical problem; I wish only, in the plainest possible sense, to ask, and to have an answer, upon this one point—how much is understood by that obscure term* "religion," when used by a Chris-

* "*That obscure term:*"—*i.e.*, not obscure as regards the *use* of the term, or its present value, but as regards its original *genesis*, or what in civil law is called the *deductio*. Under what angle, under what aspect or relation, to the field which it concerns did the term *religion* originally come forward? The general field overlooked by religion, is the ground which lies between the spirit of man and the supernatural world. At present, under the humblest conception of religion, the human spirit is supposed to be interested in such a field by the conscience and the nobler affections. But I suspect that originally these great faculties were absolutely excluded from the point of view. Probably the relation between spiritual *terrors* and man's power of propitiation, was the problem to which the word *religion* formed the answer. Religion meant apparently, in the infancies of the various idolatries, that *latreia*, or service of sycophantic fear, by which, as the most approved method of approach, man was able to conciliate the favour, or to buy off the malice of supernatural powers. In all Pagan nations it is probable that religion would, on the whole, be a degrading influence; although I see, even for such nations, two cases, at the least, where the uses of a religion would be indispensable—viz., for the sanction of *oaths*, and as a channel for gratitude not pointing to a human object. If so, the answer is easy: religion *was* degrading; but heavier degradations would have arisen from irreligion. The noblest of all idolatrous peoples, viz., the Romans, have left deeply scored in their very use of their word *religio* their testimony to the degradation wrought by any religion that Paganism could yield. Rarely, indeed, is this word employed by a Latin author, in speaking of an individual, without more or less of sneer. Reading that

tian? Only I am punctilious upon one demand—viz., that the answer shall be comprehensive. We are apt in such cases to answer elliptically, omitting, because silently presuming as understood between us, whatever *seems* obvious. To prevent *that*, we will suppose the question to be proposed by an emissary from some remote planet,—

---

word in a Latin book, we all try it and ring it, as a petty shopkeeper rings a half-crown, before we venture to receive it as offered in good faith and loyalty. Even the Greeks are nearly in the same *ἀπορίᾳ*, when they wish to speak of religiosity in a spirit of serious praise. Some circuitous form, commending the correctness of a man, *περὶ τὰ θεῖα, in respect of divine things*, becomes requisite; for all the direct terms, expressing the religious temper, are preoccupied by a taint of scorn. The word *ὅσιος* means *pious*—not as regards the gods, but as regards the dead; and even *εὐσεβής*, though not used sneeringly, is a world short of our word "religious." This condition of language we need not wonder at: the language of life must naturally receive, as in a mirror, the realities of life. Difficult it is to maintain a just equipoise in any moral habits, but in none so much as in habits of religious demeanour under a Pagan [that is, a degrading] religion. To be a coward is base; to be a sycophant is base; but to be a sycophant in the service of cowardice is the perfection of baseness; and yet this was the brief analysis of a devotee amongst the ancient Romans. Now, considering that the word *religion* is originally Roman [probably from the Etruscan], it seems probable that it presented the idea of religion under some one of its bad aspects. Coleridge must quite have forgotten this Paganism of the word when he suggested, as a plausible idea, that originally it had presented religion under the aspect of a coercion or restraint. Morality having been viewed as the prime restraint or obligation resting upon man, then Coleridge thought that religion might have been viewed as a *religatio*, a reiterated restraint, or secondary obligation. This is ingenious, but it will not do. It is cracked in the ring. Perhaps as many as three objections might be mustered to such a derivation; but the last of the three is conclusive. The ancients never *did* view morality as a mode of obligation: I affirm this peremptorily; and with the more emphasis, because there are great consequences suspended upon that question.

who, knowing as yet absolutely nothing of us and our intellectual differences, must insist (as *I* insist) upon absolute precision, so that nothing essential shall be wanting, and nothing shall be redundant.

What, then, is religion? Decomposed into its elements, as they are found in Christianity, how many *powers* for acting on the heart of man does, by possibility, this great agency include? According to my own view, four.* I will state them, and number them.

1*st*, A form of worship, a *cultus*.

2*dly*, An idea of God; and (pointing the analysis to Christianity in particular) an idea not purified merely from ancient pollutions, but recast and absolutely born again.

3*dly*, An idea of the relation which man occupies to God: and of this idea also, when Christianity is the religion concerned, it must be said, that it is so entirely remodelled as in no respect to resemble any element in any other religion. Thus far we are reminded of the poet's expression, "Pure religion *breathing* household laws;" that is, not *teaching* such laws, not formally *prescribing* a new economy of life, so much as *inspiring* it indirectly through a new atmosphere surrounding all objects with new attributes. But there is also in Christianity,

4*thly*, A *doctrinal* part, a part directly and explicitly occupied with *teaching;* and this divides into two great sections: *a*, A system of ethics so absolutely

---

* "*Four:*"—There are *six*, in one sense, of religion—viz., 5*thly*, corresponding moral affections; 6*thly*, a suitable life. But this applies to religion as *subjectively possessed* by a man, not to religion as *objectively contemplated*.

new as to be untranslateable* into either of the classical languages; and, β, A system of mysteries; as, for instance, the mystery of the Trinity, of the Divine Incarnation, of the Atonement, of the Resurrection, and others.

Here are great elements; and now let me ask, how many of these are found in the Heathen religion of Greece and Rome? This is an important question; it being my object to show that no religion *but* the Christian, and precisely through some one or two of its *differential* elements, could have been an organ of political movement.

Most divines who anywhere glance at this question, are here found in, what seems to me, the deepest of errors. Great theologians are they, and eminent philosophers, who have presumed that (as a matter of course) all religions, however false, are introductory to some scheme of morality, however imperfect. They grant you that the

* "*Untranslateable*:"—This is not generally perceived. On the contrary, people are ready to say, "Why, so far from it, the very earliest language in which the Gospels appeared, excepting only St Matthew's, was the Greek." Yes, reader, but *what* Greek? Had not the Greeks been, for a long time, colonising Syria under princes of Grecian blood—had not the Greek language (as a *lingua Hellenistica*) become steeped in Hebrew ideas—no door of communication could have been opened between the new world of Christian feeling, and the old world so deaf to its music. Here, therefore, we may observe two preparations made secretly by Providence for receiving Christianity and clearing the road before it—first, the diffusion of the Greek language through the whole civilised world (ἡ οἰκουμένη) some time before Christ, by which means the Evangelists found wings, as it were, for flying abroad through the kingdoms of the earth; secondly, the Hebraising of this language, by which means the Evangelists found a new material made plastic and obedient to these new ideas, which they had to build *with*, and which they had to build *upon*.

morality is oftentimes unsound; but still, they think that some morality there must have been, or else for what purpose was the religion? This I pronounce error.

All the moral theories of antiquity were utterly disjoined from religion. But this fallacy of a dogmatic or doctrinal part in Paganism is born out of Anachronism. It is the anachronism of unconsciously reflecting back upon the ancient religions of darkness, and as if essential to *all* religions, features that never were suspected as possible until they had been revealed in Christianity.* Religion, in the eye of a Pagan, had no more relation to morals than it had to shipbuilding or trigonometry. But, then, why was religion honoured amongst Pagans? How did it ever arise? What was its object? Object! it *had* no object; if by this you mean ulterior object. Pagan religion arose in no motive, but in an impulse. Pagan religion aimed at no distant prize ahead: it fled from a danger immediately behind. The gods of the Pagans were wicked natures; but they were natures to be feared, and to be propitiated; for they were fierce, and they were moody, and (as regarded man who had no wings) they were powerful. Once accredited as facts, the Pagan gods could not be regarded as other than terrific facts; and thus it was, that in terror, blind terror, as against power in the hands of divine wickedness, arose the ancient religions of Paganism. Because the gods were wicked, man was religious; because Olympus was cruel, earth trembled; because the divine beings were the most lawless of

* "*In Christianity:*"—Once for all, to save the trouble of continual repetitions, understand Judaism to be commemorated jointly with Christianity—the dark root together with the golden fruitage—whenever the nature of the case does not presume a contradistinction of the one to the other

Thugs, the human being became the most abject of sycophants.

Had the religions of Paganism arisen teleologically—that is, with a view to certain purposes, to certain final causes ahead; had they grown out of *forward*-looking views, contemplating, for instance, the furthering of civilisation, or contemplating some interests in a world beyond the present, there would probably have arisen, concurrently, a section in all such religions, dedicated to positive instruction. There would have been a *doctrinal* part. There might have been interwoven with the ritual of worship a system of economics, or a code of civil prudence, or a code of health, or a theory of morals, or even a secret revelation of mysterious relations between man and the Deity: all which existed in Judaism. But, as the case stood, this was impossible. The gods were mere odious facts, like scorpions or rattlesnakes, having no moral aspects whatever; public nuisances; and bearing no relation to man but that of capricious tyrants. First arising upon a basis of terror, these gods never subsequently enlarged that basis, nor sought to enlarge it. All antiquity contains no hint of a possibility that *love* could arise, as by any ray mingling with the sentiments in a human creature towards a divine one; not even sycophants ever pretended to *love* the gods.

Under this original peculiarity of Paganism, there arose two consequences, which I will mark by the Greek letters α and β. The latter I will notice in its order, first calling the reader's attention to the consequence marked α, which is this:—in the full and profoundest sense of the word *believe*, the Pagans could not be said to believe in *any* gods; but, in the ordinary sense, they did, and do, and must believe in *all* gods. As this proposition will startle some readers, and is yet closely involved in the main truth which I am now pressing—viz., the meaning and effect of a simple *cultus*, as distinguished from a high doctrinal religion, let us seek an illustration from our Indian empire. The Christian missionaries from home, when first opening their views to Hindoos, describe themselves as labouring to prove that Christianity is a *true* religion, and as either asserting, or leaving it to be inferred, that, on that assumption, the Hindoo religion is a false one. But the poor Hindoo never dreamed of doubting that the Christian was a true religion; nor will he at all infer, from your religion being true, that his own must be false. Both are true, he thinks: all religions are true; all gods are true gods; and all are *equally* true. Neither can he understand what you mean by a false religion, or how a religion *could* be false; and he is perfectly right. Wherever religions consist only of a worship, as the Hindoo religion does, there can be no competition amongst them as to truth. *That* would be an absurdity, not less nor other than it would be for a Prussian to denounce the Austrian emperor, or an Austrian to denounce the Prussian king, as a false sovereign. False! *How* false? In what sense false? Surely not as non-existing. But, at least (the reader will reply), if the religions contradict each other, one of them *must* be false. Yes; but *that* is impossible. Two religions cannot contradict each other, where both contain only a *cultus*: they could come into collision only by means of a doctrinal or directly affirmative part, like those of Christianity and Mohammedanism. But this part is what no idolatrous religion ever had, or will have. The reader must not understand me to mean that, merely as a compromise of courtesy, two professors of different idolatries would agree to recognise each other. Not at all. The truth of one does not imply the falsehood of the other. Both are true as *facts:* neither can be false in any higher sense, because neither makes any pretence to truth doctrinal.

This distinction between a religion having merely a worship, and a religion having also a body of doctrinal truth, is familiar to the Mohammedans; and they convey the distinction by a very appropriate expression. Those majestic religions (as they esteem them) which rise above the mere pomps and tympanies of ceremonial worship, they denominate "*religions of the book.*" There are of such religions three—viz., Judaism, Christianity, and Islamism. The first builds upon the Law and the Prophets, or perhaps sufficiently upon the Pentateuch; the second upon the Gospel; the last upon the Koran. No other religion can be said to rest upon a book, or to need a book, or even to admit of a book. For we must not be duped by the case where a lawgiver attempts to connect his own human institutes with the venerable sanctions of a national religion, or the case where a learned antiquary unfolds historically the record of a vast mythology. Heaps of such cases (both law and mythological records) survive in the Sanscrit, and in other Pagan languages. But these are books which build upon the religion, not books upon which the religion is built. If a religion consists only of a ceremonial worship, in that case there can be no opening for a book; because the forms and details publish themselves daily in the celebration of the worship, and are traditionally preserved from age to age, without dependence on a book. But if a religion has a doctrine, this implies a revelation or message from Heaven, which cannot in any other way secure the transmission of this message to future generations than by causing it to be registered in a book. A book, therefore, will be convertible with a doctrinal religion:—no book, no doctrine; and, again, no doctrine, no book.

Upon these principles we may understand that second consequence (marked β) which has perplexed many men—viz., why it is that the Hindoos in our own times, but, equally, why it is that the Greek and Roman idolaters of antiquity, never proselytised; no, nor could have viewed such an attempt as rational. Naturally, if a religion is doctrinal, any truth which it possesses, as a secret deposit consigned to its keeping by a revelation, must be equally valid for one man as for another, without regard to race or nation. For a *doctrinal* religion, therefore, to proselytise, is no more than a duty of consistent humanity. You, the professors of that religion, possess the medicinal fountains. You will not diminish your own share by imparting to others. What churlishness if you should grudge to others a health which does not interfere with your own! Christians, therefore, Mohammedans, and Jews originally, in proportion as they were sincere and conscientious, have always invited, or even forced, the unbelieving to their own faith: nothing but accidents of situation, local or political, have disturbed this effort. But, on the other hand, for a mere "*cultus*" to attempt conversions is nonsense. An ancient Roman could have had no motive for bringing you over to the worship of Jupiter Capitolinus; nor you any motive for going. "Surely, poor man," he would have said, "you have some god of your own, who will be quite as good for *your* countrymen as Jupiter for mine. But if you have *not*, really I am sorry for your case; and a very odd case it is: but I don't see how it could be improved by talking nonsense. You cannot beneficially, you cannot rationally, worship a tutelary Roman deity, unless in the character of a Roman; and a Roman you may become, legally and politically. Being such, you will participate in all advantages, if any there *are* of our national religion; and, without needing a process of conversion, either in substance or in form. *Ipso facto*, and without any separate choice of your own, on becoming a Roman citizen, you become a party to the Roman worship." For an idolatrous religion to proselytise would therefore be not only useless, but unintelligible.

Now, having explained *that* point, which is a great step towards the final object of my paper—viz., the investigation of the reason why Christianity *is*, which no Pagan religion ever *has* been, an organ of political movement, I will go on to review rapidly those four constituents of a religion, as they are realised in Christianity, for the purpose of contrasting them with the false shadows, or even blank negations, of these constitutents in Pagan idolatries.

First, then, as to the CULTUS, or form of the national worship:—In our Christian ritual I recognise these separate acts; viz. A, an act of Praise; B, an act of Thanksgiving; C, an act of Confession; D, an act of Prayer. In A we commemorate with adoration the *general* perfections of the Deity. There, all of us have an equal interest. In B, we commemorate with thankfulness those special qualities of the Deity, or those special manifestations of them, by which we, the individual worshippers, have recently benefited. In C, by upright confession, we deprecate. In D, we pray, or ask for the things which we need. Now, in the *cultus* of the ancient Pagans, B and C (the second act and the third) were wanting altogether. No thanksgiving ever ascended, on his own account, from the lips of an individual; and the state thanksgiving for a triumph of the national armies was but a mode of ostentatiously publishing the news. As to C, it is scarcely necessary to say that this was wanting, when I mention that penitential feelings were unknown amongst the ancients, and had no name; for *pœnitentia** means *regret*, not *penitence;* and *me pœnitet hujus facti* means, "I rue this act in its consequences," not "I repent of this act for its moral nature." A and D, the first act and the last, *appear* to be present; but are so most imperfectly. When "God is praised aright," praised by means of such deeds or such attributes as express a Divine nature, we recognise one great function of a national worship—not otherwise. This, however, we must overlook and pardon, as being a fault essential to the religion: the poor creatures did the best they could to praise their god, lying under the curse of gods so thoroughly depraved. But in D, the case is different. Strictly speaking, the ancients never prayed; and it may be doubted whether D approaches so near to what *we* mean by prayer, as even by a mockery. You read of *preces*, of *apai*, &c., and you are desirous to believe that Pagan supplications were not *always* corrupt. It is too shocking to suppose, in thinking of nations idolatrous, yet noble, that never *any* pure act of approach to the heavens took place on the part of man; that *always* the intercourse was corrupt; *always* doubly corrupt; that eternally the god was bought, and the votary was sold. Oh weariness of man's spirit before that unresting mercenariness in high places, which, neither when his race clamoured for justice, nor when it languished for pity, would listen without hire!

* In Greek, there is a word for repentance, but not until it had been re-baptised into a Christian use. *Metanoia*, however, is not that word: it is grossly to defeat the profound meaning of the New Testament, if John the Baptist is translated as though summoning the world to *repentance;* it was not *that* to which he summoned them.

How gladly would man turn away from his false rapacious divinities to the godlike human heart, that so often would yield pardon *before* it was asked, and for the thousandth time that would give without a bribe! In strict propriety, as my reader knows, the classical Latin word for a prayer is *votum;* it was a case of contract, of mercantile contract; of that contract which the Roman law expressed by the formula—*Do ut des.* Vainly you came before the altars with empty hands. "But *my* hands are pure." Pure, indeed! would reply the scoffing god; let me see what they contain. It was exactly what you daily read in morning papers, viz.,—that, in order to appear effectually before that Olympus in London which rains rarities upon us poor abject creatures in the provinces, you must enclose "an order on the Post-office or a reference." It is true that a man did not always register his *votum* (the particular offering which he vowed on the condition of receiving what he asked) at the moment of asking. Ajax, for instance, prays for light in the *Iliad,* and he does not then and there give either an order or a reference. But you are much mistaken if you fancy that even light was to be had *gratis.* It would be "carried to account." Ajax would be "debited" with that "advance."

Yet, when it occurs to a man that, in this *Do ut des,* the general *Do* was either a temple or a sacrifice, naturally it occurs to ask what *was* a sacrifice? I am afraid that the dark murderous nature of the Pagan gods is here made apparent. Modern readers, who have had no particular reason for reflecting on the nature and management of a sacrifice, totally misconceive it. They have a vague notion that the slaughtered animal was roasted, served up on the altars as a banquet to the gods; that these gods by some representative ceremony "made believe" to eat it; and that finally (as dishes that had now become hallowed to divine use), the several joints were disposed of in some mysterious manner: burned, suppose, or buried under the altars, or committed to the secret keeping of rivers. Nothing of the sort: when a man made a sacrifice, the meaning was, that he gave a dinner. And not only was every sacrifice a dinner-party, but every dinner-party was a sacrifice. This was strictly so in the good old ferocious times of Paganism, as may be seen in the *Iliad:* it was not said, "Agamemnon has a dinner-party to-day," but "Agamemnon sacrifices to Apollo." Even in Rome, to the last days of Paganism, it is probable that some slight memorial continued to connect the dinner-party [*cœna*] with a divine sacrifice; and thence partly arose the sanctity of the hospitable board; but to the east of the Mediterranean the full ritual of a sacrifice must have been preserved in all banquets, long after it had faded to a form in the less superstitious West. This we may learn from that point of casuistry treated by St Paul—whether a Christian might lawfully eat of things offered to idols. The question was most urgent; because a Christian could not accept an invitation to dine with a Grecian fellow-citizen who still adhered to Paganism, *without* eating things offered to idols. The whole banquet was dedicated to an idol. If he would not take *that*, he must continue *impransus*. Consequently the question virtually amounted to this: were the Christians to separate themselves altogether from those whose interests were in so many ways entangled with their own, on the single consideration that these persons were heathens? To refuse their hospitalities *was* to separate, and with a hostile expression of feeling. That would be to throw hinderances in the way of Christianity: the religion could not spread rapidly under such repulsive prejudices; and dangers, that it became un-Christian to provoke, would thus multiply against the infant faith. This being so, and as the gods were really the only parties invited who got nothing at all of the banquet, it becomes a question of some interest,—what *did* they get? They were merely mocked, if they had no compensatory interest in the dinner! For surely it was an inconceivable mode of honouring Jupiter, that you and I should eat a piece of roast beef, leaving to the god's share only the mockery of a *Barmecide* invitation, assigning him a chair which everybody knew that he would never fill, and a plate which might as well have been filled with warm water? Jupiter got *something*, be assured; and what *was* it? This it was,—the luxury of inhaling the groans, the fleeting breath, the palpitations, the agonies, of the dying victim. This was the dark interest which the wretches of Olympus had in human invitations to dinner; and it is too certain, upon comparing facts and dates, that, when left to their own choice, the gods had a preference for *man* as the victim. All things concur to show, that precisely as you ascend above civilisation, which continually increased the limitations upon the gods of Olympus, precisely as you go back to that gloomy state in which their true propensities had power to reveal themselves, was man the genuine victim for *them*, and the dying anguish of man the best "nidor" that ascended from earthly banquets to *their* nostrils. Their stern eyes smiled darkly upon the throbbings of tortured flesh, as in Moloch's ears dwelt like music the sound of infants' wailings.

Secondly, as to the birth of a new idea respecting the nature of God:—It may not have occurred to every reader, but none will perhaps object to it, when once suggested to his consideration, that, as is the god of any nation, such will be that nation. God, however falsely conceived of by man, even though splintered into fragments by Polytheism, or disfigured by the darkest mythologies, is still the greatest of all objects offered to human contemplation. Man, when thrown upon his own delusions, may have raised to himself, or may have adopted from others, the very falsest of ideals, as the true image and reflection of what he calls god. In his lowest condition of darkness, terror may be the moulding principle for spiritual conceptions; power, the engrossing attribute which he ascribes to his deity; and this power may be hideously capricious, or associated with vindictive cruelty. It may even happen that his standard of what is highest in the divinity should be capable of falling greatly below what an enlightened mind would figure to itself as lowest in man. A more shocking monument, indeed, there cannot be than this, of the infinity by which man may descend below his own capacities of grandeur: the gods, in some systems of religion, have been such and so monstrous by excesses of wickedness, as to insure, if annually one hour of periodical eclipse should have left them at the mercy of man, a general rush from their own worshippers for strangling them as mad dogs. Hypocrisy, the cringing of sycophants, and the credulities of fear, united to conceal this misotheism; but we may be sure that it was widely diffused through the sincerities of the human heart. An intense desire for kicking Jupiter, or for hanging him, if found convenient, must have lurked in the honourable Roman heart, before the sincerity of human nature could have extorted upon the Roman stage a public declaration, that their supreme gods were capable of enormities which a poor, unpretending human creature [homuncio] would have disdained. Many times the ideal of the divine nature, as adopted by Pagan races, fell under the contempt, not only of men superior to the national superstition, but of men partaking in that superstition. Yet, with all those drawbacks, an ideal *was* an ideal. The being set up for adoration as god, *was* such upon the whole to the worshipper; since, if there had been any higher mode of excellence conceivable for *him*, that higher mode would have virtually become his deity. It cannot be doubted, therefore, that the nature of the .national divinities indicated the qualities which ranked highest in the national estimation; and that being contemplated continually in the spirit of veneration, these qualities must have worked an extensive conformity to their own standard. The mythology sanctioned by the ritual of public worship, the features of moral nature in the gods distributed through that mythology, and sometimes commemorated by gleams in that ritual, domineered over the popular heart, even in those cases where the religion had been a derivative religion, and not originally moulded by impulses breathing from the native disposition. So that, upon the whole, such as were the gods of a nation, such was the nation: given the particular idolatry, it became possible to decipher the character of the idolaters. Where Moloch was worshipped, the people would naturally be found cruel; where the Paphian Venus, it could not be expected that they should escape the taint of a voluptuous effeminacy.

Against this principle there could have been no room for demur, were it not through that inveterate prejudice besieging the modern mind,—as though all religion, however false, implied some scheme of morals connected with it. However imperfectly discharged, one function even of the Pagan priest (it is supposed) must have been,—to guide, to counsel, to exhort, as a teacher of morals. And had *that* been so, the practical precepts, and the moral commentary coming after even the grossest forms of worship, or the most revolting mythological legends, might have operated to neutralise their horrors, or even to allegorise them into better meanings. Lord Bacon, as a trial of skill, has attempted something of that sort in his *Wisdom of the Ancients.* But all this is modern refinement, either in the spirit of playful ingenuity or of ignorance. I have said sufficiently that there was no *doctrinal* part in the religion of the Pagans. There was a *cultus*, or ceremonial worship: *that* constituted the sum-total of religion in the idea of a Pagan. There was a necessity, for the sake of guarding its traditional usages, and upholding and supporting its pomp, that official persons should preside in this *cultus: that* constituted the duty of the priest. Beyond this ritual of public worship, there was nothing at all; nothing to believe, nothing to understand. A set of legendary tales undoubtedly there was, connected with the mythologic history of each separate deity. But in what sense you understood these, or whether you were at all acquainted with them, was a matter of indifference to the priests; since many of these legends were variously related, and some had apparently been propagated in ridicule of the gods rather than in their honour.

With Christianity a new scene was opened. In this religion the *cultus*, or form of worship, was not even the primary business, far less was it the exclusive business. The worship flowed as a direct consequence from the new idea exposed of the divine nature, and from the new idea of man's relations to this nature. Here were suddenly unmasked great doctrines, truths positive and directly avowed; whereas, in Pagan forms of religion, any notices which then were, or seemed to be, of circumstances surrounding the gods, related only to matters of fact or accident, such as that a particular god was the son or the nephew of some other god; a truth, if it *were* a truth, wholly impertinent to any interest of man.

As there are some important truths, dimly perceived or not at all, lurking in the idea of God—an idea too vast to be navigable as yet by the human understanding, yet here and there to be coasted—I wish at this point to direct the reader's attention upon a passage which he may happen to remember in Sir Isaac Newton: the passage occurs at the end of the *Optics*, and the exact expressions I do not remember; but the sense is what I am going to state: Sir Isaac is speaking of God; and he takes occasion to say, that God is not good, but goodness; is not holy, but holiness; is not infinite, but infinity. This, I apprehend, will have struck many readers as merely a rhetorical *bravura;* sublime, perhaps, and fitted to exalt the feeling of awe connected with so unapproachable a mystery, but otherwise not throwing any new light upon the darkness of the idea as a problem before the intellect. Yet indirectly perhaps it *does*, when brought out into its latent sense by placing it in juxtaposition with Paganism. If a philosophic theist, who is also a Christian, or who (*not* being a Christian) has yet by his birth and breeding become saturated with Christian ideas and feelings,* attempts to realise the idea of supreme

* "*Not being a Christian, has yet become saturated with Christian ideas:*"—This case is far from uncommon; and undoubtedly, from having too much escaped observation, it has been the cause of much error. Poets I could mention, if it were not invidious to do so, who, whilst composing in a spirit of burning enmity to the Christian faith, yet rested for the very sting of their pathos upon

Deity, he becomes aware of a double and contradictory movement in his own mind whilst striving towards that result. He demands, in the first place, something in the highest degree generic; and yet again in the opposite direction, something in the highest degree individual; he demands on the one path a vast ideality, and yet on the other in union with a determinate personality. He must not surrender himself to the first impulse, else he is betrayed into a mere *anima mundi:* he must not surrender himself to the second, else he is betrayed into something merely human. This difficult antagonism of what is most and what is least generic, must be maintained, otherwise the idea, the possible idea, of that august unveiling which takes place in the Judaico-Christian God, is absolutely in clouds. Now, this antagonism utterly collapses in Paganism. And to a philosophic apprehension, this peculiarity of the heathen gods is more shocking and fearful than what at first sight had seemed most so. When a man pauses for the purpose of attentively reviewing the Pantheon of Greece and Rome, what strikes him at the first with most depth of impression and with most horror is, the *wickedness* of this Pantheon. And he observes with surprise that this wickedness, which is at a furnace-heat in the superior gods, becomes fainter and paler as you descend. Amongst

---

ideas that but for Christianity could never have existed. Translators there have been, English, French, German, of Mohammedan books, who have so coloured the whole vein of thinking with sentiments peculiar to Christianity, as to draw from a reflecting reader the exclamation, "If this can be indeed the product of Islamism, wherefore should Christianity exist?" If thoughts so divine can indeed belong to a false religion, what more could we gain from a true one?

the semi-deities, such as the Oreads or Dryads, the Nereids or Naiads, he feels not at all offended. The odour of corruption, the *sæva mephitis*, has by this time exhaled. The uproar of eternal outrage has ceased. And these gentle divinities, if too human and too beset with infirmities, are not impure, and not vexed with ugly appetites, nor instinct of quarrel: they are tranquil as are the hills and the forests; passionless as are the seas and the fountains which they tenant. But, when he ascends to the *dii majorum gentium*, to those twelve gods of the supreme house, who may be called, in respect of rank, the Paladins of the classical Pantheon, secret horror comes over him at the thought that demons, reflecting the worst aspects of brutal races, ever *could* have levied worship from his own. It is true they do so no longer as regards *our* planet. But what *has* been apparently *may* be. God made the Greeks and Romans of one blood with himself; he cannot deny that *intellectually* the Greeks—he cannot deny that *morally* the Romans—were amongst the foremost of human races; and he trembles in thinking that abominations, whose smoke ascended through so many ages to the *supreme* heavens, may, or might, so far as human resistance is concerned, again become the law for the noblest of his species. A deep feeling, it is true, exists latently in human beings of something perishable in evil. Whatsoever is founded in wickedness, according to a deep misgiving dispersed amongst men, must be tainted with corruption. *There* might seem consolation; but a man who reflects is not quite so sure of *that*. As a commonplace resounding in schools, it may be justly current amongst us, that what is evil by nature or by origin must be transient. But *that* may be because evil in all human things is partial, is heterogeneous; evil mixed with good; and the two natures, by their mutual enmity, must enter into a collision which may possibly guarantee the final destruction of the whole compound. Such a result may not threaten a nature that is purely and totally evil, that is *homogeneously* evil. Dark natures there may be, whose *essence* is evil, that may have an abiding root in the system of the universe not less awfully exempt from change than the mysterious foundations of God.

This is dreadful. Wickedness that is immeasurable, in connection with power that is superhuman, appals the imagination. Yet this is a combination that might easily have been conceived; and a wicked god still commands a mode of reverence. But that feature of the Pagan Pantheon which I am contrasting with this—viz., that no Pagan deity is an *abstraction*, but a vile *concrete*, impresses myself with a subtler sense of horror; because it blends the hateful with a mode of the ludicrous. For the sake of explaining myself to the non-philosophic reader, I beg him to consider what is the sort of feeling with which he regards an ancient river-god, or the presiding nymph of a fountain. The impression which he receives is pretty much like that from the monumental figure of some allegoric being, such as Faith or Hope, Fame or Truth. He hardly believes that the most superstitious Grecian seriously believed in such a being as a distinct personality. He feels convinced that the sort of personal existence ascribed to such an abstraction, as well as the human shape, are merely modes of representing and drawing into unity a variety of phenomena and agencies that seem *one*, by means of their unintermitting continuity, and because they tend to one common purpose. Now, from such a symbolic god as this let him pass to

Jupiter or Mercury, and instantly he becomes aware of a revolting individuality. He sees before him the opposite pole of deity. The river-god had too little of a concrete character. Jupiter has nothing else. In Jupiter you read no incarnation of any abstract quality whatever: he represents nothing whatever in the metaphysics of the universe. Except for the accident of his power, he is merely a man. He has a *character*, that is, a tendency or determination to this quality or that in excess; whereas a nature truly divine must be *in equilibrio* as to all qualities, and comprehend them all, in the way that a *genus* comprehends the subordinate *species*. He has even a personal history; he has passed through certain adventures, faced certain dangers, and survived hostilities that, at one time, were doubtful in their issue. No trace, in short, appears, in any Grecian god, of the generic. Whereas we, in our Christian ideas of God, unconsciously, and without thinking of Sir Isaac Newton, realise Sir Isaac's conceptions. We think of Him as having a sort of allegoric generality, liberated from the bonds of the individual; and yet, also, as the most awful among natures, having a conscious personality. He is diffused through all things, present everywhere, and yet not the less present locally. He is at a distance unapproachable by finite creatures; and yet, without any contradiction (as the profound St Paul observes), "not very far" from every one of us. And I will venture to say that many a poor old woman has, by virtue of her Christian innoculation, Sir Isaac's great idea lurking in her mind; as, for instance, in relation to any of God's attributes; suppose holiness or happiness, she feels (though analytically she could not explain) that God is not holy or is not happy by way of participation, after the manner of other beings—

that is, He does not draw happiness from a fountain separate and external to Himself, and common to other creatures, He drawing more and they drawing less; but that He Himself *is* the Fountain: that no other being can have the least proportion of either one or the other but by drawing from that Fountain; that as to all other good gifts, that as to life itself, they are, in man, not on any separate tenure, not primarily, but derivatively, and only in so far as God enters into the nature of man; that "we live and move" only so far and so long as the incomprehensible union takes place between the human spirit and the fontal abyss of the Divine. In short, here, and here only, is found the outermost expansion, the centrifugal, of the τὸ catholic, united with the innermost centripetal of the personal consciousness. Had, therefore, the Pagan gods been less detestable, neither impure nor malignant, they could not have won a salutary veneration—being so merely concrete individuals.

Next, it must have degraded the gods (and have made them instruments of degradation for man) that they were, one and all, incarnations; not, as even the Christian God is, for a transitory moment and for an eternal purpose; but essentially and by overruling necessity. The Greeks could not conceive of spirituality. Neither can *we*, metaphysically, assign the conditions of the spiritual; but practically, we all feel and represent to our own minds the agencies of God, as liberated from bonds of space and time, of flesh and of resistance. This the Greeks could *not* feel, could *not* represent. And the only advantage which the gods enjoyed over the worm and the grub was, that they (or at least the Paladins amongst them—the twelve supreme gods) could pass fluently from one incarnation to another.

Thirdly, out of that essential bondage to flesh arose a dreadful suspicion of something worse: in what relation did the Pagan gods stand to the abominable phenomenon of death? It is not by uttering pompous flatteries of ever-living and *αμβροτος αει*, &c., that a poet could intercept the searching jealousies of human penetration. These are merely oriental forms of compliment. And here, by the way, as elsewhere, we find Plato vehemently confuted; for it was the undue exaltation of the gods, and not their degradation, which must be ascribed to the frauds of poets. Tradition, and no poetic tradition, absolutely pointed to the grave of more gods than one. But, waiving all *that* as liable to dispute, one thing we know, from the ancients themselves, as open to no question, that all the gods were *born;* were born infants; passed through the stages of helplessness and growth; from all which the inference was but too fatally obvious. Besides, there were grandfathers, and even great-grandfathers in the Pantheon: some of these were confessedly superannuated; nay, some had disappeared. Even men, who knew but little of Olympian records, knew this at least for certain, that more than one dynasty of gods had passed over the golden stage of Olympus, had made their *exit*, and were hurrying onward to oblivion. It was matter of notoriety, also, that all these gods were and had been liable to the taint of sorrow for the death of their earthly children (as the Homeric Jupiter for Sarpedon, Thetis for Achilles, Calliope, in Euripides, for her blooming Rhesus); all were liable to fear; all to physical pain; all to anxiety; all to the indefinite menaces of a danger* not measurable. Look

* "*Danger not measurable:*"—It must not be forgotten that all the superior gods passed through an infancy (as Jove, &c.), or even

ing backwards or looking forwards, the gods beheld enemies that attacked their existence, or modes of decay (known and unknown) which gnawed at their roots. All this I take the trouble to insist upon: not as though it could be worth any man's trouble, at this day, to expose (on its own account) the frailty of the Pantheon, but with a view to the closer estimate of the Divine idea amongst men, and by way of contrast to the power of that idea under Christianity: since I contend that, such as is the God of every people, such, in the corresponding features of character, will be that people. If the god (like Moloch) is fierce, the people will be cruel; if (like Typhon) a destroying energy, the people will be gloomy; if (like the Paphian Venus) libidinous, the people will be voluptuously effeminate. When the gods are perishable, man cannot have the grandeurs of his nature developed; when the shadow of death sits upon the highest of what man represents to himself as celestial, essential blight will sit for ever upon human aspirations. One thing only remains to be added on this subject: why were not the ancients more profoundly afflicted by the treacherous gleams of mortality in their gods? How was it that they could forget, for a moment, a revelation so full of misery? Since not only the character of man partly depended upon the quality of his god, but also, and *à fortiori*, his destiny upon the destiny of his god. But the reason of his indifference to the divine mortality was,—because, *at any rate*, the Pagan man's connection with the gods terminated at his own death. Even selfish men would reconcile themselves

---

an adolescence (as Bacchus), or even a maturity (as the majority of Olympus during the insurrection of the Titans); surrounded by perils that required not strength only, but artifice, and even abject self-concealment, to evade.

to an earthquake which should swallow up all the world; and the most unreasonable man has professed his readiness, at all times, to die with a dying universe,—*mundo secum per eunte, mori*.

III. But, *thirdly*, the gods being such, in what relation to them did man stand? It is a fact hidden from the mass of the ancients themselves, but sufficiently attested, that there was an ancient and secret enmity between the whole family of the gods and the human race. This is confessed by Herodotus as a persuasion spread through some of the nations amongst which he travelled: there was a sort of truce, indeed, between the parties; temples, with their religious services, and their votive offerings, recorded this truce. But below all these appearances lay deadly enmity, to be explained only by one who should know the mysterious history of both parties from the eldest times. It is extraordinary, however, that Herodotus should rely, for this account, upon the belief of distant nations, when the same belief was so deeply recorded amongst his own countrymen in the sublime story of Prometheus. Much* of the sufferings endured by Prometheus was on account of man, whom he had befriended; and, *by* befriending, had defeated the malignity of Jove. According to some, man was even created by Prometheus; but no accounts, until lying Platonic philosophers arose, in far later times, represented man as created by Jupiter.

Now let us turn to Christianity; pursuing it through the functions which it exercises in common with Paganism, and also through those which it exercises separately and incommunicably.

* "*Much*,"—not all: for part was due to the obstinate concealment from Jupiter, by Prometheus, of the danger which threatened his throne in a coming generation.

I. As to the *Idea of God*,—how great was the chasm dividing the Hebrew God from all gods of idolatrous birth, and with what starry grandeur this revelation of *Supreme* Deity must have wheeled upwards into the field of human contemplation, when first surmounting the steams of earth-born heathenism, I need not impress upon any Christian audience. To their *knowledge* little could be added. Yet to *know* is not always to *feel*; and without a correspondent depth of feeling, there is in moral cases no effectual knowledge. Not the understanding is sufficient upon such ground, but that which the Scriptures in their profound philosophy entitle the "understanding heart." And perhaps few readers will have adequately appreciated the prodigious change effected in the theatre of the human spirit by the transition, sudden as the explosion of light, in the Hebrew cosmogony, when, from the caprice of a fleshly god, in one hour man mounted to a justice that knew no shadow of change; from cruelty mounted to a love which was inexhaustible; from gleams of *essential* evil, to a holiness that could not be fathomed; from a power and a knowledge, under limitations so merely and obviously* human, to the same agencies lying underneath creation, as a root below a plant. Not less awful in power was the transition from the limitations of space and time to ubiquity and eternity, from the familiar to the mysterious, from the incarnate to the spiritual. These enormous transitions were fitted to work changes of answering mag-

* "*So merely and obviously human:*"—It is a natural thought, to any person who has not explored these recesses of human degradation, that surely the Pagans must have had it in their power to invest their gods with all conceivable perfections, quite as much as we that are *not* Pagans. The thing wanting to the Pagans, he will think, was the *right:* otherwise as regarded the *power*.

nitude in the human spirit. The reader can hardly make any mistake as to this. He *must* concede the changes. What he will be likely to misconceive, unless he has reflected, is—the immensity of these changes. And another mistake, which he is even more likely to make, is this: he will imagine that a new idea, even though the idea of an object so vast as God, cannot become the ground of any revolution more than intellectual—cannot revolutionise the moral and active principles in man, consequently cannot lay the ground of any political movement. We shall see. But next, that is,—

II. Secondly, as to the idea of man's relation to God, this, were it capable of disjunction, would be even more of a revolutionary idea than the idea of God. But the one idea is enlinked with the other. In Paganism, as I have said, the higher you ascend towards the original fountains of the religion, the more you leave behind the frauds, forgeries, and treacheries of philosophy; so much the more clearly you descry the odious truth—that man stood in the relation of a superior to his gods, as respected all moral qualities of any value, but in the relation of an inferior as respected physical power. This was a position of the two parties fatal, by itself, to all grandeur of moral aspirations. Whatever was good or corrigibly bad, man saw associated with weakness; and power was sealed and guaranteed to absolute wickedness. The evil disposition in man to worship success was strengthened by this mode of superiority in the gods. Merit was disjoined from prosperity. Even merit of a lower class, merit in things morally indifferent, was not so decidedly on the side of the gods as to reconcile man to the reasonableness of their yoke. They were compelled to acquiesce in a government which they did not regard as just. The gods were stronger, but not much;

they had the unfair advantage of standing over the heads of men, and of wings for flight or for manœuvring. Yet even so, it was clearly the opinion of Homer's age, that in a fair fight, the gods might have been found liable to defeat. The gods again were generally beautiful: but not more so than the *élite* of mankind; else why did these gods, both male and female, continually persecute our race with their odious love? which love, be it observed, uniformly brought ruin upon its objects. Intellectually the gods were undoubtedly below men. They pretended to no great works in philosophy, in legislation, or in the fine arts, except only that, as to one of these arts, viz., poetry, a single god vaunted himself greatly in simple ages. But he attempted neither a tragedy nor an epic poem. Even in what he did attempt, it is worth while to follow his career. His literary fate was what might have been expected. After the Persian war, the reputation of his verses rapidly decayed. Wits arose in Athens, who laughed so furiously at his style and his metre, in the Delphic oracles, that at length some echoes of their scoffing began to reach Delphi; upon which the god and his inspired ministers became sulky, and finally took refuge in prose, as the only shelter they could think of from the caustic venom of Athenian malice.

These were the miserable relations of man to the Pagan gods. Everything, which it is worth doing at all, man could do better. Now it is some feature of alleviation in a servile condition if the lord appears by natural endowments superior to his slave; or at least it embitters the degradation of slavery if he does *not*. Greatly, therefore, must human interests have suffered had this jealous approximation of the two parties been the sole feature noticeable in the relations between them. But there was a worse. There was an original enmity between man and the Pantheon; not the sort of enmity which we Christians ascribe to our God; *that* is but a figure of speech: and even there is a derivative enmity; an enmity founded on something in man *subsequent* to his creation, and having a ransom annexed to it. But the enmity of the heathen gods was original—that is, to the very nature of man, and as though man had in some stage of his career been their rival; which indeed he was, if we adopt Milton's hypothesis of the gods as ruined angels, and of man as created to supply the vacancy thus arising in heaven.

Now, from this dreadful scheme of relations between the human and divine under Paganism, turn to the relations under Christianity. It is remarkable that even here, according to a doctrine current amongst many of the elder divines, man was naturally superior to the race of beings immediately ranking above him. Jeremy Taylor notices the obscure tradition, that the angelic order was, by original constitution, inferior to man; but this original precedency had been reversed for the present, by the fact that man, in his higher nature, was morally ruined, whereas the angelic race had not forfeited the perfection of *their* nature, though otherwise an inferior nature. Waiving a question so inscrutable as this, we know, at least, that no allegiance or homage is required from man towards this doubtfully superior race. And when man first finds himself called upon to pay tributes of this nature as to a being illimitably his superior, he is at the same moment taught by a revelation that this awful superior is the same who created him, and that, in a sense more than figurative, he himself is the child of God. There stand the two relations, as declared in Paganism and in Christianity,—both probably true. In the former, man is the essential enemy of the gods, though sheltered by some conventional arrangement; in the latter, he is the son of God. In his own image God made him; and the very central principle of his religion is, that God for a great purpose assumed his own human nature: a mode of incarnation which could not be conceivable, unless through some divine principle common to the two natures, and forming the *nexus* between them.

With these materials it is, and others resembling these, that Christianity has carried forward the work of human progression. The ethics of Christianity it was,—new ethics and unintelligible, in a degree as yet but little understood, to the old Pagan nations,—which furnished the rudder or guidance for a human revolution; but the mysteries of Christianity it was,—new Eleusinian shows, presenting God under a new form and aspect, presenting man under a new relation to God,—which furnished the oars and sails, the moving forces, for the advance of this revolution.

It was my intention to have shown how this great idea of man's relation to God, connected with the previous idea of God, had first caused the state of *slavery* to be regarded as an evil. Next, I proposed to show how *charitable institutions*, not one of which existed in Pagan ages, hospitals, and asylums of all classes, had arisen under the same idea brooding over man from age to age. Thirdly, I should have attempted to show, that from the same mighty influence had grown up a *social* influence of woman, which did not exist in Pagan ages, and will hereafter be applied to greater purposes. But, for want of room, I confine myself to saying a few words on war, and the mode in which it will be extinguished by Christianity.

WAR.—This is amongst the foremost of questions that

concern human progress, and it is one which, of all great questions (the question of slavery not excepted, nor even the question of the slave-*trade*), has travelled forward the most rapidly into public favour. Thirty years ago there was hardly a breath stirring against war, as the sole natural resource of national anger or national competition. Hardly did a wish rise, at intervals, in that direction, or even a protesting sigh, over the calamities of war. And if here and there a contemplative author uttered such a sigh, it was in the spirit of mere hopeless sorrow, that mourned over an evil apparently as inalienable from man as hunger, as death, as the frailty of human expectations. Cowper, about sixty years ago, had said—

> "War is a game which, were their subjects wise,
> Kings would not play at."

But Cowper would not have said this had he not been nearly related to the Whig house of Panshanger. Every Whig thought it a duty occasionally to look fiercely at kings, saying—"D——, who's afraid?" pretty much as a regular John Bull, in the lower classes, expresses his independence by defying the peerage.—"A lord! do you say? what care I for a lord? I value a lord no more than a button top;" whilst, in fact, he secretly reveres a lord as being usually amongst the most ancient of landed proprietors, and, secondly, amongst the richest. The scourge of kingship was what Cowper glanced at, rather than the scourge of war; and, in any case, the condition which he annexed to his suggestion of relief is too remote to furnish much consolation for cynics like myself, or the reader. If war is to cease only when subjects become wise, we need not contract the scale of our cannon-founderies until the millennium. Sixty years ago, therefore, the abolition of war looked as unprosperous a speculation as Dr Darwin's scheme for improving our British climate by hauling out all the icebergs from the polar basin in seasons when the wind sate fair for the tropics; by which means these wretched annoyers of our peace would soon find themselves in quarters too hot to hold them, and would disappear as rapidly as sugar-candy in children's mouths. Others, however, inclined rather to the Ancient Mariner's scheme, by shooting an albatross :—

> "'Twas right, said they, such birds to shoot,
> That bring the frost and snow."

Scarcely more hopeless than these crusades against frost were any of the serious plans which had then been proposed for the extirpation of war. St Pierre contributed "*son petit possible*" to this desirable end, in the shape of an essay towards the idea of a perpetual peace; Kant, the great professor of Königsberg, subscribed to the same benevolent scheme *his* little essay under the same title; and others in England subscribed a guinea each to the fund for the suppression of war. These efforts, one and all, spent their fire as vainly as Darwin spent his wrath against the icebergs: the icebergs are as big and as cold as ever; and war is still, like a basking snake, ready to rear his horrid crest on the least rustling in the forests.

But in quarters more powerful than either purses of gold or scholastic reveries, there has, since the days of Kant and Cowper, begun to gather a menacing thunder-cloud against war. The nations, or at least the great leading nations, are beginning to set their faces against it. War, it is felt, comes under the denunciation of Christianity, by the havoc which it causes amongst those who bear God's image; of political economy, by its destruction of property and human labour; of rational logic, by the frequent absurdity of its pretexts. The wrong which is put forth as the ostensible ground of the particular war is oftentimes not of a nature to be redressed by war, or is even forgotten in the course of the war and secondly, the war prevents another course which *might* have redressed the wrong—viz., temperate negotiation, or neutral arbitration. These things were always true, and indeed, heretofore, more flagrantly true: but the difference in favour of our own times is, that they are now felt to be true. Formerly the truths were seen, but not felt: they were inoperative truths, lifeless, and unvalued. Now, on the other hand, in England, America, France, societies are rising for making war upon war; and it is a striking proof of the progress made by such societies that, some two years ago, a deputation from one of them being presented to King Louis Philippe, received from him—not the sort of vague answer which might have been expected, but a sincere one, expressed in very encouraging words.* Ominous to himself this might have been thought by the superstitious, who should happen to recollect the sequel to a French king, of the very earliest movement in this direction: the great (but to this hour mysterious) design of Henry IV., in 1610, was supposed by many to be a plan of this very nature, for enforcing a general and permanent peace on

* "*Encouraging words:*"—and rather presumptuous words, if the newspapers reported them correctly: for they went the length of promising that he, separately, as King of the French, would coerce Europe into peace. But, from the known good sense of the king, it is more probable that he promised his *negative* aid,—the aid of not personally concurring to any war which might otherwise be attractive to the French government.

Christendom, by means of an armed intervention; and no sooner had it partially transpired, through traitorous evidence, or through angry suspicion, than his own assassination followed.

Shall I offend the reader by doubting, after all, whether war is not an evil still destined to survive through several centuries? Great progress has already been made. In the two leading nations of the earth, war can no longer be made with the levity which provoked Cowper's words two generations back. France is too ready to fight for mere bubbles of what she calls glory. But neither in France nor England could a war now be undertaken without a warrant from the *popular* voice. This is a great step in advance; but the final step for its extinction will be taken by a new and Christian code of international law. This cannot be consummated until Christian philosophy shall have traversed the earth, and re-organised the structure of society.

But finally, and (as regards extent, though not as regards intensity of effect) far beyond all other political powers of Christianity, is the power, the *demiurgic* power of this religion over the kingdoms of human opinion. Did it ever strike the reader, that the Greeks and Romans, although so frantically republican, and, in *some* of their institutions, so democratic, yet, on the other hand, never developed the idea of *representative* government, either as applied to legislation or to administration? The elective principle was widely used amongst them. Nay, the nicer casuistries of this principle had been latterly discussed. The separate advantages of open or of secret voting had been the subject of keen dispute in the political circles of Rome; and the art was well understood of disturbing the natural course of the public suffrage, by varying the modes of combining the voters under the different forms of the Comitia. Public authority and jurisdiction were created and modified by the elective principle; but never was this principle applied to the creation or direction of public opinion. The senate of Rome, for instance, like our own sovereign, represented the national majesty, and, to a certain degree, continued to do so for centuries after this majesty had received a more immediate representative in the person of the reigning Cæsar. The senate, like our own sovereign, represented the grandeur of the nation, the hospitality of the nation to illustrious strangers, and the gratitude of the nation in the distribution of honours. For the senate continued to be the fountain of honours, even to Cæsar himself: the titles of Germanicus, Britannicus, Dalmaticus, &c. (which may be viewed as peerages), the privilege of precedency, the privilege of wearing a laurel diadem, &c. (which may be viewed as the Garter, Bath, Thistle), all were honours conferred by the senate. But the senate, no more than our own sovereign, ever represented, by any one act or function, the public opinion. How was this? Strange, indeed, that so mighty a secret as that of delegating public opinions to the custody of elect representatives, a secret which has changed the face of the world, should have been missed by nations applying so vast an energy to the whole theory of public administration. But the truth, however paradoxical, is, that in Greece and Rome no body of public opinions existed that could have furnished a standing-ground for adverse parties, or that consequently could have required to be represented. In all the dissensions of Rome, from the secessions of the Plebs to the factions of the Gracchi, of Marius and Sylla, of Cæsar and Pompey; in all the ϛασεις of the Grecian republics,—

the contest could no more be described as a contest of opinion, than could the feuds of our buccaneers in the seventeenth century, when parting company, or fighting for opposite principles of dividing the general booty. One faction has, another sought to have, a preponderant share of power; but these struggles never took the shape, even in pretence, of differences that moved through the conflict of principles. The case was always the simple one of power matched against power, faction against faction, usage against innovation. It was not that the patricians deluded themselves by any speculative views into the refusal of intermarriages with the plebeians: it was not as upon any opinion that they maintained the contest (such as at this day divides ourselves from the French upon the question of opinion with regard to the social rank of literary men), but simply as upon a fact: they appealed to evidences, not to speculations; to usage, not to argument. They were in possession, and fought against change, not as inconsistent with a theory, but as hostility to an interest. In the contest of Cæsar with the oligarchic knavery of Cicero, Cato, and Pompey, no possible exercise of representative functions (had the people possessed them) could have been applied beneficially to the settlement of the question at issue. Law and the abuses of law, good statutes and evil customs, had equally thrown the public power into a settlement fatal to the public welfare. Not any decay of public virtue, but increase of poverty amongst the inferior citizens, had thrown the suffrages, and consequently the honours and powers of the state, into the hands of some forty or fifty houses, rich enough to bribe, and bribing systematically. Cæsar, undertaking to correct a state of disease which would else have convulsed the republic every third year by civil war, knew that no arguments could be available against a competition of mere interests. The remedy lay, not through opposition speeches in the senate, or from the rostra,—not through pamphlets or journals,—but through a course of intense cudgelling. This he happily accomplished; and by that means restored Rome for centuries,—not to the aspiring condition which she once held, but to an immunity from annual carnage, and in other respects to a condition of prosperity which, if less than during her popular state, was greater than any else attainable after that popular state had become impossible from changes in the composition of society.

Here, and in all other critical periods of ancient republics, we shall find that opinions did not exist as the grounds of feud, nor could by any dexterity have been applied to the settlement of feuds. Whereas, on the other hand, with ourselves for centuries, and latterly with the French, no public contest has arisen, or does now exist, without fighting its way through every stage of advance by appeals to public opinion. If, for instance, an improved tone of public feeling calls for a gradual mitigation of army punishments, the quarrel becomes instantly an intellectual one; and much information is brought forward which throws light upon human nature generally. But in Rome such a discussion would have been stopped summarily, as interfering with the discretional power of the Prætorium. To take the *vitis* or cane from the hands of the centurion was a perilous change; but, perilous or not, must be committed to the judgment of the particular imperator, or of his legatus. The executive business of the Roman exchequer, again, could not have been made the subject of public discussion; not only because no sufficient material for judgment could, under the want of a public press, have been gathered, except from the parties interested in all its abuses, but also because these parties (a faction amongst the equestrian order) could have effectually overthrown any counter-faction formed amongst parties not personally *affected* by the question. The Roman institution of *clientela*—which had outlived its early uses,—does anybody imagine that this was open to investigation? The influence of murderous riots would easily have been brought to bear upon it, but not the light of public opinion. Even if public opinion could have been evoked in those days, or trained to combined action, insuperable difficulties would have arisen in adjusting its force to the necessities of the Roman provinces and allies. Any arrangement that was practicable would have obtained an influence for these parties, either dangerous to the supreme section of the empire, or else nugatory for each of them selves. It is a separate consideration, that through total defect of cheap instruments for communication, whether personally or in the way of thought, public opinion must always have moved in the dark: what I chiefly assert is, that the feuds bearing at all upon public interests never *did* turn, or could have turned, upon any collation of opinions. And two things must strengthen the reader's conviction upon this point,—viz., first, that no public meetings (such as with us carry on the weight of public business throughout the empire) were ever called in Rome; secondly, that in the regular and "official" meetings of the people, no *social* interest was ever discussed, but only some *political* interest.

Now, on the other hand, amongst ourselves, every question that is large enough to engage public interest, though it should begin as a mere comparison of strength with strength, almost immediately travels forward into a comparison of rights with rights, or of duty with duty. A mere fiscal question of restraint upon importation from this or that particular quarter, passes into a question of colonial rights. Arrangements of convenience for the management of the pauper, or the debtor, or the criminal, or the war-captive, become the occasions of profound investigations into the rights of persons occupying those relations. Sanatory ordinances for the protection of public health,—such as quarantine, fever hospitals, draining, vaccination, &c.,—connect themselves, in the earliest stages of their discussion, with the general consideration of the duties which the state owes to its subjects. If education is to be promoted by public counsels, every step of the inquiry applies itself to the consideration of the knowledge to be communicated, and of the limits within which any section of religious partisanship can be safely authorised to interfere. If coercion, beyond the warrant of the ordinary law, is to be applied as a remedy for local outrages, a tumult of opinions arises instantly as to the original causes of the evil, as to the sufficiency of the subsisting laws to meet its pressure, and as to the modes of connecting enlarged powers in the magistrate with the *minimum* of offence to the general rights of the subject.

Everywhere, in short, some question of duty and responsibility arises to face us in any the smallest public interest that *can* become the subject of public opinion. Questions, in fact, that fall short of this dignity; questions that concern public convenience only, and do not wear any moral aspect, such as the bullion question, never *do* become subjects of public opinion. It cannot be said in which direction lies the bias of public opinion. In the very possibility of interesting the public judgment is involved the certainty of wearing some relation to moral principles. Hence the ardour of our public disputes; for no man views without concern a great moral principle darkened by party motives, or placed in risk by accident: hence the dignity and benefit of our public disputes; hence, also, their ultimate relation to the Christian faith. We do not, indeed, in these days, as did our homely ancestors in the sixteenth and seventeenth centuries, cite texts of Scripture as themes for senatorial commentary or *exegesis*; but the virtual reference to Scriptural principles is now a thousand times more frequent. The great principles of Christian morality are now so interwoven with our habits of thinking, that we appeal to them no longer *as* Scriptural authorities, but as the natural suggestions of a sound judgment. For instance, in the case of any wrong offered to the Hindoo races, now so entirely dependent upon our wisdom and justice, we British* immediately, by our solemnity of investigation, testify our sense of the deep responsibility to India with which our Indian supremacy has invested us. We make no mention of the Christian oracles. Yet where, then, have we learned this doctrine of far-stretching responsibility? In all Pagan systems of morality there is the vaguest and slightest appreciation of such relations as connect us with our colonies.

* "*We British*:"—It may be thought that, in the prosecution of Verres, the people of Rome acknowledged something of the same high responsibility. Not at all. The case came before Rome, not as a case of injury to a colonial child, whom the general mother was bound to protect and avenge; but as an appeal, by way of special petition, from Sicilian clients. It was no grand political movement, but simply judicial. Verres was an ill-used man, and the victim of private intrigues. Or, whatever *he* might be, Rome certainly sate upon the cause, not in any character of maternal protectress taking up voluntarily the support of the weak, but as a sheriff assessing damages in a case forced upon his court by the plaintiff.

But, from the profound philosophy of Scripture, we have learned that no relations whatever, not even those of property, can connect us with even a brute animal but that we contract concurrent obligations of justice and mercy.

In this age, then, public interests move and prosper through conflicts of opinion. Secondly, as I have endeavoured to show, public opinion cannot settle powerfully upon any question that is *not* essentially a moral question. And, thirdly, in all moral questions, we, of Christian nations, are compelled, by habit and training, as well as other causes, to derive our first principles, consciously or not, from the Scriptures. It is therefore through the *doctrinality* of our religion that we derive arms for all moral questions; and it is as moral questions that any political disputes much affect us. The daily conduct, therefore, of all great political interests throws us unconsciously upon the first principles which we all derive from Christianity. And, in this respect, we are more advantageously placed, by a very noticeable distinction, than the professors of the two other doctrinal religions. The Koran having pirated many sentiments from the Jewish and the Christian systems, could not but offer some rudiments of moral judgment; yet, because so much of these rudiments is stolen, the whole is incoherent, and does not form a *system* of ethics. In Judaism, again, the special and insulated situation of the Jews has unavoidably impressed an exclusive bias upon its principles. In both codes the rules are often of restricted and narrow application. But in the Christian Scriptures the rules are so comprehensive and large as uniformly to furnish the major proposition of a syllogism; whilst the particular act under discussion, wearing perhaps some modern name, naturally is not directly mentioned: and to bring this, in the minor proposition, under the principle contained in the major is a task left to the judgment of the inquirer in each particular case. Something is here entrusted to individual understanding; whereas in the Koran, from the circumstantiality of the rule, you are obliged mechanically to rest in the letter of the precept. The Christian Scriptures therefore, not only teach, but train the mind to habits of *self*-teaching in all moral questions, by enforcing more or less of activity in applying the rule; that is, in subsuming the given case proposed under the Scriptural principle.

Hence it is certain, and has been repeatedly illustrated, that whilst the Christian faith, in collision with others, would inevitably rouse to the most active fermentation of minds, the Mohammedan (as also doctrinal but unsystematical) would have the same effect in kind, but far feebler in degree; and an idolatrous religion would have no such effect at all. Agreeably to this scale, some years ago, a sect of reforming or fanatical Mohammedans in Bengal* commenced a persecution of the surrounding Hindoos. At length a reaction took place on the part of the idolaters; but in what temper? Bitter enough, and so far alarming as to call down a government interference with troops and artillery, but yet with no signs of *religious* retaliation. That was a principle of movement which the Hindoos could not understand: their retaliation was simply to the personal violence they had suffered. Such is the inertia of a mere *cultus*. And, in the other extreme, if we Christians, in our intercourse with both Hindoos and Mohammedans, were not sternly reined up by the vigilance of the local governments, no long time would pass before all India would be incurably convulsed by disorganising feuds.

* At Baraset, if I remember rightly.

NOTES ON GILFILLAN'S LITERARY PORTRAITS.*

GODWIN—FOSTER—HAZLITT

It is no duty of a notice so cursory to discuss Mr Godwin as a philosopher. Mr Gilfillan admits that in this character he did not earn much popularity by any absolute originality; and of such popularity as he may have snatched surreptitiously without it, clearly all must have long since exhaled before it could be possible for "a respectable person" (p. 15) to demand of Mr Gilfillan, "*Who's Godwin?*" A question which Mr Gilfillan justly thinks it possible that "some readers" of the present day (November 1845) may repeat. That is, we must presume, *not* who is Godwin the novelist? but who is Godwin the political philosopher? In that character he is now forgotten. And yet in *that* he carried one single shock into the bosom of English society, fearful but momentary, like that from the electric blow of the gymnotus; or, perhaps, the intensity of the brief panic which, fifty years ago, he impressed on the public mind, may be more adequately expressed by the case of a ship in the middle ocean sud-

* *A Gallery of Literary Portraits.* By George Gilfillan.

denly scraping with her keel a ragged rock, hanging for one moment as if impaled upon the teeth of the dreadful *sierra;* then, by the mere *impetus* of her mighty sails, grinding audibly to powder the fangs of this accursed submarine harrow, leaping into deep water again, and causing the panic of ruin to be simultaneous with the deep sense of deliverance. In the *quarto* (that is, the original) edition of his *Political Justice*, Mr Godwin advanced against thrones and dominations, powers and principalities, with the air of some Titan slinger or monomachist from Thebes and Troy, saying—"Come hither, ye wretches, that I may give your flesh to the fowls of the air." But in the second or *octavo* edition—and under what motive has never been explained—he recoiled, absolutely, from the sound himself had made: everybody else was appalled by the fury of the challenge, and, through the strangest of accidents, Mr Godwin also was appalled. The second edition, as regards principles, is not a re-cast, but absolutely a travesty of the first; nay, it is all but a palinode. In this collapse of a tense excitement I myself find the true reason for the utter extinction of the *Political Justice*, and of its author considered as a philosopher. Subsequently he came forward as a philosophical speculator in the *Enquirer* and elsewhere; but here it was always some minor question which he raised, or some mixed question, rather allied to philosophy than philosophical. As regarded the main creative *nisus* of his philosophy, it remained undeniable that, in relation to the hostility of the world, he was like one who, in some piratical ship, should drop his anchor before Portsmouth—should defy the navies of England to come out and fight, and then, whilst a thousand vessels were contending for the preference in blowing him out of the seas, should suddenly slip his cables and run.

But it is as a novelist, not as a political theorist, that Mr Gilfillan values Godwin; and specially for his novel of *Caleb Williams*. Now, if this were the eccentric judgment of one unsupported man, however able, and had received no countenance at all from others, it might be injudicious to detain the reader upon it. It happens, however, that other men of talent have raised *Caleb Williams* to a station in the first rank of novels; whilst many more, amongst whom I am compelled to class myself, can see in it no merit of any kind. A schism, which is really perplexing, exists in this particular case; and, that the reader may judge for himself, I will state the outline of the plot, out of which it is that the whole interest must be supposed to grow; for the characters are nothing, being mere generalities, and very slightly developed. Thirty-five years it is since I read the book; but the nakedness of the incidents makes them easily rememberable.—Falkland, who passes for a man of high-minded and delicate honour, but is, in fact, distinguished only by acute sensibility to the opinion of the world, receives a dreadful insult in a most public situation. It is, indeed, more than an insult, being the most brutal of outrages. In a ball-room, where the local gentry and his neighbours are assembled, he is knocked down, kicked, dragged along the floor, by a ruffian squire named Tyrrel. It is vain to resist; he himself is slightly built, and his antagonist is a powerful man. In these circumstances, and under the eyes of all the ladies in the county witnessing every step of his humiliation, no man could severely have blamed him, nor would our English law have severely punished him, if, in the frenzy of his agitation, he had seized a poker and laid his assailant dead upon the spot. Such allowance does the natural feeling of men,—such allowance does the sternness of the judgment-seat,—make for human infirmity when tried to extremity by devilish provocation. But Falkland does not avenge himself thus: he goes out, makes his little arrangements, and, at a later hour of the night, he comes by surprise upon Tyrrel, and murders him in the darkness. Here is the first vice in the story. With any gleam of generosity in his nature, no man in pursuit of vengeance would have found it in such a catastrophe. That an enemy should die by apoplexy, or by lightning, would be no gratification of wrath to an impassioned pursuer: to make it a retribution for *him*, he must himself be associated to the catastrophe in the consciousness of his victim. Falkland for some time evades or tramples on detection. But his evil genius at last appears in the shape of Caleb Williams; and the agency through which Mr Caleb accomplishes his mission is not that of any grand passion, but of vile eavesdropping inquisitiveness. Mr Falkland had hired him as an amanuensis; and in that character Caleb had occasion to observe that some painful remembrance weighed upon his master's mind; and that something or other—documents or personal memorials connected with this remembrance—were deposited in a trunk visited at intervals by Falkland. But of what nature could these memorials be? Surely Mr Falkland would not keep in brandy the gory head of Tyrrel; and anything short of *that* could not proclaim any murder at all, much less the particular murder. Strictly speaking, nothing *could* be in the trunk of a nature to connect Falkland with the murder more closely than the circumstances had already connected him; and those circumstances, as we know, had been insufficient. It puzzles one, therefore, to imagine any evidence which the trunk could yield, unless there were secreted within it some known personal property of Tyrrel's; in which case the aspiring Falkland had committed a larceny as well as a murder. Caleb, meantime, wastes no labour in hypothetic reasonings, but resolves to have ocular satisfaction in the matter. An opportunity offers: an alarm of fire is given in the day-time; and whilst Mr Falkland, with his people, is employed on the lawn manning the buckets, Caleb skulks off to the trunk; feeling, probably, that his first duty was to himself, by extinguishing the burning fire of curiosity in his own heart, after which there might be time enough for his second duty, of assisting to extinguish the fire in his master's mansion. Falkland, however, misses the absentee. To pursue him, to collar him, and, we may hope, to kick him, are the work of a moment. Had Caleb found time for accomplishing his inquest? I really forget; but no matter: either now, or at some luckier hour, he does so: he becomes master of Falkland's secret; consequently, as both fancy, of Falkland's life. At this point commences a flight of Caleb, and a chasing of Falkland, in order to watch his motions, which forms the most spirited part of the story. Mr Godwin tells us that he derived this situation, the continual flight and continual pursuit, from a South American tradition of some Spanish vengeance. Always the Spaniard was riding *in* to any given town on the road, when his destined victim was riding *out* at the other end; so that the relations of "whereabouts" were never for a moment lost: the trail was perfect. Now, this might be possible in certain countries; but in England!—heavens! could not Caleb double upon his master, or dodge round a gate (like Falkland when he murdered Mr Tyrrel), or take a headlong plunge into London, where the scent might have lain cold for forty years?* Other accidents by thousands would interrupt the chase. On the hundredth day, for instance, after the flying parties had become well known on the road, Mr Falkland would drive furiously up to some King's Head or White Lion, putting his one question to the waiter, "Where's Caleb?" And the waiter would reply, "Where's Mr Caleb, did you say, sir? Why, he went off at five by the Highflyer, booked inside the whole way to Doncaster; and Mr Caleb is now, sir, precisely forty-five miles ahead." Then would Falkland furiously demand "four horses on;" and then would the waiter plead a contested election in excuse for having no horses at all. Really, for dramatic effect, it is a pity that the tale were not translated forward to the days of railroads. Sublime would look the fiery pursuit, and the panic-stricken flight, when racing from Fleetwood to Liverpool, to Birmingham, to London; then smoking along the Great Western, where Mr Caleb's forty-five miles ahead would avail him little, to Bristol, to Exeter; thence doubling back upon London, like the steam leg in Mr H. G. Bell's admirable story.

But, after all, what was the object, and what the result of all this racing? Once I saw two young men facing each other upon a high road, but at a furlong's distance, and playing upon the foolish terrors of a young woman, by continually heading her back from one to the other, as alternately she approached towards either. Signals of some dreadful danger in the north being made by the

---

* "*Forty years:*"—so long, according to my recollection of Boswell, did Dr Johnson walk about London before he met an old Derbyshire friend, who also had been walking about London with the same punctual regularity for every day of the same forty years The *nodes* of intersection did not come round sooner.

northern man, back the poor girl flew towards the southern, who, in *his* turn, threw out pantomimic warnings of an equal danger to the south. And thus, like a tennis-ball, the simple creature kept rebounding from one to the other, until she could move no farther, through sheer fatigue; and then first the question occurred to her—What was it that she had been running from? The same question seems to have struck at last upon the obtuse mind of Mr Caleb; it was quite as easy to play the part of hunter as that of hunted game, and likely to be cheaper. He turns therefore sharp round upon his master, who in *his* turn is disposed to fly, when suddenly the sport is brought to a dead lock by a constable, who tells the murdering squire that he is "wanted." Caleb has lodged informations; all parties meet for a final "reunion" before the magistrate; Mr Falkland, oddly enough, regards himself in the light of an ill-used man; which theory of the case, even more oddly, seems to be adopted by Mr Gilfillan; but, for all that he can say, Mr Falkland is fully committed: and as laws were made for every degree, it is plain that Mr Falkland (however much of a pattern man) is in some danger of swinging. But this catastrophe is intercepted: a novelist may raise his hero to the peerage; he may even confer the Garter upon him; but it shocks against usage and courtesy that he should hang him. The circulating libraries would rise in mutiny if he did. And therefore it is satisfactory to believe (for all along I speak from memory) that Mr Falkland reprieves himself from the gallows by dying of exhaustion from his travels.

Such is the fable of *Caleb Williams*, upon which, by the way, is built, I think, Colman's drama of *The Iron Chest*. I have thought it worth the trouble (whether for the reader or for myself) of a flying abstract; and chiefly with a view to the strange collision of opinions as to the merit of the work; some, as I have said, exalting it to the highest class of novels, others depressing it below the lowest of those which achieve any notoriety. They who vote against it are in a large majority. The Germans, whose literature offers a free port to all the eccentricities of the earth, have never welcomed *Caleb Williams*. Chenier, the ruling *littérateur* of Paris, in the days of Napoleon, when reviewing the literature of his own day, dismisses Caleb contemptuously as coarse and vulgar. It is not therefore to the German taste; it is not to the French. And as to our own country, Mr Gilfillan is undoubtedly wrong in supposing that it "is in every circulating library, and needs more frequently than almost any novel to be replaced." If this were so, in presence of the immortal novels which for one hundred and fifty years have been gathering into the garners of our English literature, I should look next to see the race of men returning from venison and wheat to their primitive diet of acorns. But I believe that the number of editions yet published would at once discredit this account of the book's popularity. Neither is it likely, *à priori*, that such a popularity could arise even for a moment. The interest from secret and vindictive murder, though coarse, is undoubtedly deep. What would make us thrill in real life,—the case, for instance, of a neighbour lying under the suspicion of such a murder,—would make us thrill in a novel. But then it must be managed with art, and covered with mystery. For a long time it must continue doubtful both as to the fact, and the circumstances, and the motive. Whereas, in the case of Mr Falkland, there is little mystery of any kind; not much, and only for a short time, to Caleb; and none at all to the reader. who could have relieved the curiosity of Mr Caleb from the first, if he were placed in communication with him.

Differing so much from Mr Gilfillan as to the effectiveness of the novel, I am only the more impressed with the eloquent images and expressions by which he has conveyed his own sense of its power. Power there must be, though many of us cannot discern it, to react upon us through impressions so powerful in other minds. Some of Mr Gilfillan's impressions, as they are clothed in striking images by himself, I will here quote :—" His" (Godwin's) " heat is never that of the sun with all his beams around him; but of the round rayless orb seen shining from the summit of Mont Blanc, still and stripped in the black ether. He has more passion than imagination. And even his passion he has learned more by sympathy than by personal feeling. And amid his most tempestuous scenes you see the calm and stern eye of philosophic analysis looking on. His imagery is not copious, nor always original; but its sparseness is its strength: the flash comes sudden as the lightning. No preparatory flourish or preliminary sound; no sheets of useless splendour: each figure is a fork of fire, which strikes, and needs no second blow. Nay, often his images are singularly commonplace, and you wonder how they move you so, till you resolve this into the power of the hand which jaculates its own energy in *them*." And again, " His novels resemble the paintings of John Martin, being a gallery—nay, a world—in themselves. In both, monotony and mannerism are incessant: but the monotony is that of the sounding deep, the mannerism that of the thunderbolts of heaven. Martin might append to his one continual flash of lightning, which is present in all his pictures—now to reveal a deluge, now to garland the brow of a fiend—now to rend the veil of a temple, and now to guide the invaders through the breach of city—the words, *John Martin, his mark.* Godwin's novels are not less terribly distinguished to those who understand their cipher—the deep scar of misery branded upon the brow of the 'victim of society.'"

And as to the earliest of these novels, the *Caleb Williams*, he says, "There is about it a stronger suction and swell of interest than in any novel we know, with the exception of one or two of Sir Walter's. You are in it ere you are aware. You put your hand playfully into a child's, and are surprised to find it held in the grasp of a giant. It becomes a fascination. Struggle you may, and kick, but he holds you by his glittering eye." In reference, again, to *St Leon*, the next most popular of Godwin's novels, there is a splendid passage upon the glory and pretensions of the ancient alchemist, in the infancy of scientific chemistry. It rescues the character from vulgarity, and displays it idealised, as sometimes, perhaps, it must have been. I am sorry that it is too long for extracting; but, in compensation to the reader, I quote two very picturesque sentences, describing what, to Mr Gilfillan, appears the quality of Godwin's style:—"It is a smooth succession of short and simple sentences, each clear as crystal, and none ever distracting the attention from the subject to its own construction. It is a style in which you cannot explain how the total effect rises out of the individual parts, and which is forgotten as entirely during perusal as is the pane of glass through which you gaze at a comet or a star." Elsewhere, and limiting his remark to the style of the *Caleb Williams*, he says finely:—"The writing, though far from elegant or finished, has in parts the rude power of those sentences which criminals, martyrs, and maniacs scrawl upon their walls or windows in the eloquence of desperation."*

These things perplex me. The possibility that any individual in the minority can have regarded Godwin with such an eye seems to argue that we of the majority must be wrong. Deep impressions seem to justify themselves. *We* may have failed to perceive things which *are* in the object; but it is not so easy for others to perceive things which are *not;* or, at least, hardly in a case like this, where (though a minority) these "others" still exist in number sufficient to check and to confirm each other. On the other hand, Godwin's name seems sinking out of remembrance; and he is remembered less by the novels that succeeded, or by the philosophy that he abjured, than as the man that had Mary Wolstonecraft for his wife, Mrs Shelley for his daughter, and the immortal Shelley as his son-in-law.

JOHN FOSTER.

Mr Gilfillan perhaps overrates the power of this essayist, and the hold which he has upon the public mind. It is singular, meantime, that whatever might be its degree, much or little, originally his influence was due to an accident of position which in some countries would have tended to destroy it. He was a dissenter. Now, in England, *that* sometimes operates as an advantage. To dissent from the established form of religion, which could not affect the value of a writer's speculations, may easily become the means of diffusing their reputation, as well as

* "*Desperation:*"—Yet, as *martyrs* are concerned in the picture, it ought to have been said, "of desperation and of farewell to earth," or something equivalent.

of facilitating their introduction. And in the following way: The great mass of the reading population are absolutely indifferent to such deflexions from the national standard. The man, suppose, is a baptist: but to be a baptist is still to be a Protestant, and a Protestant agreeing with his countrymen in everything essential to purity of life and faith. So far there is the most entire neutrality in the public mind, and readiness to receive any impression which the man's powers enable him to make. There is, indeed, so absolute a carelessness for all inoperative shades of religious difference lurking in the background, that even the ostentatiously liberal hardly feel it a case for parading their liberality. But, on the other hand, his own sectarian party are as energetic to push him forward as all others are passive. They favour him as a brother, and also as one whose credit will react upon their common sect. And this favour, pressing like a wedge upon the unresisting neutrality of the public, soon succeeds in gaining for any able writer among sectarians an exaggerated reputation. Nobody is against him; and a small section acts *for* him in a spirit of resolute partisanship.

To this accident of social position, and to his connection with the *Eclectic Review*, Mr Foster owed his first advantageous presentation before the public. The misfortune of many an able writer is, not that he is rejected by the world, but that virtually he is never brought conspicuously before them: he is not dismissed unfavourably, but he is never effectually introduced. From this calamity at the outset Foster was saved by his party. I happened myself to be in Bristol at the moment when his four essays were first issuing from the press; and everywhere I heard so pointed an account of the expectations connected with Foster by his religious party that I made it a duty to read his book without delay. It is a distant incident to look back upon; gone by for more than thirty years; but I remember my first impressions, which were these:—1*st*, That the novelty or weight of the thinking was hardly sufficient to account for the sudden popularity, without some *extra* influence at work; and 2*dly*, That the contrast was remarkable between the uncoloured style of his general diction, and the brilliant felicity of occasional images embroidered upon the sober ground of his text. The splendour did not seem spontaneous, or growing up as part of the texture within the loom; it was intermitting, and seemed as extraneous to the substance as the flowers which are chalked for an evening upon the floors of ball-rooms.

Subsequently I remarked two other features of difference in his manner, neither of which has been overlooked by Mr Gilfillan—viz., 1*st*, The unsocial gloom of his eye, travelling over all things with dissatisfaction; 2*d* (Which in our days seemed unaccountable), the remarkable limitation of his knowledge. You might suppose the man, equally by his ignorance of passing things and by his ungenial moroseness, to be a specimen newly turned out from the silent cloisters of La Trappe. A monk he seemed by the repulsion of his cloistral feelings, and a monk by the superannuation of his knowledge. Both peculiarities he drew in part from that same sectarian position, operating for evil, to which, in another direction as a conspicuous advantage, he had been indebted for his favourable public introduction. It is not that Foster was generally misanthropic; neither was he, as a sectarian, "a good hater" at any special angle—that is, he was not a zealous hater; but, by temperament, and in some measure by situation, as one pledged to a polemic attitude by his sect, he was a general disliker and a general suspecter. His confidence in human nature was small; for he saw the clay of the composite statue, but not its gold; and apparently his satisfaction with himself was not much greater. Inexhaustible was his jealousy; and for that reason his philanthropy was everywhere checked by frost and wintry chills. This blight of asceticism in his nature is not of a kind to be briefly illustrated, for it lies diffused through the texture of his writings. But of his other monkish characteristic, his abstraction from the movement and life of his own age, I may give this instance, which I observed by accident about a year since in some *late* edition of his Essays. He was speaking of the term *Radical* as used to designate a large political party; but so slightly was he acquainted with the history of that party, so little had he watched the growth of this important interest in our political system, that he supposes the term "Radical" to express a mere scoff or movement of irony from the antagonists of that party. It stands, as he fancies, upon the same footing as "Puritan," "Roundhead," &c., amongst our fathers, or "Swaddler," applied to the Evangelicals amongst ourselves. This may seem a trifle; nor do I mention the mistake for any evil which it can lead to, but for the dreamy inattention which it argues to what was most important in the agitations around him. It may cause nothing; but how much does it presume? Could a man, interested in the motion of human principles or the revolutions of his own country, have failed to notice the rise of a new party which loudly proclaimed its own mission and purposes in the very name which it assumed! The term "Radical" was used elliptically: Mr Hunt, and all about him, constantly gave out that they were reformers who went to the *root—radical* reformers; whilst all previous political parties they held to be merely masquerading as reformers, or, at least, wanting in the determination to go deep enough. The party-name "Radical" was no insult of enemies: it was a cognisance self-adopted by the party which it designates, and worn with pride; and whatever might be the degree of *personal* weight belonging to Mr Hunt, no man who saw into the composition of society amongst ourselves could doubt that his principles were destined to a most extensive diffusion—were sure of a permanent settlement amongst the great party interests—and, therefore, sure of disturbing thenceforwards for ever the previous equilibrium of forces in our English social system. To mistake the origin or history of a word—is nothing; but to mistake it when that history of a word ran along with the history of a *thing* destined to change all the aspects of our English present and future—implies a sleep of Epimenides amongst the shocks which are unsettling the realities of earth.

The four original essays by which Foster was first known to the public are those by which he is still best known. It cannot be said of them that they have any *practical* character calculated to serve the uses of life. They terminate in speculations that apply themselves little enough to any business of the world. Whether a man should write memoirs of himself cannot have any personal interest for one reader in a myriad. And two of the essays have even a misleading tendency. That upon "Decision of Character" places a very exaggerated valuation upon one quality of human temperament, which is neither rare nor at all necessarily allied with the most elevated features of moral grandeur. Coleridge, because he had no business talents himself, admired them preposterously in others; or fancied them vast when they existed only in a slight degree. And, upon the same principle, I suspect that Mr Foster rated so highly the quality of decision in matters of action chiefly because he wanted it himself. Obstinacy is a gift more extensively sown than Foster was willing to admit. And *his* scale of appreciation, if it were practically applied to the men of history, would lead to judgments immoderately perverse. Milton would rank far below Luther. In reality, as Mr Gilfillan justly remarks, "Decision of character is not strictly a moral power; and it is extremely dangerous to pay that homage to any intellectual quality which is sacred to virtue alone." But even this estimate must often tend to exaggeration; for the most inexorable decision is much more closely connected with bodily differences of temperament than with any superiority of mind. It rests too much upon a physical basis; and of all qualities whatever, it is the most liable to vicious varieties of degeneration. The worst result from this essay is not merely speculative: it trains the feelings to false admirations; and upon a path which is the more dangerous, as the besetting temptation of our English life lies already towards an estimate much too high of all qualities bearing upon the active and the practical. We need no spur in that direction.

The essay upon the use of technically religious language seems even worse by its tendency, although the necessities of the subject will for ever neutralise Foster's advice. Mr Gilfillan is, in this instance, disposed to defend him: "Foster does not ridicule the use, but the abuse, of technical language, as applied to divine things; and proposes, merely as an experiment, to translate it, in ccommodation to fastidious tastes." Safely, however, it may be assumed, that in all such cases, the fastidious taste is but another aspect of hatred to religious themes,— hatred which there is neither justice nor use in attempting to propitiate. Cant words ought certainly to be proscribed, as degrading to the majesty of religion: the word "prayerful," for instance, so commonly used of late years, seems objectionable; and such words as "savoury," which is one of those cited by Foster himself, are absolutely abominable, when applied to spiritual or intellectual objects. It is not fastidiousness, but manliness and good feeling, which are outraged by such vulgarities. On the other hand, the word "grace" expresses an idea so exclusively belonging to Christianity, and so indispensable to the wholeness of its philosophy, that any attempt seek for equivalent terms of mere human growth, or amongst the vocabularies of mere worldly usage, must terminate in conscious failure, or else in utter self-delu- on. Christianity, having introduced many ideas that e absolutely new, such as *faith*, *charity*, *holiness*, the nature of *God*, of human *frailty*, &c., is as much entitled (nay, as much obliged and pledged) to peculiar language and terminology as chemistry. Let a man try if he can find a word in the market-place fitted to be the substitute for the word *gas* or *alkali*. The danger, in fact, lies exactly in the opposite direction to that indicated by Foster. No fear that men of elegant taste should be revolted by th use of what, after all, is Scriptural language; for it is plain that he who *could* be so revolted wants nothing seriously with religion. But there is great fear that any general disposition to angle for readers of *extra* refinement, or to court the effeminately fastidious by sacrificing the majestic simplicities of Scriptural diction, would and must end in a ruinous dilution of religious truths. Along with the characteristic language of Christian philosophy would exhale its characteristic doctrines.

WILLIAM HAZLITT.

This man, who would have drawn in the scales against a select vestry of Fosters, is for the present deeper in the world's oblivion than the man with whom I here connect his name. *That* seems puzzling. For if Hazlitt were misanthropic, so was Foster; both as writers were splenetic and more than peevish; but Hazlitt requited his reader for the pain of travelling through so gloomy an atmosphere by the rich vegetation which his teeming intellect threw up as it moved along. The soil in *his* brain was of a volcanic fertility; whereas, in Foster, as in some tenacious clay, if the life were deep, it was slow and sullen in its throes. The reason for at all speaking of them in connection is, that both were essayists; neither in fact writing anything of note *except* essays, moral or critical; and both were bred at the feet of dissenters. But how different were the results from that connection Foster turned it to a blessing, winning the jewel that is most of all to be coveted, peace and the *fallentis semita vitæ*. Hazlitt, on the other hand, sailed wilfully away from this sheltering harbour of his father's profession,—for sheltering it might have proved to *him*, and *did* prove to his youth,—only to toss ever afterwards as a drifting wreck at the mercy of storms. Hazlitt was not one of those who *could* have illustrated the benefits of a connection with a sect,—*i.e.*, with a small confederation hostile by position to a larger; for the hostility from without, in order to react, presumes a concord from within. Nor does *his* case impeach the correctness of what I have said on that subject in speaking of Foster. He owed no introduction to the dissenters; but it was because he *would* owe none. The Ishmaelite, whose hand is against every man, yet smiles at the approach of a brother, and gives the salutation of "Peace be with you!" to the tribe of his father. But Hazlitt smiled upon no man, nor exchanged tokens of peace with the nearest of fraternities. Wieland, in his *Oberon*, says of a benign patriarch—

"*His* eye a smile on all creation beam'd."

Travestied as to one word, the line would have described Hazlitt—

His eye a scowl on all creation beam'd.

This inveterate misanthropy was constitutional; exasperated it certainly had been by accidents of life, by disappointments, by mortifications, by insults, and still more by having wilfully placed himself in collision from the first with all the interests that were in the sunshine of this world, and with all the persons that were then powerful in England. But my impression was, if I had a right to *have* any impression with regard to one whom I knew so slightly, that no change of position or of fortunes could have brought Hazlitt into reconciliation with the fashion of this world, or of this England, or "this now." It seemed to me that he hated those whom hollow custom obliged him to call his "friends," considerably more than those whom notorious differences of opinion entitled him to rank as his enemies. At least within the ring of politics this was so. Between those particular Whigs whom literature had connected him with, and the whole gang of *us* Conservatives, he showed the same difference in his mode of fencing and parrying, and even in his style of civilities, as between the domestic traitor, hiding a stiletto among his robes of peace, and the bold enemy who sends a trumpet before him, and rides up sword-in-hand against your gates. *Whatever is*—so much I conceive to have been a fundamental lemma for Hazlitt—*is wrong*. So much he thought it safe to postulate. *How* it was wrong might require an impracticable investigation; you might fail for a century to discover; but *that* it was wrong he nailed down as a point of faith, that could stand out against all counter-presumptions from argument, or counter-evidences from experience. A friend of his it was, a friend wishing to love him, and admiring him almost to extravagance, who told me, in illustration of the dark sinister gloom which sate for ever upon Hazlitt's countenance and gestures, that involuntarily when Hazlitt put his hand within his waistcoat (as a mere unconscious trick of habit), he himself felt a sudden recoil of fear, as from one who was searching for a hidden dagger. Like "a Moor of Malabar," as described in the *Faery Queen*, at intervals Hazlitt threw up his angry eyes and dark locks, as if wishing to affront the sun, or to search the air for hostility. And the same friend, on another occasion, described the sort of feudal fidelity to his belligerent duties which in company seemed to animate Hazlitt, as though he were mounting guard on all the citadels of malignity, under some *sacramentum militaire*, by the following trait,—that, if it had happened to Hazlitt to be called out of the room, or to be withdrawn for a moment from the current of the general conversation by a fit of abstraction, or by a private whisper to himself from some person sitting at his elbow, always, on resuming his place as a party to what might be called the public business of the company, he looked round him with a mixed air of suspicion and defiance, such as seemed to challenge every body by some stern adjuration into revealing whether during his own absence or inattention, anything had been said demanding condign punishment at his hands "Has any man uttered or presumed to insinuate," he seemed to insist upon knowing, "during this *interregnum*, things that I ought to proceed against as treasonable to the interests which I defend?" He had the unresting irritability of Rousseau, but in a nobler shape; for Rousseau transfigured every possible act or design of his acquaintances into some personal relation to himself. The vile act was obviously meant, as a child could understand, to injure the person of Rousseau, or his interests, or his reputation. It was meant to wound his feelings, or to misrepresent his acts calumniously, or secretly to supplant his footing. But, on the contrary, Hazlitt viewed all personal affronts or casual slights towards himself as tending to something more general, and masquing, under a pretended horror of Hazlitt the author, a real hatred, deeper than it was always safe to avow, for those social interests which he was reputed to defend. "It was not Hazlitt whom the wretches struck at; no, no; it was democracy, or it was freedom, or it was Napoleon, whose shadow they saw in the rear of Hazlitt; and Napoleon, not for anything in him that might be really bad, but in revenge of that consuming wrath against the thrones of Christendom, for which (said Hazlitt) let us glorify his name eternally."

Yet Hazlitt, like other men, and perhaps with more bitterness than other men, sought for love and for intervals of rest, in which all anger might sleep, and enmity might be laid aside like a travelling dress, after tumultuous journeys:—

"Though the sea-horse on the ocean
Own no dear domestic cave,
Yet he slumbers without motion
On the still and halcyon wave.

"If, on windy days, the raven
Gambol like a dancing skiff,
Not the less he loves his haven
On the bosom of a cliff.

"If almost with eagle pinion
O'er the Alps the chamois roam,
Yet he has some small dominion,
Which, no doubt, he calls his home."

But Hazlitt, restless as the sea-horse, as the raven, as the chamois, found not their respites from storm; he sought, but sought in vain. And for *him* the closing stanza of that little poem remained true to his dying hour; in the person of the "Wandering Jew," *he* might complain,—

"Day and night my toils redouble:
Never nearer to the goal,
Night and day I feel the trouble
Of the wanderer in my soul."

Domicile he had not round whose hearth his affections might gather; rest he had not for the sole of his burning foot. One chance of regaining some peace, or a chance, as he trusted, for a time, was torn from him at the moment of gathering its blossoms. He had been divorced from his wife, not by the law of England, which would have argued criminality in *her*, but by Scottish law, satisfied with some proof of frailty in himself. Subsequently he became deeply fascinated by a young woman in no very elevated rank, for she held some domestic office of superintendence in a boarding-house kept by her father, but of interesting person, and endowed with strong intellectual sensibilities. She had encouraged Hazlitt; had gratified him by reading his works with intelligent sympathy; and, under what form of duplicity it is hard to say, had partly engaged her faith to Hazlitt as his future wife, whilst secretly she was holding a correspondence, too tender to be misinterpreted, with a gentleman resident in the same establishment. Suspicions were put aside for a time; but they returned, and gathered too thickly for Hazlitt's penetration to cheat itself any longer. Once and for ever he resolved to satisfy himself. On a Sunday, fatal to him and his farewell hopes of domestic happiness, he had reason to believe that she, whom he now loved to excess, had made some appointment out-of-doors with his rival. It was in London; and through the crowds of London Hazlitt followed her steps to the rendezvous. Fancying herself lost in the multitude that streamed through Lincoln's-Inn-Fields, the treacherous young woman met her more favoured lover without alarm, and betrayed, too clearly for any further deception, the state of her affections by the tenderness of her manner. *There* went out the last light that threw a guiding ray over the storm-vexed course of Hazlitt. He was too much in earnest, and he had witnessed too much to be deceived or appeased. "I whistled her down the wind," was his own account of the catastrophe; but, in doing so, he had torn his own heart-strings, entangled with her "jesses." Neither did he, as others would have done, seek to disguise his misfortune. On the contrary, he cared not for the ridicule attached to such a situation amongst the unfeeling: the wrench within had been too profound to leave room for sensibility to the sneers outside. A fast friend of his at that time, and one who never ceased to be his apologist, described him to me as having become absolutely maniacal during the first pressure of this affliction. He went about proclaiming the case, and insisting on its details, to every stranger that would listen. He even published the whole story to the world in his *Modern Pygmalion*. And people generally, who could not be aware of his feelings, or the way in which this treachery acted upon his mind as a ratification of all other treacheries and wrongs that he had suffered through life, laughed at him, or expressed disgust for him as too coarsely indelicate in making such disclosures. But there was no indelicacy in such an act of confidence, growing, as it did, out of his lacerated heart. It was an explosion of frenzy. He threw out his clamorous anguish to the clouds, and to the winds, and to the air; caring not *who* might listen, *who* might sympathise, or *who* might sneer. Pity was no demand of his; laughter was no wrong: the sole necessity for *him* was—to empty his overburdened spirit.

After this desolating experience, the exasperation of Hazlitt's political temper grew fiercer, darker, steadier. His *Life of Napoleon* was prosecuted subsequently to this, and perhaps under this remembrance, as a reservoir that might receive all the vast overflows of his wrath, much of which was not merely political, or in a spirit of bacchanalian partisanship, but was even morbidly anti-social. He hated, with all his heart, every institution of man, and all his pretensions. He loathed his own relation to the human race.

It was but on a few occasions that I ever met Mr Hazlitt myself; and those occasions, or all but one, were some time subsequent to the case of female treachery which I have here described. Twice, I think, or it might be three times, we walked for a few miles together: it was in London, late at night, and after leaving a party. Though depressed by the spectacle of a mind always in agitation from the gloomier passions, I was yet amused by the pertinacity with which he clung, through bad reasons or no reasons, to any public slander floating against men in power, or in the highest rank. No feather, or dowl of a feather, but was heavy enough for *him*. Amongst other instances of this willingness to be deluded by rumours, if they took a direction favourable to his own bias, Hazlitt had adopted the whole strength of popular hatred which for many years ran violently against the King of Hanover, at that time Duke of Cumberland. A dark calumny had arisen against this prince amongst the populace of London, as though he had been accessory to the death of his valet. This valet (Sellis) had in fact attempted to murder the prince; and all that can be said in palliation of his act is, that he *believed* himself to have sustained, in the person of his beautiful wife, the heaviest dishonour incident to man. How that matter stood I pretend not to know; the attempt at murder was baffled, and the valet then destroyed himself with a razor. All this had been regularly sifted by a coroner's inquest; and I remarked to Hazlitt that the witnesses seemed to have been called indifferently from all quarters likely to have known the facts; so that, if this inquest had failed to elicit the truth, we might, with equal reason, presume as much of all other inquests. From the verdict of a jury, except in very peculiar cases, no candid and temperate man will allow himself to believe any appeal sustainable; for, having the witnesses before them face to face, and hearing the *whole* of the evidence, a jury have always some means of forming a judgment which cannot be open to him who depends upon an abridged report. But on this subject Hazlitt would hear no reason. He said—"No; all the princely houses of Europe have the instinct of murder running in their blood;—they cherish it through their privilege of making war, which being wholesale murder, once having reconciled themselves to *that*, they think of retail murder, committed on you or me, as of no crime at all." Under this obstinate prejudice against the duke, Hazlitt read everything that he did, or did *not* do, in a perverse spirit. And in one of these nightly walks he mentioned to me, as something quite worthy of a murderer, the following little trait of casuistry in the royal duke's distribution of courtesies. "I saw it myself," said Hazlitt, "so no coroner's jury can put me down." His royal highness had rooms in St James's, and one day, as he was issuing from the palace into Pall-Mall, Hazlitt happened to be immediately behind him; he could therefore watch his motions along the whole line of his progress. It is the custom in England, wheresoever the persons of the royal family are familiar to the public eye, as at Windsor, &c., that all passengers in the streets, on seeing them, walk bareheaded, or make some signal of dutiful respect. On this occasion all the men who met the prince took off their hats, the prince acknowledging every such obeisance by a separate bow. Pall-Mall being finished, and its whole harvest of royal salutations gathered in, next the duke came to Cockspur Street. But here, and taking a station close to the crossing, which daily he beautified and polished with his broom, stood a negro sweep. If human at all, which some peopled doubted, he was pretty nearly as abject a representative of our human family divine as can ever have existed. Still he was held to be a man by the law of the land, which would have hanged any person, gentle or simple, for cutting his throat. Law (it is certain) conceived him to be a man, however poor a one; though medicine, in an under tone, muttered some-

N 2.

times a demur to that opinion. But here the sweep *was*, whether man or beast, standing humbly in the path of royalty; vanish he would not; he was (as the *Times* says of the Corn League) "a great fact," if rather a muddy one; and though, by his own confession (repeated one thousand times a-day), both "a nigger" and a sweep, ["Remember poor nigger, your honour! remember poor sweep!"] yet the creature could take off his rag of a hat and earn the bow of a prince as well as any white native of St James's. What was to be done? A great case of conscience was on the point of being raised in the person of a paralytic nigger; nay, possibly a state question,—Ought a son of England,* could a son of England, descend from his majestic pedestal to gild with the rays of his condescension such a grub, such a very doubtful grub, as this? Total Pall-Mall was sagacious of the coming crisis; judgment was going to be delivered; a precedent to be raised; and Pall-Mall stood still, with Hazlitt at its head, to learn the issue. How if the black should be a Jacobin, and (in the event of the duke's bowing) should have a bas-relief sculptured on his tomb, exhibiting an

---

* "*Son of England*:"—*i.e.*, prince of the blood in the *direct*, and not in the collateral line. I mention this for the sake of some readers who may not be aware that this beautiful formula, so well known in France, is often transferred by the French writers of memoirs to our English princes, though little used amongst ourselves. Gaston, Duke of Orleans, brother of Louis XIV., was "a *son* of France," as being a child of Louis XIII. But the son of Gaston, viz., the Regent Duke of Orleans, was a *grandson* of France. The first wife of Gaston, our Princess Henrietta, was called "*Fille* d'Angleterre," as being a daughter of Charles I. The Princess Charlotte, again, was a *daughter* of England; her present majesty, a *grand-daughter* of England. But all these ladies collectively would be called, on the French principle, the children of England.

English prince and a German king, as two separate personages, in the act of worshipping his broom? Luckily it was not the black's province to settle the case. The Duke of Cumberland, seeing no counsel at hand to argue either the *pro* or the *contra*, found himself obliged to settle the question *de plano;* so, drawing out his purse, he kept his hat as rigidly settled on his head as William Penn and Mead did before the recorder of London. All Pall-Mall applauded: *contradicente* Gulielmo Hazlitt, and Hazlitt only. The black swore that the prince gave him half-a-crown; but whether he regarded this in the light of a godsend to his avarice, or a shipwreck to his ambition—whether he was more thankful for the money gained, or angry for the honour lost—did not transpire. "No matter," said Hazlitt, "the black might be a fool; but I insist upon it that he was entitled to the bow, since all Pall-Mall had it before him, and that it was unprincely to refuse it." Either as a black or as a scavenger, Hazlitt held him "qualified" for sustaining a royal bow: as a black, was he not a specimen (if rather a damaged one) of the *homo sapiens* described by Linnæus? As a sweep, in possession (by whatever title) of a lucrative crossing, had he not a kind of estate in London? Was he not, said Hazlitt, a fellow-subject, capable of committing treason, and paying taxes into the treasury? Not perhaps in any direct shape, but indirect taxes most certainly on his tobacco—and even on his broom?

These things could not be denied. But still, when my turn came for speaking, I confessed frankly that (politics apart) my feeling in the case went along with the Duke's. The bow would not be so useful to the black as the half-crown: he could not possibly have both; for how could any man make a bow to a beggar when in the act of giving him half-a-crown? Then, on the other hand, this bow, so useless to the sweep, and (to speak by a vulgar adage) as superfluous as a side-pocket to a cow, would re-act upon the other bows distributed along the line of Pall-Mall, so as to neutralise them one and all. No honour could continue such in which a paralytic negro sweep was associated. This distinction, however, occurred to me; that if, instead of a prince and a subject, the royal dispenser of bows had been a king, he ought *not* to have excluded the black from participation; because, as the common father of his people, he ought not to know of any difference amongst those who are equally his children. And in illustration of that opinion, I sketched a little scene which I had myself witnessed, and with great pleasure, upon occasion of a visit made to Drury Lane by George IV. when regent. At another time I may tell it to the reader. Hazlitt, however, listened fretfully to me when praising the deportment and gracious gestures of one conservative leader; though he had compelled *me* to hear the most disadvantageous comments on another.

As a lecturer, I do not know what Hazlitt was, having never had an opportunity of hearing him. Some qualities in his style of composition were calculated to assist the purposes of a lecturer, who must produce an effect oftentimes by independent sentences and paragraphs; who must glitter and surprise; who must turn round within the narrowest compass, and cannot rely upon any sort of attention that would cost an effort. Mr Gilfillan says, that "he proved more popular than was expected by those who knew his uncompromising scorn of all those tricks and petty artifices which are frequently employed to pump up applause. His manner was somewhat abrupt and monotonous, but earnest and energetic." At the same time, Mr Gilfillan takes an occasion to express some opinions, which appear very just, upon the unfitness (generally speaking) of men whom he describes as "fiercely inspired" for this mode of display. The truth is, that all genius implies originality, and sometimes uncontrollable singularity, in the habits of thinking, and in the modes of viewing as well as of estimating objects; whereas a miscellaneous audience is best conciliated by that sort of talent which reflects the average mind, which is not overweighted in any one direction, is not tempted into any extreme, and is able to preserve a steady, rope-dancer's equilibrium of posture upon themes where a man of genius is most apt to lose it.

It would be interesting to have a full and accurate list of Hazlitt's works, including, of course, his contributions to journals and encyclopædias. These last, as shorter and oftener springing from an *impromptu* effort, are more likely than his regular books to have been written with a pleasurable enthusiasm: and the writer's proportion of pleasure in such cases very often becomes the regulating law for his reader's. Amongst the philosophical works of Hazlitt, I do not observe that Mr Gilfillan is aware of two that are likely to be specially interesting. One is an examination of David Hartley, at least as to his law of association. Thirty years ago, I looked into it slightly; but my reverence for Hartley offended me with its tone; and afterwards, hearing that Coleridge challenged for his own most of what was important in the thoughts, I lost all interest in the essay. Hazlitt unavoidably having heard Coleridge talk on this theme, must have approached it with a mind largely preoccupied as regarded the weak points in Hartley, and the particular tactics for assailing them. But still the great talents for speculative research which Hazlitt had from nature, without having given to them the benefit of much culture or much exercise, would justify our attentive examination of the work. It forms part of the volume which contains the *Essay on Human Action;* which volume, by the way, Mr Gilfillan supposes to have won the special applause of Sir James Macintosh, then in Bengal. This, if accurately stated, is creditable to Sir James's generosity; for in this particular volume it is that Hazlitt makes a pointed assault, in sneering terms, and very unnecessarily, upon Sir James as a lecturer at Lincoln's Inn.

The other little work unnoticed by Mr Gilfillan is an examination (but under what title I cannot say) of Lindley Murray's English Grammar. This may seem, by its subject, a trifle; yet Hazlitt could hardly have had a motive for such an effort but in some philosophic perception of the ignorance betrayed by many grammars of our language, and continually by that of Lindley Murray; which Lindley, by the way, though resident in England, was an American. There is great room for a useful display of philosophic subtlety in an English grammar, even though meant for schools. Hazlitt could not *but* have furnished something of value towards such a display. And if (as I was once told) his book was suppressed, I imagine that this suppression must have been purchased by some powerful publisher interested in keeping up the current reputation of Murray.

"Strange stories," says Mr Gilfillan, "are told about his [Hazlitt's] latter days, and his deathbed." I know not whether I properly understand Mr Gilfillan. The stories which I myself have happened to hear were not so much "strange," since they arose naturally enough out of pecuniary embarrassments, as they were afflicting in the turn they took. Dramatically viewed, if a man were speaking of things so far removed from our own times and interests as to excuse that sort of language, the circumstances of Hazlitt's last hours might rivet the gaze of a critic as fitted harmoniously, with almost scenic art, to the whole tenor of his life; fitted equally to rouse his wrath, to deepen his dejection, and in the hour of death to justify his misanthropy. But I have no wish to utter a word on things which I know only at second-hand, and cannot speak upon without risk of misstating facts or doing injustice to persons. I prefer closing this section with the words of Mr Gilfillan :—

"Well, says Bulwer, that of all the mental wrecks which have occurred in our era, this was the most melancholy. Others may have been as unhappy in their domestic circumstances, and gone down steeper places of dissipation than he; but they had meanwhile the breath of popularity, if not of wealth and station, to give them a certain solace." What had Hazlitt of this nature? Mr Gilfillan answers,— "Absolutely nothing to support and cheer him. With no hope, no fortune. no *status* in society; no certain popularity as a writer, no domestic peace, little sympathy from kindred spirits, little support from his political party, no moral management, no definite belief; with great powers and great passions within, and with a host of powerful enemies without, it was his to enact one of the saddest tragedies on which the sun ever shone. Such is a faithful portraiture of an extraordinary man, whose restless intellect and stormy passions have now, for fifteen years, found that repose in the grave which was denied them above it.' Mr Gilfillan concludes with expressing his conviction, in which I desire to concur, that both enemies and friends will *now* join in admiration for the man; "both will readily concede *now* that a subtle thinker, an eloquent writer, a lover of beauty and poetry, and man and truth, one of the best of critics, and not the worst of men, expired in William Hazlitt." *Requiescat in pace!*

FALSIFICATION OF ENGLISH HISTORY.

I AM myself, and always have been, a member of the Church of England, and am grieved to hear the many attacks against the Church [frequently most illiberal attacks] which not so much religion as political rancour gives birth to in every third journal that I take up. This I say to acquit myself of all dishonourable feelings, such as I would abhor to co-operate with, in bringing a very heavy charge against that great body in its literary capacity. Whosoever has reflected on the history of the English constitution must be aware that the most important stage of its development lies within the reign of Charles I. It is true that the judicial execution of that prince has been allowed by many persons to vitiate all that was done by the heroic parliament of November 1640; and the ordinary histories of England assume as a matter of course that the whole period of parliamentary history through those times is to be regarded as a period of confusion. Our constitution, say they, was formed in 1688–9. Meantime it is evident to any reflecting man that the Revolution simply re-affirmed the principles developed in the strife between the two great parties which had arisen in the reign of James I., and had ripened and come to issue with each other in the reign of his son. Our constitution was not a birth of a single instant, as they would represent it, but a gradual growth and development through a long tract of time. In particular, the doctrine of the king's vicarious responsibility in the person of his ministers, which first gave a sane and salutary meaning to the doctrine of the king's personal irresponsibility [" The king can do no wrong"], arose undeniably between 1640 and 1648. This doctrine is the main pillar of our constitution, and perhaps the finest discovery that was ever made in the theory of government. Hitherto the doctrine *that the King can do no wrong* had been used not to protect the indispensable sanctity of the king's constitutional character, but to protect the wrong. Used in this way it was a maxim of Oriental despotism, and fit only for a nation where law had no empire. Many of the illustrious patriots of the Great Parliament saw this and felt the necessity of abolishing a maxim so fatal to the just liberties of the people. But some of them fell into the opposite error of supposing that this abolition could be effected only by the direct negation of it; *their* maxim accordingly was—" The king *can* do wrong," *i.e.*, is responsible in his own person. In this great error even the illustrious wife of Colonel Hutchinson participated;*

* This is remarked by her editor and descendant, Julius Hutchinson, who adds some words to this effect:—" That *if* the patriots of that day were the inventors of the maxim [*the king can do no wrong*], we are much indebted to them." The patriots certainly did not invent the maxim, for they found it already current: but they gave it its new and constitutional sense. I refer to the book, however, as I do to almost all books in these notes, from memory; writing most of them in situations where I have no access to books. By the way, Charles I., who used the maxim in the most odious sense, furnished the most colourable excuse for his own execution.

and accordingly she taxes those of her own party who scrupled to accede to the new maxim, and still adhered to the old one, with unconscientious dealing. But she misapprehended their meaning, and failed to see where they laid the emphasis: the emphasis was not laid, as it was by the royal party, on the words "can do no *wrong*"—but on "The king:" that is, wrong may be done; and in the king's name; but it cannot be the king who did it [the king cannot constitutionally be supposed the person who did it]. By this exquisite political refinement the old tyrannical maxim was disarmed of its sting; and the entire redress of all wrong, so indispensable to the popular liberty, was brought into perfect reconciliation with the entire inviolability of the sovereign, which is no less indispensable to the popular liberty. There is, moreover, a double wisdom in the new sense: for not only is one object [the redress of wrong] secured in conjunction with another object [the king's inviolability] hitherto held irreconcilable,—but even with a view to the first object alone a much more effectual means is applied, because one which leads to no schism in the state, than could have been applied by the blank negation of the maxim; *i.e.*, by lodging the responsibility exactly where the executive power [*ergo* the power of resisting this responsibility] was lodged. Here, then, is one example in illustration of my thesis—that the English constitution was in a great measure gradually evolved in the contest between the different parties in the reign of Charles I. Now, if this be so, it follows that for constitutional history no pe

He constantly maintained the irresponsibility of his ministers; but, if that were conceded, it would then follow that the king must be made responsible in his own person:—and that construction led of necessity to his trial and death.

riod is so important as that: and indeed, though it is true that the Revolution is the great era for the constitutional historian, because he there first finds the constitution fully developed as the "bright consummate *flower*," and. what is equally important, he there first finds the principles of our constitution *ratified* by a competent authority,—yet, to trace the *root* and growth of the constitution, the three reigns immediately preceding are still more properly the objects of his study. Briefly, the *root* of our constitutional settlement was in the three reigns of Charles I., of Charles II., and of James II.; but its manifestation by fruits and blossoms was in 1689. In proportion, then, as the reign of Charles I. is important to the history of our constitution, in that proportion are those to be taxed with the most dangerous falsifications of our history who have misrepresented either the facts or the principles of those times. Now I affirm that the clergy of the Church of England have been in a perpetual conspiracy since the era of the restoration to misrepresent both. As an illustration of what I mean I refer to the common edition of *Hudibras*, by Dr Grey; for the proof I might refer to some thousands of books. Dr Grey's is a disgusting case: for he swallowed with the most anile credulity every story, the most extravagant that the malice of those times could invent, against either the Presbyterians or the Independents: and for this I suppose, amongst other deformities, his notes were deservedly ridiculed by Warburton. But, amongst hundreds of illustrations more respectable than Dr Grey's, I will refer the reader to a work of our own days, the *Ecclesiastical Biography* [in part a republication of *Walton's Lives*], edited by the present master of Trinity College, Cambridge, who is held in the highest esteem wherever he is known, and is, I am persuaded, perfectly conscientious, and as impartial as in such a case it is possible for a high churchman to be. Yet so it is that there is scarcely one of the notes having any political reference to the period of 1640–1660 which is not disfigured by unjust prejudices; and the amount of the moral which the learned editor grounds upon the documents before him is this,—that the young student is to cherish the deepest abhorrence and contempt of all who had any share on the parliamentary side in the "confusions" of the period from 1640 to 1660: that is to say, of men to whose immortal exertions it was owing that the very Revolution of 1688, which Dr W. will be the first to applaud, found us with any such stock of political principles or feelings as could make a beneficial revolution possible. Where, let me ask, would have been the willingness of some Tories to construe the flight of James II. into a virtual act of abdication, or to consider even the most formal act of abdication binding against the king,—had not the great struggle of Charles's days gradually substituted in the minds of all parties a rational veneration of the king's *office* for the old superstition in behalf of the king's *person*, which would have protected him from the effects of any acts, however solemnly performed, which affected injuriously either his own interests or the liberties of his people. Tempora mutantur: *nos et mutamur in illis*. Those whom we find in fierce opposition to the popular party about 1640 we find still in the same personal opposition fifty years after, but an opposition resting on far different principles: insensibly the principles of their antagonists had reached even them; and a courtier of 1689 was willing to concede more than a patriot of 1630 would have ventured to ask. Let me not be understood to mean that true patriotism is at all more shown in supporting the rights of the people than those of the king; as soon as both are defined and limited, the last are as indispensable to the integrity of the constitution—as the first; and popular freedom itself would suffer as much, though indirectly, from an invasion of Cæsar's rights—as by a more direct attack on itself. But in the 17th century the rights of the people were as yet *not* defined; throughout that century they were gradually defining themselves—and, as happens to all great practical interests, defining themselves through a course of fierce and bloody contests. For the kingly rights are almost inevitably carried too high in ages of imperfect civilisation; and the well-known laws of Henry VII., by which he either broke or gradually sapped the power of the aristocracy, had still more extravagantly exalted them. On this account it is just to look upon democratic or popular politics as identical in the 17th century with patriotic politics. In later periods the democrat and the patriot have sometimes been in direct opposition to each other; at that period they were inevitably in conjunction. All this, however, is in general overlooked by those who either write English history or comment upon it. Most writers *of* or *upon* English history proceed either upon servile principles, or upon no principles; and a good *Spirit of English History*, that is, a history which should abstract the tendencies and main results [as to laws, manners, and constitution] from every age of English history, is a work which I hardly hope to see executed. For it would require the concurrence of some philosophy with a great deal of impartiality. How idly do we say, in speaking of the events of our own time which affect our party feelings,—"We stand too near to these events for an impartial estimate; we must leave them to the judgment of posterity!" For it is a fact, that of the many books of memoirs written by persons who were not merely contemporary with the great civil war, but actors and even leaders in its principal scenes—there is hardly one which does not exhibit a more impartial picture of that great drama than the histories written at this day. The historian of Popery does not display half so much zealotry and passionate prejudice in speaking of the many events which have affected the power and splendour of the Papal See for the last thirty years, and under his own eyes, as he does when speaking of a reformer who lived three centuries ago—of a Bible translator into a vernacular tongue who lived five centuries ago—of an Antipope—of a Charlemagne or a Gregory the Great still further removed from himself. The recent events he looks upon as accidental and unessential; but in the great enemies or great founders of the Romish temporal power, and in the history of their actions and their motives, he feels that the whole principle of the Romish cause and its pretensions are at stake. Pretty much under the same feeling have modern writers written with a rancorous party spirit of the political struggles in the 17th century: here they fancy that they can detect the *incunabula* of the revolutionary spirit: here some have been so sharpsighted as to read the features of pure Jacobinism; and others*

* Amongst these Mr D'Israeli (the father of the Right Honourable Benjamin D'Israeli) in one of the latter volumes of his *Curiosities of Literature* has dedicated a chapter or so to formal proof of this proposition. A reader who is familiar with the history of that age comes to the chapter with a previous indignation, knowing what sort of proof he has to expect. This indignation is not likely to be mitigated by what he will there find. Because some one madman, fool, or scoundrel makes a monstrous proposal—which dies of itself unsupported, and is in violent contrast to all the acts

have gone so far as to assert that all the atrocities of the French Revolution had their direct parallelisms in acts done or countenanced by the virtuous and august Senate of England in 1640! Strange distortion of the understanding which can thus find a brotherly resemblance between two great historical events, which of all that ever were put on record stand off from each other in most irreconcilable enmity,—the one originating, as Coleridge has observed, in excess of principle: the other in the utter defect of all moral principle whatever; and the progress of each being answerable to its origin! Yet so it is. And not a memoir-writer of that age is reprinted in this but we have a preface from some red-hot Anti-jacobin warning us with much vapid commonplace from the mischiefs and eventual anarchy of too rash a spirit of reform, as dis-

---

and the temper of those times—this is to sully the character of the parliament and three-fourths of the people of England. If this proposal had grown out of the spirit of the age, that spirit would have produced many more proposals of the same character and acts corresponding to them. Yet upon this one infamous proposal, and two or three scandalous anecdotes from the libels of the day, does the whole *onus* of Mr D'Israeli's parallel depend. *Tantamne rem tam negligenter?*—In the general character of an Englishman I have a right to complain that so heavy an attack upon the honour of England and her most virtuous patriots in her most virtuous age should be made with so much levity: a charge so solemn in its matter should have been prosecuted with a proportionate solemnity of manner. Mr D'Israeli refers with just applause to the opinions of Mr Coleridge: I wish that he would have allowed a little more weight to the striking passage in which that gentleman contrasts the French Revolution with the English Revolution of 1640–8. However, the general tone of honour and upright principle which marks Mr D'Israel's work encourages me and others to hope that he will cancel the chapter—and not persist in wounding the honour of a great people for the sake of a parallelism, which—even if it were true—is a thousand times too slight and feebly supported to satisfy the most accommodating reader.

played in the French Revolution,—*not* by the example of that French Revolution, but by that of our own in the age of Charles I. The following passage from the Introduction to Sir William Waller's *Vindication*, published in 1793, may serve as a fair instance: "He" (Sir W. Waller) "was indeed at length sensible of the misery which he had contributed to bring on his country" (by the way, it is a suspicious circumstance that Sir William* first became sensible that his country was miserable when he became sensible that he himself was not likely to be again employed; and became fully convinced of it when his party lost their ascendancy); "he was convinced, by fatal experience, that anarchy was a bad step towards a perfect government; that the subversion of every establishment was no safe foundation for a permanent and regular constitution; he found that pretences of reform were held up by the designing to dazzle the eyes of the unwary, &c.; he found, in short, that reformation by popular insurrection must end in the destruction, and cannot tend to the formation, of a regular government." After a good deal more of this well-meaning cant, the Introduction concludes with the following sentence—the writer is addressing the Reformers of 1793, amongst whom—"Both leaders and followers," he says, "may together reflect—that upon speculative and visionary reformers" (*i.e.*, those of 1640) "the severest punishment which God in his vengeance ever yet inflicted—was to curse them with the

* Sir William and his cousin Sir Hardress Waller were both remarkable men. Sir Hardress had no conscience at all; Sir William a very scrupulous one; which, however, he was for ever tampering with—and generally succeeded in reducing into compliance with his immediate interest. He was, however, an accomplished gentleman; and as a man of talents worthy of the highest admiration.

complete gratification of their own inordinate desires." I quote this passage—not as containing anything singular, but for the very reason that it is *not* singular: it expresses, in fact, the universal opinion: notwithstanding which I am happy to say that it is false. What "complete gratification of their own desires" was ever granted to the "reformers" in question? On the contrary, it is well known (and no book illustrates that particular fact so well as Sir William Waller's) that as early as 1647 the army had too effectually subverted the just relations between itself and parliament—not to have suggested fearful anticipations to all discerning patriots of that unhappy issue which did in reality blight their prospects. And when I speak of an "unhappy issue," I would be understood only of the immediate issue: for the remote issue was—the Revolution of 1688, as I have already asserted. Neither is it true that even the immediate issue was "unhappy" to any extent which can justify the ordinary language in which it is described. Here, again, is a world of delusions. We hear of "anarchy," of "confusions," of "proscriptions," of "bloody and ferocious tyranny." All is romance; there was no anarchy, no confusions, no proscriptions, no tyranny in the sense designed. The sequestrations, forfeitures, and punishments of all sorts which were inflicted by the conquering party on their antagonists went on by due course of law; and the summary justice of courts-martial was not resorted to in England: except for the short term of the two wars, and the brief intermediate campaign of 1648, the country was in a very tranquil state. Nobody was punished without an open trial; and all trials proceeded in the regular course, according to the ancient forms, and in the regular courts of justice. And as to "tyranny," which is meant chiefly of the acts of

Cromwell's government, it should be remembered that the Protectorate lasted not a quarter of the period in question (1640–1660); a fact which is constantly forgotten even by very eminent writers, who speak as though Cromwell had drawn his sword in January 1640—cut off the king's head—instantly mounted his throne—and continued to play the tyrant for the whole remaining period of his life. Secondly, as to the *kind* of tyranny which Cromwell exercised, the misconception is ludicrous: continental writers have a notion, well justified by the language of English writers, that Cromwell was a ferocious savage, who built his palace of human skulls and desolated his country. Meantime, he was simply a strong-minded, rough-built Englishman, with a character thoroughly English, and exceedingly good-natured. Gray valued himself upon his critical knowledge of English history; yet how thoughtlessly does he express the abstract of Cromwell's life in the line on the village Cromwell,—"Some Cromwell, guiltless of his country's blood!" How was Cromwell guilty of his country's blood? What blood did he cause to be shed? A great deal was shed, no doubt, in the wars (though less, by the way, than is imagined): but in those Cromwell was but a servant of the parliament; and no one will allege that he had any hand in causing a single war. After he attained the sovereign power no more domestic wars arose: and as to a few persons who were executed for plots and conspiracies against his person, they were condemned upon evidence openly given and by due course of law. With respect to the general character of his government, it is evident that, in the unsettled and revolutionary state of things which follows a civil war, some critical cases will arise to demand an occasional "vigour beyond the law"—such as the Roman government allowed in allowing the dictatorial power. But in general Cromwell's government was limited by law: and no reign in that century, prior to the Revolution, furnishes fewer instances of attempts to tamper with the laws—to overrule them—to twist them to private interpretations—or to dispense with them. As to his major-generals of counties, who figure in most histories of England as so many *Ali Pachas* that impaled a few prisoners every morning before breakfast—or rather as so many ogres that ate up good Christian men, women, and children alive, they were disagreeable people, who were disliked much in the same way as our commissioners of the income-tax were disliked in the memory of us all; and heartily they would have laughed at the romantic and bloody masquerade in which they are made to figure in the English histories. What, then, was the "tyranny" of Cromwell's government, which was confessedly complained of even in those days? The word "tyranny" was then applied not so much to the mode in which his power was administered (except by the prejudiced) as to its origin. However mercifully a man may reign, yet if he have no right to reign at all, we may in one sense call him a tyrant; his power not being justly derived, and resting upon an unlawful (*i.e.*, a military) basis. As a usurper, and one who had diverted the current of a grand national movement to selfish and personal objects, Cromwell was and will be called a tyrant; but not in the more obvious sense of the word. Such are the misleading statements which disfigure the History of England in its most important chapter. They mislead by more than a simple error of fact: those which I have noticed last involve a moral anachronism; for they convey images of cruelty and barbarism such as could not co-exist with the national civilisation at that time; and whosoever has not corrected this false picture by an acquaintance with the English literature of that age must necessarily image to himself a state of society as rude and uncultured as that which prevailed during the wars of York and Lancaster—*i.e.*, about two centuries earlier. But those with which I introduced this article are still worse, because they involve an erroneous view of constitutional history, and a most comprehensive act of ingratitude: the great men of the Long Parliament paid a heavy price for their efforts to purchase for their descendants a barrier to irresponsible power and security from the anarchy of undefined regal prerogative: in these efforts most of them made shipwreck of their own tranquillity and peace; that such sacrifices were made unavailingly (as it must have seemed to themselves), and that few of them lived to see the "good old cause" finally triumphant, does not cancel their claims upon our gratitude, but rather strengthen them by the degree in which it aggravated the difficulty of bearing such sacrifices with patience. But whence come these falsifications of history? I believe from two causes; first (as I have already said), from the erroneous tone impressed upon the national history by the irritated spirit of the clergy of the Established Church: to the religious zealotry of those times—the church was the object of especial attack; and its members were naturally exposed to heavy sufferings; hence their successors are indisposed to find any good in a cause which could lead to such a result. It is their manifest right to sympathise with their own order in that day; and in such a case it is almost their duty to be incapable of an entire impartiality. Meantime they have carried this much too far; the literature of England must always be in a considerable proportion lodged in their hands; and the extensive means thus placed at their disposal for injuriously colouring that important part of history they have used with no modesty or forbearance. There is not a page of the national history, even in its local subdivisions, which they have not stained with the atrabilious hue of their wounded remembrances: hardly a town in England, which stood a siege for the king or the parliament, but has some printed memorial of its constancy and its sufferings; and in nine cases out of ten the editor is a clergyman of the Established Church, who has contrived to deepen "the sorrow of the time" by the harshness of his commentary. Surely it is high time that the wounds of the seventeenth century should close in the nineteenth; that history should take a more commanding and philosophic station; and that brotherly charity should now lead us to a saner view of constitutional politics, or a saner view of politics to a more comprehensive charity. The other cause of this falsification springs out of a selfishness which has less claim to any indulgence—viz., the timidity with which the English Whigs of former days and the party to whom they* succeeded, constantly shrank from acknowledging any alliance with the great men of the Long Parliament under the nervous horror of being confounded with the regicides of 1649. It was of such urgent importance to them, for any command over the public support, that they should acquit themselves of any sentiment of lurking toleration for regicide, with which their enemies never failed to load them, that no mode of abjuring it seemed sufficiently emphatic to them: hence

* Until after the year 1688 I do not remember ever to have found the term Whig applied except to the religious characteristics of that party; whatever reference it might have to their political distinctions was only secondary and by implication.

it was that Addison, with a view to the interest of his party, thought fit when in Switzerland to offer a puny insult to the memory of General Ludlow: hence it is that even in our own days no writers have insulted Milton with so much bitterness and shameless irreverence as the Whigs; though it is true that some few Whigs, more however in their literary than in their political character, have stepped forward in his vindication. At this moment I recollect a passage in the writings of a modern Whig bishop*—in which, for the sake of creating a charge of falsehood against Milton, the author has grossly mistranslated a passage in the *Defensio pro Pop. Anglicano*: and if that bishop were not dead, I would here take the liberty of rapping his knuckles—were it only for breaking Priscian's head. To return to the clerical feud against the Long Parliament,—it was a passage in a very pleasing work of this day (*Ecclesiastical Biography*) which suggested to me the whole of what I have now written. Its learned editor (Doctor Wordsworth, brother of the great poet), who is incapable of uncandid feelings except in what concerns the interests of his order. has adopted the usual tone in regard to the men of 1640 throughout his otherwise valuable annotations: and somewhere or other (in the life of Hammond, according to my remembrance) he has made a statement to this effect:—That the custom prevalent among children in that age of asking their parents' blessing was probably first brought into disuse by the Puritans. Is it possible to imagine a perversity of prejudice more unreasonable? The unamiable side of the patriotic character in the seventeenth century was unquestionably its religious bigotry; which, however,

* Watson, Bishop of Llandaff.

had its ground in a real fervour of religious feeling and a real strength of religious principle somewhat exceeding the ordinary standard of the nineteenth century. But, however palliated, their bigotry is not to be denied; it was often offensive from its excess, and ludicrous in its direction. Many harmless customs, many ceremonies and rituals that had a high positive value, their frantic intolerance quarrelled with: and for my part I heartily join in the sentiment of Charles II.—applying it as *he* did, but a good deal more extensively, that their religion "was not a religion for a gentleman:" indeed all sectarianism, but especially that which has a modern origin—arising and growing up within our own memories, unsupported by a grand traditional history of persecutions—conflicts—and martyrdoms, lurking moreover in blind alleys, holes, corners, and tabernacles, must appear spurious and mean in the eyes of him who has been bred up in the grand classic forms of the Church of England or the Church of Rome. But because the bigotry of the Puritans was excessive and revolting, is *that* a reason for fastening upon them all the stray evils of omission or commission for which no distinct fathers can be found? The learned editor does not pretend that there is any positive evidence, or presumption even, for imputing to the Puritans a dislike to the custom in question: but because he thinks it a good custom, his inference is, that nobody could have abolished it but the Puritans. Now, who does not see that if this had been amongst the usages discountenanced by the Puritans, it would on that account have been the more pertinaciously maintained by their enemies in church and state? Or even if this usage were of a nature to be prohibited by authority,—as the public use of the liturgy, organs, surplices, &c.,—who does not see that with regard to *that*, as well as to other Puritanical innovations, there would have been a reflux of zeal at the restoration of the king which would have established them in more strength than ever? But it is evident to the unprejudiced that the usage in question gradually went out in submission to the altered spirit of the times. It was one feature of a general system of manners, fitted by its piety and simplicity for a pious and simple age, and which therefore even the seventeenth century had already outgrown. It is not to be inferred that filial affection and reverence have decayed amongst us because they no longer express themselves in the same way. In an age of imperfect culture all passions and emotions are in a more elementary state—speak a plainer language—and express themselves *externally:* in such an age the frame and constitution of society is more picturesque; the modes of life rest more undisguisedly upon the basis of the absolute and original relation of things,—the son is considered in his sonship, the father in his fatherhood; and the manners take an appropriate colouring. Up to the middle of the seventeenth century there were many families in which the children never presumed to sit down in their parents' presence. But with us, in an age of more complete intellectual culture, a thick disguise is spread over the naked foundations of human life; and the instincts of good taste banish from good company the expression of all the profounder emotions. A son, therefore, who should kneel down in this age to ask his papa's blessing on leaving town for Brighton or Bath would be felt by himself to be making a theatrical display of filial duty, such as would be painful to him in proportion as his feelings were sincere. All this would have been evident to the learned editor in any case but one which regarded the Puritans: they were, at any rate.

to be molested; in default of any graver matter, a mere fanciful grievance is searched out. Still, however, nothing was effected; fanciful or real, the grievance must be connected with the Puritans: here lies the offence, there lie the Puritans: it would be very agreeable to find some means of connecting the one with the other; but how shall this be done? Why, in default of all other means, the learned editor *assumes* the connection. He leaves the reader with an impression that the Puritans are chargeable with a serious wound to the manners of the nation in a point affecting the most awful of the household charities; and he fails to perceive that for this whole charge his sole ground is, that it would be very agreeable to him if he *had* a ground. Such is the power of the *esprit de corps* to palliate and recommend as colourable the very weakest logic to a man of acknowledged learning and talent! In conclusion, I must again disclaim any want of veneration and entire affection for the Established Church: the very prejudices and injustice with which I tax the English clergy have a generous origin; but it is right to point the attention of historical students to their strength and the effect which they have had. They have been indulged to excess; they have disfigured the grandest page in English history; they have hid the true descent and tradition of our constitutional history; and, by impressing upon the literature of the country a false conception of the patriotic party in and out of Parliament, they have stood in the way of a great work,—a work which, according to my ideal of it, would be the most useful that could just now be dedicated to the English public, —viz., *a philosophic record of the revolutions of English History*. The English Constitution, as proclaimed and ratified (but not created) in 1688–9, is in its kind the noblest work of the human mind working in conjunction with Time, and what in such a case we may allowably call Providence. Of this *chef d'œuvre* of human wisdom it were desirable that we should have a proportionable history. For such a history the great positive qualification would be a philosophic mind: the great negative qualification would be this [which to the Established clergy may now be recommended as a fit subject for their magnanimity], viz., complete conquest over those prejudices which have hitherto discoloured the greatest era of patriotic virtue, by contemplating the great men of that era under their least happy aspect,—namely, in relation to the Established Church.

Now that I am on the subject of English History, I will notice one of the thousand misstatements of Hume's, which becomes a memorable one from the stress which he has laid upon it, and from the manner and situation in which he has introduced it. Standing in the current of a narrative, it would have merited a silent correction in an unpretending note: but it occupies a much more assuming station; for it is introduced in a philosophical essay; and being relied on for a particular purpose with the most unqualified confidence, and being alleged in opposition to the very highest authority [viz., the authority of an eminent person contemporary with the fact], it must be looked on as involving a peremptory defiance to all succeeding critics who might hesitate between the authority of Mr Hume, at the distance of a century from the facts, and Sir William Temple, speaking to them as a matter within his personal recollections. Sir William Temple had represented himself as urging, in a conversation with Charles II., the hopelessness of any attempt on the part of an English king to make himself a despotic and absolute monarch except, indeed, through the affections of his people.* This general thesis he had supported by a variety of arguments; and, amongst others, he had described himself as urging this—that even Cromwell had been unable to establish himself in unlimited power, though supported by a military force of *eighty thousand men*. Upon this Hume calls the reader's attention to the extreme improbability which there must beforehand appear to be in supposing that Sir W. Temple—speaking of so recent a case, with so much official knowledge of that case at his command, uncontradicted moreover by the king, whose side in the argument gave him an interest in contradicting Sir William's statement, and whose means of information were paramount to those of all others—could under these circumstances be mistaken. Doubtless the reader will reply to Mr Hume, the improbability *is* extreme, and scarcely to be invalidated by any possible counter-authority, which, at best, must terminate in leaving an equilibrium of opposing evidence. And yet, says Mr Hume, Sir William was unquestionably wrong, and grossly wrong. Cromwell never had an army at all approaching to the number of eighty thousand. Now here is a sufficient proof that Hume had never read Lord Clarendon's account of his own life: this book is not so common as his *History of the Rebellion*; and Hume had either not met with it, or had neglected it. For, in the early part of this work, Lord Clarendon, speaking of the army which was assembled on Blackheath to welcome the return of Charles II.,

* Sir William had quoted to Charles a saying from Gourville (a Frenchman whom the king esteemed, and whom Sir William him self considered the only foreigner he had ever known that understood England) to this effect: "That a king of England, who will be the man of his people, is the greatest king in the world; but if he will be something more, by G— he is nothing at all."

says that it amounted to fifty thousand men; and when it is remembered that this army was exclusive of the troops in all garrisons—of the forces (six thousand at least) left by Monk in Scotland—and, above all, of the entire army in Ireland—it cannot be doubted that the whole would amount to the number stated by Sir William Temple. Indeed Charles II. himself, in the year 1678 (*i.e.*, about four years after this conversation), as Sir W. Temple elsewhere tells us, "in six weeks' time raised an army of twenty thousand men, the completest, and in all appearance the bravest, troops that could be anywhere seen, and might have raised many more; and it was confessed by all the Foreign Ministers that no king in Christendom could have made and completed such a levy as this appeared in such a time." William III., again, about eleven years afterwards, raised twenty-three regiments with the same ease and in the same space of six weeks. It may be objected indeed to such cases, as in fact it *was* objected to the case of William III. by Howlett in his sensible *Examination of Dr Price's Essay on the Population of England*, that, in an age when manufactures were so little extended, it could never have been difficult to make such a levy of men, provided there were funds for paying and equipping them. But, considering the extraordinary funds which were disposable for this purpose in Ireland, &c., during the period of Cromwell's Protectorate, we may very safely allow the combined authority of Sir William Temple, of the king, and of that very prime minister (Clarendon) who disbanded Cromwell's army, to outweigh the single authority of Hume at the distance of a century from the facts. Upon any question of fact, indeed, Hume's authority is none at all; for he never pretended to any research.

END OF ELEVENTH VOLUME.

CPSIA information can be obtained
at www.ICGtesting.com
Printed in the USA
LVHW040341110522
718423LV00001B/267

9 783375 000684